APR - 5 1991			
JAN 20, 2006			

The Collaborators

Reginald Hill

The Collaborators

The Countryman Press, Inc.
Woodstock, Vermont

First U.S. edition, 1989

Copyright © 1987 by Reginald Hill

First published in Great Britain 1987
by William Collins Sons & Co. Ltd

LIBRARY OF CONGRESS CATALOGING IN PUBLICATION DATA

Hill, Reginald.
　The collaborators / Reginald Hill.—1st U.S. ed.
　　p.　　cm.
　"First published in Great Britain, 1987, by William　Collins Sons &
Co. Ltd."—T.p. verso.
　ISBN 0-88150-138-7
　1. World War, 1939-1945—Fiction.　2. World War, 1939-1945—
Underground movements—France—Fiction.　I. Title.
PR6058.I448C65 1989　　　　　　　　　　　　　　　　88-31573
823'.914—dc 19　　　　　　　　　　　　　　　　　　　CIP

Printed in the United States of America

The Countryman Press
Woodstock, Vermont
05091

Car la collaboration, comme le suicide,
comme le crime, est un phenomène normal.

Jean-Paul Sartre,
Qu'est-ce qu'un collaborateur?

Chacun son Boche

Communist rallying cry,
August 1944

PROLOGUE
March 1945

Sur mes refuges détruits
Sur mes phares écroulés
Sur les murs de mon ennui
J'écris ton nom

Paul Éluard, *Liberté*

1

She dreamt of the children.

They were picnicking on the edge of a corn field, Pauli hiding from his sister, Céci giggling with delight as she crawled through the forest of green stalks. Now she too was out of sight, but her happy laughter and her brother's encouraging cries drifted back to their mother, dozing in the warm sunshine.

Suddenly there was silence, and a shadow between her and the sun, and a shape leaning over her, and a hand shaking her shoulder.

She sat up crying, 'Jean-Paul!'

'On your feet, Kraut-cunt. You've got a visitor.'

It was the fat wardress with the walleye who pulled her upright off the palliasse. A man in a black, badly-cut suit was standing before her. Without hesitation or embarrassment she sank to her knees and stretched out her hands in supplication.

'Please, sir, is there any news of my children? I beg you, tell me what has happened to my children!'

'Shut up,' said the wardress. 'Here, put on this hat.'

'Hat?' She was used to cruelty but not to craziness. 'What do I want with a hat? Is the magistrate bored with the sight of my head?'

'Your examination's over, woman. Haven't you been told? She should have been told!'

He spoke with a bureaucratic irritation which had little to do with human sympathy. The wardress shrugged and said, 'She'll have been told. She pays little heed this one unless you mention her brats. Now, put on the hat like the man says. See, it's like one of them Boche helmets, so it should suit you.'

9

She was holding an old cloche hat in dirty grey felt.

'Why must I wear a hat? This is lunacy!'

'Janine Simonian,' said the man. 'The examining magistrate has decided that your case must go for trial before the Court of Justice set up by the Provisional Government of the Republic. I am here to conduct you there. Put on the hat. It will hide your shame.'

Janine Simonian was still on her knees as if in prayer. Now she let her arms slowly fall and leaned forward till she rested on her hands like a caged beast.

'My shame?' she said. 'Oh no. To hide *yours*, you mean!'

Impatiently the wardress dropped the hat on her skull, but immediately Janine tore it off and hurled it at the official.

'No! Let them see what they've done to me. I'll strip naked if you like so they can see the lot. Let them see me as I am!'

'That will be the purpose of your trial,' said the official, retrieving the hat. 'Now, if you please, madame.'

'*Madame*, is it? What a lot of changes! A hat, and *madame*. What's wrong with Kraut-cunt? Or Bitch-face? Or Whore? Oh, Jesus Christ!'

She screamed as the wardress twisted her arms behind her and locked them together with handcuffs so tight that they crushed the delicate wrist-bones beneath the emaciated flesh.

'You'll hear worse than that before the trial's over, dearie, never you fret,' said the wardress, ramming the hat down over her brow with brutal force. 'Now, on your feet and follow the nice man, though it's a waste of time and money, if you ask me. Straight out and shot, that was the best way for your kind. I don't know how they missed you.'

'Keep your mouth shut, woman,' ordered the court officer. 'You're a Government employee. Show some respect for the law.'

The wardress glared resentfully at his back as she urged Janine after him.

'Jumped up fart-in-a-bottle,' she muttered.

She got her revenge twenty minutes later as they paused outside the courtroom. Suddenly Janine lunged her head at the jamb. She gave her skull a sickening crack but she dislodged the hat. The official stooped to pick it up, but before he could retrieve it, the wardress had pushed Janine through the doorway.

On the crowded public benches, the ripple of expectancy surged momentarily into a chorus of abuse then almost instantly faded into an uneasy silence.

They had been expecting to see a woman they could hate. Instead they found themselves looking at a creature from another world, whose pale, set face, eroded to the bone line by hunger and cold, was completely dehumanized by the high, narrow dome of the shaven skull. In the six months since that first punitive shaving, her head had been razored three times more as an anti-vermin measure. Now the shadows of regrowing hair, and the scars and sores where the razor had been wielded with deliberate or accidental savagery, gave her skull the look of a dead planet. Even the jury, selected for their unblemished Resistance records, looked uneasy. There were only four of them. The new Courts of Justice were desperately overworked and personnel had to be spread thin. Janine, indifferent to change or reaction, fixed her gaze on the single presiding judge and cried, 'Please, Your Honour, I don't care what you do to me, but if you have any news of my children, please tell me. Surely I've a right to know, a mother's right.'

For a moment the plea touched almost every heart, but at the same time it made her human again and therefore vulnerable, and they had come to wound.

'Probably the little bastards've gone back to Berlin with their dad!' a voice called out.

Eager for release from their distracting sympathy, the majority of those present burst into laughter. But this died away as a man on the benches reserved for witnesses leapt to his feet and cried angrily, 'You're wrong!

Take that back! The father of this whore's children was a hero and a patriot. Don't slander him or his children. He couldn't help his wife and they can't help their mother.'

Again the courtroom was reduced to silence under the contemptuous gaze of the speaker, a man of about thirty with prematurely greying hair and a face almost as pale and intense as the prisoner's. He leaned heavily on a stick, and on the breast of his smart black business suit he wore the ribbons of the Médaille de la Résistance and the Croix de l'Ordre de la Libération.

This time the judge, a grey-faced, tired man of perhaps fifty, broke the silence.

'Monsieur Valois,' he said. 'We are delighted to see you restored to health and honoured to have you in court, particularly as your testimony is, I understand, essential to the prosecution of the case.'

Now his tone changed from polite respect to quiet vehemence.

'However, you must remember that during the course of this trial you are as much subject to the discipline of our country's laws as the prisoner herself. Therefore I would respectfully ask that you offer your testimony in due order and form.'

Christian Valois subsided slowly and the judge let his weary gaze move unblinkingly over the public benches. He had lost count of how many of these cases he had had to deal with since the Courts of Justice had finally creaked into operation here in Paris last October. He knew there was work enough to keep him busy for months, perhaps years to come. Well, it was necessary; justice required that those who had betrayed their country's trust should be brought to account, and the people demanded it. But it was well for the people to know too that the days when the Resistance wrote its own laws were past, and the judiciary was back in control.

Satisfied that his point was made he said, 'Now let us proceed.'

12

There was some legal preamble, but finally, in an intense silence, the charges were read.

'Janine Simonian, born Crozier, you are accused that between a date unknown in 1940 and the liberation of Paris in August 1944 you gave aid and comfort to the illegal occupying forces of the German Army; that during the whole or part of this same period you acted as a paid informant of the secret intelligence agencies of the said forces; that you provided the enemies of your country with information likely to assist them in defeating operations and arresting members of the FFI; and more specifically, that you revealed to *Hauptmann* Mai, counter-intelligence officer of the German *Abwehr*, details of a meeting held in June 1944, and that as a result of this betrayal the meeting was raided, several resistants were captured and subsequently imprisoned, tortured and deported, and your own husband, Jean-Paul Simonian, was brutally murdered.'

The official reading the charges paused and the spectators filled the pause with a great howl of hatred. Janine heard all the abuse the wardress had promised.

She looked slowly round the room as if searching for someone, her gaze slipping as easily over the anxious faces of her parents as all the rest.

'Janine Simonian, you must plead to these charges. How do you plead? Guilty or not guilty?'

She sighed deeply, seemed to shrug her thin shoulders and spoke inaudibly.

'The court must be able to hear the prisoner's plea.'

Again that shrug as if all this was irrelevant.

But now her eyes had found a face to fix on, the pale, drawn features of the man called Christian Valois, and she raised her voice just sufficiently to be heard.

'Guilty,' she said wearily. 'I plead guilty.'

PART ONE
June 1940

Ils ne passeront pas!

> Marshal Henri Philippe Pétain,
> *Verdun 1916*

1

The poplar-lined road ran arrow-straight from north to south.

At dawn it was empty. The rising sun barred its white surface with the poplars' shadows so that it lay like an elopcr's ladder against the ripening walls of corn.

Now a car passed down it fast.

A few minutes later there was another.

Both cars had their roof-racks piled high with luggage.

The sun climbed higher, grew hotter. By ten there was a steady stream of south-bound traffic. By eleven it had slowed to a crawl. And it no longer consisted solely of cars.

There were trucks, vans, buses, taxis; horse-drawn carts and pony-drawn traps; people on foot pushing handcarts, barrows, prams and trolleys; men, women and children and babes in arms; rich and poor, old and young, soldiers in blue, priests in black, ladies in high heels, peasants in sabots; and animals too, dogs and cats and smaller pets nursed by loving owners, cows, geese, goats and hens driven by fearful farmers; here in truth was God's plenty.

By midday the stream was almost static, setting up a long ribbon of heat-haze which outshimmered the gentler vibration above the ripening corn. Cars broke down under the strain and were quickly pushed into the ditch by those behind. Janine Simonian sat in her tiny Renault, terrified that this would soon be her fate. The engine was coughing like a sick man. She glanced at her two small children and tried to smile reassuringly. Then she returned her gaze to the dark-green truck ahead of her and concentrated on its tailboard, as if by will alone she hoped to create a linkage and be towed along in its wake.

Her lips moved in prayer. She'd done a lot of praying in the past few weeks.

So far it hadn't worked at all.

There were four of the green trucks, still nose to tail as they had been since they set off from Fresnes Prison that morning.

In the first of them, unbeknown to Janine, sat her cousin, Michel Boucher. It was to his sister, Mireille, living in what seemed like the pastoral safety of the Ain region east of Lyon, that she was fleeing.

Boucher himself wasn't fleeing anywhere, at least not by choice. And given the choice, he wouldn't have thought of his sister, whom he hadn't seen for nearly ten years. Besides, he hated the countryside.

Paris was the only place to be, in or out of gaol. Paris was his family, more than his sister and her peasant husband, certainly more than his cousin and her fearful mother. Bloody shop-keepers, they deserved to be robbed. And bloody warders, they needed some sense kicked into them.

Rattling his handcuffs behind him he said, 'Hey, Monsieur Chauvet, do we have to have these things on? If them Stukas come, we're sitting ducks.'

'Shut up,' commanded the warder without much conviction.

He was thinking of his family. They were stuck back there in Paris with the Boche at the gate while he was sitting in a truck conveying a gang of evacuated criminals south to safety. Something was wrong somewhere!

'Know what this lot looks like?' said another prisoner, a thin bespectacled man called Pajou. 'A military convoy, that's what. Just the kind of target them Stukas like. We'd be better off walking.'

'You think your mates would be able to spot you at a couple of hundred miles an hour, Pajou?' said the warder viciously. 'No, my lad, you'll be getting your Iron Cross posthumously if the bastards come!'

Pajou looked indignant. He'd been a charge hand at a

munition factory near Metz. A year before, he had been sentenced to eight years for passing information about production schedules to German Military Intelligence. He had always loudly protested his innocence.

Before he could do so now, Boucher rattled his cuffs again and pleaded, 'Come on, chief, you know it's not right. If them Stukas come, it's like we were staked out for execution.'

The warder, Chauvet, opened his mouth, but before he could speak, Pajou cried, 'Listen! Look!'

Looking and listening were almost the same thing. Two black spots expanded like ink stains in the clear blue sky in a crescendo of screaming engines; then came the hammering of guns, the blossoming of explosions; and the long straight river of refugees fountained sideways into the poplar-lined ditches as the Stukas ran a blade of burning metal along the narrow road.

Boucher saw bullets ripping into the truck behind as he dived over the side. With no protection from his arms, he fell awkwardly, crashing down on one shoulder and rolling over and over till a poplar trunk soaked up his impetus.

'Jesus Christ!' he groaned as he lay there half-stunned. All around were the cries and moans of the terror stricken and the wounded. How long he lay there he did not know, but it was that other sound, heard only once but now so familiar, that roused him. The Stukas were returning.

Staggering to his feet he plunged deeper into the field which lay beyond the roadside ditch. What crop it held he could not say. He was no countryman to know the difference between corn and barley, wheat and rye. But the sea of green and gold stems gave at least the illusion of protection as the Stukas passed.

Rising again, he found he was looking into Pajou's pallid face. His spectacles were awry and one lens was cracked but an elastic band behind his head had kept them in place.

'You all right, Miche?'

'Yeah.'

'What now?'

19

Why the man should offer him the leadership, Boucher did not know. He hardly knew Pajou and didn't care for what he did know. Robbing the rich was one thing, selling your country another.

But people often deferred to him, probably simply because of his appearance. Over six foot tall, Titian-haired, eagle-nosed, he had the kind of piratical good looks which promised excitement and adventure. Also he was known from his name as Miche the Butcher, and if his easy-going manner made anyone doubt his capacity for violence, his sheer bulk generally inhibited them from testing it.

But Pajou's question was a good one. What now? Run till they found a friendly blacksmith?

'Hold on,' said Boucher.

An image from his mad flight from the road had returned to him.

He retraced his steps to the roadside. Lying in the ditch just as he had remembered was the warder. There was no sign of a bullet wound, but his head was split open. Despite the freedom of his arms, he must have fallen even more awkwardly than Boucher.

The bloody head moved, the eyes opened and registered Boucher, who raised his booted foot threateningly. With a groan, Chauvet closed his eyes and his head fell back.

Squatting down with his back to the body, Boucher undid the man's belt, then fumbled along it till he came to the chain which held his ring of keys. It slid off easily.

Standing up, he found that Pajou had joined him.

Looking down at the unconscious warder, he said admiringly, 'Did you do that? Christ, you can handle yourself, can't you, Miche?'

'Let's go,' said Boucher shortly.

They set off once more into the green-gold sea, sinking into it like lovers after a couple of hundred metres.

It took ten minutes working back to back to unlock the cuffs from Pajou's wrists, two seconds then to release Boucher.

20

Released, Pajou was a different man, confident of purpose.

'Come on,' he said, massaging his wrists.

'Where, for Christ's sake?'

'Back to Paris, of course,' said Pajou in surprise. 'With the Germans in Paris, the war's over.'

'Tell that to them back there,' said Boucher curtly gesturing towards the road.

'They should've stayed at home,' said Pajou. 'There'll be no fighting in Paris, you'll see. It'll be an open city. Once the peace starts, it'll be a German city.'

Boucher considered the idea. He didn't much like it.

'All the more reason to be somewhere else,' he growled.

'You think so?' said Pajou. 'Me, I think there'll be work to do, money to be made. Stick with me, Miche. The *Abwehr* will be recruiting likely lads with the right qualities, and they're bloody generous, believe me!'

'So you did work for them,' said Boucher in disgust. 'All that crap about being framed! I should've known.'

'It didn't harm anybody,' said Pajou. 'If anything, it probably saved a few lives. The Krauts were coming anyway. Whatever helped them get things over with quickest was best for us, I say. It's them silly military bastards who went on about the Maginot Line that should've been locked up. We must've been mad to pay any heed to a pathetic old fart like Pétain . . . Jesus Christ!'

Boucher had seized him by his shirt front and lifted him up till they were eye to eye.

'Careful what you say about the Marshal, friend,' he growled. 'He's the greatest man in France, mebbe the greatest since Napoleon, and I'll pull the tongue out of anyone who says different.'

'All right, all right,' said Pajou. 'He's the greatest. Come on, Miche, let's not quarrel. Like I say, stick with me, and we'll be all right. What's the difference between robbing the Boche and robbing our own lot? What do you say?'

For answer Boucher flung the smaller man to the ground and glowered down at him.

21

'I say, sod off, you nasty little traitor. Go and work for the Boche if you must, and a lot of joy I hope you both get from it. Me, I'll stick to honest thieving. I may be a crook, but at least I'm a French bloody crook! Go on, get out of my sight, before I do something I probably won't be sorry for!'

'Like kicking my head in like you did that warder's?' mocked Pajou, scrambling out of harm's way. 'Well, please yourself, friend. If you change your mind any time, you know how to find me! See you, Miche.'

He got to his feet and next moment was gone.

Michel Boucher sat alone in the middle of a field of waving cereal. It was peaceful here, but it was lonely. And when the bright sun slid out of the blue sky, he guessed it would also be frightening.

This was no place for him. He was a creature of the city, and that city was Paris. Pajou had been right in that at least. There was nowhere else to go.

The difference was of course that he would return as a Frenchman, ready to resist in every way possible the depredations of the hated occupiers.

Feeling almost noble, he rose to his feet and, ignoring the path trampled by Pajou, began to forge his own way northward through the ripening corn.

2

Janine Simonian had dived into the ditch on the other side of the road as the Stukas made their first pass. Like her cousin, she had no arm free to cushion her fall. The left clutched her two-year-old daughter, Cécile, to her breast; the right was bound tight around her five-year-old son, Pauli. They lay quite still, hardly daring to breathe, for more than a minute. Finally the little girl began to cry.

The boy tried to pull himself free, eager to view the vanishing planes.

'Pauli! Lie still! They may come back!' urged his mother.

'I doubt it, madame,' said a middle-aged man a little further down the ditch. 'Limited armaments, these Boche planes. They'll blaze away for a few minutes, then it's back to base to reload. No, we won't see those boys for a while now.'

Janine regarded this self-proclaimed expert doubtfully. As if provoked by her gaze, he rose and began dusting down his dark business suit.

'Maman, why do we have to go to Lyon?' asked Pauli in the clear precise tone which made old ladies smile and proclaim him 'old-fashioned'.

'Because we'll be safe down there,' said Janine. 'We'll stay with your Aunt Mireille and Uncle Lucien. They don't live in the city. They've got a farm way out in the country. We'll be safe there.'

'We won't be safe in Paris?' asked the boy.

'Because the Boche are in Paris,' answered his mother.

'But Gramma and Granpa stayed, didn't they? And Bubbah Sophie too.'

'Yes, but Granpa and Gramma have to look after their shop . . .'

'More fool them,' interrupted the middle-aged expert. 'I fought in the last lot, you know. I know what your Boche is like. Butchering and looting, that's what's going on back there. Butchering and looting.'

With these reassuring words, he returned to his long limousine, which was standing immediately behind Janine's tiny Renault. He was travelling alone. She guessed he'd sent his family ahead in plenty of time and been caught by his own greed in staying behind to cram the packed limo with everything of value he could lay his hands on.

Janine reprimanded herself for the unkind thought. Wasn't her own little car packed to, and above, the roof with all her earthly possessions?

23

Others were following the businessman's example and beginning to return to the road. There didn't seem to have been any casualties in this section of the long procession, though from behind and ahead drifted cries of grief and pain.

'Come on, madame! Hurry up!' called the man, as if she were holding up the whole convoy.

'In a minute!' snapped Janine, who was busy comforting her baby and brushing the dust out of her short blonde fuzz of childish hair.

Pauli rose and took a couple of steps back on to the road where he stood shading his eyes against the sun which was high in the southern sky.

'They *are* coming back,' he said in his quiet, serious voice.

It took a couple of seconds for Janine to realize what he meant.

'Pauli!' she screamed, but her voice was already lost in the explosion of a stick of bombs only a couple of hundred metres ahead. And the blast from the next bowled her over back into the protecting ditch.

Then the screaming engines were fading once more.

'Pauli! Pauli!' she cried, eyes trying to pierce the brume of smoke and dust which enveloped the road, heart fearful of what she would see when she did.

'Yes, maman,' said the boy's voice from behind her.

She turned. Her son, looking slightly surprised, was sitting in the corn field.

'It flew me through the air, maman,' he said in wonderment. 'Like the man at the circus. Didn't you see me?'

'Oh Pauli, are you all right?'

For answer he rose and came to her. He appeared unscathed. The baby was crying again and the boy said gravely, 'Let me hold her, maman.'

Janine passed the young girl over. Céci often reacted better to the soothing noises made by her brother than to her mother's ministrations.

Turning once more to the road, Janine rose and took a

couple of steps towards the car. And now the smoke cleared a little.

'Oh Holy Jesus!' she prayed or swore.

The bomb must have landed on the far side of the road. There was a small crater in the corn field and a couple of poplars were badly scarred and showed their bright green core, almost as obscene as torn flesh and pulsating blood.

Almost.

The businessman lay across the bonnet of his ruined car. His head was twisted round so that it stared backward over his shoulders, a feat of contortion made possible by the removal of a great wedge of flesh from his neck out of which blood fountained like water from a garden hose.

As she watched, the pressure diminished, the fountain faded, and the empty husk slid slowly to the ground.

'Is he dead, maman?' enquired Pauli.

'Quickly, bring Céci. Get into the car!' she shouted.

'I think it's broken,' said the boy.

He was right. A fragment of metal had been driven straight through the engine. There was a strong smell of petrol. It was amazing the whole thing hadn't gone up in flames.

'Pauli, take the baby into the field!'

Opening the car door she began pulling cases and boxes on to the road. She doubted if the long procession of refugees would ever get moving again. If it did, it was clear her car was going to take no part in it.

She carried two suitcases into the corn field. As she returned a third time, there was a soft breathy noise like a baby's wind and next moment the car was wrapped in flames.

Pauli said, 'Are we going back home, maman?'

'I don't know,' she said wearily. 'Yes. I think so.'

'Will papa be there?'

'I don't think so, Pauli. Not yet.'

If there'd been the faintest gleam of hope that Jean-Paul would return before the Germans, she could never have left. But the children's safety had seemed imperative.

25

She looked at the burning car, the bomb craters, the dead businessman. So this was safety!

'Maman, will the Germans have stopped butchering and looting now?' asked the boy.

'Pauli, save your breath for walking.'

And in common with many others who had found there is a despair beyond terror, she set off with her family back the way they had come.

3

Under the Arc de Triomphe, a cat warmed herself at the Eternal Flame. Then, deciding that the air on this fine June morning was now balmy enough to be enjoyed by a sensitive lady, she set off down the Champs-Élysées. She looked neither to left nor right. There was no need to. Sometimes she sat in the middle of the road and washed herself. Sometimes she wandered from one pavement to the other, hoping to find tasty scraps fallen beneath the café tables. But no one had eaten here for at least two days and the pavements were well scavenged. Finally, when she reached the Rond Point, she decided like a lady of breeding whose servants have deserted her that she'd better start fending for herself and bounded away among the chestnut trees where the beat of a bird's wing was the first sign of life she'd seen since sunrise.

Christian Valois too was reduced to getting his own breakfast, in his family's spacious apartment in Passy. Four days earlier the Government had packed its bags, personal and diplomatic, and made off to Bordeaux. With them had gone Valois's parents, his young sister, and the maid-of-all work. Léon Valois was a member of the Chamber of Deputies and a fervent supporter of Pétain. By training a lawyer, he reckoned there weren't many things, including wars, which couldn't be negotiated to a satisfactory compromise. His son, though a civil servant in the Ministry of Finance, was a romantic. To him the move to Bordeaux was a cowardly flight. He refused to leave Paris. Neither his father's arguments nor his mother's hysterics could move him. Only his sister, Marie-Rose's tears touched his heart, but couldn't melt his resolve.

At work he got less attention. His superior, Marc du Prat, smiled wearily and said, 'Try not to spill too much blood on my office carpet.' Then, pausing only to remove the Corot sketch which was his badge of culture, he left.

For three days Christian Valois had conscientiously gone to work, even though he had nothing to do and no one for company. The Ministry occupied part of the great Palace of the Louvre. What was happening in the museum he did not know, but in his section overlooking the Rue de Rivoli, it was eerily quiet, both inside and out.

This morning, because he found himself very reluctant to go in at all, he had forced himself out of bed even earlier than usual. But when he arrived at the Louvre almost an hour before he was officially due, the thought of that silent dusty room revolted him and his feet took him with little resistance down towards the river.

He saw few signs of life. A car crossed an intersection some distance away. Two pedestrians on the other side of the street hugged the wall and looked down as they passed. A priest slipped furtively into St Germain-l'Auxerrois as though he had a secret assignation with God.

Then he was on the quay, looking at the endless, indifferent Seine.

Was he merely a posing fool? he asked himself moodily as he strolled along. Perhaps his father was right. With the army in flight or simply outflanked, the time for heroics was past. It was time for the negotiators to save what they could from the débâcle. Perhaps the Germans wouldn't even bother to send their army into Paris. Perhaps in the ultimate act of scorn they would occupy the city with a bus-load of clerks!

27

At least I should feel at home then, he told himself bitterly.

He had crossed to the Île de la Cité. When he reached the Pont du Change, he headed for the Right Bank once more, half-resolved that he would waste no more time on this foolishness. If he truly wanted to be a hero he should have fled, not to Bordeaux, but to England or North Africa, and looked for a chance to fight instead of merely making gestures.

So rapt was he that his feet were walking in time with the noise before his mind acknowledged it. Once acknowledged, though, he recognized it at once, for he had heard it often, echoing in his dreams like thunder in a dark sky ever since the war had passed from threat to reality, and his imagination had not deceived him. It was the crash of marching feet, powerful and assured, striking sparks off the paving stones as if they made an electrical connection between the conquerors and the conquered. He stopped and leaned against the low parapet of the bridge, overcome by his own mental image.

Then suddenly he could see as well as hear them, and the reality was even more devastating. In columns of three they were striding into the Place du Châtelet, passing beneath the Colonne du Palmier whose gilded Victory seemed to spread her angelic wings wider and hold her triumphal wreaths higher in greeting to these new and mightier victors.

Now they were on the bridge and coming towards him, trio after trio of strong young men, their faces beneath their heavy helmets grave with victory. Past him they strode with never a sideways look. He turned to follow their progress, saw the leaders halt before the Palace of Justice, saw them turn to face it, saw the great gates swing open and the gendarme on duty stand aside as the first Germans entered.

Now once more it was essential he should be at his desk.

He walked as fast as he could without breaking into an undignified trot which might be mistaken for fear. By the

28

time he reached the Louvre the Rue de Rivoli had come to life once more, but what a life! No colourful drift of shoppers and tourists, but a rumbling, roaring procession of trucks and tanks and cars and motor-cycles; and above all, of marching men, an endless stream of grey, like ash-flaked lava flowing inexorably, all-consumingly, through the streets of Pompeii.

Seated at last at his desk, he realized his calf-muscles were shaking. He experienced the phenomenon distantly as though the trembling were external and did not have its source in his own physical core.

Minutes passed, perhaps an hour.

Suddenly, without hearing anything, he knew they were in the building. He'd grown used to its emptiness, its sense of sleeping space.

Now . . .

Noise confirmed his intuition. Footsteps; steel on marble; regular, swift; certain.

The trembling in his legs grew wilder and wilder. It was beginning to spread through the whole of his body, must surely be evident now in his arms, his shoulders, his face. He tried to control it but couldn't, and prayed, not out of fear but shame, that they would not after all find him.

But now the steps were close. Doors opening and shutting. And at last, his.

In that self-same moment the trembling stopped.

It was the young soldier who looked in who showed the shock of his discovery, clearly taken aback to find anyone here.

'Yes?' said Valois testily.

The young man levelled his rifle, turned his head and called, 'Sir! Here's someone!'

More footsteps, then a middle-aged warrant officer came into the room, pushing the soldier's rifle up with irritation.

'Who the hell are you?' he said in execrable French.

'Valois. Junior Secretary, Ministry of Finance.'

'You what? I thought this was a museum. Where's all the pictures?'

'That's another part of the Palace. This wing holds the Ministry of Finance.'

'Does it, now? Don't suppose you keep any money here, though!' the man laughed.

Valois did not reply.

'No. Thought not. All right. Don't go away. Someone may want to talk to you.'

Turning to the soldier, the man commanded, 'Stay on guard outside!'

The soldier left. The warrant officer gave the mockery of a salute. 'Carry on with your work, Monsieur Valois,' he said smiling.

Then he was gone.

Valois slowly relaxed. The trembling was starting again, but less violently now. He felt a sudden surge of exultation through his body.

He had seen the enemy face to face and had not flinched.

But best of all, he had felt the upwelling of such a powerful hatred that it must surely spring from a reservoir deep enough to sustain him through the long, bitter and dangerous struggle that lay ahead. He'd been right not to flee to Bordeaux or even England. Here was where the real resistance to the Boche would start. Whatever the future held for France, the worst it could hold for Christian Valois was a hero's death.

Suddenly he felt a surge of something much stronger than exultation move through his body. He rose and hurried to the door. The young soldier regarded him with alarm and brought his rifle up.

Making a desperate and humiliating mime, Christian pushed past him. There were driving forces stronger than either terror or patriotism. He was discovering a truth rarely revealed in song or saga, that even heroes have to crap.

PART TWO

June–December 1940

Fuyez les bois et les fontaines
Taisez-vous oiseaux querelleurs
Vos chants sont mis en quarantaines
C'est le règne de l'oiseleur
Je reste roi de mes douleurs

> Louis Aragon, *Richard II*
> *Quarante*

1

There was no getting away from it, thought Günter Mai.
Even for an *Abwehr* lieutenant who was more likely to see
back alleys than front lines, it was nice to be a conqueror.
Not nice in a brass-banded, jack-booted, *Sieg Heil*ing sort
of way. But nice to be here in this lovely city, in this elegant
bedroom in this luxurious hotel which for the next five?
ten? twenty? years would be the Headquarters of Military
Intelligence in Paris.

He gazed out across the sun-gilt rooftops to the distant
mast of the Eiffel Tower and saluted the view with his
pipe.

'Thank you, Paris,' he said.

Behind him someone coughed, discreet as a waiter, but
when he turned he saw it was his section head, Major
Bruno Zeller.

'Good morning, Günter,' said the elegant young man.
'I missed you at breakfast. Can my keeper be ill, I asked
myself.'

'Morning, sir. I wasn't too hungry after last night's
celebration.'

'You mean you *ate* as well as drank?' said Zeller lounging
gracefully on to the bed. 'You amaze me. Now tell me, do
you recall a man called Pajou?'

Mai's normally round, amiable face lengthened into a
scowl. A hangover reduced his Zeller-tolerance dramatically. In his late twenties, he had long got over the irritation
of having to 'sir' someone several years his junior. Such
things happened, particularly if you were the son of an
assistant customs officer in Offenburg and 'sir' was heir to
some turreted castle overhanging the Rhine, not to men-

tion a distant relative of Admiral Canaris, head of the *Abwehr*.

But that didn't entitle the cheeky child to wander at will into your bedroom and lie across your bed!

'Pajou. Now let me see,' said Mai. Yes, of course, he remembered him well. But having remembered, it now suited him to play the game at his speed. From his dressing-table he took a thick black book. It was an old Hitler *Jugend Tagebuch* which he'd never found any use for till he started in intelligence work. Now, filled with minuscule, illegible writing, it was the repository of all he knew. He guessed Zeller would pay highly for a fair transcript. He saw the young man's long, manicured fingers beat an impatient tattoo on the counterpane. The movement caught the light on his heavy silver signet ring, reminding Mai of another source of irritation. The signet was the family heraldic device, basically a Zed crossed by a hunting horn. On first noticing it, Mai had remarked unthinkingly that he had seen a similar device on some brass buttons which he thought came from a coat belonging to his grandfather. Zeller had returned from his next visit to his widowed mother delighted with the news, casually introduced, that there had been an under-keeper called Mai working on the family's Black Forest estate till he'd gone off to Offenburg to better himself. 'And here's his grandson, still working for the family in a manner of speaking! Strange how these things work out, eh, Günter?'

Thereafter he often referred to Mai as 'my keeper', though it had to be said he didn't share the joke with other people.

Mai took it all in good part – except when he had a hangover. Basically he quite liked the young major. Also there were other shared pieces of knowledge which dipped the scales of power in his favour.

One, unusable except in the direst emergency, was that Zeller was as queer as a kosher Nazi and was no doubt already looking for some Gallic soulmate to criminally waste his precious Aryan seed on.

Another, and more important for everyday working, was that Mai was twice as good at the job as his boss, though Zeller compensated by taking twice the credit.

He began to read from the book.

'Pajou, Alphonse. Worked for the National Armaments Company. I recruited him in Metz in '38. No political commitment, in it purely for the money. Got greedy, took risks and got caught. Tried and gaoled just before the war. Lucky for him. Any later and he'd have got the guillotine. So, what about him?'

'It seems he got an early release, unofficially I guess, and would like to make it official by re-entering our employ. He's not very trusting, however. The duty sergeant says he insisted on dealing with you when he rang earlier this morning.'

'Why didn't he put the call through then?' asked Mai.

'The sergeant says that you left instructions last night that you weren't to be disturbed by anything less than a call from the Führer and not even then if he wanted to transfer the charge.'

Mai grimaced behind a puff of smoke.

'Sorry about that, sir. Look, I'm not sure Pajou's the kind of man we want just now. Basically he's a nasty piece of work and he's not even a native Parisian. What we ought to be doing now, before the first shock fades and people begin to take notice, is establishing a network of nice ordinary citizens who'll feed us with intelligence just for the sake of reassurance that the dreadful Hun is a nice ordinary chap like themselves.'

'Clever thinking, Günter. But in the end we'll doubtless need the nasties, so we might as well recruit Pajou now. If we don't no doubt the SD will when they arrive.'

The *Sicherheitsdienst* was the chief Nazi intelligence gathering service. With France under military control, the SD ought not yet to have a presence, let alone a function.

'*When!*' said Mai. 'I heard the bastards were already settling in at the Hôtel du Louvre. And I'm sure I saw

35

Fiebelkorn in the restaurant last night – in civvies, of course, not his fancy SS colonel's uniform.'

'Let's hope it was a drunken delusion,' said Zeller with a fastidious shudder.

'One thing, if they've started showing their faces, it means the fighting's definitely over. Right, sir, I'll talk to Pajou if he rings back.'

'No, you'll talk to him face to face,' said Zeller, rising gracefully. 'He left word that he would look for you by the Medici Fountain at ten-thirty this morning. That gives you just half an hour.'

'But breakfast . . .' objected Mai, genuinely indignant.

'I thought you weren't hungry. Anyway a good keeper should have been doing the rounds of his estate at the crack of dawn. Let me know how you get on, won't you?'

With a smile and a sort of waving salute, Zeller left.

'Go stuff yourself,' murmured Mai, but he began to get ready. Zeller expected obedience in small matters, and though Mai had been looking forward to his favourite hangover cure of sweet black coffee and half a dozen croissants, it wasn't worth the risk of irritating him into some petty revenge.

He clattered through the lobby of the hotel trying to look brisk and businesslike, but once out into the gentle morning sunlight, he slowed to strolling pace. Sod Pajou. He could wait. What was more, he *would* wait. He wasn't selling information today, he was applying for a job!

It was good to see how things were coming back to normal. The Bon Marché emporium which he could see at the far side of the garden opposite the hotel had re-opened and looked to be doing good business. He must go on a shopping expedition himself soon. Victory or no victory, there'd soon be shortages he guessed. And a nice supply of silks and perfume would be useful on his next home leave.

He strolled on, taking deep breaths of the rich enchanted air. His mind, ever ready to deflate, reminded him that at this hour of the morning the air would normally have been rich indeed – with the stench of exhaust fumes.

You see how we're improving things already! he mentally addressed the city.

Gradually he became aware that the air was indeed richly scented. Wandering by half-memory, he had turned into the Rue d'Assas. It ought to lead him roughly towards the Luxembourg. In any case, he liked the sound of the name. Eventually he reached a narrow crossroads where the Rue Duguay-Trouin entered and the Rue de Fleurus intersected the Rue d'Assas. Looking left, he could see down to the Gardens. But his nose was turning him away to the right. He followed it along the narrow street till his eyes could do their share of the work and identify the source of that rich, warm smell.

It was a baker's shop, not very big, but dignified by the words *Boulangerie Pâtisserie* parading above the windows in ornate lettering, and decorated by glass-covered designs around the door which featured a sturdy farmer and his elegant wife and promised 'Pains Français et Viennois, Pains de Seigle, Chaussons aux Pommes et Gâteaux Secs'.

On the glass of the door was engraved 'Crozier Père et Fils depuis 1870', underlined by a triangle of curlicues, eloquent of the pride with which that first Crozier had launched his business seventy years before. The same year in which, if Mai's history served him well, the Franco–Prussian war began. Perhaps other occupying Germans had been customers at this shop!

The shop window was fairly bare. But the smell of baking was rich and strong.

He pushed open the door and went in. There was one customer, one of those Frenchwomen of anything between fifty and a hundred who wear black clothes of almost Muslim inclusiveness whatever the weather. She was being served by a stout woman in middle age with the kind of flesh that looked, not unfittingly, as if it had been moulded from well-kneaded dough.

The black-swathed customer looked in alarm at Mai's uniform, said abruptly, 'Good morning, Madame Crozier,' and left.

'Good morning, Madame Duval,' the stout woman called after her. 'Monsieur?'

Her attempt at sang-froid failed miserably.

He set about allaying her fears.

'Madame,' he said in his rolling Alsatian French. 'I have been drawn here by the delectable odours of what I'm sure is your superb baking. I would deem it an honour if you would allow me to purchase a few of your croissants.'

The woman's doughy features stretched into a simper.

'Claude!' she shouted.

The door behind her opened, admitting a great blast of mouth-watering warmth and a man cast in the same mould, and from the same material, as his wife.

'What?' he demanded. Then he saw the uniform, and his face, which would have made him a fortune in the silent movies, registered fearful amazement.

'Good day, monsieur,' said Mai. 'I was just telling your wife how irresistible I found the smell of your baking.'

'Claude, are there any more croissants? The officer wants croissants,' said Madame Crozier peremptorily.

'No, I'm sorry . . .' began the man.

'Well, make some, Claude,' commanded the wife. 'If the officer would care to wait, it will only take a moment.'

The man went back into the kitchen and the woman brought Mai a chair. As she returned to the counter the door burst open. A good-looking woman of about twenty-five with dishevelled fair hair and a pale smudged face rushed in. She was carrying a child of about two years and at her heels was a boy a few years older.

She cried, 'Maman, are you all right? Madame Duval said the Boche were here!'

'Janine!' exclaimed the woman. 'What are you doing back? Why aren't you in Lyon? Oh the poor baby! Is she ill?'

The child in arms had begun to cry. Madame Crozier reached over the counter and took her in her arms with much cooing.

'No, she's just hungry,' said the girl, then broke off abruptly as for the first time she noticed Mai sitting quietly in the corner, almost hidden by the door. She was not however the first of the newcomers to notice him. The young boy's eyes had lit on him as soon as he came in and the lad had thereafter fixed him with a disconcertingly level and unblinking gaze.

Mai got to his feet.

'I'm sorry, madame,' he said. 'Please do not let me disturb this reunion.'

'No, wait,' cried Madame Crozier. 'Claude! Where are those croissants?'

'They're coming, they're coming!' came the reply, followed almost immediately by the opening of the door. Once again Mai had the pleasure of seeing that cinematic amazement.

'Janine!' cried Crozier. 'What're you doing here? Why've you come back?'

'Because the Boche dropped bombs and fired bullets at everyone on the road,' cried Janine vehemently. 'They could see we were a real menace. Men, women, children, animals, all running south in terror. Oh yes, we were a real menace!'

Sighing, Mai put on his cap. Not even the best croissants in the world were worth this bother.

'But you're not hurt, are you? And the children are all right? Claude, the officer's croissants!'

The man put the croissants in a bag and handed it to Mai. He reached into his pocket. The woman said, 'No, no. Please, you can pay next time.'

A good saleswoman thought Mai approvingly. Ready to risk a little for good will and the prospect of a returning customer. The young woman was regarding him with unconcealed hostility. As he took the croissants he clicked his heels and made a little bow just as Major Zeller would have done. She too might as well have her money's worth.

He left the shop, pausing in the doorway as if deciding which way to go. Behind him he heard the older woman say, 'Oh look at the poor children, they're like little gypsies. And you're not much better, Janine.'

'Mother, we've been walking for days! We slept in a barn for two nights. Has there been any news of Jean-Paul?'

'No, nothing. Now come and sit down and have something to eat. Pauli, child, you look as if you need fattening for a week. Claude, coffee!'

Mai left, smiling but thoughtful. These French! Some of his masters believed that, properly handled, they could be brought into active partnership with their conquerors. With the baker and his wife it might be possible. Be correct, avoid provocative victory parades, use clever propaganda, offer them a fair armistice and business as usual; yes they might grumble, but only as they grumbled at their own authorities. But they'd co-operate.

Alas, not all the French were like Monsieur and Madame Crozier. Take that girl, so young, so child-like, but at the same time so fierce!

He turned left at the Bassin in the Luxembourg Gardens. As he skirted the lush green lawn before the Palace, he saw two German soldiers on guard duty. They were looking towards him and he remembered he was still in uniform. The sooner he got out of it the better. One of the joys of being an *Abwehr* officer was the excuse it gave for frequently wearing civilian clothes. The sentries offered a salute. He returned it, realized he was still clutching a croissant, grinned ruefully and bore right to the Medici Fountain.

Slowly he made his way alongside the urn-flanked length of water to take a closer look at the sculpture. In the centre of three niches a fierce-looking bronze fellow loomed threateningly above a couple of naked youngsters in white marble. Us and the French! he told himself, crumbling a croissant for the goldfish.

A hand squeezed his elbow. He started, turned and saw

a thin bespectacled man showing discoloured teeth in a smile at once impudent and ingratiating.

'Hello, lieutenant. Didn't use to be able to creep up on you like that!'

'Hello, Pajou,' said Mai coldly.

The man turned up the ingratiating key.

'I was really glad when I realized you were in town, lieutenant. That Mai's a man I can trust, a man I can talk to. So here I am, reporting for duty. Do you think you can use me?'

Mai returned his gaze to the crouching cyclops, Polyphemus, poised so menacingly over the entwined figures of Acis and Galatea.

'Yes, Pajou,' he sighed. 'I very much fear we can.'

2

Sophie Simonian was praying for her son when a knock at the door and a voice calling, 'Bubbah Sophie, it's me, Janine,' made her hope for a second that her prayers had been answered.

Leaning heavily on a silver-topped cherry cane, she went to the door, opened it, and knew at once that there was no good news in her daughter-in-law's face. On the other hand, there was no bad news either, thanks be to God for small mercies.

'Bubbah, how are you? You look well,' said Janine embracing her. 'Is there any news of Jean-Paul?'

'Nothing. No news at all. Sit down, my dear. Where are the children?' In sudden alarm, 'There is nothing wrong with the children? Why are you back in Paris?'

'No, they're fine, really. Pauli sends his love, and Céci too. I'll bring them round soon. But I thought I'd come myself first so we can have a good talk.'

Quickly she described her abortive flight, her slow return. Unlike her own parents, Sophie had approved her decision to leave, though refusing (thank God!) Janine's offer to take her too. Nearly seventy with a rheumatic knee, a return on foot would have been quite beyond her. Besides, she'd done her share of refugeeing almost forty years before, after the great pogrom of 1903 in Kishinev. France had offered a new life in every sense. It was here in Paris when hope seemed dead that at last she had conceived and given birth to a son. Iakov Moseich he was named after his father, and Jean-Paul, to tell the world he was a native-born Frenchman.

Her husband had died of a heart attack in 1931. Jean-Paul had wanted to abandon his university place due to be taken up the following year and get a job to look after his mother. She had told him scornfully that his father would have struck him for such self-indulgent sentimentality. It was time to start acting like a real Frenchman and not a joke-book Jewish son.

He certainly took her at her word, she later told herself ironically. During the next few years, he abandoned his religion, declared himself an atheist, flirted with the Communist Party, and announced that he was going to marry Janine Crozier. This last was perhaps the biggest shock of all. Some left-wing intellectual shiksa from the university she could have understood. But this wide-eyed child, of parents whose attitudes were as offensive to his new political religion as to his old racial one, was a complete surprise. When finally she had been unable to contain the question, 'Why! Why! Why do you want to marry this child? She isn't even pregnant!' he had given her the only reply which could silence her: 'Because whenever I see her, I feel happy.'

But six years and two grandchildren later, Sophie was completely converted, and during this trying time she had derived much comfort from her daughter-in-law.

As Janine finished her tale, there was a knock at the door and a man's voice called reassuringly, 'It's only me, Madame Simonian. Christian.'

Janine opened the door. Christian Valois was standing there, in his arms a dark ginger cat with a smudge of black hair around his nose.

'Janine!' he said. 'Is there news?'

Janine shook her head and said, 'No. Nothing. Hello, Charlot, you're fatter than ever!'

The cat purred as she scratched him and then jumped out of Valois's arms and bounced on to Sophie's lap.

'I met him on the stairs,' said Valois, kissing the old lady. 'You've heard nothing either, madame? Of course not. Why doesn't he write to one of us?'

His voice was full of concern which slightly irritated Janine. True, he was a very old friend of Jean-Paul's, but this hardly entitled him to put his concern on a level with, if not above, that of a wife and a mother.

'We are going to have some tea, Christian. Will you stay?' said Sophie.

'Just for a moment. I have to get back.'

'Back where?' asked Janine in surprise. 'Surely there is no work for you to do. I thought everyone to do with the Government had run off to Bordeaux?'

'I stayed,' said Valois shortly.

In fact, his gesture in staying on at the Ministry was proving rather a strain. It hadn't taken the Germans long to realize that he had neither authority nor function. A friendly *Wehrmacht* officer had suggested that if he was worried about his pay, he'd quite happily sign a weekly chitty certifying that the undermentioned civil servant had attended his place of work. This kindly condescension was far more infuriating than any hostility or threat could have been.

'That was brave,' said Janine sincerely.

Valois's thin sallow face flushed. He opened his mouth, realized he was going to say something pompous about duty, bit it back and said instead, 'Thank you.'

The two young people smiled at each other. Sophie Simonian noted this with approval. She liked young Christian and it had always seemed a shame that he and Janine

43

didn't get on. A man's first loyalty was to his family, but he needed his friends too, much more than a woman did.

As they sat and drank their tea, Janine told her story once more. Valois frowned as she told of the German planes attacking the refugee column.

'Bastards!' he said.

'It's war,' said Sophie. 'What do you expect? Stop the war is the only way to stop the killing.'

'You think so? Perhaps. Only the war will not stop, will it?'

'But the Marshal is talking with the Germans about a truce,' cried Janine. 'It was on the wireless.'

'Truce? Defeat, you mean. Is that what you want?' demanded Valois.

'No! I mean, I don't know. I hate the Germans, I want to see them thrown out of France, of course I do. But the only way for Jean-Paul to be safe is for the fighting to stop! I mean it's stupid, he's out there on the Maginot Line somewhere and all the Germans are here in France behind him! I mean it's just so bloody, bloody stupid!'

She was close to tears. Sophie put her arm around her and frowned accusingly at Valois.

'I'm sorry,' he said. 'You know I'm worried about Jean-Paul too. Listen, there will be a truce, an armistice, something like that, I'm sure. He'll be safe. But that's not what I mean when I say the war won't end. De Gaulle's gone to England, a lot of them have. I heard him on the British radio saying that he would fight on no matter what happened back here.'

'De Gaulle? Who's he?' asked Janine.

'He's a general, a friend of the Marshal's.'

'But the Marshal wants a truce, doesn't he?'

'That's right.'

'And everyone says the Boche will be in England soon too. There's nothing to stop them, is there? What does this de Gaulle do then? Go to America?' asked Janine scornfully.

'At least there's someone out there not giving up,' said Valois.

He finished his tea and stood up. Janine saw his gaze drift round the room coming to rest on the large silver menorah on the window sill.

'Are the other apartments still occupied?' he asked casually.

Sophie said, 'A lot went. Soon they'll be back when they see it's safe, no doubt. Madame Nomary, the concierge, is still in the basement. Like me, too old to run. And Monsieur Melchior is still upstairs.'

'Melchior?'

'You must have seen him,' said Janine. 'The writer. Or artist. Or something like that. At least he dresses that way, you know, flamboyantly. I think he's . . .'

'He likes the men more than the ladies is what she doesn't care to say in front of silly old Bubbah,' mocked Sophie. 'But he's a gentleman and very quiet, especially since the war. I think he's been hiding up there, poor soul. Why so interested in my neighbours, Christian?'

'No reason. I must go, Madame Sophie. Take care.'

'I'd better go too and rescue maman from the kids,' said Janine, jumping up. 'Bye, Bubbah. I'll bring Pauli and Céci next time.'

'Be sure you do, child. God go with you both.'

Outside in the steepsided canyon of the Rue de Thorigny they walked in silence for a little way.

Finally Janine said, 'What's worrying you about Sophie, Christian?'

He shot her a surprised glance then said, 'I thought I was a better actor! It's nothing. I was just wondering how I could suggest that it might be politic not to, well, advertise her Jewishness . . .'

'In the Marais? Don't be silly. And why would you say such a thing?'

'You must have heard how the Boche treat Jews. Some of the stories . . .'

'But that's in Germany,' protested Janine. 'They wouldn't dare do anything here, not to Frenchmen. The people wouldn't let it happen!'

'You think not? I hope so,' he said doubtfully.

'I'm glad you didn't say anything, though. It would really have worried Bubbah.'

'It wasn't just her I was concerned about,' said Christian gently.

'Me? Why should it worry . . . oh my God. Jean-Paul, you mean? If they capture Jean-Paul . . .'

She stood stricken.

'I'm sorry,' he said. 'It probably won't happen. And he'll be a prisoner-of-war in any case, under the Geneva Convention . . . where are you going?'

She'd set off at a pace that was more of a trot than a walk. Looking back over her shoulder she cried, 'I've got to get back to the children, see they're all right. Goodbye, Christian.'

'Goodbye,' he said. 'I'll call . . .'

Already she was out of earshot. He headed west, frowning, and in a little while turned on to the Rue de Rivoli. He walked with his shoulders hunched, his head down, and did not see, or at least did not acknowledge seeing, the huge red and black swastika banners which fluttered everywhere like prospectors' flags to mark out what the Germans were claiming for their own.

3

'Hey kid, what's your name?'

Pauli looked up at the man who'd just appeared in the doorway of the little courtyard behind the baker's. He was a big man with long red hair, a longer beard and a strong curved nose. He looked as if he'd been living rough and as he moved nearer, Pauli realized he smelt that way too.

'Pauli,' he said. 'Well, Jean-Paul, really. But maman calls me Pauli.'

'Pauli, eh? Maman, you say? Would that be Janine?'

'Yes, that's maman's name,' said the boy.

'Well, I'll be blowed. And look at the size of you! Little Janine's boy! Well, I'm your Uncle Miche, Pauli. Not really your uncle, more your half-cousin, but uncle will do nicely till I've stood out in the rain long enough to shrink to your size.'

This reversal of the usual adult clichés about growing up into a big boy amused and reassured Pauli. He stood his ground as the big man moved forward and rested a hand on his head. He noticed with interest that this new and fascinating uncle did indeed seem to have been standing out in the rain. His shapeless grey trousers and black workman's jacket were damp with the moisture which the morning sun was just beginning to suck up from the high roofs. Here in the confined yard, it was still shadowy and chill. Michel Boucher shivered but with a controlled shiver like an animal vibrating its flesh for warmth.

'Why don't we go inside and surprise Uncle Claude?' he said. 'I bet it's nice and warm in the bakehouse!'

It was. There were two huge ovens, one down either side of the vaulted ochre-bricked building and both were going full blast. Claude Crozier was removing a trayful of loaves from one of them to add to the morning's bake already cooling on the long central table. Boucher looked at the regiments of bread with covetous eyes and said, 'Morning, Uncle Claude. How's it been with you? Christ, there's a grand smell in here!'

The baker almost dropped his tray in surprise.

'Who's that? Michel, is that you? What the blazes are you doing here?'

'Just passing, uncle, and I thought I'd pay my respects.'

'Kind of you, but just keep on passing, eh? Before your aunt sees you.'

47

Crozier was not a hard man but his nephew was an old battle, long since lost. The baker had been more than generous in the help he gave his widowed sister to bring up her two children. But when within the space of a year, their mother had died of TB, Mireille had married a farmer on holiday and gone to live in the Ain region, and Miche had got two years' juvenile detention for aggravated burglary, Louise broke her disapproving silence and said, 'Enough's enough. Not a penny more of our hard-earned money goes to that ne'er-do-well. He'll never be more than a crook, you'll see.'

Now here he was again.

'You can't stay,' said Crozier urgently.

'Oh I won't stay, uncle,' said Boucher. 'Just long enough for a bite of breakfast, eh?'

The baker's consternation at this prospect changed to terror as the door to the shop opened and his wife came in.

She stopped dead at the sight of Boucher.

'Morning, Auntie Lou,' he called cheerfully. 'Just dropped in to pay my respects. And have a bite of breakfast.'

He took a couple of steps nearer the tray of new-baked bread as he spoke.

'My God!' cried the woman, peering closely at him. 'You're wet! You're dirty! You're unshaven! And you smell!'

Her tone was triumphant as well as indignant. There were few pleasures dearer to her bourgeois heart than being justified in a fit of moral indignation.

'Yes, well, I've been down on my luck a bit,' said Boucher.

Suddenly Pauli moved forward to the table, picked up a roll and presented it to the man.

'Thanks, kid,' he said, already shedding crumbs with the second syllable.

'Pauli, what are you doing! How dare you?' thundered Louise.

'Maman, what's going on? Why're you shouting at Pauli?'

Janine, attracted by her mother's bellow, had appeared in the doorway. She looked at Boucher without recognition.

'I just gave Uncle Miche a roll,' explained the little boy tearfully.

'Hello, Cousin Janine. This is a good lad you've got here,' said Boucher. He stuffed the rest of the roll into his mouth. 'Delicious! Well, I'll be on my way. Don't want to outstay such a generous welcome. Cheers, kid.'

He patted Pauli on the head again, gave a mock military salute and left.

Pauli ran to his mother and said, 'Maman, he was all wet. He says he stands out in the rain to shrink.'

'You'll have to do something about that boy,' said Louise, annoyed at feeling in the wrong. 'The sooner he gets off to school, the better.'

Janine glared at her mother, then turned and ran back into the shop. A moment later they heard the shop door open and shut.

She met her cousin as he came out of the passage which led into the rear yard.

'Here,' she said, stuffing a note into his hand. 'It's not much, but I haven't got much.'

He looked at the money, making little effort to hide his surprise.

'Thanks, cousin,' he said. 'Things have changed, eh?'

'What do you mean?'

'Last time we met, you were still at school, I think. You told me you weren't permitted to speak to degenerates. Exact words!'

Janine flushed, then laughed as she saw Boucher was laughing at her.

'People grow up,' she said.

'Not me,' he said. 'Not if I can help it.'

'What *are* you doing, Miche?'

'I'm not sure,' he said. 'I thought somehow, when this

49

lot started, I'd be fighting the Boche, slate wiped clean sort of thing. But the first flic who recognized me came charging after me waving his cuffs! So I've had to keep my head down. It's been a bit rough, but it'll get sorted sooner or later I don't doubt.'

'Haven't you got anywhere to stay?' asked Janine sympathetically.

'No. Well, I was all right at first. I shacked up . . . I mean lodged with an old friend. Arlette la Blonde, stage name, does an exotic dance at the Golden Gate, I don't expect you know her. Well, that was all right, only a few days back, they opened up again and well, late hours and that, it wasn't convenient, you know these show people . . .'

He tailed off as he realized that this time she was laughing at him.

'You mean she brings friends back for the night and they don't care to find your head on the pillow already!'

'Yeah, that's it,' he said grinning. Then he stopped grinning.

'I could have hung on there, slept days. Only I found she was bringing back Krauts! That really got up my nose! So I slung my hook.'

'You won't have to be so choosy, Miche. Not now they're our friends.'

'Friends? What do you mean?'

'Haven't you heard? It was on the radio this morning. An armistice was signed yesterday.'

'Armistice? Signed by who? Not by the Marshal! He'd not sign an armistice with these bastards. Not the Marshal.'

'Yes,' said Janine. 'Pétain signed it. At Compiègne. In the same railway carriage.'

'Bloody hell,' said Boucher shaking his head in bewilderment.

'Janine!' called her mother's voice from inside.

'I'd better go.'

'Yeah. Sure. Thanks, cousin. We'll keep in touch, eh?'

50

She smiled, pecked his cheek and went inside.

Boucher turned and walked away, not paying much attention to direction. Despite his experiences, he'd still gone on hoping that somewhere in this mess there was going to be a chance for a sort of patriotic redemption. But now it was over before it had really begun and he was back to being a full-time wanted man.

He paused to take stock of his surroundings. He'd almost reached the Boulevard Raspail. There was a car coming towards him. It didn't look particularly official, but any car you saw on the streets nowadays was likely to be official. He coughed in his hand, covering his face, just in case.

But the car was slowing. It pulled into the kerb just in front of him. His head still lowered, he increased his pace as he went by. A door suddenly opened. His legs tensed themselves to break into a run.

'Miche? Miche Boucher? It *is* you!'

He paused, glanced back, turned.

'Bloody hell,' he said. 'Pajou.'

4

Maurice Melchior carefully examined his black velvet jacket for dust or hairs. Satisfied, he slipped his slender arms into it, spent some time adjusting the angle of his fedora, then stood back from the mirror to get the total effect.

Stunning, was the only possible verdict. He was a creature perfectly in balance, at that ideal point in his thirties where youth still burnt hot enough to melt the mature, and maturity already glowed bright enough to dazzle the young.

He tripped light as a dancer down the rickety staircase

in this tall old house. On the floor below he met Charlot, the ginger cat belonging to old Madame Simonian. Charlot wanted attention. It was hard to resist those appealing eyes, but, 'Not when I'm wearing the black velvet, my dear,' explained Melchior.

A few moments later he was out in the sunshine.

This was not the first time he had been out since the Boche came, but his previous expeditions had been furtive, frightened things, at dusk, well wrapped up, to buy a few provisions and scuttle back to his lair. Really, a man of his sensibility should have fled as soon as the invasion became a certainty, but as usual he'd put off the decision till the sight of all those jostling refugees made it quite impossible.

And what had happened? Nothing! Life, he had gradually been reassured, was going on much as before for those courageous souls who had refused to be panicked into craven flight. Today he was going out in broad daylight and not just round the corner to the grocer's shop. Today he was strolling south, leaving the Marais behind, and heading where he truly belonged.

The Left Bank! Saint-Germain-des-Prés! Everything he dreamt of was here . . . to hear his wit applauded at the Deux Magots, to have his custom valued at the Tour d'Argent . . . Dreams indeed. But even though he could rarely afford the latter and was barely admitted to the outermost circles of the former, merely to cross the river once more felt like coming home. If it hadn't been that the dear old man who had set him up in his little flat in the Rue de Thorigny all those years ago had arranged in his will for the rent to be paid as long as he stayed, he'd have moved across the river long since.

After his first exhilaration at being back in his old haunts, a certain uneasiness began to steal over him. Everything was so quiet. Not many people about and next to no traffic, except for the odd German truck which still sent him diving into the nearest doorway. He found himself thinking of going home.

Then he drew himself up to his full five feet seven inches and cried, 'No!'

Whatever this day brought forth, Maurice Melchior, aesthete, intellectual, wit, man of letters, gourmet, not to mention homosexual and Jew, would be there to greet it.

Overcome with admiration for his own courage, he stepped unheeding off the pavement. There was a screech of brakes and a car slewed to a halt across the road. It didn't actually touch Melchior but sheer shock buckled his knees and he sat down. Out of the driver's window a man in grey uniform began to shout at him in German. It wasn't difficult to get his gist.

'Be quiet,' said an authoritative voice. 'Monsieur, I hope you're not hurt.'

And Maurice Melchior looked up to see a Nordic god stooping over him with compassion and concern in his limpid blue eyes.

'My name is Zeller. Bruno Zeller. Call me Bruno. And you, monsieur . . . Melchior?'

They had come to a café on the Boulevard Saint-Michel where Melchior used to meet, or seek, student friends. The vacation and the situation combined to make it empty at the moment and the patron had been delighted to have their custom, greeting Melchior by his name, a fact which seemed to impress the German.

'Yes. Melchior's my name! Magus that I am! Bearing gifts of gold! From the East I come!'

It was a little verse from a Nativity Play which he used occasionally to quiz his Christian friends. Zeller laughed in delight.

'But call me Maurice,' he went on. 'Cigarette?'

He offered his gold case, inscribed (at his own expense) *'To Maurice – In remembrance of times past – Marcel.'*

'English,' he said. 'I hope you don't mind.'

'Not at all,' said Zeller. 'I have no prejudice.'

He smiled then let his gaze fall to the case which Melchior had left on the table.

He read the inscription and said, 'Good Lord. Is that . . . ?'

'What? Oh, yes. Dear Marcel. I was very young of course. A child. And he was old . . . ah, that cork-lined bedroom . . .'

He spent the next hour idly reminiscing about the past. His conversation was liberally laced with references to great figures of the worlds of art and literature. Nor was his familiarity altogether feigned. Though a gadfly, he'd been fluttering around the Left Bank too long not to have been accepted as a denizen.

Zeller was clearly impressed. Melchior soon had him placed as an intelligent and reasonably educated man by German standards, but culturally adolescent. Paris was to him the artistic Mecca which held all that was most holy. He needed a guide, Melchior needed a protector. They were made for each other.

But he mustn't overdo it. Was that a flicker of doubt in those lovely blue eyes as he mentioned that his mother, a laundress in Vincennes, had been mistress to both Renoir *and* Zola? He quickly asked a question about the German's family. The story which came back of a widowed mother living a reclusive life in the family castle high above the Rhine had to be true or Zeller's invention outstripped his own!

'Major Zeller. I thought it was you.'

A black Mercedes had drawn in at the kerb close to their pavement table. A man was looking out of the open rear window. He had a heavy, florid face with watery eyes in which hard black pupils glistened like beads of jet. Melchior felt something unpleasantly hypnotic in their gaze. Perhaps Zeller felt it also for he rose with evident reluctance from his chair and went to the car. But when he spoke, his tone wasn't that of a man controlled.

'Ah, Colonel Fiebelkorn. On leave? I hope you have long enough to take in all the sights.'

Melchior recognized aristocratic insolence when he heard it.

'The interesting ones.' The cold eyes slipped to Melchior. 'A guide is always useful. Why don't you introduce me to your friend, major?'

'This is *Abwehr* business,' said Zeller coldly. But Melchior had already come forward. He examined Fiebelkorn with interest. In his fifties, a powerful personality, he guessed. In the lapel of his civilian jacket he wore a tiny silver death's head. Too, too Gothic!

'Maurice Melchior,' he said, holding out his hand.

'Walter Fiebelkorn,' said the German, taking it and squeezing gently.

Good Lord, thought Melchior. Two out of two! If all German officers were like this pair, this could yet be France's finest hour!

'I'm glad the security of the Fatherland is in such safe hands,' said Fiebelkorn. 'Major, Monsieur Melchior. Till we meet again.'

As the car drew away, Melchior said testingly, 'Nice man.'

'If you can think that, you're a fool.'

'Oh dear. And that will never do if I'm to be a secret agent, will it?'

His boldness worked. Zeller laughed and took his arm.

'Let's see if we can find something better suited to your talents,' he said.

5

As the summer ended and the sick time of autumn began, Pauli caught measles. Soon afterwards Céci went down with them too. It was a worrying time but at least it focused Janine's mind outward from her daily increasing fears for Jean-Paul.

There were all kinds of rumours about French prisoners,

the most popular being that now the war was over they'd be sent home any day. But the long trains had rolled eastward since then carrying millions into captivity. Only the sick and the maimed came home, but at least most families with a missing man had learned if he were dead or alive.

But Jean-Paul Simonian's name appeared on no list.

It was to her father that Janine turned for support and sympathy. She had never forgotten the look on her mother's face when she'd run into the shop those seven years before and announced joyously that she and Jean-Paul were to be married. It had been her father then who had comforted her and made her understand just how many of his wife's prejudices had been roused in a single blow.

Briefly, by being an anti-clerical, intellectual, left-wing Jewish student, Jean-Paul Simonian was offensive in every particular. The fact that his religious targets included Judaism was a small mitigation, and getting a job as a teacher was a slightly larger one. Charm, which he always had, and children, which they quickly had, had finally sown the seeds of a truce with his mother-in-law, but it was a delicate growth and peculiar in that Jean-Paul's absence seemed to threaten it more than his presence had ever done.

Louise Crozier's attitude to the Germans was soon another point of issue.

'That nice lieutenant from the Lutétia was asking after the children this morning,' said Madame Crozier one lunchtime.

'The fat Boche? What business is it of his?' said Janine.

'He was only being polite,' retorted her mother. 'You might try it too. Politeness never hurt anyone. He always comes in on pastry day and asks for three of your brioches. I told him you hadn't done any. He wasn't at all put out but asked, very concerned, how the children were. I think he's charming.'

'He's a pig like the rest of them,' said Janine, who was tired and irritable. She had got very little sleep the previous night. 'I don't see why you encourage them to come into the shop.'

'Don't talk stupid!' said her mother. 'The war's over, so who's the enemy now? All right, the Germans are here in Paris, but they've behaved very correctly, you can't deny that. All that talk about burning and looting and raping! Why, the streets are safer now than they've ever been!'

'How can you talk like that!' demanded Janine. 'They've invaded our country, killed our soldiers. They nearly killed me and the kids. They've probably killed my husband or at best they've locked him up. And you talk as if they've done us a favour by coming here!'

'I don't think your mother really meant that, dear,' said Claude Crozier mildly.

'Permit me to say for myself what I mean!' said his wife. 'Listen, my lady, I run a business here. I don't pick my customers, they pick me. And we don't have to like each other either. But I tell you this, there's a lot of our French customers I like a lot less than Lieutenant Mai.'

'Maman,' said Pauli at the door. 'Céci's crying.'

'Shall I go?' offered Louise.

'No thanks,' said Janine. 'She doesn't speak German yet.'

She left the room, pushing her son before her.

'She gets worse,' said Madame Crozier angrily. 'I don't know where she gets it from. Not my side of the family, that's sure.'

'It's a worrying time for her what with the children being ill and no news of Jean-Paul,' said her husband.

'If you ask me, she'll be better off if she never gets any news of him,' said the woman.

'Louise! Don't talk like that!'

'Why not?' said Madame Crozier, a little ashamed and therefore doubly defiant. 'It was a mistake from the start.'

'He's a nice enough lad,' said Crozier. 'And there was never any fuss about religion. The children are being brought up good Catholics, aren't they?'

'That's no credit to him,' replied Madame Crozier, who

57

had never seen what consistency had to do with a reasoned argument. 'You can't respect a man who doesn't respect his own heritage, can you? There's someone come into the shop. Are you going to sit on your backside all day?'

With a sigh, Crozier rose and went through into the shop. A moment later he returned, followed by Christian Valois.

'She's upstairs with the little girl,' he said. 'I'll tell her you're here.'

'Thank you. Hello, Madame Crozier.'

Christian was a little afraid of Janine's mother. One of the things he admired about Jean-Paul was his mocking indifference to his in-laws. 'They're made of dough, you know,' he'd said. 'Put 'em in an oven and they'd rise!'

Louise for her part was ambivalent in her attitude to Valois. True, he was one of her son-in-law's clever-clever university chums. But he came from a good Catholic family, had a respectable job in the Civil Service, and was unfailingly polite towards her.

'Sit down,' she said. 'How are your charming parents?'

She'd never met them but knew that Valois senior was an important deputy. That was how to get the good jobs; have a bit of influence behind you! She felt envy but no disapproval.

'They are safe and well, madame,' said Valois. 'My father continues to look after the country's interests in Vichy.'

He spoke with a bitter irony which seemed to be lost on Madame Crozier.

Janine came in.

'Christian, is there news?'

'Nothing, I'm afraid. But my contacts in the Foreign Ministry are still trying. And I've written to my father asking him to help.'

She turned away in disappointment and flopped into a chair. He looked at her with exasperation. Clearly she regarded his efforts on Jean-Paul's behalf as at best coldly bureaucratic, at worst impertinently intrusive. His sacrifice

58

of pride and principle in writing to his father for assistance meant nothing to her. Why Jean-Paul had ever hitched himself to someone like this, he couldn't understand. A silly shop-girl, good for a few quick tumbles.

He said brusquely, 'There's another matter.'

'Yes?' said Janine indifferently.

'Perhaps a word in private.'

'Come through into the shop,' said Janine after a glance at her mother, who showed no sign of moving.

In the shop, Valois said, 'Have you seen Madame Simonian lately?'

'Not for a while. I usually take the children on Sundays, but they've been ill. Why? She hasn't heard anything, has she?'

The sudden eagerness in her voice irritated Valois once more.

'No,' he said. 'It's her I'm worried about. I went to see her earlier. The concierge said she'd just gone down to the greengrocer's so I went after her. I found her having an argument with a German sergeant who'd seen her pulling down the JEWISH BUSINESS poster the greengrocer had put in his window.'

'What poster's that?' interrupted Janine.

'Don't you pay attention to anything? It's been decreed that all Jewish shopkeepers have to put up these posters. Fortunately the sergeant clearly thought there weren't many medals in arresting a seventy-year-old woman for threatening him with a bunch of celery, so he was glad to let me smooth things over.'

'Yes,' she said, taking in his neat dark suit and his guarded bureaucratic expression. 'You'd be good at that, Christian. Personally I think you'd have done better to join in bashing the Boche with the celery. If we all did that, we'd soon get things back to normal!'

'All? Who are these *all*?' wondered Valois.

'People. You don't think any real Frenchman's going to sit back and let the Boche run our lives for us, do you?'

He said, 'Janine, it's real Frenchmen who are putting

their names to these decrees. I'll tell you something else that real Frenchmen have done. It's been suggested – that's the word used – *suggested* to publishing firms that they might care to do a voluntary purge on their lists, get rid of unsuitable authors such as German exiles, French nationalists, British writers, and of course Jews. They've *all* agreed! No objections. Not one!'

'Oh, those are intellectuals with their heads in the clouds, or businessmen with their noses in the trough,' said Janine wearily. 'It's the ordinary people I'm talking about. They won't let themselves be mucked around by these Boche. Just wait. You'll see. But thanks for telling me about Sophie. I'll keep an eye on her.'

As she spoke, Valois realized just how much on edge she was; emotionally frayed by worry about Jean-Paul, physically exhausted by her work in the shop combined with sleepless nights looking after the kids, and doubtless worn down by the simple strain of daily life with the formidable Louise.

Behind him the shop door opened and a German officer came in. He was a stocky fellow of indeterminate age with an ordinary kind of face, were it not for a certain shrewdness of gaze which made you think that every time he blinked, his eyes were registering photographs.

'Good day, Ma'm'selle Janine,' he said in excellent French. 'I hope the children are improving. I was asking after them when I talked with your excellent mother earlier. I thought perhaps a few chocolates might tempt their appetites back to normal . . .'

He proffered a box of chocolates. Janine ignored it and glanced furiously at Valois. She was angry that after what she'd just been saying, the civil servant should see her on such apparently familiar terms with this Boche. Feeling herself close to explosion, she took a deep breath and said, 'No thank you, lieutenant. I don't think they will help.'

'Oh,' said Günter Mai, nonplussed.

He regarded her assessingly, placed the box carefully on the counter and said, 'Forgive the intrusion. Perhaps your

dear mother, or you yourself, might enjoy them. You'll
be doing me a favour.'

He patted his waistline ruefully, touched his peak in the
shadow of a salute and brought his heels gently together
in the echo of a click.

It was the gentle mockery of these gestures plus the
diplomatic courtesy with which he'd received her rejection
that finally triggered off the explosion.

She pushed the chocolates back across the counter with
such force that the box flew through the air, struck him on
the chest and burst open, scattering its contents all over
the floor.

'Why don't you sod off and take your sodding chocolates
with you?' she shouted. 'We don't want them, do you
understand? I can look after my own kids without any help
from the likes of you.'

The door from the living quarters burst open.

'What's going on!' demanded Madame Crozier. 'What's
all the noise?'

'It's nothing, madame. The young lady is upset. Just a
little misunderstanding,' said Mai with a rueful smile.

'I've been telling your Boche friend a few home truths,'
cried Janine. 'You talk to him if you want, maman. Me,
I've had enough!'

She pushed her way past her mother and disappeared.

'Janine! Come back here!' commanded Madame Crozier. 'Lieutenant, I'm so sorry, you must forgive her, take
no notice, she's overwrought. Excuse me.'

She turned and went after her daughter. Soon angry
voices drifted back into the shop where Mai and Valois
stood looking at each other.

'And you are . . . ?' said Mai courteously.

'Valois. Of the Ministry of Finance.'

'Ah. Not in Vichy, monsieur?'

'Finance remains in Paris.'

'Of course. Good day, Monsieur Valois.'

No salute or heel clicking this time. He turned and left
the shop. Christian Valois went to the door and watched

him stroll slowly along the pavement. His back presented an easy target. With a shock of self-recognition, Valois found himself imagining pulling out a gun and pumping bullets into that hated uniform. But if he had a gun would he have the nerve to use it? He realized he was trembling.

Behind him, Louise re-entered, her face pink with emotion.

'Has he gone? Such behaviour! I don't know where she gets it from, not my family, I'm sure. She's never been the same since she married that Jew.'

She sank to her knees and began collecting chocolates. Janine came in. Ignoring her mother, she said, 'Christian, no need to worry about Sophie. Soon as the children are well enough, I'll be coming to stay with her. Will you tell her that, please? I'll be round later to sort things out.'

'It's a very small flat,' said Valois. 'You'll be awfully crowded.'

'Not as crowded as we are here, knee deep in Boches and their hangers-on.'

'Listen to her. Such ingratitude, she'll get us all killed,' muttered Louise, crawling around in search of stray chocolates.

Pauli came in and looked curiously at his crawling grandmother.

'What's gramma doing?' he asked.

'Rooting for truffles,' said Janine. 'Goodbye, Christian.'

Stepping gingerly over Louise, Christian Valois left the bakery. As he walked along the empty street, he began to smile, then to chuckle out loud.

Unobserved in a doorway on the other side, Günter Mai smiled too.

6

In October, a census of Jews was announced. They were required to report in alphabetical order to their local police station. When Janine expressed unease, Sophie laughed and said, 'It's our own French police I shall see, not the Germans. In any case, would the Marshal have met with Herr Hitler and shaken his hand if there was need to worry?'

Janine too had taken comfort from the meeting at Montoire. If things were getting back to normal, surely prisoners must soon be released? He wasn't dead . . . he couldn't be dead . . .

At the police station there was a long queue. When she reached its head, Sophie filled in her registration form with great care. Only at the *Next of Kin* section did she hesitate. Something made her look over her shoulder. Behind her, winding around the station vestibule and out of the door, stretched the queue. Conversation was low; most didn't speak at all, but stood with expressions of stolid resignation, every now and then shuffling forward to whatever fate officialdom had devised for them.

'Come on, old lady,' said a gendarme. 'What's the hold-up?'

She put a stroke of the pen through *Next of Kin*.

'What? No family?'

'A son. Until the war.'

'I'm sorry. Thank God it's all over for the rest of us. Now sign your name and be on your way.'

It felt good to be out in the street again and her confidence rapidly returned as she walked home as briskly as her rheumatic knee permitted.

As she reached the apartment building, Maurice Melchior emerged, resplendent in a long astrakhan coat which he'd been given by accident from the cloakroom at the Comédie-Française the previous winter and at last felt safe in wearing.

'Good day, Madame Simonian. And how are you? Taking the air?'

Piqued at being accused of such unproductive activity, Sophie said sharply, 'No, monsieur. I've been to register.'

'Register?' He raised his eyebrows. 'How quaint! Good day, madame!'

Melchior set off at a brisk pace, eager to put as much distance as possible between himself and this silly old Jewess who'd gone voluntarily to put her name on an official census-list. How desperate people were to convince themselves that everything was normal. Normal! All they had to do was stroll along the boulevards and look in the shop windows. Everything had gone. Ration coupons had been introduced the previous month. And the forecast was for a long, hard winter. The only people who had any cause for complacency were the black-marketeers.

I must make some contacts, thought Melchior. But not today. Today he had more immediate and personal worries.

Bruno was close to dumping him, that was the brutal truth. A couple of nights earlier they'd visited the Deux Magots where Melchior, rather full of Bruno's excellent brandy, had spotted Cocteau in a corner.

'Do I know him? Blood-brothers, dear boy! Of course I'll introduce you.' And he'd set off across the room, big smile, outstretched hand, with Bruno in close formation. The Great Man (pretentious shit!) had thrust an empty bottle into the outstretched hand and said, 'Another of the same, waiter. A bit colder this time,' and all his arse-licking cronies had set up a jeering bray.

Zeller turned on his heel and stormed out of the door. By the time Melchior got out, he was in his car. The engine drowned Maurice's attempts at explanation and apology, and as he grasped the door handle, the car accelerated away, pulling him to his knees in the gutter.

Perhaps it was the supplicatory pose; or perhaps Zeller was reminded of the circumstances of their first meeting. He stopped the car, reversed and opened the door.

'Get in,' he said.

They drove away at high speed up the Rue de Rennes and turned into the Boulevard Raspail.

'Are we going to the Lutétia?' asked Melchior.

'Yes.'

Melchior relapsed into a nervous silence. Once before he had suggested provocatively that Bruno should take him to dine at the Lutétia. The German had said coldly, 'The only Frenchmen who come into *Abwehr* Head-quarters are agents or prisoners. It can be arranged.'

Now Melchior recalled that moment and shivered.

The trouble was things hadn't been going well for some weeks. As life returned to something like normal it had grown increasingly difficult to maintain his claim to be at the artistic heart of things. Name-dropping was only successful if the names dropped kept a decent distance from the city. But many had returned, and even when they were polite, they made it very clear they were not intimate with him. Usually he was able to bluff it out but a snub like tonight's was too unambiguous for bluff.

They entered the hotel by a side-door. It was clear he wasn't going to see the public rooms. 'Who's duty officer?' Zeller demanded of an armed corporal.

'Lieutenant Mai, sir.'

'Fetch him.'

When Günter Mai arrived, annoyed at having been dragged from his dinner, he recognized Melchior instantly but concealed the fact. His superior's sexual impulses were his own affair as long as they didn't compromise the section's security. As soon as the inevitable happened and Zeller found himself a 'friend', Mai had done a thorough check. In the light of official Party attitudes to Jews and perverts, Maurice Melchior was not an ideal companion for a German officer. But it was clear he hadn't a political thought in his head. Motivated entirely by hedonistic self-interest, conceited, cowardly, the little queer posed no security risk at all. But what on earth was he doing here?

'This is Monsieur Melchior,' said Zeller. 'I'll be interviewing him immediately. Is there a room?'

'Of course, sir,' said Mai. 'This way.'

In the sparsely furnished room, Zeller waited till Mai had closed the door behind him, then said, 'Let's talk seriously, Maurice.'

'Delighted. But why have you brought me here?'

'So you'll understand quite clearly what I'm saying to you,' said Zeller softly. 'Maurice, you haven't been honest with me, have you? You've been a naughty boy.'

'Always willing to oblige,' laughed Melchior.

'Shut up! It seems that far from being the celebrity you claim, you're a nobody. Worse, you're a bit of a laughing stock. That's your bad luck, but by your idiocy, you've got me involved in it too. I don't care to be made to look ridiculous, Maurice. Getting mixed up with you was a mistake. Some people can forget mistakes. I can't. I need to correct them.'

'What do you mean, Bruno?' demanded Melchior nervously.

'You're going to have to start earning your keep,' said Zeller spitefully. 'As a cultural guide, you're a dead loss. As a sexual partner, you have your moments, but frankly, with the exchange rate the way it is, I can afford troupes of prettier, younger, more athletic friends than you, and there's no shortage of offers. So that leaves only one avenue.'

'What's that, Bruno?' asked Melchior, his mouth dry.

'When we first met, you asked if I was going to make an agent out of you. Like you, I took it as a joke. But by Christ, Maurice, the joking time is over. Those big ears and sharp eyes of yours must be good for something. From now on, if you want protection – and the alternative, let me assure you, is persecution – you're going to earn your keep. Do you understand me?'

Hell hath no fury like a German officer made to feel ridiculous, thought Günter Mai who was listening in the next room. But trying to make an agent out of a creature like Melchior, that really *was* ridiculous. There could be trouble there. Should he try to warn Zeller? He thought not. It would mean admitting his knowledge. And Zeller probably wouldn't listen. Besides, he thought with a smile, a bit of trouble wouldn't do that gilded youth any harm at all.

A not unkind man, Günter Mai might have been rather more concerned, though not much, if he could have shared Melchior's growing panic as October turned to November and Zeller's threats became more and more dire. He tried to explain how terribly difficult it was for someone like himself to become an agent. He was more than willing to oblige, dear Bruno must believe that, but the kind of gossip he was so expert at collecting was not, alas, the kind which held much interest for the guardians of military security.

But at last a break had come. There were rumours everywhere that, angered by the complacent acceptance by their elders of the German Occupation, the university students were planning some kind of demonstration on November 11th, armistice day. Melchior spent all his spare time in the cafés on the Boul' Miche where once he had sought the occasional pick-up. The youngsters were happy enough to let him pay for their drinks, but laughed behind his back at his efforts to draw them. Did someone who had so shamelessly flaunted his Aryan nancy-boy really believe they were going to spill their plans for a few cups of coffee?

But there were others who noticed and did not discount his efforts so scornfully.

On November 10th, he was sitting disconsolately in the café where he'd taken Bruno after their first meeting. The owner no longer greeted him by name now his usual clientele were back, and not even free coffee seemed able to buy him company today. As one student had explained, thinking to be kind, 'You've grown so dull, Maurice, since you stopped trying to screw us.'

He rose and left. As he walked along the rain-polished pavement observing with distaste the spattering of his mirror-like shoes, footsteps came hurrying after him. He looked round to see a youngster he knew as Émile approaching. He was a pale, sick-looking boy, and shabby even by student standards. When he caught up, he glanced behind him furtively, then drew Maurice off the boulevard into a doorway.

'Monsieur,' he said. 'I need money.'

'I'm sorry,' said Melchior. 'A couple of francs is all I have . . .'

'I need a thousand. Five hundred at the very least.'

Melchior looked at him sharply. This was obviously no ordinary touch.

He said, 'Even if I had such a sum, which I don't, why should I loan it to you?'

'Not loan. Pay. Look, monsieur, everyone knows you're very interested in the plans for our demo tomorrow. Well, I can tell you it's not going to wait till tomorrow. Come midnight tonight, and you'll be able to see to read, if you're in the right places. I know those places.'

'But that'll mean breaking the curfew.'

'It's not the only thing that will be broken,' said Émile. 'Come on. Are you in the market or not?'

'Why are you doing this?' asked Melchior.

'Because if I don't, I'll be flung off my course by the weekend, if I don't get flung off a bridge first by the people I owe money to.'

These were reasons Melchior could understand. He said, 'I'd need proof.'

'For God's sake, what's proof? I've got a copy of the plan with timings and locations, if that's what you mean.'

'I'll tell you what,' said Melchior who despite everything was quite enjoying getting into his role. 'You give me the plan. If it works out, I'll pay you five hundred francs tomorrow.'

'Go and screw yourself, you little fairy,' said Émile angrily. 'You don't imagine I'm going to trust someone like you!'

Melchior smiled, unhurt, and said significantly, 'It wouldn't be me you were trusting, Émile. Your payment would be guaranteed, believe me.'

The youngster weighed this up. Strange, thought Melchior. He knows I mean the Germans and he'll doubtless end up by deciding he can trust them more than he'd trust me.

He was right.

'OK,' said the student reluctantly. 'Payment tomorrow morning, nine sharp, the Tuileries Gardens, by the Orangerie. And it'll be the full thousand for extended credit, all right?'

'Agreed,' said Melchior, holding out his hand.

A folded sheet of paper was put into it, then Émile turned on his heel and hurried away into the gathering dusk.

Melchior walked along, studying the paper. There were going to be torchlight processions starting in the Place de la Bastille at 11.30. And once the authorities' attention had been concentrated on the processions, the Embassy, in the Rue de Lille, and the Hôtel de Ville were going to be the objects of the main demos at midnight. Melchior practically danced along the pavement in his elation. No hint of such early activity had emerged hitherto. This would be a real coup for Bruno. Surely he must show his gratitude by restoring their relationship?

But now as quickly as it had come, his joy faded as a sense of revulsion swept over him. What the hell was he doing? Giving this to Bruno meant hundreds of youngsters could be walking into a trap. And the Boche wouldn't be gentle, that was sure. No! He wouldn't do it. Bruno could go jump in the Seine!

He walked on, feeling incredibly noble.

Then he heard the sound of breaking glass. He turned a corner and saw a tobacconist's with its window shattered. Pasted on the door was a now familiar sign saying JEWISH BUSINESS. Two youths with the armbands of the Parti Populaire Français were standing laughing on the pavement. They fell silent as he walked past. Then he heard their footsteps coming after him. Faster and faster he walked till he was almost running.

Finally, exhausted by effort and fear, he stopped and turned.

He was alone. But he had left his feeling of nobility far behind.

7

Every year on November 11th, Sophie Simonian went to the Tomb of the Unknown Warrior to leave some flowers and make her own personal thanksgiving.

'Bubbah, this year say thanks at home or in the synagogue,' urged Janine.

Sophie looked at her in surprise and said, 'Why should I change the habit of twenty years, child? I owe it to Iakov for his safe return.'

Realizing she had no hope of winning the argument, Janine insisted on accompanying her, leaving the children in the care of a neighbour.

As their train pulled into l'Étoile métro station, she saw that the platforms were crowded and the crush of people getting into the carriage prevented the two women from getting out. When Sophie began to grow agitated, a middle-aged man who'd just entered said, 'Take it easy, old lady. You're better off down here than up there. You'd not be let out of the station anyway!'

'What's going on?' demanded Janine.

'Chaos,' he said. 'There's been demonstrations, students mainly. The Boche are clearing the streets, and not being too gentle about how they do it.'

They managed to get off at the next station. Janine wanted to cross platforms and head straight home, but Sophie ignored her pleas and, clutching her small posy of Michaelmas daisies, marched out of the station and turned up the avenue towards l'Étoile.

Janine half-expected to find a howling mob. Instead what she saw was a lot of people, scattered enough for passage among them to be relatively easy, and not making a great deal of mob-noise. But the atmosphere felt electric.

'Janine! Madame Simonian! What are you doing here?'

It was Valois, his sallow face flushed with excitement.

Janine told him and Sophie flourished her posy.

'I'd get rid of those,' said Valois. 'The Boche seem allergic to flowers. Oh Christ, here they come!'

An armoured car was moving steadily down the centre of the avenue with soldiers fanning out on either side. They held their rifles at the port and their trotting feet kept perfect time so that the thud of the boots was a powerful heart-beat under the panicking cries of the crowd.

People started to scatter and run.

'Come on!' urged Valois.

But Sophie had neither the strength nor the inclination to flee and the best Janine could manage was to pull her behind an advertising stand which would at least part the advancing line.

The soldiers broke, re-formed, passed on. Except one, a cadaverous, pock-faced man who looked frightened enough to be brutal.

'Go on,' he snarled. 'Fuck off out of it quick! Run! Run! Run!'

He thrust at them with his rifle as he spoke. Janine and Valois tried to protect Sophie but she pushed between them.

'I'm going to the tomb,' she said clearly. 'To lay these flowers.'

71

She held out the posy. The soldier looked at it in puzzlement as if imagining it was being offered to him. Then he struck it from her grasp and said, 'Get off out of it, you old bag. I won't tell you again.'

'You bastard!' cried Valois. Before he could move, Janine flung her arms round him. She could see the soldier was keyed up enough to shoot.

'We must get Sophie away,' she urged.

Valois's tense body relaxed. 'You're right,' he said. 'There'll be time for that.'

They hurried the old lady to the station. A sergeant and two privates were lounging there, cheerfully waving back anyone still trying to emerge. When they saw that the newcomers wanted to go in, they politely stood aside.

'That's right, darling,' said the sergeant. 'Home's best today. I wish I was coming with you!'

And the soldiers' mocking laughter followed them down the stairs.

Half a mile away, a German corporal was growing very irritated. He'd been up since before midnight, first of all lying in wait to quell an assault on the Embassy which never happened. Then, when at last he was stood down, he'd just had time to have some breakfast and stretch himself out on his bunk before he was ordered out again to deal with some real demonstrations. All was quiet now, and he could be thinking of getting back to that bunk if this funny little twerp would stop babbling at him in broken German.

Maurice Melchior had woken up to a terrifying silence. No one was talking about midnight marches and torchlight processions and assaults on the Embassy. He was supposed to meet Zeller early to collect Émile's pay-off, but he had the sense not to keep that appointment. He did go to the Orangerie, however, and hung around in growing despair till news of the disturbances at l'Étoile had brought him hurrying here, hoping against hope that somehow *his* disturbances had moved on in space and time.

The corporal grew angry. The little fairy was apparently taking the piss about last night's abortive ambush! Only his eagerness to get to bed stopped him from arresting him. He turned away. The Frenchie grasped his shoulder! That did it. He turned and hit him in the gut. Melchior sank to the ground. The corporal swung back his foot.

'No,' said a voice from a staff-car which had drawn up alongside.

Through tear-clouded eyes, Melchior recognized a face. No. *Two* faces. One, looking at him through the window, was Colonel Fiebelkorn's. The other, less frightening but more incredible, belonged to a man getting out of the car. He looked at Melchior and smiled as he walked past. It was Émile.

'Monsieur Melchior,' said Fiebelkorn opening the door. 'Won't you join me?'

For days there were rumours of pitched battles, hundreds killed, thousands arrested. The truth was less dramatic. No deaths, a few injuries, and only one arrest on a serious charge.

'Some poor devil miles away from the demos got jostled by a drunken Boche and jostled back. Now he's facing the death penalty for violence against the German Army! At least it'll show people what kind of monsters we're up against.'

'Isn't that a big price to pay for an illustration?' wondered Janine.

'Don't give me that bourgeois sentimental crap,' retorted Valois.

'All I mean is a man's life seems more important to me than anything else.'

'Oh yes? And to get Jean-Paul home safe and sound, how many death-warrants would you be prepared to sign? One? Two? Three? A hundred?'

'I don't know. That's different. It would depend . . . I don't know!'

'It's a question of objectives and priorities, isn't it?' said Valois bleakly.

'Christian, are you a communist?' asked Janine.

'Don't be silly,' he replied, suddenly gay. 'Didn't you know, the communists are Herr Hitler's friends, bound to him by formal agreement? They're finding it even harder to be consistent than you are!'

It was true. This seemed a time of inconsistencies. On December 15th the Marshal had his vice-president, Laval, arrested. Abetz, the German ambassador, immediately went to Vichy to have him released. Meanwhile, at midnight on December 16th, a gun carriage rumbled through the curfew-emptied snow-feathered streets flanked by a mixed escort of French and German soldiers. On the carriage was a coffin containing the body of the Duke of Reichstadt, Napoleon's only son, exhumed from the imperial vault in Vienna, and returned at Hitler's own behest to be set at his father's side in Les Invalides. For a short while Bayreuth came to Paris and under the flaming torches of this Wagnerian stage-setting, all the civic dignitaries, French and German alike, shivered through their walk-on parts. This conciliatory gesture was followed a week later by the execution of the man arrested during the November demonstrations.

Then it was Christmas.

'You must go to your parents, for the children's sake, especially, but for your own sake too,' said Sophie firmly.

'But what about you?' said Janine.'Why should you be left alone at Christmas?'

Sophie laughed merrily.

'What are you saying? An old Jewess *alone* at Christmas? What's Christmas to me, liebchen?'

'All right, I'll go,' said Janine. Then she added, guiltily aware that despite her objection she had really made up her mind before Sophie spoke, 'I was going to anyway.'

'I knew you were,' said the old lady laughing. 'You're a good daughter.'

74

'You think so?' said Janine doubtfully. 'I don't always feel it. I don't feel grown-up yet. Adults should be prepared to suffer the consequences of their own decisions, shouldn't they? In any case, it's me who has the rows with maman, but it's papa and the children who suffer the consequences.'

Sophie shook her head.

'Yes, when I first knew you, that was very much how you were. But you've grown a lot since then, child. And you're still growing.'

'Am I? Have I far to go, Bubbah?' she asked, half-mocking, half-serious.

'Further than I care to see, it sometimes feels,' said the old lady, for a moment very frail and distant. But before Janine could express her concern, Sophie laughed and said with her usual energy, 'And when I said you were a good daughter, I meant to me as well as to Madame Crozier.'

The welcome they received on Christmas Eve made Janine ashamed that she could even have dreamt of staying away. Louise burst into tears of joy at seeing them and later, while she was out of the room putting the children to bed, Claude said confidentially to his daughter, 'If you'd not come here, we were going to come round to see you tomorrow.'

'Maman too? But she said she'd never visit Sophie's flat again.'

Never set foot in that heathen temple had been the precise phrase.

'I told her it was Christmas and she'd have to swallow her pride,' said Claude. 'She shouted at me a bit, but deep down she wanted to be told.'

'Yes,' said Janine ruefully. 'I know how she feels.'

The truce lasted all that evening and even survived Janine's amazement the next morning at the way in which rationing and growing food shortages did not seem to have affected her mother's preparations for Christmas dinner. Probably all over Paris, housewives were performing similar miracles, she assured herself. But she had a feeling this miracle had started with a bit more than a few loaves and fishes.

Just on midday with the house rich with the smell of baking and boiling and roasting, the door burst open to admit a tall, broad-shouldered, red-bearded man, resplendent in a beautifully cut suit, pale grey almost to whiteness, a virginal silk shirt and a flowered necktie fastened with a diamond-studded gold pin. He had the look of a pirate king dressed up for his bosun's wedding. On his arm was an elegantly furred woman with tight black curls, a great deal of make-up, bright-red nail varnish and a good figure, slightly thickening with rather heavy thighs.

'My God, Miche, is that you?' said Janine.

'Cousin Janine, how are you, girl?' Boucher cried, stooping to give her a kiss which went a little way beyond the cousinly. His beard was soft and fragrant with attar of roses.

'I hoped you'd be here. I've brought a few things for the kids. Hey, this is Hélène Campaux, by the way. La Belle Hélène, eh? She dances at the Folies. Some mover! Now where are those kids? And where's the old folks?'

'I think they're in the bakehouse,' said Janine. 'I'll go and tell them . . .'

Warn them, she meant. But it was too late.

The door opened.

Madame Crozier stopped dead in her tracks when she saw the newcomers.

Then spreading her arms, she cried, 'Michel, my dear. You've come!'

And with an expression of amazement which matched anything her father ever produced, Janine saw these old antagonists embrace with all the fervour of dear friends, long parted.

It soon became clear that the reconciliation had taken place some time before and obviously had much to do with Cousin Miche's new affluence. He presided over the feast like a red-bearded Father Christmas, commandeering Pauli's help to fetch in from a rakish Hispano-Suiza bottles

of champagne, a smoked ham, a tub of pâté de foie gras
and a whole wheel of Camembert. In addition there were
the promised presents, a huge fairy doll for Céci and a
football and a penknife for Pauli.

Janine demurred at the knife.

'He's far too young. He'll cut himself.'

'Nonsense!' said her cousin. 'Me, I was carrying daggers
and knuckle-dusters at his age!'

This reference to his criminal past, far from offending
Louise, provoked her into peals of laughter. But she went
on to say, 'Janine's right. He's too young for a knife.'

Pauli said, 'Maman, it's not all a knife. It's got all kinds
of things.'

He demonstrated, pulling out one after another a cork-
screw, a bottle-opener, a screw-driver, a gimlet.

'I can't cut myself with these,' he said earnestly. 'If I
promise not to open the blade till I'm old enough, can I
keep it? Please, maman?'

He fixed his unblinking wide-eyed gaze upon her, not
beseeching, but inviting her to retreat before the logic of
his argument.

As usual, there seemed nothing else to do.

'All right,' she said. 'Only, Pauli, *I'll* decide when you're
old enough, you understand?'

'Yes, maman.'

'Then promise.'

'I promise,' he said solemnly.

'Janine, are you sure? He's only a child,' protested
Louise. 'You're far too soft, I always said.'

'Except when you said I was too hard,' retorted Janine.

This small crack in good will was smoothly papered over
by Hélène, who said, 'Isn't it lovely to see them opening
their presents? I just long to have children of my own,
Janine. You're so lucky to have this beautiful pair.'

She sounded as if she meant it and Janine found herself
warming to her. Soon they were deep in domestic conversation, while Madame Crozier busied herself being the
perfect hostess, and Boucher and Monsieur Crozier talked

nostalgically about the great cyclists of the thirties. One thing that no one mentioned was the immediate past or the foreseeable future. The Paris – indeed the France – that lay outside the door might not have existed. Christmas, always a game, was being played with extra fervour this year.

Only a child to whom all play is reality could not grasp the rules of this game. Pauli ate his dinner silently, and drank his wine and water, and looked after his little sister who still found it hard to discriminate between nose and mouth. And all the time he hardly ever took his eyes off Michel Boucher. But Janine knew, and the knowledge wrenched her heart, that it was his father he was seeing.

And now her own father, as if catching the thought, broke the rules too and said quietly when Pauli had taken his sister to the lavatory, 'Any news of Jean-Paul?'

Janine shook her head. Boucher said, 'That man of yours not turned up yet? That's lousy. Have you tried the Red Cross?'

'I've tried everything,' said Janine dully. She listed all her channels of enquiry. Hélène put her hand over hers and squeezed sympathetically, while Boucher snorted his opinion of civil servants and bureaucracy.

Then Louise came in with brandy and chocolates and the subject was shelved.

When the time came for the visitors to go, Janine showed them out. After he had put Hélène in the car, Miche came back to the shop doorway and kissed her in a fairly cousinly manner.

'It's been great today,' he said.

'That's good, Miche. And it was lovely having you and Hélène here.'

'Yeah. Surprising too, eh?' He laughed. 'I saw your face! Thing is I've always liked your dad. He's been good to me over the years, more than the rest of you know. All the family I've got, you Croziers. It was meeting Hélène that made me realize a man needed a family. So when I started doing well enough to get round Auntie Lou, I thought, what the hell. I can put up with her funny little ways.'

'I'm glad, Miche. You and Hélène are really serious then?'

'Do me a favour!' he said. 'I'm too young to be *really* serious. But serious enough. Look, Jan, none of my business, but about Jean-Paul, if you like I'll have a word with my new boss, see if he can help.'

'Your new boss. Who's that, Miche?' asked Janine suspiciously.

'Doesn't matter, if he can help, does it?' laughed Boucher. 'And if he can't, then it doesn't matter either. I'll be in touch. Hey, what are you doing on New Year's Eve? Fancy going to a party?'

'I don't think so, Miche,' said Janine. 'I'm not really in the party mood at the moment.'

'No? On second thoughts, you probably wouldn't enjoy this one anyway,' he said with a grin. 'Cheers, kids. Pauli, you look after your mother now. *Wiedersehen!*'

And as Janine frowned her displeasure, he smiled, shrugged and said, 'When in Rome, sweetie, do like they do in Berlin. *Leb'wohl!*'

8

So the year drew to its close. Winter like the Germans came swiftly, hit hard, felt as if it was here to stay.

'I'll tell you something, Günter,' said Major Zeller. 'I never thought it would be so easy.'

'Victory, you mean?'

'No. Not victory in the field, anyway. It was always possible that *that* would be easy. No, the remarkable thing is the degree to which we have got ourselves accepted.

More than accepted. Welcomed! I actually feel at home in this city, a visitor rather than a conqueror.'

He paused, then went on, 'It would please me, Günter, if from time to time as I spoke to you, that you gave a little nod of agreement or let something other than lugubrious doubt light up that gamekeeper face of yours.'

'Sorry,' said Mai.

'You don't agree?'

'It's early days, sir,' said Mai. 'You knock a man down, he may be concussed and in shock for a long time afterwards. He may even believe that he didn't really mind being knocked down. But you'd better wait till he's fully himself again before deciding if you really want him holding the ladder while you're cleaning windows.'

Zeller regarded him curiously.

'Cleaning windows? How quaint you sometimes are, Günter. I do hope you will not put your quaintness forward as official *Abwehr* thinking tonight. The SD are keen enough to undermine us without giving them ammunition in the Embassy.'

'I'll try to remember my manners, sir. I expect in any case I've only been invited to hand out drinks to the distinguished foreign guests. Is Monsieur Melchior attending on our ticket, by the way?'

A glittering New Year reception was being held at the Embassy. All the main sections of the Occupying Authority had been asked to submit suggestions for the guest list. Mai knew very well that there was more chance of Zeller suggesting Winston Churchill than Melchior. The major was still being ribbed by officers in those units put on alert for the non-existent midnight disturbances. He was convinced that somehow the SD had been behind the fiasco to make the *Abwehr* look ridiculous. Mai didn't discount the possibility but didn't reckon Melchior would have had the nerve to fool Zeller knowingly.

'I should prefer not to hear that revolting creature's name mentioned, lieutenant,' said Zeller dangerously. 'I don't know where he's been hiding for the past weeks, but when he finally crawls out of his hole, he's going to wish he'd burrowed down the centre of the earth.'

Going to give him a spanking, are we? thought Mai. But the look on his superior's face convinced him it would be unwise even to hint he found the matter more amusing than tragic.

That night as he stood in the most obscure corner of the huge reception room in the Embassy, feeling itchy and uncomfortable in his dress uniform, he wondered if perhaps Zeller hadn't been right about one thing. Looking round the glittering assembly, it was easy to believe that all the richest, most influential members of the Parisian ruling classes were here. Women in elegant billows of silk and satin, necks and bosoms gleaming with gold or dazzling with diamonds; men in tail-suits that actually fitted, some with the medals of other campaigns in other wars pinned proudly on their chests; smiling, dancing, drinking, joking with their conquerors. Could it be that Zeller was right? Could they not only have won the war, but somehow managed to win the peace?

As if summoned by his thoughts, the major appeared. He looked vital, assured, handsome, a true conqueror.

'Enjoying yourself, Günter? The perfect end to a perfect year, wouldn't you say? Triumph after triumph! There's been nothing like it since Augustan Rome!'

'Remember, you are mortal, major.'

'What?'

'Didn't the Romans use to set a slave close behind the conqueror in his triumph to whisper as he acknowledged the cheers of the crowd, *Remember, you are mortal?*'

'Did they? And is that the role you think God's allocated you?' said Zeller sarcastically. 'No, I shouldn't think so. Basically you're too arrogant a bastard to think of yourself as a slave.'

Mai smiled. He wasn't about to be provoked into a public row with his superior. That kind of fight was no-contest.

In any case, he definitely hadn't been picked to remind Zeller of his human frailty that night. God had chosen

81

quite another champion. Mai knew this because, over the major's shoulder, he could see him approaching. And soon they could both hear his voice, fluting its deflating message.

'Bruno, dear boy! I thought it was you, so unmistakable from behind! I'm so glad you could make it!'

Zeller swung round to confirm with his eyes what his ears found incredible.

'What in the name of God are you doing here?' he cried, bewilderment as yet stronger than rage.

Maurice Melchior raised his eyebrows.

'I'm having a really delightful time, that's what.'

He turned round, his elegant silken dinner jacket giving a quick flash of a brilliant scarlet lining.

'Walter, I told you he'd be here. Bruno, my dear, you know my friend, Walter, of course. But let's be formal, I know how much protocol matters to you military boys. Lieutenant-Colonel Fiebelkorn, may I have the honour of presenting you to Major Bruno Zeller?'

Mai saw the delight trembling through Melchior's whole body as he made the introduction. Even clearer was the fury that held Zeller stiff, his fists clenched so tight that the silver signet ring stood out like a weapon. Melchior could live to rue the day he had made the major an enemy.

But as Günter Mai looked at the SS colonel's impassive face and unblinking watery gaze, he felt a sudden certainty that it had been a far more dangerous day for Melchior when he had made Fiebelkorn his friend.

Across the room, a gorgeous French film star fanned her nearly naked breasts and complained how warm it was. A gallant Panzer officer immediately leant forward, drew back the heavy brocaded curtains and began to wrestle with a window.

'The black-out! Remember the black-out!' called some-one.

'The black-out?' said the Panzer officer. 'Why bother? There's no danger up there unless Churchill starts sending trained pigeons from Trafalgar Square!'

There was a burst of laughter which became general as

this shaft of Aryan wit was passed around the room and for a while the open curtain was forgotten, allowing the brilliance of the many chandeliers to spill its diamantine glory into the darkness outside.

A crowd had gathered earlier in the Rue de Lille to see the notables arrive, but as midnight approached, despite a rumoured assurance that the curfew would be suspended for this night, most of the watchers had drifted away to their own houses and their own meditations on the dying year.

A few remained, however. Among them was Janine Simonian. She had felt compelled to get out of Sophie's tiny flat that night. She'd let herself drift but hadn't been surprised to find herself in the University quarter. She had been brought here first by Jean-Paul. It was here that her eyes had been opened to a world outside the bakery, a world of ideas and imagination, of criticism and curiosity. Finally the memories had become too much and to escape them she joined the watchers in the Rue de Lille.

'What's happening?' she asked someone.

'It's a ball, just like the old days,' was the reply.

At that moment the curtain was drawn back and the spectators could see right into the reception hall. Music drifted out, and laughter. Elegant women in expensive clothes were drinking with attentive men in formal evening dress or colourful dress uniforms. It was a scene of assurance and power; it stated more forcibly than marching troops or rumbling gun carriages that we, here, inside, are the conquerors and will be for ever; while you, outside, are for ever the conquered.

A flurry of snow passed overhead, leaving flakes on her cheeks like tears. The last watchers began to depart. Someone said, 'Happy New Year,' but no one replied.

Janine said, 'Jean-Paul, wherever you are, Happy New Year, my love.'

Then she too turned and walked slowly away from the light.

PART THREE
February–December 1941

Dans une telle situation, il n'y a que
le premier pas qui coûte.

Madame du Deffand

1

If it wasn't the coldest February in years, to most Frenchmen it felt like it.

Monsieur Édouard Scheffer of Strasbourg sat in the Café Balzac near the Quai de Grenelle métro station and shivered. Not even two thicknesses of overcoat, a Homburg hat and frequent additions to his vile coffee from a gun-metal hip flask could keep him warm. The patron, who valued his custom, was apologetic. He and Monsieur Scheffer had done a few small blackmarket deals in the couple of months since Miche the Butcher had introduced them, so he was sure that Monsieur would appreciate the problem of fuel shortage.

The seated man nodded and thought of his beautifully warm room at the Lutétia. Bruno Zeller would never undertake assignments which involved freezing to death. In fairness it was difficult to imagine Zeller being able to pass himself off as anything other than a German officer, but just now Günter Mai didn't feel like being fair.

The door opened. Two figures entered. One was Boucher, the other was the girl. Boucher peered down the long shadowy room in search of him. He always sat at the furthermost end near the kitchen door, partly for security, partly to avoid the draught.

Now Boucher saw him. Spoke to the girl. Pointed.

She looked, saw, recognized.

In that instant he could see she'd had no idea who she was going to meet. He'd assumed Boucher would have told her, and he'd been surprised when nevertheless the redhead had confirmed the meet was on. But all that he'd read into this was that the girl was desperate, and desperate people made easy recruits.

She was trying to leave but her cousin was hanging on to her arm. Mai willed him to let her go. If she was forced to confront him now, his cover could be blown and he found Édouard Scheffer very useful.

She was coming. Damn. He signalled the patron to bring more coffee. The girl arrived and glowered down at him.

'Darling, how good to see you. Not still angry with me, are you?'

She was taken aback. The patron, arriving with the coffee, grinned lecherously, scenting a lovers' quarrel. Angrily she sat in the chair he ostentatiously pulled out for her.

Mai took out his flask and poured an ounce of liquor into her glass.

'I don't like schnapps,' she said. But he noted with approval that she waited till the patron retired out of earshot.

'Me neither,' he said. 'That's why I carry cognac.'

She drank, enjoyed, didn't try to hide it. Or perhaps couldn't. Not the best quality of a prospective agent, an inability to hide your feelings, thought Mai. Still he wasn't really thinking of her as a Mata Hari.

'I didn't know it was you,' said Janine.

'You wouldn't have come?' asked Mai.

She shook her head then added, 'Not because of the shop, what happened that time, but . . .'

'Because I'm not a general, someone important? I take your point.'

She was much calmer now. It didn't surprise him. This was what he was noted for – baiting, hooking, playing, and not so much landing the little fish as persuading it to jump out of the water.

He produced his pipe, held it up in a token request for permission, and lit it. Women often found a pipe reassuring.

'That's right,' she said. 'Someone important.'

He studied her through his pipe smoke. On her entry to the café he had thought she was plumper than he remembered. Now he realized that like himself she was just wearing several layers of clothes against the cold and was in fact rather thinner than he recalled. It was a good face, not beautiful but intriguing, full of life and mobility despite the wasting effects of this long winter.

'Don't you even want to talk about your problem?' he asked.

'There's nothing to talk about.'

'Oh? You've managed to track down Corporal Jean-Paul Simonian of the Light Infantry then?'

She went red with shock and anger.

'He shouldn't have told you,' she said. 'He had no right.'

'He didn't tell me anything,' said Mai. 'I got the details elsewhere.'

For a moment she looked puzzled then it dawned.

'Maman!' she said. 'She's been talking to you, hasn't she?'

He was right. She was no fool. He nodded.

'Mothers like to talk about their children,' he said. 'Even when they quarrel. She doesn't blame you. She told me you were on edge because you'd no idea what had happened to your husband. So when Miche said you had a problem, I guessed.'

'Very clever,' said Janine. 'What else did maman say? That I'd be better off if Jean-Paul never came back?'

Mai shrugged, a good French shrug.

'He mightn't, you know that? In fact it's the likeliest explanation.'

'Of course I know that.'

Her anger had faded. She drank her spiked coffee. He drew on his pipe. He could see she was building an equation, checking what it meant. At last she shook her head. There was neither relief nor disappointment in her voice when she spoke.

'This is a waste of time. For both of us. I'll be honest with you. Since Miche arranged this meeting, I've been wondering why any German should even think of helping me. There's only one possible reason. He'd want me to

89

agree to be an informer, a spy, something like that.'

She paused. He asked, 'And what had you decided?'

'I decided anyone who got me as a spy would have made a bad bargain,' she said with an unexpected flash of humour. 'Though I suppose, now that I know Miche's boss isn't a stranger, there could be another possibility.'

It took him a couple of seconds to work it out. He had to make an effort to keep the surprise out of his face, but Janine put his thoughts into words.

'But I daresay that German officers have found easier ways of getting girls. Anyway, the point is, now I've seen you, there's no point. I can't see a mere lieutenant being any more useful to me than the Red Cross or a Vichy deputy. So thank you for the drink and goodbye.' She rose to leave.

He didn't try to stop her.

She walked straight past Boucher at the bar without saying a word.

'Hey, Janine,' he cried, going after her. 'What's up?' he demanded as he overtook her in the street. 'Won't he help?'

'He's a lieutenant, Miche. A nobody. You should have told me. What can someone like that do?'

'Look, I'm sorry,' he said walking fast to keep up with her. 'You're probably right. Except that he strikes me as a clever sod, despite appearances, and my mate, Pajou – he's the one who got me the job – he reckons old Günter really runs half the show at the Lutétia.'

She stopped and turned to face him.

'This job of yours, what is it exactly?' she asked.

'It's all above board,' he assured her. 'We help the authorities recover things. Food that's been hoarded, valuables that have been hidden, illegally I mean.'

'You help the Boche to loot!'

'No,' he said with genuine indignation. 'It's just recovery. People abandon their houses, make no proper provision for storing delicate antiques, the authorities take care of them.'

'Rich Jews' villas, you mean? And what do you know about delicate antiques, Miche?'

He grinned and said, 'Not much. But they have experts to deal with things like that. And it's not just Jewish stuff either. I reckon it's a lot of rubbish this stuff about the Boche being down on the Jews. So there's a bit of trouble sometimes, but there's never been any shortage of our lot ready to have a go at the Jews. Ask your mum-in-law. I bet she can tell a tale or two. It just goes to show.'

It struck Janine that what her cousin was really wanting to show was that he was quite justified in working for the Germans. And it struck her also that she was feeling rather holier-than-thou for someone who had lain awake all night debating just what she would agree to in return for hard information about Jean-Paul.

But it had all been a waste of time. She was running out of hope. That was the point she was trying to steer away from in this idle chatter with Miche.

She didn't realize she was crying till Miche said, 'Hey come on. No weeping. Not outside anyway. You'll get icicles on your cheeks. Let's get you home. Tell you what, why don't I use my influence and see if I can dig you up some proper fuel, and perhaps a kilo of best steak so you can all feast your faces tonight?'

He dropped her in the Rue de Thorigny promising to be back within the hour. He meant it too. Miche the Butcher had a soft heart. But he was even softer when it came to resolution.

As he drove along the Rue Montmartre toward his well-stocked, well-fuelled apartment, he saw a familiar small but exquisitely packed figure, swaying along beneath an explosion of golden hair.

'Arlette!' he called. 'Arlette! How's it going?'

She looked in surprise at the impressive car pulling into the kerb, then recognized Boucher.

'Miche, it's you. God, you're doing all right, aren't you?'

'Not bad,' he grinned. 'Long time, no see.'

In fact he hadn't seen Arlette since she'd put him up

when he came back to Paris last June. They'd parted in a quarrel. He recalled throwing some very nasty names at her, not because she'd needed him out of her room so that she could ply her trade, but because he realized her new customers were Germans.

Well, he'd been a patriot then. Still was, only the Marshal had changed the shape of patriotism.

'Fancy a drink?' he said.

'Why not? My place or yours?'

Hélène was at his place. She was dancing tonight and liked to have a good rest. He'd been quite looking forward to disturbing her. On the other hand it would probably be a kindness not to.

'Yours,' he said. 'Hop in.'

Janine had watched him drive away: assertive, positive, athletic. She'd felt envious. What must it be like to be a man and be able to adapt your environment to your needs instead of having to mould your needs to your environment! These men could do anything! Finding a lost husband, or providing food and fuel within the hour, it was all one to them.

But as she shivered hungrily to bed that night, she made a bitter adjustment to her conclusion.

Promising to find a husband; *promising* to provide warmth and nourishment; *promising* to come back from the wars safe and sound and soon; it was these resounding promises that were all one to them. All vibrant with sincerity, and all completely vain.

2

It was an April evening, but the wind that met Christian Valois head on as he cycled back to the family apartment in Passy was full of sleet. He carried his bike up the stairs and into the apartment with him. Cars had practically vanished from the streets. There was little petrol to be had and, in any case, you needed a special *Ausweis* from the Germans to use one, so bikes were now pricey enough to attract the professional thief.

As he took off his sodden coat, the phone rang.

The line was poor and the female voice at the other end was faint and intermittent.

'Hello! Hello! I can't hear you. Who is that?'

Suddenly the interference went and the voice came loud and clear.

'It's me, your sister, idiot!'

'Marie-Rose! Hello. How are you?'

'I'm fine. Listen, quickly, in case we get cut off. Are you coming down this weekend? Please, you must, it's my birthday, or had you forgotten?'

She was seventeen on Saturday. Seventeen. A good age, even in awful times. But could he bear to go to Vichy? His parents had urged him frequently to join them, or at least to come for a visit. So far he had refused. But Marie-Rose's birthday was different. Despite her youthful impertinence his sister adored him and he was very fond of her.

He said, 'I don't know. The weather, it's so awful . . .'

'Damn the weather! Please, please, it won't be the same without you.'

'I'll see,' he said. 'I won't promise but I'll see.'

Shortly afterwards they were cut off.

The next morning, spring finally exploded with all the violence of energy too long restrained. On the Friday afternoon, he caught the train to Vichy.

At the crossing point into the Free Zone, they were all ordered out to have their papers checked. Valois had had no difficulty in getting an *Ausweis*. When your father was a Vichy deputy and you were a respectable civil servant, you were regarded as quite safe, he thought moodily.

Not everyone was as lucky. Somewhere along the platform an argument had broken out. Voices were raised, German and French. Suddenly a middle-aged man in a dark business suit broke away from a group of German soldiers, ran a little way down the platform, then scrambled beneath the train.

Valois jumped into the nearest carriage to look out of the further window. The man was on his feet again, running across the tracks. He was no athlete and he was already labouring. A voice cried, 'Halt!' He kept going. A gun rattled twice. He flung up his arms and fell.

He wasn't dead, but hit in the leg. Two soldiers ran up to him and pulled him upright. He screamed every time his injured leg touched the ground as he half-hopped and was half-dragged the length of the train to bring him back round to the platform.

Valois turned furiously from the window and made for the platform door. There was a man sitting in the compartment who must have got back in after him.

He said, 'I shouldn't bother.'

Valois paused, realizing he recognized the man.

'I'm sorry? It's Maître Delaplanche, isn't it?'

'You recognize me?'

The lawyer's face, which was the living proof of his Breton peasant ancestry, screwed up in mock alarm.

'You're often in the papers, and I attended several meetings you spoke at when I was a student.'

'Did you? Ah yes. I seem to recall you now.' Face screwed up again in an effort of recollection as unconvincing as his alarm. 'Valois, isn't it? Christian Valois. Of course. I knew your father when he practised, before politics took him over.'

Delaplanche was well known in legal circles as a pleader of underdog causes. Whenever an individual challenged the State, his opinion if not his counsel would be sought. He had spoken on a variety of socialist platforms but always refused to put the weight of his reputation behind any programme except in his own words, 'the quest for justice'.

'Nice to meet you,' said Valois. 'Excuse me.'

'I shouldn't bother,' repeated the lawyer as Valois

94

opened the door on to the platform. 'I presume you're going to make a fuss about the chap they've just shot? I'll tell you his story. His papers were obviously forged. He made a run for it and got shot. He'll turn out to be a blackmarketeer, or an unregistered Jew, or perhaps even an enemy agent. All you'll do is draw attention to yourself and get either yourself or, worse still, the whole train delayed here a lot longer.'

'That's bloody cynical!' snapped Valois. 'I thought you were famous for fighting the underdog's battles.'

'Against the law, not against an army,' said Delaplanche. 'Against an army, all the underdog armed with the law does is get fucked!'

He smiled with the complacency of one who was famous for his earthy courtroom language. On the platform German voices were commanding the passengers back on to the train. Delaplanche picked up a newspaper and began reading it. Feeling defeated, Valois stepped down on to the platform but only to return to his own compartment.

His gloom lasted till the train pulled into the station at Vichy, but lifted at the sight of his sister, long black hair streaming behind her, running down the platform to greet him.

They embraced. Since he last saw her she'd become a young woman and a very beautiful one. She tucked her arm through his in delight and led him to where their mother was waiting.

'Where's father?' asked Valois as they approached.

'Busy. He sends his apologies.'

'No. I understand. Without his constant efforts, the country would be ground down under the conqueror's heel.'

'Shut up and behave! I don't want my birthday spoilt!'

He just about managed to obey the injunction, but there were difficult moments. Vichy disgusted him with its opulent façades all draped with tricolours. Everywhere he looked, red, white and blue, like make-up on a leprous

95

face. He preferred the stark truth of those swastikas he could see from his office window flapping lazily over the arcades of the Rue de Rivoli. The people, most of them, were the same. 'Like characters on a film set,' he told his sister. 'Or worse. Vichy is like a folk-tale village in a pop-up book. Only a child thinks it's really magic.'

'I agree,' said Marie-Rose. 'It's so boring here. That's why I want to come back to Paris with you!'

He looked at her in alarm. This was the first he'd heard of this idea and the more he thought about it, the less he liked it. In Paris, by himself, his decisions only concerned himself; it was a time of danger and it would get worse.

He tried to explain this to Marie-Rose and they quarrelled. But by way of compensation, he found an area of common ground with his father who was absolutely opposed to any such move.

Indeed he and his father kept the peace till the time came to part. His mother presented him with a bag full of 'goodies' and his father with a piece of paper.

'It's a permit to use the car, the Renault. I'll want to use it myself whenever I come to Paris and it's absurd for it to stand in the garage all the time, so I got a permit for you too.'

His instinct was to tear the paper in half and it showed on his face.

'What's the matter?'

'Father, have you any idea what it's like in Paris? The kind of people who're still driving around in cars, well, they're not the kind of people I want to be associated with. There's still a war on, father, believe me!'

'No, there's an armistice on, *you'd* better believe *me!*' snapped Léon Valois. 'Face up to reality, even if you don't like it. The facts are that the Germans are in control and likely to stay that way. With or without us, they'll rule. Without us . . . well, I dread to think how it might be. With us, we can restrain, influence, perhaps eventually control! They're a rigid race, good for soldiering, poor for politics. Believe me, Christian, my way's the only way to build a future for France!'

He spoke with passionate sincerity but there was no place for them to meet. The one good thing about their quarrel was that it reunited him with his sister just as *their* row had temporarily brought him closer to his parents. She kissed him tenderly at parting and asked, 'Is it really so awful under the Boche? I worry about you.'

'Oh it's not so bad really,' he assured her.

'No? Well, no matter what you say, one day I'll surprise you and come and see for myself!'

She grinned in a most unseventeen-like way and hugged him once more with a childish lack of restraint before he got on the train.

He leaned out of the window and waved as long as he could see her on the platform. As he turned to sit down, the compartment door opened.

'We meet again,' said Delaplanche. 'How was your trip? What did you think of Vichy?'

His eyes glanced at Madame Valois's bagful of expensive cans, as if he were reading the labels through the cloth, and when they returned to Valois, he felt as if the man could see through to the car permit in his pocket.

'I'll tell you what I thought of Vichy,' he said savagely.

Delaplanche listened in silence. Finished at last, Valois waited for approval.

'I hope you're not always so indiscreet,' was all the lawyer said. 'Especially with strangers.'

'Strangers? But . . .'

'What do you know of me?'

'I know your reputation. I've read about, listened to you. I know you're a man of the people, a socialist, some even say a . . .'

'Communist? Yes, some do say that. Of course, if I were a communist, that would put me in the German camp, wouldn't it?'

'No! On the contrary . . .'

'But Russia and Germany have a non-aggression pact.'

'Yes, but that hardly means the communists support the Nazis!'

'No. But wasn't it enough to stop you from joining the communists just when you were teetering on the edge?'

The paper went up again. And the rest of the journey passed in silence, with the lawyer reading and Valois brooding on the man's apparent detailed knowledge of his own background.

Their farewells in Paris were perfunctory. Valois felt tired yet restless. It had been an unsettling weekend and it was with a sense of relief and homecoming that he entered the apartment building. Perhaps his outrage at the idea of the car permit ought to extend to his use of his parents' large well-appointed flat, but he was glad to find his mind could accommodate this as comfortably as it accommodated him.

The old lift had become an uncertain vehicle with lack of maintenance and power irregularities, so he headed for the staircase, ill-lit by a shrouded bulb to comply with the black-out regulations. The apartment was one floor up. He could hear a distant wireless playing music. It was a lively popular piece, but the distance, the hour and his own mood made it a melancholy sound. He sighed as he reached his landing.

Then fatigue and melancholy vanished in a trice, for terror lets no rival near the throne. There was a man crouched in the shadow of his door with a submachine gun under his arm. It was too late to retreat. The waiting man had seen him.

'Monsieur Christian Valois?'

'Yes.'

'I've got a message for you.'

The man moved forward into the dim light. And the machine gun became a wooden crutch under his left arm. And the lurking assassin became a haggard, grey-haired man in a baggy suit.

'A message? Who the hell from?' demanded Valois, trying to cover his fear with aggression.

'A friend,' said the man. 'Jean-Paul Simonian. Can we go inside? I'm dying of thirst!'

3

'But he's alive?' demanded Janine for the sixth or seventh time.

'Yes, yes, yes, how many times do I have to tell you!' said Christian Valois with growing irritation. 'He got shot in the head. He was critically ill for a long time but now he's recovering. He's in a military hospital near Nancy, but soon he'll be shipped off to join the rest of them at some camp in Germany. But he *is* alive, he *is* all right.'

'Why did he contact you, not me? Why didn't he get in touch earlier? Why doesn't he write instead of sending messages by this man Pivert?'

Janine knew how absurd all these questions must sound, but they forced themselves out against her will. The truth was, at first she didn't believe it, *couldn't* believe it, when Valois, unnaturally flushed with suppressed excitement, had burst in, crying, 'He's alive! Jean-Paul's alive!' Finally, as details of the story began to adhere, there had started these other emotions, erupting like jets of steam from a hot spring, scalding, unforecastable, uncontrollable. Doubt was there, panic, fear, anger and plain resentment. Then the door opened and Pauli, attracted by the noise, rushed in crying, 'Maman, what's the matter? Are you ill?'

'No, Pauli. It's your father. He's alive!'

For a moment the little boy stood perfectly still. Then he sat on the floor and began to cry, not the silent, half-concealed tears she had grown used to, but howling like his little sister.

'Pauli!' she said, kneeling beside him and hugging him

close. 'It's all right, my love. It's all right. Daddy's alive!'

And suddenly it *was* all right. Her sobs joined the child's and at last her emotions ran as clear as her joyful tears.

'I'm sorry, Christian,' she said a little later as they sat and drank a glass of wine. 'I didn't dare to believe you. Do you understand that? Now quickly, now I'm calm, before Sophie comes back from shopping, tell me it all again so I can break the news to her the best way possible.'

Corporal Major Pivert's story had been told with an old soldier's rough directness. He had been second in command of the section in which Jean-Paul was serving. They had held out for a day and a half against a ferocious onslaught.

'Most of the Boche just went round us, leaving half a company to mop us up. Well, we showed the bastards! Mind you, we took a pounding. It brought us real close together. We'd been a tight-knit group before, got on well despite all our differences, but being under heavy attack together, losing some of your mates, that really binds you close as cement. It's a grand feeling, but Christ, the pain of it, when another of your mates gets hit. You see, you're all one. Every wound, every scream, every death, it's yours. Do you see what I mean?'

Christian said, 'I think so, I'm trying . . .'

The old soldier regarded him keenly and said, 'You've had no service, have you, sir? You can't understand without knowing it for yourself.'

Valois flushed and said, 'Go on.'

'It hit Simonian bad. His best mate, a young lad from Auxerre, died in his arms, spilling his guts all over him. I think he'd have gone over the top himself then, trying to take the bastards on single-handed, but the lieutenant stopped him. He was a good lad, that lieutenant. Fucking children they're putting in charge now, I said when I first saw him. But he was all right.

'Finally the lieutenant decided to call it a day. Our wireless had packed up, see, and for a long time we thought it was like the first war again, with us part of a long line running all the way from the sea to Switzerland. Little Verdun, that's what I called the place we was. Except we found when we got the wireless going again, that just about every other bugger had packed up and gone home, or they were sitting on their arses waiting to be rounded up and trucked off east. Well, now the case was altered. Simonian was keen to go on fighting at first, but the lieutenant persuaded him for the sake of his mates to give it up. So we made a white flag, but before we shoved it up, the lieutenant said, "Hold on. Simonian, take this," and he handed over the dead lad from Auxerre's pass-book. "What for?" asks Simonian. "So you can chuck your own away," says the lieutenant. "I was in Berlin before the war and I assure you that you'll be better off not to have the name Iakov Moseich Simonian in your pass-book when the Boche get round to checking their prisoners." "No," says Simonian. "I'm not using these papers, I'm not having his parents told he's alive and well and a prisoner when he's lying dead and unburied out here." "Please yourself," says the lieutenant. "But let's have a look at your own book then." And he takes it and he scratches and tears it, then hands it back, looking right scruffy but no worse than many another after what we'd been through. "There," he says. "You've been christened in every sense!" And I glanced at the book and saw that all that remained of his name was Jean-Paul Simon!

'Now we waved the flag. The only trouble was that Fritz seemed to be a bit short-sighted. Or more like a bit short-tempered for all the bother we'd caused. So they just shot the flag to pieces and us with it. There were only four of us left alive and of these, only me and Simonian lasted long enough to get to hospital, me with one foot shot off and him with a bullet in his head.

'And that was it, more or less. They were sawing bits off me for the next few months till they'd got as far as they could go. I didn't even know Jean-Paul was still alive till a month or so back when I was getting around on my crutch and ran into him, so to speak, in a wheelchair. He didn't seem to recognize me at first but when we got to talking, I could see it all gradually coming back to him. The thing was, he was still down in the books as Jean-Paul Simon. I asked one of the nurses about him. She said it was sad, he never said anything about his past life and there didn't seem to be any next of kin to inform. At least he was getting better, though he'd been very ill. Well, I guessed that he was just playing dumb because, having changed his name, he could hardly start talking about a family called Simonian, could he? And from what I heard people saying, the lieutenant had been right. Iakov Moseich was not a good label to wear in the heart of Bocheland, which is where he'll likely end up.

'Me, well, there was no use sending a one-legged man to a POW camp, even the Boche could see that. So they decided to discharge me back home. When I told Jean-Paul, he asked me to get in touch with you, Monsieur Valois, and tell you he was alive and well. He didn't want to risk putting anything down on paper in case I got searched. So here I am and that's my message!'

'By the time he finished it was nearly curfew or I'd have come round last night,' concluded Valois. 'He slept in the flat and this morning I sent him off with some money.'

'Did you get his address? Can I talk to him?' demanded Janine.

'Of course,' said Valois. 'Though not straightaway, eh? I'll fix it up later. There's still a slight risk now, and it's best not to take chances.'

This wasn't the real reason, but Janine in her joy and excitement was easily persuaded to accept it. The truth was that Valois had other cause to feel uneasy about a meeting between Pivert and Janine. He'd censored all references to the mental scarring left by Jean-Paul's wound.

'I knew he was married with kiddies,' Pivert had said. 'You talk about these things when you're under fire like

102

we'd been. But first time I mentioned them in the hospital, he just looked blank. Another time he talked about them, but like he was talking about something in a dream. Most of the time he just wanted to talk about our old comrades. I had to go through how each of them died, he was so desperate to believe that some others might have survived.

'But you he seemed to remember all the time, sir. You and his old mother. He said to contact you first so you could break it to the old lady. Good news can sometimes shock even more than bad, can't it?'

Good news so mixed with cause for unease certainly could, decided Valois. And he had taken it upon himself to convey only the joyous essentials of the tale to Janine and his reward was to see her face light up like a spring dawn.

When Sophie returned from shopping, complaining bitterly about the lack of most things and the price of the rest, Valois diplomatically withdrew. They needn't have worried, however. She short-circuited Janine's tentative approach to the subject with a crisp, 'What's this? You've got news of Jean-Paul, haven't you? Well, praise be to God, he's alive!'

'Bubbah! How did you know?' demanded Janine amazed.

'Know? I've always known! And how did I know you were going to tell me? Well, I've not seen your eyes sparkle like that for over a year, so I didn't think you were going to tell me he was dead! Come here, child!'

Laughing and crying together, Janine fell into the old woman's arms.

After joy came decision. Day to day existence had gone out of the window. There was now a future to be planned. Janine wanted to sit down and write a long loving letter to Jean-Paul straightaway and once more found herself at odds with Christian.

'You can't just write,' he said. 'Letters are censored. I don't know how much danger Jean-Paul would be in if they discovered his background, but they'd certainly sit up and take notice if they did find out he'd been misleading them about his name. So it can't help him if suddenly out of the blue he starts getting letters from his family, can it?'

To Janine's surprise and disappointment, Sophie supported Valois. 'There are stories told in the schul of what these Nazis have done in Germany. If my son is soon to go into one of these prisoner camps, better he go as Jean-Paul Simon, Catholic, I think.'

'But we have to let him know that we're all well, Bubbah, you, me and the children!' cried Janine. 'And if we don't contact him straightaway, how will we ever know where they send him? Oh, don't let's lose him again so soon after finding him! Couldn't I travel to Nancy to see him? Christian, couldn't your father help me to get an *Ausweis*?'

Valois shook his head in exasperation.

'Please, I beg of you, Janine. Do nothing without consulting me first, eh? Look at it this way. The Germans have got themselves a prisoner, an ordinary soldier of no particular importance, called Jean-Paul Simon. The only danger is from us, his friends, if we draw the Germans' attention to him in any way.'

Suddenly all Janine's other emotions were blanked out by a single memory. Up to now she'd completely forgotten her interview with the *Abwehr* lieutenant. Now Valois's warning brought it all back. Just how much had her mother told Mai about Jean-Paul?

She shook her head. What did it matter? The *Abwehr* were hardly going to concern themselves with one French soldier who, as Mai had pointed out, was probably dead.

'Are you all right?' asked Valois.

'Fine. It's just the excitement. So tell me, what *do* we do?'

'Here's my idea. The only person who can contact Jean-Paul without drawing undue attention is Pivert. So let's send a parcel through the Red Cross with a note allegedly from Pivert saying he's not forgotten his old fellow-patient. In the note, Pivert can say that he's safely back in Paris, and has found his own family, Sophie, Janine, Pauli and Céci, safe and well. And he can tell Jean-Paul to write to him, care of my address. It's a risk, but not much of one and we've got to give him an excuse to write back. How does that sound to you?'

Janine considered. It sounded cautious, reasonable, well-planned. It sounded so many things she found it hard to be but which she knew she was going to have to learn.

'It sounds all right,' she said.

When Christian left she accompanied him to the street door. He was in a quiet mood which contrasted with his excitement as the bearer of good news earlier. She guessed he was still worried that by some impulsive act she might endanger Jean-Paul. The thought annoyed her. Didn't he know that while there was an ounce of strength in her body she would fight for Jean-Paul? Then she thought, of course he knows it, just as I know that while there's any strength left in his mind, he will be fighting alongside me.

'I'll be in touch then,' he said.

Awkwardly he leaned forward and kissed her cheek. She jerked her head back and for a second he thought she was going to thrust him away. Then her arms went round his shoulders and she pulled him close.

'Thank you, Christian,' she whispered. 'Thank you for being such a good friend.'

Before he could think of what to reply, she released him and slipped back into the house.

He stood in the doorway for a while after she'd gone, not thinking anything in particular but savouring the memory of her slim, strong body pressed against his like the reverberation of music after the players have laid their instruments down.

Then he smiled as if at some recognition of his own foolishness and set off walking towards the centre of town.

4

Maurice Melchior was bored with his job.

He was bored with the countryside. He was bored with bumping around in a smelly army truck. And he was bored with his companion, SS Sergeant Hans Hemmen, who had no conversation whatsoever. What he did have was a certain Nordic beauty but when Maurice had let his hand brush those firm swelling buttocks on an early excursion, Hemmen had bent his fingers back till they almost broke.

Also, though this he kept very well hidden, he was beginning to get a little bored with his patron, Colonel Walter Fiebelkorn. The man had a certain hard wit, but little refinement. His sexual demands were sadly unimaginative and always contained a strong element of humiliation. And if only he looked like Hemmen!

It was of course Walter who'd got him attached to the SS's Art Preservation Section. Everyone was at it, the SS, the *Abwehr*, the Embassy, not forgetting visiting notables like Goering. Melchior had eased his early pangs of conscience by assuring himself there was real preservation work to be done in places where the owners had been too concerned with packing everything portable to worry about protecting what wasn't. Winter was the worst enemy. Delicate inlays developed a bloom, the frames of fine old pianos warped into discord, the pigment of paintings cracked and flaked. Yes, there was work to be done here.

But in the end it came down to looting.

This was brought home to him beyond all doubt one glorious June day in a villa on the Heights of the Seine. The usual anonymous delation had told them that the owner had gone for a long 'holiday' in Spain. The tipster must have been very keen for the house to be 'preserved' as he had evidently informed the *Abwehr* preservation group too. Melchior recognized one of them, a big piratical red-head who occasionally visited old Madame – or perhaps young Madame – Simonian in the flat below. He seemed an amiable fellow, which was more than could be said for his mate, a nauseating little man called Pajou whose bloodshot eyes behind their thick frames never stopped moving.

It was Pajou who said, as the argument reached its height, 'Look, let's not be silly about this. We're all in the same game, aren't we? Spin of a coin, winner takes the lot.'

Hemmen rejected the offer angrily, but it turned out to be merely a time-wasting tactic anyway, to give an *Abwehr* captain time to turn up and throw his rank about. Hemmen, with the weight of the SS behind him, refused to be intimidated, while Melchior retired in disgust.

All in the same game indeed! Whatever game he was in, it certainly wasn't that little rat's. His indignation led him into temptation. There was a beautiful piece of Nevers *verre filé* in a niche, a tiny figurine of a young girl strewing flowers from a basket. She probably represented Spring, one of a set, overlooked when the family packed and ran. Its intrinsic value was not great but it gave him great pleasure to look at. What would its fate be if it fell into the hands of either set of looters? And if preservation really was their job, who would preserve it more lovingly than he?

Checking that Hemmen was too immersed in the row to keep his usual distrustful eye on him, Melchior slipped the figurine into his pocket.

Five minutes later it became clear that the sergeant too had merely been playing for time. A staff-car drew up outside the villa and Colonel Walter Fiebelkorn got out.

Now there was no contest but Fiebelkorn seemed ready to be a good winner.

'We are after all in the same line of business, my dear captain,' he said echoing Pajou's words, but with a wider meaning. 'We both look after our fatherland's security in our different ways. This is merely a diversion, not something to sour friendship over. Why don't we simply divide the spoil? You take the ground floor, we take the rest.'

It was not an offer the *Abwehr* man could refuse even though it was clearly based on Hemmen's intelligence that the ground floor had been almost entirely cleared, the upper floors much less so.

It didn't take Pajou and Boucher long to remove what little remained downstairs. Fiebelkorn watched with an impassive face.

'All done?' said the disgruntled captain.

'Not quite,' said Pajou.

'What else is there?'

'If we are to have everything from down here, what about the figurine that little fairy's got in his pocket?'

All eyes turned to Melchior. He felt no fear yet, only irritation that in his eagerness to be sure he was unnoticed by Hemmen, he'd ignored Pajou's shifty gaze.

'Oh this?' he said. 'Sorry.'

He held out the little Spring.

'This is a serious offence, colonel,' said the *Abwehr* captain, delighted to have captured the initiative from the SS. 'Theft of works of art sequestered to the State is punishable by death.'

'You want him killed?' asked Fiebelkorn indifferently.

'Well, no,' said the captain. 'I just wanted to be sure the SS would take the serious view I think this case demands. Examples should be made.'

'I agree,' said Fiebelkorn. 'Sergeant.'

Hemmen approached Melchior, his eyes alight with pleasure. In his hand he held his machine pistol. For a terrible second, Maurice felt sure he was going to be shot. Then the figurine was swept out of his outstretched hand by the dully gleaming barrel. Before it hit the floor, the gun had swept back, catching Melchior along the side of his face. He felt no immediate pain, only a warm rush of blood down his ravaged cheek. Then the barrel came back, laying open his temple this time, and now he felt pain. His scream seemed to incense Hemmen, who drove his knee into the little Frenchman's groin and as he collapsed sobbing to the ground began to kick furiously at his chest and stomach.

Melchior rolled this way and that in his effort to avoid the blows, finally fetching up at Fiebelkorn's feet.

He looked up into that blank face and choked, 'Walter . . . please . . .'

Perhaps something moved in those dead eyes, but the voice was perfectly calm as the SS man said, 'Well, captain, is this sufficient to satisfy the *Abwehr*'s understandable demand for an example to be set?'

'Yes. Enough,' said the captain unsteadily.

'Good. Rest assured, if our friend here troubles us again, we will not be so merciful.'

To Melchior remembering the moment later, the most horrifying thing was to recognize that Fiebelkorn had been utterly sincere. In his eyes this beating had been an act of mercy. But just now he had no thought for anything but pain. He lay very still, heard footsteps leaving the room, heard them more distantly mounting the marble stairway. Then silence. Then a hand on his shoulder. He screamed in terror.

'Come on, my little hero,' said Michel Boucher's voice. 'You've got a lot to learn about thieving, my friend. Here, let's clean you up a bit.'

A large red kerchief was applied with surprising gentleness to his cheek.

'Now, can you stand? We'll get you out of here before Attila returns.'

Unsteadily he rose. Something crunched beneath his feet. He looked down and saw the little Spring had strewn her flowers at last.

He liked to think some of the tears in his eyes were for that.

'Aren't you the chap who lives upstairs from old Sophie?'

asked Boucher as he helped him out. 'My cousin's married to her son who's missing.'

'Melchior's my name, sage that I . . .' His words drowned in blood.

'Christ Almighty, Miche,' said Pajou as he saw the big red-head half-carrying the groaning figure towards their truck. 'What the hell do you think you're doing with that dirty little fairy?'

'Well, I'll tell you what, Paj,' said Boucher laying Melchior gently in the back of the truck. 'It's nearly midsummer day and I just fancied a little fairy of my own, OK? So now drive carefully, or me and my friend here might just take it into our minds to make an example out of *you*.'

'Today,' said Günter Mai, 'is the twenty-first of June, the longest day. Hereafter begins the darkness.'

'I hope I don't detect a metaphor,' said Bruno Zeller sardonically.

'Why? Can they arrest you for metaphors now?'

He was rather drunk, but it had seemed ungracious not to take full advantage of the major's unexpected hospitality, particularly when it involved the Tour d'Argent's superb duck, with wine to match. He looked out of the window. Below he could see the Seine darkly gleaming, with willow reflections reaching up to form an osier cage with their own realities. In such a cage his ex-gamekeeper grandfather had kept a blackbird. It never sang till one day by accident Mai had set it free. Such a torrent of bubbling music poured from its golden beak as it sped away that he forgot to be afraid of the consequences till the old man's angry blows reminded him.

'You're strangely rapt, my friend,' said Zeller. 'Not more metaphors?'

'Perhaps. Tell me, Bruno, sir, what precisely am I doing here?'

'In Paris, you mean?' said Zeller, deliberately misunderstanding.

'No. I know what I'm doing in Paris. There's a war on, remember?'

'Really?' Zeller looked round the crowded room. 'Hard to believe, isn't it?'

'Not if you look out of the window. Out there, under every roof, there's at least one person who knows he or she is fighting a war.'

'So you do have X-ray vision! It explains such a lot.'

'The major is pleasant. But in a way he's right. Even here I can look towards the kitchen and see them spitting in the soup.'

'How fortunate we avoided the soup then,' said Zeller, suddenly impatient. 'But you're right. There is of course a reason for our little tête-à-tête. Günter, you're one of the best men we've got. Well, I know you know it. I just wanted you to be sure that your superiors know it too.'

'Good Lord,' said Mai. 'This isn't a party to celebrate my promotion, is it?'

'The lieutenant is facetious,' said Zeller. 'Now, a serious question. What do you think the greatest danger is to the *Abwehr*'s work?'

'Easy,' said Mai without hesitation. 'The SD.'

'Explain.'

'A military occupation with a *Wehrmacht* chain of command is not to their taste. To them security is not just a means of keeping the peace but putting their ideology into action. Where our areas of work overlap, their best way to complete control is to discredit us and through us the military administration. Also men like your friend Fiebelkorn honestly believe that the only safe condition for an occupied country is one of constant terror.'

'Don't mention that bastard to me,' said Zeller. 'That trick of his with that runt Melchior last November was just a beginning. Listen, Günter. I've been unofficially authorized to organize a small section to keep an eye on whatever the SD are getting up to. Forewarned is forearmed. I'd value your assistance.'

Mai sipped his wine and said, 'You realize the best you

111

can hope for is a delaying action? Behind us we've got generals, and of course an admiral. They've got politicians. It's no contest.'

'So you won't help?'

'Of course I will. You knew that before you ordered this excellent dinner. In fact I've taken a step or two in that direction already. Though, as doubtless you know, I should imagine our work load's going to be increased quite a bit after tomorrow.'

The remark was made so casually that Zeller found himself nodding in melancholy agreement till its implications struck home.

'What the hell do you mean?' he demanded.

Mai laughed aloud at Zeller's evident discomfiture.

'What's the matter, major? Can't ask how I know what I shouldn't without admitting you know what you shouldn't also? Come now. The world is full of birds that sing more sweetly than even an admiral's parrot!'

Zeller shook his head in disbelief. Finally a slow smile spread across his face and he signalled to a waiter.

'Cognac,' he said. 'The oldest, the finest. Günter, you may be a disgusting and impudent peasant, but by God, I picked the right man when I picked you!'

The following morning the news was broadcast with triumphant music all over Europe. The German Army had invaded Russia. The civilized world was invited to applaud, and to join in, the great crusade against Communism.

It was a Saturday morning and Christian Valois did not have to go into the office. He was drinking his morning coffee when the bell of his apartment sounded.

It should have surprised him to find the lawyer Delaplanche on his doorstep, but it didn't.

'Heard the news?'

'Yes' – not asking which news.

'The case is altered, I think.'

'I suppose so' – not asking which case.

'Like to talk?'

112

'I'm sorry. Come in. Let me get you some coffee.'

The lawyer sat down and looked around the luxuriously appointed room.

'Nice place,' he said.

'It's my parents',' said Valois shortly, pouring the coffee.

'No need to be defensive,' laughed Delaplanche. 'There's no harm in enjoying comfort, as long as you fight for other people's right to enjoy it too. You will fight, I take it?'

'For comfort?'

'For people's right to enjoy it. And other things.'

'Let's get one thing straight. Are you a communist, Monsieur Delaplanche?'

'I'm a Frenchman and a patriot, isn't that all that matters?' Surprisingly, the blunt Breton didn't make the words sound in the least ironic.

'What do you want with me?'

'Nothing. I thought you might like to join a party tonight.'

'Join . . .?'

'I mean a celebration party,' said Delaplanche, grinning. 'Or if you prefer, an anniversary party. Don't you remember? A year today the armistice was signed. For a year we've been citizens of the Third Reich. Anyway, come if you like. The Café Carvallo, Rue Saint-Honoré, you know it? No need to wear cloak and dagger. It really is a celebration. My secretary is getting engaged. But there will be a couple of people there I'd like you to meet. Seven o'clock. These things start early because of the curfew.'

He emptied his coffee cup, rose, shook hands and made for the door. As he reached it the bell rang. When Valois opened the door, he found Janine on the doorstep, her face flushed from haste.

'Christian, I must talk to you. Oh, I'm sorry.'

She had spotted Delaplanche. The lawyer smiled at her, said, 'Madame. Goodbye, Monsieur Valois,' and left.

'Wasn't that Maître Delaplanche?' said Janine when Valois had closed the door.

'You know him?'

'I've seen his photograph in the paper. Christian, I'm sorry to bother you but something's happened.'

She flopped down in a chair, her face crumbling with worry, her limbs slack and sprawling yet still strangely graceful.

'You've had some news about Jean-Paul?' he guessed, full of concern.

'Yes. No. I mean indirectly. Perhaps. Oh, I'll have to tell you.'

Wretchedly she told him of her earlier meeting with Günter Mai.

'It was my idiot cousin's idea. I should never have listened. Then to find maman's been blabbing all my business to this Boche. And all the time Jean-Paul's been trying to keep his real name quiet!'

'No harm done,' Christian soothed her. 'What could this man find out? If Jean-Paul fooled the Boche in the hospital, no mere *Abwehr* lieutenant's going to work it out from Paris!'

'I know. But then why does he want to see me again this afternoon?'

Miche had brought her the message, grinning like an ape, expecting thanks.

'I had to talk to you, Christian. I can't go, I can't!'

She put her hands to her face, which was wet with tears. He caught her wrists and drew her hands away. Leaning close, he said urgently, 'You must go, Janine. You must hear what he has to say.'

'Must I?' she said, looking at him like a child eager for guidance.

Their faces were very close.

'Yes. You must.'

He leaned forward the last six inches and kissed her on each salty cheek. Then, springing upright, he said, 'And never fear! Soon the *Abwehr* and all the rest of their secret police are going to have other things to worry about.'

'What do you mean?'

'Haven't you heard? Hitler's attacked Russia. He's set the French communists free.'

'Is that good?'

He looked down at her and found himself smiling.

His feelings about her had become strangely muddled. He was still convinced that she was no wife for his friend, yet there was about her a directness, a simplicity, a lack of intellectual complication which he could now see might attract a complex mind like Jean-Paul's. And she was attractive physically too. Once he had not thought so. Now, skinny from the effects of worry and of want, dishevelled, tearstained, seated with complete unselfconsciousness in a little-girl pose with knees spread wide and arms dangling between, she touched both his heart and his senses.

He knew in that moment that whatever proposals Delaplanche was about to make to him, he would accept. Janine and all those like her represented the raw emotional energy of France which without direction and protection would burn itself out uselessly, or be blown out by the Boche.

'Yes,' he said softly. 'That is very good indeed.'

5

By four o'clock that Saturday afternoon, Günter Mai was just about recovering from his excesses at the Tour d'Argent. He had woken early to a horrified mental re-run of all his indiscretions of the night before. Had he really told that joke about Hitler, Goering, Goebbels and Himmler in the Jewish whore-house? And should he be consoled by the memory of Zeller laughing so much he almost choked on a piece of Roquefort?

He had fallen asleep again and when he woke up the second time about ten a.m. things had seemed a little better. If he had been indiscreet, so had Zeller. Each was the other's only witness, and jokes about the Party leaders were possibly less dangerous than plots to spy on the SD.

He lunched in the mess. The talk was all of the invasion of Russia. The tone was one of patriotic fervour and great optimism. Mai said seriously, 'I daresay there'll be transfers soon,' and left in the ensuing lull.

He thought of going round to the Crozier boulangerie for a pipe and a coffee. It was a visit easy to justify on professional grounds. Louise gossiped freely about life and events in the neighbourhood. At the very least he could use her as a sounding board for opinion. Not that he needed a sounding board. Any fool could tell that the good times were over. An opportunity had been missed. With the Marshal and Vichy in their pocket, they should have the majority of ordinary people with them now. Instead fear and resentment were growing, and his visits to the Croziers were as much for relaxation as information.

But somehow the awareness that he was seeing their daughter later that afternoon kept him away. Instead he walked the rest of his hangover off and got to the Café Balzac half an hour early.

Miche Boucher was there. Mai frowned. He quite liked Miche, but he didn't want him hanging around while he talked to Janine.

'Hello, Monsieur Scheffer,' the redhead greeted him. 'What are you having?'

They sat and talked for a little while. Mai used the opportunity to pump Boucher about his work with the *Abwehr* purchasing section. It was always useful to know what one's colleagues were getting up to.

Gradually it became apparent that Boucher had deliberately sought him out and was working round to asking his advice. Finally he got to the point.

'The thing is,' he said, 'Pajou's been going on for a bit about making a move. He's got his fingers in every pie, that one, and he's evidently been talking to some of your lot at the Rue des Saussaies, you know, the Gestapo. He reckons he can get a better deal there, more freedom of action, a wider brief. He wants me to move over with him. He says things like . . .'

He hesitated, then went on with a rush, '. . . like the *Abwehr*'s on its way out and this time next year, it'll be all Gestapo and we'd better be in at the ground floor. Now, me, I'm a bit bewildered by all this. I mean, you and the Gestapo, you're all the same lot, right? I mean, you're all Boche, sorry, Germans. So what's he getting at? I'm happy with Purchasing. It's easy work and there's plenty of perks. Pajou says that in this new job, there'd be more perks, though. Because we'd be dealing mostly with people not things. I don't get that myself. I mean, you can't cream off people, can you?'

Mai smiled to himself at the man's naïve openness – and then reminded himself that men like Boucher had a strong instinct for knowing exactly how far they could go with those in authority. He mustn't confuse an astute estimate of his own tolerance with naïvety.

He said, 'I think what Pajou means is if you're bringing in a hundred crates of champagne, you can perhaps "lose" four or five for yourself. But if you're bringing in a man, and he happens to have a hundred crates of champagne in his cellar, you can probably help yourself to the lot.'

Boucher digested this.

'Yes,' he said. 'I thought it was something like that. Bringing men in, I mean, not things.'

'That would bother you?' said Mai.

'I don't know,' said Boucher honestly. 'Depends who it was. Look, what do you think? Pajou's a bit of a sod, but he's not often wrong. I mean, this business of the *Abwehr* being on the way out. What's that mean?'

'I really don't know,' said Mai easily, his mind racing. 'There are admittedly some rivalries, bound to be. I'll tell you what, Miche. I'd like to help you. You're a nice chap and you've helped me a lot. So why not go along with

Pajou? At the same time, keep in touch with me, tell me what you're up to, and I'll give you the benefit of whatever inside knowledge I have. All right?'

Boucher considered, then began to smile. If Mai had had any thought of recruiting an unconscious spy, that smile removed it. Boucher knew exactly what he was being asked to do.

'You want a sort of scout in the opposition dressing room, is that it?' he asked. 'All right, you're on. You scratch my back, I'll scratch yours. Now I'd best be off before Janine gets here. Take care!'

He lifted his great length out of the chair and, with a cheerful wave, departed.

Mai sipped his coffee and reflected not without complacency on the happy knack he seemed to have of turning up aces. He wanted a nose in SD operations and almost immediately one turned up. Of course it was an absurd waste of time and expertise. Keeping the peace here required the full co-operation of all the security arms. Even then he doubted if they'd contain the reaction which he reckoned was shortly due. Competition instead of co-operation would make their task almost impossible, but it wasn't his choice.

'Monsieur Scheffer?' It was Janine who'd arrived unnoticed.

'Sorry,' he said, half-rising. 'Please, sit down. Patron, some coffee here.'

He looked at her thoughtfully. She was nervous. Perhaps in the expectation of news; perhaps simply because Boche officers, even in civilian clothes, made her nervous.

He said, 'How is your family?'

'The children are fine. I expect you see more of my parents than I do.'

The sudden flash amused him. Even in her nervousness she couldn't control her dislike of himself and of her parents' conciliatory attitude towards him. He wondered again how he might use her.

'And your friend, Monsieur Valois? How is he?'

118

This clearly came as a surprise. There was something like alarm in her face. That was interesting.

'You know Christian?'

'I met him at your parents' shop, remember? When you had the accident with the chocolates.'

'Yes,' she said, flushing. 'I remember. He's well, I think. Now, please, why have you asked to see me?'

'Why? Simply because you asked me for my help in the first place and I felt it only polite to offer a progress report. But if you'd rather we didn't proceed any further . . .'

He let his hurt tone fade away into a hurt expression. He could see that a need stronger than dislike and resentment was keeping her in her seat.

'No. Go on. Now I'm here . . .' The words emerged with difficulty.

'All right. As you requested, I put in train certain enquiries as to the whereabouts of your husband, Private Jean-Paul Simonian, or to give him his full name, Iakov Moseich Jean-Paul Simonian.'

He paused. She felt faint but held herself perfectly still. He knew Jean-Paul's full name. Surely her mother wouldn't have told him that? Miche . . . ? But Miche didn't know Jean-Paul at all, could hardly know his full name.

The lieutenant's next words confirmed her worst fears.

'I obtained from French military records a full list of those in your husband's unit. Then I circulated a request to all POW camps and other holding centres for information on prisoners from this unit and in particular one called Iakov Moseich Jean-Paul Simonian.'

Again the almost sensual dwelling on the name. The man was a monster.

'It's an unusual name, that, madame. For a Frenchman. But that made it all the easier to check.' He paused, then went on. 'I'm sorry to report that all responses were negative.'

She tried desperately to conceal her relief, or to let it emerge as disappointment.

119

'You mean there's no trace?'

'None. I'm sorry.'

'Yes. Well, thank you, lieutenant.'

She was being polite now he couldn't help her! He watched her prepare to go.

Then he said, 'However, I did encounter one odd thing. A military hospital in Lorraine. They'd had a couple of patients from your husband's unit.'

Slowly she sank back into her chair. Should she speak? Dare she speak? Dare she keep quiet?

'Yes?' she said.

'One of them was on the unit roll I had. But for some reason the other wasn't. A man called Jean-Paul Simon.'

He spoke the name with precisely the same intonation he'd used before, as if savouring the syllables on his tongue. She sat perfectly still, trying to keep all emotion from her usually expressive face, fearing that her very lack of expression would in itself be a giveaway. She felt his eyes on her, his will pressing her to speak. She could think of no words that would not be a betrayal and yet her silence too seemed vibrant with guilt.

Then Günter Mai laughed.

'Which just goes to show how useless official records are! I'm sorry I haven't been able to help, Madame Simonian, truly sorry. But don't give up hope. I checked casualty lists too and there's no sign of your husband's name there either. So, keep hoping. Now let's have some more coffee, shall we?'

6

Three shots rang out. The street sloped steeply down from the Place Pigalle. The fleeing man had got up a good speed and when he was hit, he cartwheeled dramatically across the pavement and smashed through a shop window. Two German soldiers lounging outside a café laughed and applauded. But Maurice Melchior, leaning on the bar inside, started so violently that he knocked a bottle off the counter.

'Relax, monsieur,' said the proprietor. 'It's just a film they're making.'

Melchior's hand went up to the still pink scar on his cheek, a gesture he found it hard to control when anything made him nervous.

'They're still making films?' he said when he was sure his voice wouldn't shake.

'Why not?' The man shrugged. 'Actors too must live. And directors must live very well. It's one of Monsieur Yerevan's. He'll probably be in for his coffee shortly.'

Maurice tried not to show he was impressed. Serge Yerevan made highly successful gangster films. They had once been introduced, but so briefly and so inconsequentially that he'd probably made no more impression on the great man than a flapped-away fly.

Well, all that was changed now. Even this disfiguring scar fitted in with his new role.

'Come on,' he snapped. 'I haven't got all day. Let's do business.'

Silently the café owner handed over an envelope. It allegedly contained 50,000 francs but he slipped it under his waistcoat without counting. When you were an accredited agent of Miche the Butcher's blackmarket business, you didn't need to count.

'Same order next month,' said the proprietor.

'We'll have to see,' said Melchior doubtfully. 'The booze should be OK but I don't know how long we can keep spuds down to eight francs the kilo. As for the steak . . . !'

The owner looked sullen, then said, 'Filthy Boche!' which was the nearest he dared come to a protest against his supplier. Melchior smiled, accepted the offer of a pastis and took it to a table just inside the door.

At last things were going right for Maurice Melchior.

Boucher had taken a fancy to him, not *that* kind of fancy as he'd found out to his cost when he squeezed the big man's knee to encourage him to surmount his suspected shyness. 'Think I'm after your lily-white body, do you?' boomed Boucher. Next thing, Melchior felt himself spun round and then he screamed in pain as a large boot was driven against his buttocks.

'That's the only contact I want with your bum,' said Boucher. 'Now let's work out how you really can be useful to me, shall we?'

Thus had begun a period of unprecedented contentment and prosperity. Boucher seemed to be able to get his hands on almost anything and Melchior discovered in himself an unsuspected talent for judging what the market would bear, then squeezing a little extra.

The door opened and a group of people came in. Melchior recognized Serge Yerevan at once. He had a Middle Eastern look about him, a thin swarthy face, long nose, jet black hair and wide mobile mouth. Hanging on to his arm was his current mistress, the film star, Marie Ribot, with a face more striking than beautiful, and wickedly pointed breasts which had set something of a fashion.

As they passed Melchior's table, Yerevan caught his eye. A wide smile of recognition stretched his mouth, and he came forward with his hand outstretched.

'Maurice! It *is* you. Don't you remember me? Serge Yerevan. I had the pleasure of meeting you once, at one of Coco Chanel's do's, wasn't it?'

It wasn't. It had been a much more plebeian occasion, but it was hardly worth contradiction. Nor did Melchior believe for one moment that Yerevan would have spared him a single glance now without (a) foreknowledge and (b) motivation. The first must have come from the café owner. And the second must have to do with the man's assurance that Melchior could get hold of anything.

Complimenting himself on not being taken in, Melchior was nevertheless delighted to be made much of publicly by a man like Yerevan, who now sat down and talked animatedly, dropping famous names as though assuming they figured among Melchior's acquaintance also. In the end, they got to the point: a lament on the difficulty of getting hold of really good Havana cigars, a promise by Melchior that he'd keep his eyes open. It was a small order, in the nature of a test run really. Melchior approved such caution, knew that it could lead to higher things. But thought of caution made him realize how long he'd been sitting there. 'Don't hang around when you've got the cash,' advised Boucher. 'If possible pick it up early, and move off quick!' Well, he'd been early today, but now he was late.

He stood up abruptly and shook hands with Yerevan.

'I'll be in touch,' he said. The film director looked rather surprised. Melchior was not displeased at his unpremeditated abruptness. That'll show him I'm not trade, he thought.

'Hold on,' said Yerevan suddenly.

He reached forward and grasped Melchior's chin gently, moved his head this way and that.

'Did you ever have a test?' he wondered.

'A film test? No.'

'I'm surprised. Such excellent bone structure. Perhaps we can arrange something. And I love the scar.'

Having won back the initiative, he now stood up himself and brought his face very close to Melchior's.

'Meanwhile, see what you can do about the cigars. I know you'll do me a good price, one Jew to another, eh?'

Kissing him lightly on the cheek, Yerevan joined his friends at the bar.

Melchior left, feeling both flattered and outmanoeuvred. Outside he paused. He felt he was being watched. He looked at the two soldiers at the pavement table, but they were only interested in contemplating some men across the road replacing the shattered film window with real glass. No danger there. It must all be in the mind.

Then he saw him, only a few feet away, almost hidden

by a lamp post, his face expressionless, his calm unblinking gaze fixed on Melchior.

It took a couple of seconds for full recognition. Then he stepped quickly forward and said, 'Hello. It's Pauli isn't it! From the old lady's flat? What are you doing here? Run away from home, have you?'

Pauli Simonian slowly shook his head. The truth was, he was a great wanderer and spent a large part of his time, while his mother thought he was just round the corner playing with friends, exploring interesting quarters of the city. No one paid much attention to a small boy who probably belonged to one of the nearby adults, and he had long ago mastered the art of travelling free on all forms of public transport.

'I have to meet maman,' he said. 'She's shopping back there.'

He spoke very convincingly. To his surprise, the little man laughed out loud.

'Good try, Pauli, but your maman's not the type to come shopping here, even if there was anything here to shop for. No, you're on the loose, doing a bit of exploring, aren't you? I used to like that myself when I was a boy. But I think maybe you've come far enough today. I'd better get you back home. There's some very strange characters here, you know.'

Melchior was not being ironic. His own tastes were stoutly post-adolescent and he had a pitiless contempt for those who fancied children. Taking Pauli firmly by the hand he led him up the steep street towards the métro station. As they walked, Melchior chatted away because he was incapable of being quiet in company. And because he was not used to talking to children, he talked as he would to anyone, which was just right. Pauli listened, fascinated even when he didn't understand.

'This is Pigalle you're in, Pauli. There are those who affect to find beauty in low life and romance in squalor but I must confess I feel that an area like this requires the transforming power of art at its most magical, indeed at its most distorting. Look at that ghastly pair of tarts over there! Still I presume they do well enough for the undiscerning Boche. Call it sex if you like, my dear, I prefer to call it bayonet practice. No, this is no place for you to be, Pauli. There's nothing here for a young man of feeling.'

They entered the métro station. Pauli would have used one of his usual tricks to travel for nothing, but Melchior held him firmly and bought their tickets. The platform was crowded and soon Melchior was holding forth on the injustice of a man of his sensibilities having to travel like a bullock being transported to market. But Pauli was no longer listening. His attention had been caught by a young man a few feet away whose face was set in an expression of ferocious concentration.

Close to the young man, a little nearer the edge of the platform, was a German officer. He had a fresh, open face and his lips were pursed to whistle some tune or other, whether merry or sad Pauli could not hear. For the train was here now, decelerating noisily as it emerged from the tunnel. Even as it halted, the waiting travellers were surging forward to the unopened doors. The young Frenchman too stepped forward, bringing his hand out of his jacket pocket. Clutched in it was a small pistol. Pauli saw him raise it to half-way up the officer's spine. The young man's face was working palely. The pressure of his finger on the trigger was visible through the whole length of his arm, yet he did not seem able to find that last milligram of strength which would release the hammer. A small stout man with uneven teeth showing beneath a ragged moustache suddenly lurched forward and grabbed at the gun. When his hands closed over the younger man's he made no effort to divert the weapon but instead added his strength to the trigger finger. The gun fired. And fired again as the small man renewed his pressure. The first shot was almost inaudible. But some instinct immediately made those around fall into a wondering silence through which the second shot ripped with angry force. A woman shrieked. Blood spurted out of the officer's tunic spattering the hands of both his assailants. The German fell slowly forward. The small man turned away dragging the pale-faced younger man with him. The crowd surged away from the falling body like water driven from the centre of a pool by a heavy stone. The fleeing men came straight past Pauli. Melchior turned to see what was happening and was pushed aside by the fugitives, but he did not protest as he took in the bleeding twitching body only a few feet away. For a second he thought he'd wandered back into the make-believe world of Yerevan's gangster film, but it was not a very long second.

'Oh my God!' he cried, raising his hands to his face to block out the sight. Then he screamed in greater horror as he saw there was blood on his jacket sleeve where the assassins had brushed against him.

Two German soldiers from further up the platform forced their way to the body. A gendarme came clattering down the furthermost stairway, blowing his whistle. People were shouting, gesticulating, pointing. It seemed to Melchior they were pointing at him. In a blind panic he turned and began forcing his way towards the staircase up which the killers had vanished. The flight was totally instinctive but not altogether illogical. He had under his shirt 50,000 francs in dirty notes which he had no way of explaining. These were not the reason why he ran, but once having started running, they were a very good reason not to stop.

But suddenly there was a better reason to change his mind.

Almost at the staircase he heard a clicking noise behind him and a German voice called, 'Halt, or I fire!'

He halted, turned; a German soldier with his rifle at the ready came running towards him. Behind him was a gendarme. The soldier thrust the muzzle of his weapon into Melchior's belly. The gendarme cried breathlessly, 'Is this one of them?'

Melchior regarded them helplessly and for once speechlessly. He felt like a model posed by David for a figure of Guilt.

126

Then a small figure pushed between the gendarme and the soldier and rushed up to him, crying, 'Uncle! Uncle! I'm here! I lost sight of you, I was so frightened!'

Lowering his half-raised arms, Melchior clasped Pauli to his breast and said, 'There, there, it's all right, it's all right,' and raising his eyes to the gendarme, 'I lost him in the crowd, there was such a panic, I thought he'd got knocked over or run away.'

The gendarme rolled his eyes in exasperation.

'Come on!' he said to the soldier. 'This way!'

And the two of them ran off up the stairs.

The journey home was silent. But as they walked towards the apartment house, Melchior said, 'Perhaps we'd better not say anything to your mother, Pauli.'

'No, monsieur.'

'It would just worry her. You know how mothers worry.'

'Yes, monsieur.'

'Good. That's settled.'

As they parted outside Sophie Simonian's door, Melchior gravely offered the little boy his hand.

'And thank you, Pauli,' he said. 'Thank you very much.'

That evening as his mother tucked him up in bed, Pauli said in a low voice so as not to disturb his sister who was already fast asleep, 'Maman, is there still a war on, like when the Boche blew up our car?'

'No!' said Janine, taken aback. 'Not here, anyway.'

'Are the Boche our friends then?'

'No!' said Janine with even more vehemence. 'You can trust a friend, can't you? You must never trust a Boche!'

It was guilt that made her so vehement. In the two months since her last interview with Mai, she'd debated what he'd said in her mind a thousand times. Had he been laughing at her, knowing full well who Jean-Paul Simon was? Or was he really too stupid to make the connection?

Whatever the truth, she'd decided not to tell Christian all of what had happened, merely assuring him that Mai

127

had confirmed there was no trace of Jean-Paul in any official records. This decision was based on fear that Christian might advise against attempting further contact with Jean-Paul if he thought the Boche were on to him. Not that there'd been any contact yet. Christian had sent a parcel and letter, allegedly from Pivert, telling Jean-Paul in veiled terms that all was well, but there'd been no reply. A second letter had gone off. Still there was silence.

'Is Monsieur Valois not coming tonight?' asked Pauli.

Valois's visits were regular and this was one of his nights.

'Yes, he is late,' said Janine, smiling. Christian nearly always brought the children something, a precious sweet or an apple, whatever he could get hold of. 'Don't worry. If he comes, I'll send him in to see if you're awake! Good night now.'

She left the room still smiling. It was good when Pauli behaved like the child he was!

Behind her, Pauli lay in the dark. His eyelids were pressed tight in pretence of sleep, but his ears were straining and it wasn't until the clock in the living-room struck eleven and his mother tiptoed into the shared room that he really fell asleep, persuaded at last that there was no chance now of opening his eyes to find Christian Valois leaning over him, offering him a red-skinned apple with the same outstretched hand he had last seen in the métro, stained with the blood of the German soldier he and his accomplice had just shot down.

7

There was a poster on the wall of the bakery. Günter Mai recognized it from some distance away. Everybody was now familiar with the black-and-red edged notices printed in parallel columns of French and German on a dull biscuit

128

background. They were notifications that more executions had taken place.

This one, he saw as he got nearer, had been defaced. Someone had scrawled across it in thick blue letters, GERMAN BUSINESS.

Clever, he thought. An accusation against the authorities and also a parody of the notices Jewish-owned shops had to display.

He found Madame Crozier in a state of mixed indignation and apprehension.

'I really don't know what to say, lieutenant,' she protested. 'I know your boys have to put their notices up somewhere, but I hardly feel my shop is the proper place. Then when it was defaced, well, of course my natural instinct was to take it down, but that would make me to blame, wouldn't it?'

She was right. Removing or defacing official posters was a serious crime.

He said, 'I'll have a word about it.'

'Thank you, I knew I could rely on you.'

He accepted the usual invitation to step into the living-room and take a cup of coffee with Madame while Crozier put together his order.

'I went to the exhibition at the Berlitz the other day, have you been, lieutenant? You must go, it's really fascinating.'

The exhibition was called *Le Juif et la France*. Mai had seen the advertising poster as he walked down the Boulevard des Italiens a few days earlier. It showed a caricature Jew, bearded, hook-nosed, evil, digging claw-like fingers into a huge globe of the world.

'I was telling Madame Pascal about it, her whose son came back from the army *before* the armistice, he was a taxi-driver, so God knows what he's doing now, keeping very odd company from what I hear, and she said that she couldn't see the point of it, the exhibition, we were all French together, and wasn't Jesus a Jew. Well, I ask you! Jesus a Jew! Excuse me, that sounds like the shop door.'

She went out. Mai produced his Hitler *Jugend Tagebuch*

from the pocket it had stretched to bursting point and made an entry in his illegible shorthand. He was a collector of trivia, a sower of tiny seeds. From the shop he heard a voice whose words he could not catch but which he recognized. Then Madame Crozier spoke, in a low tone just audible to the sensitive ear.

'Lieutenant Mai is here.'

He listened for the sound of the street door opening and shutting. It didn't come. He smiled and put away his book. Sometimes the tiny seeds took root.

The living-room door opened and Madame Crozier re-entered.

'Here's my daughter, lieutenant. I think you've met.'

He stood up and bowed.

'Good day, Madame Simonian,' he said.

'Good day, lieutenant,' murmured Janine in a low voice.

She wants to talk to me, he thought. He'd guessed it when she didn't immediately walk out of the shop. He knew it now he saw her.

It hadn't been difficult to confirm that the patient 'Simon' and Iakov Moseich Jean-Paul Simonian were one and the same person. He'd arranged with the hospital for any correspondence for 'Simon' to be intercepted and copies of both letters now lay in his files. He'd checked Pivert's alleged return address and discovered it was Valois's. So far he had found nothing against the young man, but he had one of his feelings . . .

He felt no guilt about keeping all this to himself. He could see no advantage in letting the warped bastards who organized farces like the Berlitz exhibition know that one of their POWs was a Jew; on the other hand, the knowledge might be useful in recruiting another pair of ears and eyes to help his job here in Paris. But there'd been no rush. It was always better to get your victim to volunteer if you could.

He finished his coffee and said, 'Now I must go. Thank you for the coffee. Good day, Madame Simonian.'

He left swiftly. Janine wouldn't talk to him in front of

her mother, he knew that. She would need an excuse, so he'd provided her with one. And he smiled to himself a few seconds later as he heard her voice calling, 'Lieutenant! You forgot your cakes.'

He stopped and turned. Faintly flushed, she ran up to him, carrying a small white box.

'Thank you,' he said. 'That was kind. Though it might have been kinder to my waist to let me forget.'

She smiled. It was an effort, but she managed it. He said, 'Are you walking my way by any chance?'

'Yes. I think I am,' she said.

They walked in silence a little way.

'How are your children?' he asked, seeking a means of prompting her request for help.

'They're very well, thank you.'

'They must miss their father,' he said sympathetically.

'Yes. They do. We all do.' A pause, then it came out with a rush. 'I was wondering if perhaps your enquiries, you were kind enough to help, if anything else . . .'

The rush declined to a stumble.

'I have learnt nothing more than I knew last time we talked,' he said carefully. 'Nothing has changed.'

He could feel her scrutinizing his words, desperate for significance. She was hooked but he would need to play her very carefully. Other intelligence officers might have wondered if she was worth the effort, but Mai had a feeling that in the struggle ahead, every collabo they could lay their hands on was going to be invaluable. He had to be careful not to frighten her off. He recalled her own suspicion that it might be her body, not her loyalty he was after. It might be useful to re-activate that idea. Which would a woman find it easier to contemplate – betraying her husband or betraying her country? He'd no idea but he knew it was psychologically sound in matters of corruption to give the impression of choice, even between two evils.

He said, 'He has my sympathy, your husband, wherever he is.'

'What do you mean?' she demanded.

'It is a lonely business, being far from home, in a strange country, whatever the reason,' he said with a sigh. 'I know this from experience. You long for a little sympathy, a little kindness.'

He stopped and turned to face her. He reached out and took her cold, unresponsive hand in his.

'I hope,' he said softly, 'wherever he is, your man is finding a little kindness.'

For a moment he thought he'd overdone it and that she was going to laugh in his face or slap it hard. Then visibly she relaxed, her expression softened, her hand squeezed his and she said, 'I hope so too.'

He raised her hand slowly to his lips and kissed it. She lowered her head so that her hair fell in a fringe over her face, he guessed to hide her look of revulsion.

She said in an almost inaudible voice, 'The poor man you were telling me about, the one in hospital whose name did not appear on any official unit list . . .'

'Yes. I remember him.'

'He must be very lonely, if no one knows where he is, perhaps even who he is.'

'Yes,' said Mai. 'He's often been in my mind.'

'I could sense you were sympathetic,' said Janine with a flash of savage sarcasm. 'Perhaps it would be a kindness to find out how he is, what is planned for him when his treatment is finished.'

'You would be interested in that, madame?' he said. 'Then I'm sure I can find it out for you. Perhaps you would do me the honour of dining with me one night. Then I could report what I've managed to discover.'

'Yes, I would like that,' she said trying for brightness.

'On Friday then? Seven o'clock at the Balzac, shall we say? I look forward to that very much,' said Mai letting his face break into a smile.

She nodded and turned and almost ran away in her haste to put distance between them before he recognized her loathing and self-disgust.

He watched her go. She moved well, almost boyishly. Poor child, he thought. All upset because she thinks the big, bad Boche wants to bed her! She'll chatter like a chipmunk in her efforts to postpone the awful moment. And by the time she realizes it's the chatter not the chuff I'm after, she'll be so relieved, and so used to the idea of co-operating with the enemy, that the rest will be easy.

He resumed his walking, trying to whistle a few bars of Schubert's '*Sah ein Knab' ein Röslein stehn*', but it wouldn't come out right. He ought to be feeling happy that yet another of his little schemes was working out so well, but somehow he didn't.

8

'Christian,' said Maître Delaplanche, 'you are an imbecile. May I come in?'

Valois stood aside and let the lawyer pass by him into the flat. He'd been expecting the visit. Delaplanche had been away on another trip to the Free Zone at the time of the shooting in the métro.

Valois had been ill for a week afterwards. His colleagues at the Ministry had been most concerned. The prospect of seeing Delaplanche on his return had not made him get better any quicker.

Delaplanche held up a paper-wrapped parcel.

'A gift,' he said. 'From your mother. I met her in Vichy. We knew each other when your father and I were young lawyers. She asked if I could deliver it to you. I was only too pleased. It's such an excellent justification of my presence here.'

'Thank you,' said Valois, taking the parcel. 'Probably pâté.'

Delaplanche sat down and raised his eyebrows invitingly.

'I'm sorry,' said Valois wretchedly. 'It was a mistake, I see that now. They've taken hostages, they're threatening to shoot them. I never thought the bastards would react like this.'

'Didn't you? I did!' said the lawyer. 'At least, I hoped they would. It's the best thing that could happen for us.'

'That innocent Frenchmen should be shot down?'

'That not the most innocent of Frenchmen, or women, or even children should be able to feel safe!'

Valois sat down opposite the lawyer.

'Why burst in here calling me imbecile then?'

'Well, for a start, you don't seem to have been very good at it, do you? Oh, don't look so affronted! I understand you were all cut up about the killing. Now you seem to be ready to take offence at not being complimented on a nice job! I'll give you the same compliment I gave Theo, shall I?'

Theo was the cell leader. He was also the man who'd had to steady Valois's hand so he could pull the trigger.

'Don't blame Theo! It was my choice! My responsibility!'

Delaplanche said softly, 'I told Theo he was stupid, unfit for our work. And I tell you the same. Choice? Responsibility? What have they got to do with you any more? Listen, Christian. I didn't recruit you to run around the métro killing Krauts. All right, so you succumbed to some childish need to prove yourself – don't interrupt! – well, I take the blame for that. I'd forgotten what it is to be young and untried while the old men are boasting. I shouldn't have put you anywhere near Theo.'

'He's not being punished on my behalf, is he?' said Valois.

'Jesus! Such self-importance!' said Delaplanche. 'On the contrary, he's a great success, first-class organizer and he kills a lot of the enemy. No, he's going onward and upward, don't worry about Theo. It's just that you're going in different directions. This is going to be a long war. By the time it's finished you could be well up the ladder, in just the kind of position we need to help us rebuild the country. In the meantime, you'll be a pair of eyes and ears for us in the Finance Ministry, and probably other ministries too. Make yourself popular. No need to collaborate actively with the Boche, I don't want you tainted with *that* brush or some other ambitious young killer may rub you out! But be nice to people. Make up your differences with your father, for instance. Visit him more often. There's all kinds of useful little things to be picked up in Vichy!'

'You want me to spy on my father? For God's sake, that's a Nazi trick, isn't it?'

Delaplanche said quietly, 'I hope no one ever has to die for your sentimentality, Christian.'

The doorbell rang and Valois jumped to his feet in such alarm that the lawyer laughed.

'You might have been followed here!'

'Really. Why? And if I were, why shouldn't I be here? I've brought pâté from your mother! Also, you seem to forget, I'm not a member of any subversive group, am I? My name appears on no party lists. Now hadn't you better answer that bell?'

Reluctantly Valois went to the door and opened it. He was still half-expecting to see men in uniform there. Instead . . .

'Janine!' he cried.

The woman pushed by him, slamming the door behind her.

'Christian, can I talk to you?' she said.

Without waiting for an answer, she crossed the narrow vestibule and went into the lounge. Delaplanche looked up from the newspaper he was reading and smiled. Janine stopped dead.

'I'm sorry,' she said. 'Christian, I didn't know you had company . . .'

'Yes,' said Valois shortly. 'Can we talk later? In an hour perhaps?'

He glanced at Delaplanche, who nodded almost imperceptibly.

Janine glanced at her watch.

'Yes . . . no . . . it doesn't matter. Next time you come round . . . You haven't been to see us for a while . . .'

'I'll come soon, I promise.'

He ushered her back to the door and, lowering his voice, asked, 'Is it important? Have you had any news?'

'No. Nothing. It's just that, not seeing you for so long, I wondered if you'd heard anything . . . about your parcel, I mean . . .'

'You don't think I'd have heard something and not come round to tell you?' he said. 'But I will call soon, I promise. My love to the children. And to Madame Sophie.'

He kissed her cheek and closed the door behind her.

Back in the lounge, Delaplanche said, 'That's a striking young woman. What's particularly striking is the way she always seems to call on you whenever I'm here.'

'She's married to a close friend of mine. He's a prisoner-of-war. Also he's a Jew, but trying to keep it quiet.'

'Very wise,' observed Delaplanche. 'You will naturally do what you can. Only, try to keep your distance.'

'From my friends?'

'From the Jewish question. I've got a contact on the CGQJ. This exhibition is a major step forward in the Nazis' strategy for France. I suppose you might say we're lucky here. They still feel it necessary to propagandize. Elsewhere in Europe, they've been less particular. Have you been to the exhibition, by the way?'

'Certainly not!'

'Go and see it!' commanded Delaplanche. 'And let yourself be noticed seeing it. And if you find its crudeness shocks you, remember, as far as our German friends are concerned, this is anti-Semitism at its most subtle! Now, let's eat some pâté and get down to some real work in case your pretty little friend returns to interrupt us yet again!'

There was no chance of that. Janine had been on her way to her dinner date with Günter Mai when an overwhelming impulse to tell everything to Christian had diverted her. Now her sole concern was that she might arrive so late at the Café Balzac that Mai would not have waited.

But he was there, drinking a beer.

'I'm sorry,' she said breathlessly, tumbling into her chair. 'I was held up, the métro, some trouble . . .'

'It's all right,' he said, amused. 'You're only a quarter of an hour late. That's punctual in French terms, surely? Now, I thought we would just eat here, if that's all right?'

'That's fine,' she said.

He had expected her to be too impatient for news of her husband to wait more than a few moments, but she seemed content to exchange small talk and to tuck into the meal without questioning him. She was, he guessed, delaying the moment which would put her in his debt.

His guess was partly right. The other part was that Janine was determined to eat her fill. The more she ate here, the less hungry she would be when it came to sharing out the rations at home. But at last she was finished.

'All right, lieutenant,' she began, but paused as Mai put his finger to his lips.

'Not lieutenant. Not here,' he smiled.

'What then?'

'Édouard. Let us act like friends.'

'As long as we remember it is an act,' she said. 'What have you to tell me about my husband?'

He sipped his beer slowly. So, she was determined to start by throwing aside all pretence. It was a good move. When it came to pretending, she was no match for him.

'He is well, almost well enough to be discharged,' he said, accepting her change of rules.

'Discharged? Will they send him home?' she asked with sudden hope.

'I doubt it. If it had been a permanently crippling wound probably yes. But when there is a complete physical recovery . . .'

He stressed *physical* but she did not take him up. Instead

she said gloomily, 'But to keep him in hospital such a long time, it must have been a terrible wound.'

'There was a great deal of bodily damage, as well as the head wound,' admitted Mai. 'But the rest has healed completely, with a few scars. The head wound was the most serious, however. There was a fragment of metal lodged inside the skull. They did not dare try to remove it till the other wounds had healed and the body was strong enough to risk the operation. This is why it all took so very long.'

'You've gone into this pretty deeply,' she said.

He had in fact received a copy of 'Simon's' full medical record. What he'd said about the soldier's physical health was true, but there'd been more. The patient suffered from bouts of severe withdrawal, almost catatonic on occasions. Sometimes he had blackouts, and though there was a question mark against his claim to total amnesia, the doctor was certain that what recollection of the past he did have was disturbed and fragmentary.

He emptied the last of the wine into her glass. There was a limit of a bottle per table, but he had stuck to beer and Janine had consumed the wine greedily. Perhaps she was trying to anaesthetize herself against whatever payment she was expecting him to exact? He studied her flushed face over his glass. She met his gaze squarely. How did she see him? As the ruthless spymaster or a lecherous Hun? How did he see himself? He pushed his chair back a little way and crossed his legs.

She said flatly, 'How can you help me?'

Good girl! he thought. She was at least going to try to extract from him a promise of something more positive than his silence.

'Alas,' he said. 'Only with advice.'

Unasked, the patron surreptitiously brought them two glasses of cognac.

'To your health,' he said.

She drank deep and said, 'What advice?'

Her voice, now slightly blurred by the drink, had a note

of desperation in it. It wasn't just fear. This was the despairing voice of a woman alone, living with problems she did not care or dare to share with anyone.

He'd been intending to underline his power over her with a couple of gentle threats disguised as advice, and then to start leading her inexorably to the role of *Abwehr* informer. But now he found himself wanting to ease that pain he heard in her voice with some real advice.

He said, 'You must be patient. If the man, Simon, is your husband but wants to keep his real name hidden, then the greatest danger of betrayal comes from your actions.'

'*If?*' she said fearfully. 'What do you mean, *if?*'

'All right, it's quite clear he is your husband,' he said harshly. She wanted honesty. Let her have it. 'He's using another name presumably because he fears what might happen if it came out he was a Jew.'

'And is he right?' she asked with a calm dignity which took him by surprise. 'Is he right to be fearful?'

He met her unwavering gaze, thought of all the reservations he could make, the assurances he could offer; then he thought of his opposite number in the SD and said quietly, 'Yes, he is right to be fearful.'

She shook her head disbelievingly and said, 'There must be something I can do. His father fought in the last war. Marshal Pétain himself decorated him. Perhaps if I wrote . . .'

'Get it into your head,' he snapped. 'Any kind of fuss endangers your husband and perhaps even your family.'

'My family?' she said in alarm. 'What danger can there be to us? Bubbah Sophie's a Jew, yes, but she's an old lady. The children and I are good Catholics. As for Jean-Paul, he hates all religion.'

In exasperation Mai snapped, 'Being a little old lady is no protection, and saying you've been converted is no protection, and being brought up Catholic is no protection.'

His vehemence at last frightened her.

'Protection against what?' she demanded.

He sat back wearily and wondered how to answer.

He had seen plenty of anti-Semitic violence in Germany before the war. Here in France it was just starting. Recent terrorist acts were being blamed equally, sometimes simultaneously, on groups of fanatical Communists and Jews. The anti-Semitic press was growing ever more abusive. And, of course, the SD in its battle to take over effective control of the city from the Military Command would see pogrom both as a means and an end.

'Listen, Janine,' said Mai earnestly. 'I don't know what's going to happen, but prepare for the worst. Get yourself as watertight as possible. Start by making sure all your papers are in order. For instance, your husband's a French citizen, is he?'

'Of course he's a French citizen!' Janine said. 'Do you think he was fighting in the Foreign Legion?'

'Yes, all right,' said Mai. 'But was he born here? His parents weren't, were they? Presumably they were naturalized. Was that before or after your husband's birth? Have you or your mother-in-law got all the papers? Where is the office of record? Here in France bits of paper can still protect you to some extent. Friends in high places are useful too. And it won't harm to have a good lawyer in reserve.'

'But why? What's all this to do with me?' she asked in bewilderment. 'I don't know anyone important.'

'Monsieur Valois may be important one day,' Mai suggested. 'And already he must know important people. Isn't his father a deputy?'

'Yes, but they don't get on,' she said. 'Though, come to think of it, Christian does know Maître Delaplanche, and *he's* important, isn't he?'

It was enough to make you believe in God, thought Mai, but a God of malicious irony rather than loving kindness. Here he was enjoying helping this girl, having put aside (for the moment, anyway) all thought of using her, and instantly those lovely pale lips cough up this pearl. *Dela-*

planche. Almost certainly a communist, but too clever to have his name recorded on any list and too well connected (some said well informed) to be easily touchable. But he'd been on the *Abwehr*'s pink list of men to be watched even before Adolf decided to tear up the German–Soviet pact.

'Never heard of him,' he lied easily. 'He's well known, you say?'

'Oh yes. He's been in the papers a lot, helping ordinary people in trouble, so maybe someone like that could help Jean-Paul, is that what you mean?'

'Perhaps,' said Mai. The effort of changing back from friendly adviser to *Abwehr* officer was surprisingly hard.

'You've met this lawyer fellow, have you?' he asked.

'Yes, in a way. I've seen him a couple of times when I've called at Christian's flat. He seemed very nice.'

More brandy came, almost furtively.

Mai said, 'That's good. Bear him in mind. But I wouldn't say anything just yet. It's some time in the future you may find him useful, after you've got your husband home. For the time being, the less you say to anyone, the better, family or friends.'

His turnaround on the question of lawyers went unchallenged as she seized upon the bait he offered.

'When I've got Jean-Paul home? But you said there was no hope!'

He smiled and drooped one eyelid.

'No *official* hope,' he said. 'But who knows . . . ?'

He'd done this sort of thing a thousand times, manipulating contacts with half-promises, veiled threats, hinted bribes. It had never felt degrading before. Then he thought of German soldiers being assassinated in the métro and in the streets, of German families waiting for the postman. The link between Valois and Delaplanche might be nothing. On the other hand it could lead right into the middle of a Resistance group.

Janine set down her empty glass with a bang.

'All right,' she said in a voice of decision. 'What are the terms?'

141

'I'm sorry?'

'Look, I may not have gone to the Sorbonne, but there are some things you pick up, even working in a baker's shop. Price, profit, payment and return. Can you guarantee delivery, that's the first question.'

He didn't pretend not to understand but said, 'I'll do my best. If it can be done, I'll do it.'

'And what's the price?' she asked.

He hesitated. He suspected that she might be a lot less successful if she knew precisely what he was after than if he kept things vague and general. But she mistook the cause of his hesitation.

'You're not getting me body *and* mind,' she said. 'If it's information you want, I'll try. If it's me you want, you can have me. But don't hope for both.'

She was missing the point, but they nearly all did. They thought of one-off bargains, not appreciating that the initial exchange was merely the planting of the hook. It didn't much matter what form it took. In Janine's case bedding her would probably be as good as anything. With that family-destroying threat he could probably play her for ever more.

He looked at her and for a moment was tempted. She saw it in his eyes and looked away to hide whatever was in her own. No, that wasn't the way, he told himself, shocked that he could have entertained the idea for even a second. Before he could say anything, the patron appeared at the table and stopped to whisper in his ear.

'The flics are outside, Monsieur Scheffer,' he breathed. 'They'll be raiding us any second to check papers. I just got the signal.'

Mai didn't have to feign alarm. Not that there'd be any trouble from the police once he showed his *Abwehr* identification but he didn't doubt the sharp-eyed patron and God knows who else would spot what was going on, and bang went a well-established cover.

He said, 'Can we get out the back?'

'No. They'll have someone there. But you can hide

upstairs. Second door on the right. Lock it after you.'

His eyes flickered to their clasped hands and with a grin he added, 'There's a bed in there too!'

Mai rose, pulling the girl with him and went through a door behind the bar. There was a flight of rickety un-carpeted stairs. They went up them and into the room indicated by the patron. It was small, almost totally filled by a huge metal bedstead with a feather mattress. What light there was filtered through a threadbare curtain over the tiny window.

'Here?' she said in a small voice.

It took a second to get her meaning. She thought he'd made his choice and opted for payment in flesh rather than information! They were standing so close he could smell the brandy on her breath. He opened his mouth to tell her about the police raid but suddenly she moved forward and pressed herself against him. It was the spasmodic leap of the timid swimmer plunging into the icy pool before her nerve completely fails, but in that darkness, that silence, that isolation, it communicated itself to Mai like desire. He put his arms around her, bent his face to hers and kissed her passionately. There was little response from her lips, but his body responded with all the fervour of long deprivation. His mind was still protesting that this was wrong, in so many ways wrong, wrong professionally, wrong morally, wrong emotionally. If she'd cried out in rejection, he might still have had the will to back off; if he'd been able to see the contempt and revulsion on her face, he might have been unmanned. But the room was dark and the girl was silent except at the very moment of entry when she said desperately, 'He will come home, won't he?'

'Yes, yes, yes!' he promised wildly and thrust himself into her, exploding almost immediately in the reluctant, constricting heat of her body.

They lay side by side, not touching, not speaking, till the patron scratched at the door and whispered, 'All clear.'

Downstairs, there was no thought of returning to their

143

table. They went straight out into the street. It was still relatively early. People strolled by. Everything looked mockingly ordinary.

'You'll be in touch?' she said, clearly eager to be rid of him.

'Yes,' he said.

She walked swiftly away, not once looking back.

9

A cold October wind rattled leaves like bones down the side of the synagogue.

'Jesus, I'm frozen,' said Michel Boucher stamping his feet. 'Where is the little bastard?'

The little bastard was Pajou, who had just clambered through a forced window at the back of the building. It was size not courage which had got Pajou elected. The other three men in the group, though not as large as Boucher, were all well bulked with beer bellies. Boucher thought they were a dead loss. He'd been amazed at first to discover they weren't even getting paid. The Mouvement Social Révolutionnaire, they called themselves.

'I've never heard of it,' he told Mai in the weekly briefing he gave the *Abwehr* lieutenant on SD plans. 'Have you?'

Mai had smiled and nodded and made another note.

'He's here,' said one of the MSR men excitedly. 'He's here.'

'All right. Calm down. Let's get on. And for God's sake, not so much noise!'

He'd thought at first there wouldn't be much need for stealth. But Pajou had put him right. Even though it was an SD operation in origin, for some reason the Fritzes wanted to keep right in the background and hadn't even tipped their own Boche military patrols the wink to keep out of the way. It was all very puzzling. What did occur to him was that if he could lead this bunch of dynamite-laden idiots round the city without getting picked up, then it shouldn't be too hard for Resistance groups wanting to blow up the Boche to do the same. But he kept this thought to himself.

Inside, for a little while the darkened solemnity of the synagogue seemed to affect even the MSR men. Then one of them farted and the others laughed.

'Here, Paj, how the hell have we got mixed up with these jokers?' asked Boucher.

'You're getting paid, aren't you? Let's get these fuses laid. And keep that lot away from the detonators!' retorted Pajou.

The little man proved to be expert in the laying of charges and rounded off the job by setting a clockwork timing device.

'Aren't we going to see this shit-heap blow up then?' asked one of the MSR men, disappointed.

'There's more to do,' retorted Pajou. 'Once one goes up, the gendarmerie will likely check up on others, so we don't want to warn 'em, do we? You can watch the last one!'

As they passed silently through the door, Boucher glanced back, feeling again the peace and solemnity of the place. What's the point of it all? he wondered.

Then he felt the weight of the piece of silver plate he had pushed inside his leather tunic and thought, well, mebbe it's not all been a wasted effort!

That night six synagogues were blown up and a seventh, where the saboteur's charges didn't go off, was destroyed by the military for 'reasons of public safety' the following day.

In the collaborationist press the outrage was reported as the protest of ordinary Frenchmen, indignant at the slowness of the anti-Jewish reforms promised by their new military partners.

'But I told you what was going to happen!' fumed Günter

Mai. 'Didn't you pass it on to your chums at the Majestic?'

'Don't be insubordinate, Günter!' warned Zeller. 'Of course I passed it on.'

'Then why didn't they stop it?'

'How? By putting a permanent *Wehrmacht* guard on all the synagogues in Paris? Think of how that would have looked back in Berlin!'

'At least they could have used our advance warning to make sure everybody knows who really organized this.'

Zeller sighed wearily and said, 'You disappoint me, Günter. This is like burning the Reichstag. Of course everyone knows who *really* did it, but private knowledge and public acknowledgement are very different things. No, the SD have done well for themselves here. They've put the Military Governor in an impossible position either way. So, despite your excellent advance intelligence, it's one in the eye for the *Abwehr* too.'

'Listen, sir,' said Mai urgently. 'It isn't just a game between us and them, is it? There *is* a war on and none of this is helping us to win it! There's England uninvaded, Russia sucking up our troops like an ant-eater sucks up ants, America sitting waiting till someone gives her the push to join the war, and what's happening here in France? *We*'re spying on the SD who are trying to undermine the Military Governor's authority at the same time as they play into the hands of the Resistance by initiating a reign of terror! We're going to have to conquer this sodding country all over again, has anyone told the Führer that?'

Zeller stood up and waggled his finger in his ear.

'Strange how deaf I'm getting,' he said. 'Hardly caught a word of all that! Günter, take care of yourself, dear boy.'

He went out. Mai smiled after him. His indignation was genuinely felt, but, sober, he was not in the habit of letting his emotions control his mind. But he had to be quite sure where he stood with Zeller and a little controlled indiscretion was the best way of checking on that. The way things were going, he could see a hard road ahead and he needed to be sure who was walking along it behind him.

Later that day he was sitting having a drink with Michel Boucher, debriefing him about the aftermath of the synagogue burning.

'Fiebelkorn's going around like a dog with two cocks,' he said. 'They all arc. Me, I don't get it. What's so clever about letting off a bit of dynamite?'

'I can't say, Miche,' said Mai, who found Boucher's political thought processes at once naïve and impenetrable. 'We'll keep in touch, eh?'

'Sure. Talking of which, Auntie Lou was wondering if she'd offended you somehow. Says you've not been into the shop for ages.'

'I've been busy.'

'That's what I said. I expect she's just worried she'll mebbe not get her next lot of extra flour. I told her I'd fix her up if you let her down, but I don't think she liked my prices. Cousin Jan was asking after you too.'

'Was she? *Why?*' snapped Mai, guilt making him aggressive.

'No need to get ratty! I think she's still hoping you might be able to help with finding Jean-Paul, that's all.'

So at least the girl had had the sense to keep the news of her husband's survival to herself. Probably that was Valois's idea.

'It's not easy,' he said.

'I didn't reckon it would be,' said Boucher. 'Might cost a bit, I told Janine a while back. Only, make sure you get value for moncy.'

He knows, thought Mai. Or at least, he's guessed.

He'd made a conscious effort to avoid meeting Janine ever since he'd raped her. Yes, that was the right word; *went to bed with*, *made love to*, *had sex with*, none of these phrases would do. The act had been brief, brutish and against her wish if not her will; it deserved the most unadorned of verbs. The memory of the encounter filled him with shame.

And yet, amidst the shame, vibrating on the edges of

these pangs of self-reproach, he could recognize, had to acknowledge, desire. He wanted to do it again, not as it had happened last time, but with her body compliant and consenting and receiving as well as giving pleasure. He found himself thinking of Jean-Paul Simonian with furious resentment. For God's sake, it was almost like being jealous of the man.

'I'll be on my way then,' said Boucher.

'All right. Look, if you see Janine, tell her . . .'

'No need,' interrupted Boucher with a grin. 'Tell her yourself. I mentioned I'd be seeing you in here today. That's her just come in. See you, lieutenant!'

He rose and left, exchanging a brief word with his cousin *en route*. She came straight to the table and sat down. Mai found he was packing his pipe so full that strands of tobacco drooped down from the bowl. He expected her tone to be accusatory but when she spoke, her voice was hesitant, almost apologetic.

'I hope you don't mind. Miche said you'd be here. I know it must be hard to get things moving. Miche said, a man in your position, well, you'd need to be careful. I appreciate that, I really do, only as I knew you were going to be here, and time goes by, and we've still not heard a thing . . .'

She looked at him with a confident expectation that was harder for Mai to take than recrimination and despair.

In fact Janine was feeling far from confident. In some ways she was a shrewd judge of people and what had prompted her to be so frank with this stocky Boche with the filthy pipe and the probing eyes was a feeling that he was the kind of man who kept his bargains. But the nature of their bargain bothered her and paradoxically it was her trust in her judgement which was making her feel increasingly doubtful of his dependability. She looked at him now and couldn't see in him the kind of man who would look for the cheap, speedy thrill he must have got in that squalid room above the café. He looked so

148

comfortable and domestic. But you couldn't tell just by looking. Who could look at me and tell that I'm nothing but a tart? she asked herself scornfully.

She said, 'Please, how is he . . . ?'

'He's very well,' said Mai confidently. 'He's almost back to full health. And he's in no danger. But I've got to be careful not to attract attention to him.'

It was all lies, though it might of course be accurate. He hadn't made any more enquiries about Jean-Paul since he and Janine had last met. He'd simply tried to suppress the whole affair in his mind. Now she had revived it, damn her.

He left the woman abruptly with a promise that he'd see what could be done.

He wrestled with the problem a week longer. The stupid thing was, it wasn't really a problem. The only way he could get Jean-Paul released officially was either to confide in, or lie to, Zeller and process an official *Abwehr* request. The dangers were too great, to Jean-Paul as well as to his own career. Or was it simply that he didn't want Simonian released?

After another ten days of intermittent soul-searching, it occurred to him that he could do one thing at least. There was no need to keep on withholding Simonian's mail.

Having once made up his mind, he acted swiftly, authorizing a direct phone call to Erhard, the doctor in charge of 'Simon'.

'Give him the letters, you say? Good. About time. It's an act of sadism, keeping them from him. More Gestapo than *Abwehr*, I would once have said.'

Erhard was a prickly outspoken man, not the best qualities for survival, even in a doctor.

'Yes, I'm sorry,' said Mai. 'It was regrettably necessary. But no longer.'

'I expect you'll want to know how he reacts to his letters,' demanded Erhard grumblingly.

'No. No need,' said Mai. 'You've done enough. Thank you.'

'Oh?' This gentle response seemed to take some of the steam out of the doctor. 'Very well. It's just that pretty soon we're going to have to make our minds up and his reaction here might help.'

'Make up your minds about what?'

'About where he goes next. No point in keeping him here much longer. We need the bed.'

'And what are the alternatives?'

'POW camp or medical repatriation, of course. Not that there's much choice in this case, whatever I say. Unless there's some vital part clearly missing our admin. chief is impossible to convince, so it's the long road east for this poor bastard. It should be a medical decision, not some file-farting pen-pusher's!'

'He'll surely review the evidence first,' said Mai mildly.

'You would say that,' snorted Erhard. 'Two of a kind. This fellow keeps on trying to get transferred to Intelligence. That's where the real work's done, he says. Same bloody work, as far as I can see. Gathering information you don't know what to do with. No wonder he admires you lot. All bureaucrats under the skin!'

Here it was again, the voice of that ironic God he'd heard already in the Café Balzac, though this time disguised in the bitter tones of an over-worked doctor.

'I wonder if you could get this call transferred to your admin. officer?' said Mai.

Ten minutes later it was done. No official forms, file records, or signed requests. Hints, hesitations and half-promises, the dialect of deception which Mai seemed to have been speaking since childhood.

'You're looking pleased with yourself, Günter,' said Zeller, entering the room. 'Up to something wicked?'

'On the contrary, major,' said Mai with a smile.

150

10

Soon it was time for the French to celebrate their first full year as a subject race. In December Maurice Melchior went to a party given by Serge Yerevan at his villa in Auteil.

It was the kind of party he'd once dreamt of, crowded with social and artistic luminaries. Normally Melchior would have revelled in simply rubbing shoulders with such people but somehow tonight he felt out of sorts with this flashy, lively world so much at odds with the reality of life for most Parisians. When a very distant acquaintance in the theatre said to him coldly, 'Ah, Melchior, I heard you'd been doing well for yourself. Clearly the new regime likes the cut of your bum,' he'd flashed back angrily, 'Perhaps, monsieur. But at least I can conduct my business without having to crawl up German arseholes on the Champs-Élysées every time I move!'

This reference to the need for everything that was printed, produced, played or displayed to be approved by the *Propaganda Abteilung* on the Champs-Élysées caused a little upset. There was no German presence at the party, and a lot of stupid-Boche stories had been flying around, and generally speaking nearly everyone there was busy assuring everyone else that they were all good patriotic Frenchmen.

Yerevan covered the moment by inviting his guests to look at some rushes from his latest film. In the darkness he squeezed Melchior's shoulder and whispered, 'Hush, little Maurice. It's cruel to remind these poor cunts of what they are. Stay behind after they've gone. There's something I'd like to discuss with you.'

Business? wondered Melchior. Or could it be that the

151

signals he'd been sending out for some time were at last getting their answer? That Yerevan was bisexual was well known, but for the past few months he'd seemed quite content with Ribot.

When the party reached the point where it was going to turn either sentimental or orgiastic, Yerevan opted for the former, making a little speech about Christmas and absent friends and the gift of freedom, after which he sat at a piano and started to play carols. His guests joined in, raucously at first, but soon with tears in their eyes.

At eleven it was time for the party to break up. The curfew operated even for these people. Probably by inviting a few Germans, Yerevan could have provided everyone with an *Ausweis*, but he'd preferred not to.

'I can see my friends collaborating any day,' he explained later to Melchior. 'It's much more amusing to see them being patriotic.'

Melchior glanced uneasily at Ribot. He'd been held back from the general exodus by the director's hand on his arm. Now the big-nippled actress was glowering resentfully at him, making it clear he'd overstayed *her* welcome at least.

'You look tired, my dear,' said Yerevan to her. 'Why don't you turn in?'

This considerate suggestion was received like a threat. Pale with anger, the woman rose and stalked out of the room without a good night.

'Women,' said Yerevan, smiling. 'They don't know the difference between true sensitivity and pique, do they? Now, business. With Japan and America in the war, I'm a little concerned that the eastern trade routes may be blocked up. I'd like to be certain you can help.'

He was talking about opium.

'No problem,' assured Melchior. 'Do you want to talk prices now?'

'Later, later. In the morning will do,' said Yerevan, waving his hand dismissively. 'I just wanted reassurance. Don't you sometimes wish you were ordinary, Maurice? Still, God makes us all the way we are, and we mustn't quarrel with his disposition, must we? Come now. You'll stay the night, of course?'

He rose and offered his hand. Melchior took it and rose too. He hoped that Yerevan wasn't regarding tonight as in any sense a down payment. He might be the king of crime movies but a real life gangster like Miche the Butcher would probably come as something of a shock.

As they went up the stairs hand in hand, Maurice said, 'All that Christmas stuff from you came as a bit of a surprise.'

'Why so? We mustn't be bigots. After all, he was a good Jewish boy. And he's an example to us all.'

'How so?'

'He reminds us not to forget what most Gentiles would like to do to good Jewish boys!'

He opened a door leading into a sumptuously furnished bedroom.

'In these hard times,' he said seriously, 'we good Jewish boys must stick together.'

'Oh, I do hope not!' said Melchior.

Laughing, they went into the bedroom.

On the last day of the year, a train from the east pulled into the rain-lashed station at Compiègne. The platform was crowded with hopeful relatives and helpers from various voluntary agencies. There were supposed to be two carriages of repatriated prisoners on the train, but a murmur of disappointment rose above the wind as it was realized there was only one.

Janine had scanned every window as the train decelerated past.

'I can't see him,' she said wretchedly to Christian Valois. 'He hasn't come.'

'Don't be silly!' he said confidently. 'Of course he'll come. You can't have seen everyone!'

Uncomforted, she leaned against him and pressed her face into his shoulder. He tried to ignore the pressure of her body and concentrate on scanning the figures who were beginning to emerge from the train. He wanted desperately to spot the dear familiar figure of his friend, yet the thought kept on slipping into his mind that with Jean-Paul's return would vanish all excuse for the kind of contact, indeed for the close relationship, he and Janine were enjoying now. Jean-Paul had brought them together; now Jean-Paul would separate them. It was a good thing, he assured himself. There'd been a couple of times when he'd come close to overstepping the limits of a fraternal embrace. Thank God he had had the strength to resist. The double meaning of the phrase occurred to him and he smiled. He could think of the German he'd killed now with no qualms at all. Indeed, as he watched the line of bandaged and limping figures being helped from the train, he even felt pride.

Then he saw him.

He held his breath and didn't speak for a few moments till he was sure. Then he let it out with a sigh.

'He's here,' he said.

'What?'

'He's here.'

She turned her head slowly as if fearing a deceit. And when she saw him, she fixed her eyes on him with a desperate intensity as though fearful that even a single blink would wash him away.

He was much thinner. He was almost literally bare-headed. They must have shaved his head for the operation and the black hair was still as short as the nap on velvet. She could see the scars. One from the bullet at the side of his left temple, and the other edging from beneath the pall of hair where the surgeon's scalpel had probed. But it was still Jean-Paul, unmistakable, unbelievable, Jean-Paul. She looked at him and her heart swelled with love. She'd hated Günter Mai in the days after he had taken her, but now she forgave him. More, she laughed at him and mocked him for having asked so little of her in return for this dearest of treasures.

Jean-Paul hadn't seen her yet. He was walking slowly

154

along the platform, not like an invalid but with the slowness of uncertainty. A voluntary worker spoke to him and rested her hand on his arm, but he ignored her and walked on as if she were not there.

And now suddenly he smiled, the smile which turned his dark face from ascetic scholar to Sicilian shepherd boy. His steps speeded up. He came running towards them, heedless of the people between. She stood quite still, frozen by joy. And now for the first time in nearly two years she heard her husband's voice.

'Christian!'

Suddenly his arms were round Christian Valois's neck and his joyous face pressed hard against the shoulder where her dejected face had so recently rested.

'Jean-Paul, it's so good to see you. Good? It's bloody marvellous!' cried Valois. 'But hold on a bit. Come on, Jean-Paul, I don't think you've quite got your priorities right.'

Disengaging himself from Jean-Paul, he twisted him round so that he faced Janine.

For long silent seconds the young wife and the returned husband looked at each other and the smiles faded from both faces.

Then Jean-Paul turned to Valois and said in a puzzled tone, 'Who's she?'

PART FOUR
February–November 1942

Enfants, beaux fronts naïfs penchés autour de moi,
Bouches aux dents d'émail disant toujours: pourquoi?

Victor Hugo, *Ce qui se passait aux feuillantines*

1

Janine awoke.

For a moment she did not know where she was. The room was full of frosty radiance as dawn broke through the high sash window. Jean-Paul always slept with the curtains pulled wide. 'I'm a creature of light,' he said. 'I wake with the sun.'

Jean-Paul. She turned. There on the bolster beside her was his dear head. In the month since his return his hair had grown to a fledgling's fluff obscuring much of the scars, and his face had lost something of the wasted pallor that had turned him into his own ghost.

He turned in his sleep, stretched out his arm, draped it round her shoulders. She held her breath. He opened his eyes, saw her face so close to his and smiled. It was a smile that drew back years, the smile of a young man who knows that by an incredible stroke of fortune, here at the very start of his adult life he has got all that he needs to guarantee his happiness.

The door burst open. Céci rushed in crying, 'Maman, maman, Pauli's hid Mimi!'

Janine looked at her daughter with unusual irritation. These first moments of the day when sleep had thrown a fragile membrane over Jean-Paul's inner wounds were her most precious possession, her greatest hope for his healing. He was sitting up in bed now. The smile had gone and with it the carefree boy, as his face took on its now more normal expression of puzzled watchfulness.

'All right, all right, Céci. I'll be out in a minute,' she said.

Disappointed of her mother's sympathy, the little girl turned to her father.

159

'Papa, Pauli's very naughty,' she chimed.

Simonian looked at her then he smiled, not the same smile he had woken with but undoubtedly a smile. Janine felt a flood of relief. Though her old Jean-Paul was rarely with her for more than a few waking moments, there were at least two new Jean-Pauls. This one acknowledged formally who she was, could have animated conversations, particularly with Christian, and was able to smile at his daughter. The other, the one she feared, was a grim intense figure who clearly inhabited a world of darkness and pain the nature of which those around him could only guess at.

'Let's go and see Pauli, shall we,' he said, swinging his legs out of bed and picking up the delighted child.

Janine followed them out of the bedroom. She was always worried at any confrontation between Pauli and his father. Of all the renewed relationships this was the worst. Even at his darkest, Jean-Paul recognized his mother and Christian. Céci he had no recollection of, but as she had no recollection of him either, it didn't seem to matter. This was her papa, she was told, so that's how she treated him, leaving him no choice of response. Janine could find hope here even when things looked at their blackest. As for herself, her days swung between the joy of that morning recognition and the pain of subsequent rejections, ranging from the courteous to the totally indifferent.

But the real problem was Pauli.

She saw it now as she watched through the open door of the children's room.

'Pauli, papa says you've got to give me Mimi back,' cried Céci from the imperious heights of her father's arms.

Pauli was sitting on the floor cross-legged, his face set in the expression of almost frowning intensity he had inherited from his father. He didn't look up but reached under the bed and pulled out a battered toy poodle. This was Mimi, originally Pauli's toy, which had passed with his blessing to his sister some time ago. His reassertion of ownership was one of the disturbing symptoms of his feelings about his father. Almost since Céci's birth, he had

160

appointed himself her guide and protector. Now he had taken to treating her with a sulky indifference which sometimes came close to bullying.

'Come on, Pauli, give Céci the dog. Big boys don't play with toys like that, do they?'

Jean-Paul was making an effort but he couldn't hit the right tone. The trouble was that Pauli did remember him, and missed him, had been almost ill with excitement at the prospect of his return, and now found it impossible to understand the changes in him. Janine had tried to explain, but despite his apparent maturity in so many matters, she could see that all he felt here was a small child's hurt at being rejected. He withdrew into his pain just as his father so often withdrew into his. And neither of them emerged far enough to grasp the other's reaching hand.

Now Pauli threw the dog at his father's feet. Jean-Paul's face set. Then he put the little girl down and, pushing his way past Janine, re-entered his room.

'Pauli, hurry up and get ready for school,' she said. 'It's late.'

'Don't want to go to school,' said the boy sullenly.

'I don't want to stand here arguing,' she said grimly. 'Get ready.'

She turned and almost bumped into Christian Valois. He was dressed in his dark business suit.

'Christian, I'm sorry. I should have been getting breakfast ages ago. We've slept in.'

'So I see,' he said glancing at her body with a smile.

She looked down, realized she was wearing only a thin cotton nightdress which was hanging open almost to the waist.

'I'm sorry,' she said, putting her hands to her breast.

'Don't be. How's Jean-Paul this morning?'

'All right. You know, not black.'

'Good. I must rush. See you tonight.'

She watched him leave and thought, soon we must get out of this flat. It had been marvellous of Christian to put them up. Sophie's flat had been impossible. It was all right

161

for her to share with the children, but not for the four of them to sleep in the same room. The boulangerie offered more space, but the problem there was Louise. She and Jean-Paul had never got on well. Now their proximity might be positively dangerous. There was a violence in Jean-Paul which hadn't been there before and she did not know where it might come out.

But staying here was not a long-term solution. If Christian's parents or sister came to Paris, they would expect to stay here. And though he had never said or done anything out of order, she had seen Christian's eyes rest on her body as they'd done this morning and she knew that in fairness to him they ought to move on. But where? To find a decent place they could afford was not going to be easy. You'd think Paris would be half-empty, but far from it. The Boche set the price of things with their inflated exchange rate and property ran high.

And there was no doubt that the longer she stayed in this spacious and airy apartment the more choosy she was going to get!

She went to get dressed.

Jean-Paul had got back into bed. His face was turned away from her but she could tell by the set of his shoulders that he was drifting into that dark solitary world where no one else could follow.

She dressed swiftly. When she went back to the children's room she found Pauli already dressed.

'Good boy,' she said. 'Go and get yourself some bread while I see to Céci.'

'I don't want to go,' said Céci. 'I want to stay with papa.'

The little girl had not yet started school but usually Janine took her with them and always on mornings when she could tell that Jean-Paul was regressing.

'No, you come along, Céci,' she said. 'We'll call on grandpa and gramma and have some breakfast there, shall we?'

'Oh yes,' said Céci, easily seduced from her plan by the prospect of being spoilt at the bakery.

162

She looked in once more on Jean-Paul before they left. He was in exactly the same position. He looked to be asleep, but she knew if she walked round the bed she would find those eyes wide and staring, totally devoid of recognition.

She did not make the journey. That blank gaze still had power to overthrow her, and her life was too full of responsibilities for the indulgence of despair.

'Come on, children,' she said briskly. 'It's time to go.'

2

There was a queue outside the Crozier boulangerie. They looked defeated and depressed. Even their breath, made visible by the February air, was thin and grey and quickly vanishing.

Günter Mai turned up his collar and slipped round the back to enter via the bakehouse, where he found the baker removing a lightly loaded tray from the right-hand oven. The bigger oven on the left wall hadn't been lit for almost a year now as the shortage of fuel and flour had tightened its grip. Mai did his best to see that the Croziers got their fair share and a bit more besides but even he sometimes found it hard to compete with specialists.

'Bread ration day, is it?' he said.

'That's right,' said Crozier gloomily. 'And there's not much to go round. I hate to see the poor devils' faces when we're short. Come on through while this lot cools and we'll have a coffee and croissant.'

'Thank you,' said Mai, smiling. There was a not unattractive naïvety of outlook which Crozier seemed to share with his nephew Michel.

'How's Janine? And your grandchildren?' he asked.

'Fine,' said Crozier, face brightening.

Mai sat and listened to the baker talking proudly of Pauli and Céci and let his thoughts drift to their mother. He hadn't seen Janine since her husband's return, but of course had been kept up-to-date by her parents on his visits to the bakery.

He would really have liked to wash his hands of Janine, but God was still pushing her into his professional path. Why the hell did she have to take her family to stay at Christian Valois's apartment? Zeller assured him he was getting obsessed by that young man, but the more of a model citizen he became, the less Mai liked it. He'd felt the man's resentment bordering on hatred the only time they had met and there was no way he could square this with his reported reconciliation with his Vichy father or with his unquestioning acceptance of the collaborationist line in his work at the Ministry.

The one flaw in Valois's otherwise unblemished front was his acquaintance with Delaplanche. Even that had been explained to Zeller's satisfaction.

'He's an old acquaintance of Valois père from their law-student days and Delaplanche knows the value of not making unnecessary enemies. So when he returns from a visit to Vichy, what more natural than that he should bring back a gift of bonbons from Madame Valois for her much-missed son?'

Zeller might be right. Delaplanche was certainly the wiliest political opponent the collaborationist government had. The extreme rightists would have had him locked up, or better still shot, ages ago. But too many of the rest owed him favours, or, as an insurance against future set-backs, wanted him to owe them a favour, to make him an easy target. Perhaps this was after all the simple explanation of his link with the Valois family.

But Mai didn't think so. And now he had in Christian Valois's flat a potential agent ready to be activated. So far he'd been able to justify his inaction on the grounds that Delaplanche was still in the South doing God knew what. But word was that he was on his way back to Paris. So what now? And what kind of agent would Janine make anyway, especially when she felt her price had already been paid?

Crozier's rambling anecdote was interrupted by his wife's arrival from the shop.

'Hello, lieutenant,' she said. 'Crozier, isn't that next batch ready yet? Two lots of forged tickets I've had today. I think it's the Gelicot family in the Rue d'Auch. Wasn't the son apprenticed in the printing trade?'

Mai made a mental note. Any hint of an illicit press was of interest these days. And as often before, he wondered how conscious Madame Crozier was of what she was saying.

As he rose, Crozier said in excuse, 'We're just chatting about the children, dear.'

'I wish I had time to chat. They're fine children, which is saying a lot when you consider their father. Doesn't know his own wife half the time.'

'He's confused,' said Crozier mildly. 'He's been through a lot.'

'Has he?' snorted Louise. 'Well, I hope you'd have to go through a lot more, Crozier, before you forgot me.'

The two men's eyes met for a moment and Mai was still smiling a few minutes later as he left through the bakehouse door. Such moments of pure humour were to be treasured in these hard times.

'You're looking very happy, lieutenant.'

It was Janine who'd just come into the yard. She had her daughter in her arms, but the little girl was struggling to get down. Set on the ground, she ran instantly to Mai and waved a little bunch of winter jasmine at him.

'Are these for me?' he asked, bending down.

'No,' said Céci scornfully. 'For Gramma. I want donkey.'

'I'm sorry,' said Mai. 'I seem to be out of donkeys.'

'I want donkey like Uncle Chris,' cried the little girl.

Mai looked at Janine who said, 'Her Uncle Christian gives her donkey rides on his back. Céci, don't bother . . .'

'No bother,' said Mai. 'I work like a horse, so I might as well look like one.'

He swung the laughing child on to his shoulders and stood upright.

'She's growing fast,' he said. 'How old is she now?'

'Four. It was her birthday last week.'

'They soon grow up,' he said. 'How are you, Janine?'

'I'm fine.'

She was looking at him warily.

'Lieutenant, I'd like to thank you,' she said abruptly.

'Oh yes?' he said gruffly. Gratitude was salt to his still raw guilt.

'For getting Jean-Paul home to me,' she said. 'I can never thank you enough. Except . . . I can't do *that* again. Not now Jean-Paul's home.'

She thinks I'm capable of forcing myself on her again he thought desperately. But does she never guess what I'm really capable of?

Reaching up, he plucked the young girl from his shoulders and swung her to the ground, ruffling her hair as she ran back to her mother.

'*That* will not be required again,' he said stiffly. 'But I should like to meet and talk sometimes. As friends.'

He saw her expression and laughed without amusement.

'You'll never make the Comédie-Française,' he said. 'All right. As friendly enemies. Tonight for instance?'

She shook her head.

'Sunday then?' he pressed.

Her awareness of having no real choice shadowed her face.

'Sunday,' she said. 'But not in the evening. Evenings are difficult.'

'All right. Where? The Balzac?'

'No!' she exclaimed in alarm, then hastily added, 'I take the children out for a trip on Sunday afternoons. The Jardin d'Acclimatation in the Bois. The Porte de Sablons entrance. Two, or just after. Is that all right?'

He nodded and she caught her daughter up and carried her into the bakehouse. The little girl waved her flowers and shouted, 'Bye bye, donkey.'

Mai strolled slowly back towards the Lutétia. He'd done everything right. Every clandestine meeting she agreed to added another filament to the web she was already tangled in. But he found himself wishing he'd left earlier or she'd come later.

He realized he had reached the Lutétia without being conscious of the walk, a dangerous distraction in these days of ambush and assassination.

Corporal Vogel on duty at the door snapped to attention and said, 'Sir!'

'Yes, Vogel?'

'The lieutenant has a flower on his hat. Sir!'

He removed his Homburg and studied it. Sure enough, in the hollow lay a sprig of jasmine with three or four tiny flowerlets glowing on its stem. He smiled at the memory of Céci so light and merry on his shoulders.

He thought of putting the sprig in his lapel, saw Vogel watching him, and said, 'Corporal.'

'Sir!'

'Get rid of this for me, will you?'

Handing over the jasmine, he walked swiftly into the hotel.

3

Though Mai did not know it, Janine had been avoiding him just as keenly as he had been avoiding her. Whenever she visited her parents she always listened at the door first to make sure he wasn't there and on one occasion when he turned up later, she had hidden upstairs till he had gone.

But it couldn't go on for ever and now she was glad to have got it over. But in its place there was this new worry. He wanted to see her again. Why? His request filled her with great suspicion and not a little fear. He was not a stupid Boche as she'd thought and he was far from powerless. A mere lieutenant, yet he had managed to get Jean-Paul released. So her hope that one quick orgasm would be the price of her husband's return was probably as vain as she'd always feared it would be.

Now more than ever she wanted advice and comfort, but where could she turn? Not to Jean-Paul, that was clear. Her father perhaps? But she shied away from the thought of bringing her pain into that good, simple man's life. Christian? There was no one else. But not yet. It was best to find out first what the man wanted of her.

These thoughts ran through her mind as she got ready for her rendezvous on Sunday. Things had fallen well. Jean-Paul was having one of his better days and had gone to have lunch at his mother's. The two had always been very close even after Jean-Paul's abandonment of his religion. Janine prayed that the time they spent together would speed up his healing.

The doorbell rang. She heard Pauli's voice and came out of the bedroom. Standing on the threshold looking down at the boy with a puzzled expression was Maître Delaplanche. He was carrying some parcels.

She gave him a big smile and said, 'Christian's in the kitchen, I think. Just go through. Pauli, are you ready? I'll be with you in a couple of minutes. See that Céci is all right, will you?'

She was still worried about Pauli, but the solution seemed simple. Jean-Paul's relative normality this morning had extended to giving his son a casual peck on the cheek as he left. This unthinking, unthought-out, everyday act of affection had lit up the boy's face. That was all he needed. Love.

When she came out into the hallway, Pauli and Céci were standing hand in hand ready to go. She went to the living-room door to say goodbye to Christian but paused at the sound of quarrelling voices inside. Out of the confusion, the lawyer's suddenly rose loud and clear.

'He's a Jew? And he was in hospital under a false name? For God's sake, Christian, what are you thinking of? You're risking your career, *everything*, for a self-indulgent impulse. Get rid of them!'

Janine turned away, forcing herself to smile at the children.

'Let's go and see the monkeys, shall we?'

Valois and Delaplanche heard the door open and shut. The lawyer went to the window and watched till they emerged on to the pavement.

'Pretty little thing, in a skinny sort of way,' he said. 'There's nothing between you, I suppose?'

'You asked me that before.'

'Things change,' said Delaplanche. 'Listen, Christian, the reason I've been away so long was I got a message in Vichy inviting me to visit some friends further south. It turned out de Gaulle has sent an envoy to co-ordinate resistance. Typical bit of arrogance from that big-nosed bastard. But it makes sense to pull together. We're all being picked off too easily. So for now I'm going along with this fellow. But if de Gaulle imagines this is a step to putting him on top when the war's over, he's a fool. The future is ours so long as we have men like you willing to sit and wait.'

'I'd rather stand up and fight,' said Valois almost sullenly.

'I know. What you've got to do takes a special kind of courage. That's why you mustn't take foolish unnecessary risks like harbouring a mentally deranged Jew!'

'He's not mentally deranged,' protested Valois. 'He's the brightest man I know. All right, what he went through has done something to him. In particular, it has made him want to kill Boche. He's desperate to get an active Resistance job. If someone doesn't use him soon, I'm scared he'll just go off by himself and kill Krauts with his bare hands.'

'And get himself traced back here? Jesus.'

'Couldn't you use him? Oh, I know you don't do these things personally. Important people like you and me have to keep our hands clean. But Theo, perhaps . . .'

'Not Theo. He's too valuable now to land with a wild man. One of the peripheral groups perhaps . . . but not till he's long gone from here. Tell him anything, but get him out.'

There was the sound of a key in a lock, a door opening and shutting.

'You tell him,' said Valois. 'But choose your words carefully. He's a little on edge.'

The lounge door opened.

Delaplanche's first impression was of a slight, almost boyish figure who stood very still in the doorway, like a child too shy to interrupt the adults. But when his eyes met the man's unblinking gaze, the stillness seemed to grow vibrant with menace.

'Jean-Paul, come in. How was your mother?' said Valois.

'Well,' said Simonian. 'You're Delaplanche, aren't you?'

'That's right. You know me?'

'Only what everyone knows.'

'What's that?'

'Nothing.'

'I gather you were a guest of our German friends for over a year.'

'Oh, yes. They cared for me and healed me and sent me home,' sneered Simonian. 'I'm so grateful. Christian, where's Janine and the children?'

'They've gone for a walk. The Jardin d'Acclimatation, I think.'

'I'll see you later,' said Simonian. He turned abruptly and left.

'And that's the man you want me to employ,' said Delaplanche drily.

'I tell you, he hates the Boche!'

'Oh yes. I could feel the hate. I hope it's for the Boche! Christian, I'm all the more certain now, he's got to be moved out of here. All right, yes, I'll see if we can use him, always supposing he passes the entrance test! But he's not for you, my boy. Different worlds, different functions. The chances of that one surviving the war are minute, but you, Christian, you're the whole future of France!

'Now why don't you give me a little cognac while I sit and watch you unwrap these belated New Year presents?'

Janine was late. It was a chilly afternoon, not actually raining but with the gusty wind damp as well as cold against any exposed flesh.

There weren't many people about, just a few hardy souls whose Sunday promenade in the Bois wasn't going to be interrupted by either war or weather.

He glanced at his watch. Perhaps she wasn't coming. Then he saw her in the distance and his heart leapt as if he was a lover waiting for his lass instead of an *Abwehr* intelligence officer waiting for a woman whose body he'd already abused and whose loyalties he was planning to corrupt.

She greeted him as if it were a chance meeting, presumably for Pauli's benefit. After they'd entered the Jardin d'Acclimatation Janine wanted to turn immediately into the shelter of the Palais du Jardin d'Hiver, but Pauli said firmly, 'I've promised to show Céci the monkey-house, maman.'

'All right,' said Janine. 'But come straight back to the parrot house.'

'Yes, maman,' said Pauli and the children set off hand in hand.

'Will they be all right?' asked Mai anxiously.

'I thought you'd be pleased to be rid of them for a while.'

'Yes, but . . . they're so young.'

'I sometimes think Pauli's older than me,' said Janine

171

moodily. Then she smiled and added, 'But thanks for being
concerned. Honestly they'll be all right.'

'Will they mention me?'

'What if they do? An acquaintance met by chance.
Anyway, Jean-Paul doesn't spend much time talking to
the children. Nor to me either.'

'To Monsieur Valois then?'

She seemed to take this as an implied reproach.

'Christian's his oldest friend. Jean-Paul's memory's been
affected, you know that. He remembers the fighting and
what happened after that. And the further back he goes
the more he recalls. It's just the bit between . . .'

'The bit with you and the children in it?'

'Yes.'

'You must be very grateful to Monsieur Valois. For
letting you share his apartment, I mean. Do you plan to
stay there long?'

All Mai wanted was to establish some kind of timetable
for his campaign, but her reply intrigued him.

'I knew we couldn't rely on staying for ever but I thought
we would see the winter out. Now, I don't know.'

'Oh. Why's that?'

'Why do you think?' she said indignantly. 'It's you
people of course.'

Taken aback by the accusation, Mai protested, 'But, my
dear Janine, what have I done? Except bring your husband
home to you?'

It wouldn't do her any harm to be reminded of her
obligation.

'I know. I'm sorry. I didn't mean you personally. But
Christian's a civil servant. And of course it's the Boche
that really run the Government. So if they found out he
had someone like Jean-Paul staying in his flat, it could
mean trouble for him.'

There was no denying this was true, but it had been true
from the start. What had made it an issue now?

He asked, 'Did Monsieur Valois say this?'

'No. He's far too generous to say anything like that. I

overheard one of his friends spelling it out to him today.'

'One of his colleagues, you mean?' he said casually. But suddenly she was alert. The hunted animal too has its sensors, as finely tuned as the hunter's. To this point she had been saying nothing which she believed was new to him. It was his interest in what should not have been interesting that alerted her.

She said, 'I expect so. I didn't know the man.'

He smiled. Alert she might be, liar she wasn't. It didn't matter. All he had to do was check with the man he had watching Valois's apartment. If it turned out that Maître Delaplanche, just back from Vichy, had dropped in . . .

He felt impatient to be off, but a sudden departure would confirm any suspicions she might have. Besides it was more important than ever to keep the line on which he was playing this woman taut. It was good to feel himself in such a purely professional relationship with her.

They were in the parrot house now. It was crowded with visitors, both French and German, looking at the bright-feathered, beady-eyed birds. He turned to whisper to her that here was not a good place to continue their conversation but before he could speak, Pauli's voice called excitedly, 'Maman, maman, papa's here!'

Without looking round, Mai moved slowly away and exchanged a few joking words with a couple who were trying to get a big yellow-headed bird to talk to them. After a few moments, he pulled out his pipe, and under cover of lighting it he looked towards the doorway.

Standing there was a slim dark man. The resemblance between him and Pauli would have marked him out even if he hadn't been carrying Céci in his arms. Janine and the boy joined him now. Even at a distance it was possible to see Janine's joy at meeting him. Mai felt a crazy urge to go across and introduce himself.

'Hey, no smoking,' said an attendant pointing at a sign.

'Sorry,' said Mai. Instantly he realized he had spoken in German. It didn't matter. The attendant had moved away and no one else paid any attention. But Mai turned back

173

to the parrots and concentrated his mind on the source of this slip and that even less comprehensible urge to blow his cover.

It wasn't hard to find, but finding it brought little comfort.

It had been the sight of Janine going with such obvious joy to that man.

It had been jealousy.

4

As usual Janine paused outside the bakehouse door and listened carefully. It was a month since her last meeting with Mai and though she knew he could pick her up any time he liked, she sensed that he preferred these more casual and therefore more disarming encounters.

What he wanted from her she was still not certain. What could she know or do that would interest him professionally? But without doubt he wanted something.

Today she could hear voices inside. As she strained to identify them, Pauli's sharper ears beat her to it.

'It's Uncle Miche,' he cried and rushed through the door.

Looking more piratical than ever, Boucher was leaning up against the big, permanently closed oven talking to her father. His face split with pleasure when he saw them and he swept Pauli up in his right arm and Céci in his left and spun round with them. They screamed with delight and continued the spinning motion after he set them down.

Céci cried, 'We're moving house! We're moving house!'

'What's that?' said Claude Crozier.

'It's not certain, only Christian's found us a flat we can afford. We've just been looking at it. I liked it but I've left the men to sort out the details.'

In fact she had sensed a quarrel developing between the two men. She didn't know its origins but she knew she didn't want the children to see their father and their 'Uncle' Christian at each other's throats.

'Where is it?' asked her father.

'Quartier Mouffetard, off Rue Monge, quite close.'

'That's marvellous,' said Crozier. 'Come on, children, let's go and tell your gramma.'

Boucher pulled a handful of coins from his pocket and jingled them in his huge fist.

'Céci, are you eating your greens and helping your mother to dust? Pauli, are you doing your schoolwork and still not using the blade on that knife, like you promised?'

'Yes, Uncle Miche,' cried the children in unison.

'Then here you are,' said Boucher pouring the coins into their upraised hands. They screamed their thanks and followed their grandfather into the house.

'You shouldn't,' said Janine.

'Why not? I like to share what I've got. Listen, you should have come to me about a flat. I'd have found you somewhere a cut above the Quartier Mouffetard.'

'Thanks, Miche, but I think this will do us nicely,' she said.

He read between the words and said shrewdly, 'Jean-Paul wouldn't like it, eh?'

'Oh no, nothing like that,' she lied. In fact when Jean-Paul had got wind of Boucher's current employment, Janine had been terrified by the intensity of his reaction. In his eyes any association with the Germans was vile. 'The time will come,' he said with chilling certainty, 'when we'll purify this country. Then let them watch out.' Janine had thought of Günter Mai and shuddered.

'How's Hélène?' she asked to change the subject.

Boucher frowned.

'Fine,' he said shortly. 'No, look, to tell the truth, Jan, she's got herself pregnant.'

He spoke with such hurt indignation that Janine had to laugh.

175

'She did it all by herself, did she? Clever girl,' she said.

Boucher grinned sheepishly.

'No, I didn't mean . . . it's only that things were going so well . . . first time in my life I've really had enough money to enjoy myself without the law breathing down my neck . . . in fact in a manner of speaking I suppose I'm with the law now. Miche the Butcher a lawman, now there's a laugh.'

Janine took a deep breath. What Miche's precise job was she did not know and did not want to know.

'Do you want the baby, Miche?' she asked.

'Does Hélène want it, you mean. I think so.'

'No. Do *you* want it?'

He looked as if the question had never occurred to him.

'Me?' His face registered a growing amazement. 'Yeah, I do. I really do!'

'Then ask Hélène to marry you. Settle down. Become a citizen.'

He roared with laughter.

'Jan,' he said. 'You're a marvel. I might just do that. I just might.'

In the empty apartment off the Rue Monge, Jean-Paul Simonian and Christian Valois were quarrelling.

'You want rid of us,' said Simonian flatly.

'Nonsense. As I say, a friend mentioned this place. It's roomy, it's handy for Janine's parents, and Sophie's place isn't a million miles away across the river. And it's cheap.'

'You're quite a salesman, Christian,' said Simonian, not pleasantly.

Valois grew angry and replied, 'Look, do you want it or not? You can't stay in Passy for ever. My apartment belongs to my father. He comes back to Paris from time to time and won't take kindly to finding he can't use it. As for Janine, she needs her own place. Every woman does . . .'

'You didn't use to be so concerned about Janine,' said

Simonian. 'You used to think she was a common little shop-girl who'd somehow got her claws into me.'

'I never said that! But whatever I thought, I've seen how she loves you, how she missed you. She deserves a bit of happiness now.'

'Very touching,' mocked Simonian. 'You want us out, that's all there is to it. All I need to know is why? There was a time when you'd have filled the flat with Hottentots to annoy your father! No, it's something else that's turned you into a hypocrite. Delaplanche! Is that it? He wouldn't happen to be this friend who just happened to mention this place, would he?'

'Don't be stupid,' said Valois, aware of how unconvincing he sounded. He'd allowed his friend's illness to obscure the memory of just how sharp Jean-Paul's mind was.

'Stupid? I don't think so. I'll tell you what I do think. Delaplanche has recruited you, right? And he's given you the kind of job you like, which is sitting around doing nothing till the great revolution comes!'

Valois was filled with fury yet at the same time he acknowledged a sense of nostalgic pleasure at the edge of his rage. This was how it had been in the old days, the two of them in classrooms, in cafés, in the street, in the park, hurling arguments and insults at each other like love-letters tied to half bricks.

'At least I've made a choice, an intellectual decision.'

'To do what? Beat the Boche by sucking up to them?'

'Bastard! Who the hell do you think you are? What have *you* done since it started?'

'At least I got this *fighting*,' said Simonian, his hand flying to the livid scar on his temple. 'And I lost friends, good friends, true friends.'

'Did you now! And what did these "good friends" do for you, tell me that?'

'They died for me,' said Simonian dully. 'And before they died, they killed Germans for me. Can you match that, Christian?'

Valois, by now more hurt than he cared to admit, said with an effort at casualness, 'Well, I'm not dead, so you've got me there. But you don't have to be a soldier to kill the enemy, you know. As a matter of fact, I've killed my Boche. Oh yes. And not just blazing away out of a trench either. I waited, and picked him out, and stood behind him, and let him have it!'

He pretended his hand was a gun and made a child's banging sound.

'You did that?' said Simonian incredulous.

'You think I'm a liar as well as a hypocrite and a coward?'

'No. Of course not. I know how honest . . .'

To his dismay, Valois saw his friend was crying, not noisily but with steady tears trailing glistening spoors across his cheeks.

'Jean-Paul . . . please . . . I'm sorry . . . I don't mean to . . .'

'What? Oh shit. Am I crying again? Sometimes it just happens.'

He wiped away his tears then squatted in a corner, lit a cigarette and said seriously, 'Let me explain what it's like being me just now, Christian. It's like there's another me, the *real* me, the *essence*, walking around in my mind, like a man strolling in wooded countryside by a river on a misty day. You must forgive me if I grow poetic. I used to write poetry, remember? Surrealistic, despairing stuff. Now I live it.'

He drew on his cigarette.

'Sometimes the mist clears a little and I see people and places. Sometimes I recognize them instantly. As with you. Sometimes I know I know them, but I'm not sure *how* I know them. But I study them and it all comes back. But it comes back as knowledge, you see. Not as feeling. I can remember everything about Janine. Above all, I remember that she made me happy, the sight of her, the sound of her, the simple presence of her. And I remember the children too, well, Pauli anyway, but I can't believe that they're anything to do with me. They're part of another, unreachable world.

'Round and round I wander in this misty landscape. Sometimes the mist swirls grey and thick and I crash into trees, and thorns tear at my skin. But I don't mind this too much, for at these times I'm aware of a greater danger. I can hear the river rushing mightily, exploding in foam against huge, sharp rocks; I can feel its spray damp on my face; I know it is close, very close, and that a careless step in the wrong direction will plunge me in and see me carried away for ever.'

He paused. The two men looked at each other, one face pale with horror, the other dark with despair.

Then the darkness vanished from Jean-Paul's features to be replaced by a serene child-like smile.

'And there are times when the mist rises completely and I see everything in brilliant sunshine. Oddly enough, these moments usually occur when I'm confronted by a German in uniform and I know that what would make my happiness complete would be to kill the bastard! The trouble is I've got no weapon. I need a gun. Knives are for experts and too messy. I don't want to get caught, you see. It's not simply fear, but I reckon my life's worth a lot more than just one German's! So I need a gun, and I need help, a group. How do I find them? I hear talk of the Resistance and I read about acts of terrorism. I even heard an explosion the other day! But how do I join?'

'Advertise?' said Valois, grinning to signal the return to something like their normal relationship.

'That's what I'm doing, I think,' said Simonian, returning his grin. 'I may be ideologically shaky, but I can take orders. And I'm ready to kill. Tell him that.'

'I don't know what you're talking about,' said Valois still smiling.

'Of course you don't. And it occurs to me that Maître Delaplanche won't want to know either, not while I'm sharing a flat with his little Mister Clean. So, thank you, friend. This apartment looks very nice. Very nice indeed.

I think after all we will take it. As long as there's a bar within two minutes' walk.'

Valois glanced at his watch.

'Let's find out,' he said.

5

Winter slowly turned to spring and Parisians observed, most with pleasure, some with surprise, all the old 'firsts' – the first crocus, the first chestnut blossom, the first swallow.

Towards the end of May, Maurice Melchior saw his first yellow star.

He was sitting outside the Deux Magots feeling at one with this sunlit world. Everything was going well. As Miche the Butcher's factor he was prosperous; as Yerevan's housemate, he moved in the most fashionable circles. As for the Boche, he'd come to the conclusion that if he didn't bother them, they wouldn't bother him.

Then an old woman with a yellow star sewn to the breast of her threadbare coat walked by.

It was like a shadow crossing the sun. He forgot it almost instantly till five minutes later he saw another on a middle-aged man.

Hastily paying his bill, he jumped up and followed, overtaking him just beyond the church of Saint Germain.

'Excuse me, monsieur,' he said, but did not need to complete his question. Across the middle of the star was printed *Juif*.

'You haven't heard the new ordinance?' said the man, observing him keenly. 'You must be one of the clever ones who didn't register. Won't do you any good, monsieur. I didn't register either till one of my friendly neighbours sent a note to the Rue des Saussaies.'

With a harsh laugh the man walked on.

It was nothing to do with him, Melchior assured himself. It was just another bit of Boche bureaucracy. But whatever his mind said his stomach was telling him that everything had changed; police registers, notices in shop windows, these were flea-bites. But labelling people in the streets: this was the beginning of the plague the fleas carried.

But he was safe. Unregistered, anonymous . . . well, relatively . . . then he thought of Serge. *He* wasn't anonymous, far from it, and if there was one thing these Huns really hated it was an arty Yid! His first thought was purely selfish. If they went after Serge, they'd certainly grab him too. The safe thing to do was avoid the villa at Auteil like the plague and keep his head down till the first frenzy of pogrom was past.

And then a wave of shame swept over him. To abandon his friend, his lover, like this made him no better than the Germans.

He must at least warn Serge and try to convince him of the danger.

Half an hour later he was turning his key in the villa door.

In the hallway he halted. There were two suitcases on the hall floor. They were his. Ribot was standing half-way up the stairs. She didn't speak but nodded towards the door of Yerevan's study.

Melchior marched in. Yerevan was seated behind his white-topped desk with its modish tubular steel legs.

'Maurice,' he said. 'I'm glad you've come. There's trouble, I'm afraid. This new SS chief, Oberg, seems to have orders to come to grips with the Jewish question. I gather new measures are proposed.'

'I've seen one of them,' said Maurice indignantly. 'Yellow stars. That's what I was coming to warn you about.'

'I'm glad you see how dangerous this could be,' said Yerevan. 'I didn't want to worry you before, but in fact I've been fending off enquiries about you for some time now. I've done what I can but I can do no more. You'd best lie low for a while.'

'*I'd* best lie low? What about you?' Melchior asked in bewilderment.

'Me? Why should I lie low?' replied Yerevan, his dark handsome face wreathed in an actor's puzzlement. 'I have my work to do, Maurice, my debt to art to repay.'

This was either very great courage or very great crap. Melchior's mind assessed the alternatives, and did not need a long debate.

'What do you mean, Serge?' he demanded. 'You're as Jewish as I am! And I'll tell you something. If you dump me and I get picked up, I won't be as modest about your sacrifice in repaying your debt to art as you seem to be!'

He was ashamed of the threat as soon as he made it, but Yerevan was looking puzzled not threatened.

'What are you saying, Maurice? That I'm a Jew? How very odd.'

Now Melchior was dumbfounded.

'But you are,' he stuttered. 'You can't deny it.'

'Of course not. Simple denial would hardly be enough. No, you need the papers to prove it. See!'

From his inner pocket he produced a long envelope.

'I've just been down to the Rue des Saussaies to make sure there is no future misunderstanding. I saw your old friend, Colonel Fiebelkorn, as it happens. He was most courteous and even provided me with a little certificate to show that my papers have been examined and authenticated.'

'Authenticated? As what?'

'As proof that I am second generation French and that my family, Armenian in origin it is true, have been members of the Eastern Orthodox Church as far back as records can take us. Who knows? Perhaps if you'd been just a little less flamboyant, dear boy, we might have been able to prove you were second cousin to the Holy Father! But it's too late, I fear. So take a holiday, Maurice, lie low, that's my advice. Good luck. Don't forget to leave your key, will you?'

For once made speechless by rage, Melchior hurled the key at the smiling film director and had the pleasure of seeing him duck. Then he strode out, grabbed his cases and a moment later was standing in the warm sunlight.

He made no conscious decision as to where he was going, but his homing instinct was strong. An hour later, with only a vague recollection of a crowded, sweaty journey in the métro, the weight of his cases brought him to a halt and to awareness. He saw he was in the Rue des Coutures-Saint-Gervais. Just ahead, it intersected with the Rue de Thorigny. He was nearly home.

How pleasantly familiar and everyday things looked. A woman passed pushing a pram; an old man scuttled furtively by, clutching to his chest three carrots in a string bag; against a big double door directly opposite the intersection, some small boys urged on by an even smaller girl were playing a ball game; everything was lemony in the early evening sunlight, so calm, so ordinary.

One of the boys looked up from his game, saw him, and crossed the street to block his path before he reached the corner. It was Pauli Simonian. They hadn't met since that ghastly day in the métro.

'Hello, Pauli,' he said. 'Visiting your grandmother?'

He recalled vaguely that the family had moved out when the missing husband returned. His own visits here had been intermittent since he moved in with Serge.

'Yes, monsieur. Bubbah said if I saw you while I was playing to give you a message.'

He had been edging slowly past the boy, but now he stopped and returned. The steady unblinking brown eyes still disturbed him.

'Yes?' he said irritably.

'Bubbah says, there's a man, a German soldier, she says. He's waiting to see you.'

Melchior backed away from the corner in horror. He grasped the boy's shoulder for support as well as emphasis.

'Thanks, Pauli. I'm running up a big debt to you. And thank your grandmother too.'

He turned on his heel and walked swiftly back the way he had come.

Behind him, Pauli watched his departure with an expressionless face. Then there was the sound of discord from the playing children. He turned round. One of the boys had pushed Céci so that she fell into the gutter.

'Come on, Simonian! Your stupid sister's spoiling our game!'

Clenching his fists, Pauli ran towards them.

In the flat, Janine sat silently watching her mother-in-law sewing a yellow star on to her outdoor coat. She'd come ready to pour out her own woes, but when Sophie had told her the meaning of her task, she'd been unable to begin.

'Textile coupons, is it?' said Sophie, triumphantly. 'Not so quick, I say to myself. First go and see exactly what this thing is they want to pin on us. So I did, and when I saw it, I thought, that old piece of curtain I bought for the kitchen but never liked, that's the very colour! Why should I give good coupons for something I don't want, eh?'

'Why should you have to wear such a thing at all?' demanded Janine fiercely.

'Rules,' said the old woman calmly. 'There, how does that look?'

She held up the old coat on which the star with the word *Juif* picked out in black thread glowed like an exotic decoration.

'Boche rules!' exploded Janine. 'God, how right the Resistance are to shoot them.'

'Bullets kill people,' said Sophie. 'That can't be right. But how can a piece of yellow cloth harm me?'

'You obviously thought it might harm Monsieur Melchior,' said Janine, rather irritated by what seemed to her an unjustified complacency. 'Otherwise you wouldn't have asked Pauli to warn him about the soldier who's waiting.'

'Monsieur Melchior has broken their rules,' said Sophie sternly. 'He is a lost soul, I think, but one of our own, so

184

I will help him. But it is his own fault, certainly not that young man's sitting on the landing up there. He seems a nice boy. I gave him some tea and he was very polite. He showed me a photo of his family. His mother looked a very respectable sort of woman. I'm sure she too would show kindness to a French boy away from home.'

Janine took a deep breath. This seemed like a good cue.

She said, 'Bubbah Sophie, I wonder . . . I mean, I hope . . .'

She hesitated. It was hopeless. She couldn't do it.

Sophie Simonian folded the coat up so the star didn't show and laid it beside her chair.

'I wondered when you would at last talk to me about my son,' she said.

'I'm sorry,' said Janine, mistaking her tone. 'I didn't mean to . . .'

'Don't worry!' interrupted Sophie. 'I'm not being offended! I admire you for not coming rushing to me to weep about how changed he was in the first couple of weeks. You've given it time and that's good, that's right. Also, though, you should admire me, a Jewish mother, for keeping her mouth shut all these months! Women have won medals for less. My Iakov would never have believed it!'

She laughed as she spoke and Janine smiled with her. Suddenly it became easy, or at least easier.

'I've been wanting to talk to you for weeks,' she said. 'But there are times when, well, he seemed to be almost his old self again. I thought, it's just been the shock of the war, and being wounded, and being away from home all that time. But always he drifts off again . . .'

'Drifts off?'

'Yes. It's as if everything close around him fades away and he slips off into somewhere else. I don't mean he goes into a trance or anything, though there are times when he just sits and stares at nothing for an hour or more. No, it's as if he starts seeing things in a different way, as if

185

everything's there still, but it adds up to something different. Including me and the children.'

Sophie nodded.

'I've seen that too, though I would not have explained it in the same way. Last week when he was visiting me, we were talking about the old times. I kept on going further and further back, it's an old woman's privilege – not that I am so old, but I don't mind the privileges! – and I was talking about the days of my girlhood in Russia and suddenly Jean-Paul said, "You shouldn't have run! It was wrong to run." I asked him what he meant. He was staring at me in a very intense way. I sometimes see the same look in young Pauli, only not frightening like this was. "You should have stayed and fought them. Killed the bastards. Running's for cowards!" Well I grew angry then and told him if he was going to call his father a coward, a man who'd received a medal from the Marshal's own hand, then he need not come to visit me any more. That quickly brought him to his senses and he said he was very sorry, it was not what he meant. I believe him, but I think what he meant was perhaps worse, because he was talking about himself.'

Janine thought about this, then nodded.

'There is a lot of hate in him,' she said. 'I can feel it sometimes when we're out and we see some Germans. It's as if he needs it, as if it feeds him somehow. Does that sound stupid to you, Bubbah?'

The old woman shook her head sadly and said, 'No. Such a need, such a drive has always been in him, even as a child. He turned away from religion I think, because it was not *pure* enough, too much emotion, too much giving yourself. In the same way when he was wounded in the head, his mind closed off the section with you in it. That got rid of another weak part in him.'

'Weak? You think our love was weak?'

'The memory of happiness can weaken a man *in extremis*, I think,' said Sophie seriously. 'Perhaps he needed to turn to his strength as he lay near to death. And his strength comes from something stern and strong and unremitting, like hate.'

She sighed deeply and said, 'Listen to me, I am a silly old woman trying to talk like a wise old rabbi in the schul. Let me stick to what I know. Does he still love you? I mean, make love to you?'

Janine was taken aback. They'd never talked so frankly as this before. But there was no point in coyness.

She said, 'No. He tried two or three times.'

'You helped? I mean, you were willing?'

'Oh yes, I was willing. I was eager. I did everything I knew or had heard of, but it was no good. After the third time, he stopped trying. Now if I touch him, he rolls away. If I persist, he grows angry.'

'Do you think he goes elsewhere?'

Janine shook her head, but it wasn't a negative. It was her inner turmoil made visible as all her emotions were.

'I don't know,' she cried. 'He goes off by himself. I don't know what he does, who he sees. It could be a woman, it could be a whole army of whores. I don't know! He doesn't answer when I talk to him. Oh Bubbah, what does he do? Where does he go? Sometimes I think it would have been better if he'd never come home at all!'

Jean-Paul Simonian stood in a doorway in a narrow side-street within staggering distance of the Place de Clichy. From the building into which this side-door led came a distant rasp of raucous music. Round the corner, the building's garish front proclaimed it as the Golden Gate Club; back here where its detritus spilled over the pavement in boxes, sacks and bins, it preferred to remain anonymous.

Further down the street, and not before time, a sanitation department truck was moving slowly towards him, its loaders exchanging loud and vulgar abuse above the noise of their work. Simonian ignored them. His thoughts were concentrated entirely on the Golden Gate. He knew what it was like in there, even during daylight hours.

187

Expensive booze, loud music, close dancing and girls – any size, shape or race you wanted, any tricks you fancied, everything available as long as you had the money.

He found he was trembling in anticipation, like a young man close to having his first woman, weak with excitement, terrified of fiasco.

The sanitation truck was very close. Out of the main door of the club burst a couple of young women in a fanfare of laughter. They were closely followed by two German soldiers, flushed with drink and anticipation. As the girls turned into the side-street the soldiers caught up with them, one on either side, and putting their arms round their shoulders, formed a chorus line across the narrow pavement. The girls' heavily made-up faces split with mock-protests as the soldiers' heavy hands reached round to cup their breasts.

They were almost opposite the doorway when Simonian stepped out. The pistol he had been holding loosely in his hand came up without any conscious effort of will, and at point blank range he fired twice into the soldiers' gaping mouths. The men remained standing with blood bubbling from their paling lips, but it was only their dying grip on the women's shoulders that kept them upright. Now, screaming, the girls dragged themselves free and at last the soldiers fell.

A hand grasped Simonian's arm. He felt himself forced to mount the sanitation truck which accelerated noisily away towards the Rue de Clichy. It was only after a few minutes had passed that he realized he had come.

The truck came to a halt in what looked like a timber yard and Simonian was led through into a workshop which smelt of glue and woodshavings. A man was working at a foot-operated lathe, turning a table-leg. He was middle aged with a farmer's high colour and a Mexican bandit's droopy moustache. The truck driver, a bullet-headed man with a huge beer belly, spoke to the wood worker in a low voice.

'OK Henri,' he said when the driver finished. 'Better

get the truck back to the depot. You get paid today, don't you? Mustn't be late for that.'

With a cheerful wave, Henri left.

'Who are you?' demanded Simonian.

'Call me André. I'm in charge. What do you think? OK, eh?'

He held up the leg for inspection.

'I thought Henri was in charge.'

'Henri's in charge of entrance tests,' replied the other with a smile.

'Did I pass?'

'You'd not be here if you hadn't! But don't kid yourself you passed with flying colours, Monsieur Jean-Paul. You were told to shoot them in the back after they'd passed you. Henri tells me you stepped out and shot them in the head.'

'I'm sorry. They were my first. I wanted to see them face to face. From now on, I won't need that.'

'That's nice to know, monsieur! Also Pierre here got the impression you were tempted to shoot the girls.'

A tall lugubrious man in his twenties who was standing alongside Simonian nodded confirmation.

'Yes,' admitted Simonian. 'Whores! If anything they're worse than the Boche!'

'You think so? What stopped you shooting them?' asked André curiously.

'I had orders not to,' said Simonian flatly.

'Wrong!' laughed André. 'What would have stopped you shooting them was Pierre who'd have blown your head off if you'd tried! Look, here they are now. The blonde's Arlette. She's Pierre's friend. The little brunette's Mathilde. She's my daughter. So you did well to obey orders, monsieur!'

On cue the two women had come into the workshop. The brunette, whom he now saw was very young beneath her make-up, had clearly been upset by the ordeal and ran straightaway to hug and be comforted by her father.

The blonde, however, who was several years older,

looked completely at home in her role. She strolled towards them, a cigarette in her mouth. She blew a jet of smoke at Pierre then turned to Simonian.

'Hello,' she said. 'I'm Arlette.'

'Jean-Paul.'

'Hello, Jean-Paul.' They shook hands, her red-nailed finger caressing his palm as her sharp brown eyes took stock of his person.

'Hope to know you better,' she said languorously. 'I like a man who enjoys his work.'

Her hand brushed against the front of his trousers as she turned to Pierre and Simonian flushed with shame. André meanwhile had produced a brandy bottle and poured his daughter a drink. Now he filled another glass and brought it across to Simonian.

'Monsieur,' he said. 'You won't get much in the way of romantic, heroic gestures from us. We're serious businessmen, remember that, and our business is getting rid of the Boche. On the other hand, never miss an excuse for a drink, especially in hard times. So here's to you, Jean-Paul. Welcome aboard!'

He tossed back his drink and then said seriously, 'And now you're aboard, how do you fancy a bit of fishing?'

6

'To tell the truth, I'm getting a bit worried, lieutenant,' said Michel Boucher.

'About our little arrangement you mean? I shouldn't like to think I was causing you a problem of loyalties.'

'What? Christ no! I mean, what's telling one bunch of you lot what another bunch is doing got to do with loyalties?' enquired Boucher with no irony whatsoever. 'No, what I mean is, well, you're not going to be here for ever,

190

are you? You squareheads, sorry, Germans, I mean.'

It's a real puzzle, thought Mai. Does the fact that Boucher feels able to talk like this mean that I'm very good at my job, or hopeless at it? They were sitting at their ease on the pavement outside Le Colisée with the sun at its height crushing the shadows of the chestnut trees into pools of black around their boles. Most of the tables were full; there was a buzz of casual talk, a clinking of glasses, a flutter of white-coated waiters, and the world strolled past along the pavement of the Champs-Élysées. It was difficult not to feel relaxed and confidential and full of good will to Boucher, particularly as the man had supplied him with the excellent tobacco he was packing into his pipe.

'What then, friend Miche? Is it the thought of what your countrymen might do to you after we've gone that's bothering you?'

'*Do* to me? Why should they do anything to me?' said Boucher. 'They can't blame a man for earning a living, can they?'

He sounded quite genuine in his assertion. Perhaps he mistook his own easy-going temperament for the national character? If so, he was wrong. All over France, the German authorities were being snowed under by an avalanche of anonymous mail in which the 'easy-going' French denounced each other in the most virulent terms imaginable.

'What then?' Mai repeated.

'It's *that* lot,' said Boucher. 'Them *zazous*. I mean, a country depends for its future on the young ones. What's going to happen to France when that bunch of bananas grows up, if they ever do grow up!'

He was looking at a group of young people a few tables away. The men wore tight trousers and long jackets, with greasy hair curling over soft shirt collars. Some of them were wearing anoraks, despite the clear blue skies. Similarly, the girls favoured unseasonal fur jackets and most had umbrellas. Their stockings were striped which for

191

some reason Mai found rather titillating. Both sexes wore dark glasses and heavy, flat, unpolished shoes.

These were the zazous, the disaffected 'swinging' young. Mai had taken a long hard look at them for the *Abwehr* and pronounced no risk. True, this was an attempt to sabotage the adult world which allowed crap like wars to happen, but the attack was general, and the method a stylistic gesture.

'They're all right,' said Mai, suddenly envious of these apparently careless youngsters. 'Let them enjoy themselves while they can. They'll grow up too damn quick.'

'You think so? I doubt if they ever will,' said Boucher lugubriously. But it was not in his nature to remain depressed for long.

'Let's have another drink,' he said, producing his own bottle. No waiter ever objected. 'Slips down your throat like a whore's tongue, eh?'

Mai drank again. It wasn't yet midday and here he was, supping brandy and feeling very inclined to sit here till dark! But there was work to be done, even here.

He said, 'All right, Miche. What's new?'

'Nothing much. Since that funny little bugger – what did you say his name was? – Iceman, Eichmann? that's it – dropped in from Berlin last month, they've been chuntering on about geeing up the Yids, but you probably know more about that than I do.'

Mai frowned and nodded. Not that he knew much except that some large-scale operation was being planned by the SD from their offices in the requisitioned Canadian Embassy on the Avenue Foch.

'Anything else?' he said. 'What are you working on at the moment?'

'Nothing much,' said Boucher. 'In fact I've been neglecting my patriotic duties a bit recently. Pressure of personal business. Pajou's been moaning like mad. Threatening to take me off the payroll. Oh, don't look so worried. I'm off to the Avenue Foch in a couple of minutes to show my face. My job's safe. Pajou may be more to their taste, but he doesn't know Paris like me. He's a nut-case, Pajou. Always speaks highly of you though. Says you're the cleverest Kraut he's met.'

'Does he now?' said Mai without much enthusiasm.

'Too true!' laughed Boucher. 'Talking of old friends, there's someone else mentioned you. Seems to think you were OK too.'

Mai sensed an approach of some kind.

'Oh? Who's that?'

'Little poof called Melchior. Maurice Melchior. Says he met you a couple of times in 1940.'

Mai nodded and said, 'Yes, I remember him. Didn't he get friendly with one of your new bosses? Colonel Fiebelkorn, wasn't it?'

'For a bit, so I gather,' said Boucher. 'That's Maurice's way. He gets friendly with people for a bit, then he goes over the top and they fall out. He says his life's been one anti-climax after another, but he doesn't half enjoy the climaxes before the antis!'

He laughed affectionately. Mai regarded him with puzzlement. Surely Melchior wasn't Boucher's type.

He said, 'And what's your interest, Miche?'

'Hey, I'm not bent, if that's what you mean!' said Boucher with the lack of indignation of a man who doesn't believe his sexuality could be seriously called in question. 'I just like the little twerp. He worked for me in a manner of speaking, you know, essential supplies, nudge, wink. He was rather good at it too, only that's all behind him.'

'Why?'

'Well, he's screwed things up. For a start he's a Yid but he's not registered and he's not running around with a yellow star, which is all right if the Boche – sorry, the Germans – don't know you're a Yid, or don't care. But in his case they know *and* they care. What he needs is a long holiday in the Free Zone, if I can persuade the silly little bastard to go. So I wondered if you could fix him with an

Ausweis. I could do it myself, only Pajou would probably sniff it out, and that twat would sell his own mother for a pickled onion! What do you say?'

The man was quite incredible. His mind dealt with issues in the most pragmatic fashion. He judged people and situations as they impinged upon him personally. He found no contradiction in being a patriot, a collabo, and a crook. Like Janine, he saw things clearly and simply. The difference was, of course, that Boucher's judgements related to his own interests first and foremost, while Janine's concern was all for her family.

The thought of Janine made him prickle with anticipation.

After several weeks without seeing her he had contrived to bump into her at the bakery. When he had suggested another meeting, she hadn't demurred. Once again the rendezvous was safely out-of-doors, this time in the Jardin des Plantes which was very handy to her new apartment, and it was scheduled for this very afternoon. He tried to think of a good professional reason for the meeting but was hard pushed. So what? he asked himself.

But one member of any family was quite enough for an *Abwehr* officer to be unprofessional with.

'Sorry, Miche,' he said firmly. 'I can't see how I can help.' Then he heard himself adding the unnecessary qualifying excuse, 'I'm going home on leave in a couple of days.'

'Hey, that's good. I'm pleased for you,' said Miche benevolently. 'No sweat. I'll be away myself for a few days. Line of business, you know. So Maurice will just have to keep his head down. If he doesn't that's his own stupid fault. Otherwise we'll fix up something when we both get back. OK? Hey, it's time for the circus! Christ, I'm late already!'

A clock had struck twelve. In the distance they could hear a band – drums, trumpets and glockenspiel – playing martial music, and soon they could hear the tread of marching feet and see the eagle perched on the swastika as the standard of the Paris garrison was borne on its triumphant daily parade down the Champs-Élysées.

A couple of minutes later Boucher's Hispano-Suiza roared up the Champs, passing perilously close to the marching band whose heavy rhythms it mocked with a flourish on the horn.

It wasn't just the extra burden of commerce thrust upon him by Melchior's need to stay out of sight that was bothering Boucher. Hélène was putting pressure on him too. How was it that a glamorous dancer could suddenly become a bourgeois housewife just because she was pregnant? She would like to live in the country, she'd announced. It was better for bringing up children. Coincidentally Boucher had the chance of buying a very nice little property near Moret on the Loing from a black-market contact who'd decided the time had come to head for Spain. The price was right, but Boucher hesitated. It was such a commitment. It wasn't just putting down roots, it meant putting down capital.

He was still debating internally as he entered the group's headquarters in the Avenue Foch.

'Pajou?' he said to the man on duty in the vestibule.

'Top floor. Interrogation room,' said the man.

Boucher ran lightly up several flights to the top landing.

He could hear the splashing of water and a voice slowly counting.

He pushed open the door and looked inside.

The curtains were drawn to cut out the sunlight. Directly beneath a bare light bulb a tin tub full of water had been placed. Crouched over it, stripped to the waist, was Pajou. With both hands he was pressing the head of a kneeling figure into the water.

'Eighteen, nineteen, twenty . . . hello, Miche. Christ you've made me lose count. Where was I?'

Two young SS men, who were lounging against the wall with tunics removed and sleeves rolled up, laughed appreciatively.

'Let's say twenty-seven. Twenty-eight. Twenty-nine.

195

Thirty. Now let's see if that's dissolved that blockage in your throat, my dear.'

He dragged the head up by the hair which Boucher now saw was long and golden, and the white, water-puffed face was a woman's.

'Jesus!' he exclaimed involuntarily.

'Hey, Pajou, I think you've killed her,' said one of the SS men anxiously glancing into the shadows at the far end of the room. Boucher became aware there was another person present. It was Fiebelkorn sitting on a stool in a corner.

'No!' said Pajou. 'She's all right. Watch.'

He pressed his hand lightly into the woman's stomach and doubled her up. Suddenly she began to cough and retch water into the tub.

'There!' said Pajou triumphantly. 'What did I say?'

The woman groaned terribly and tried to flop on to the floor, but Pajou held her up. Her head moved from side to side and her eyes fixed on Boucher not in appeal but because behind him was the open door and the glimmer of daylight on the landing.

The return of animation to her face far from reassuring Boucher brought a new horror as incredibly but insistently these bloated features overlaid and merged with another very different image.

'Oh Jesus Christ!' he exclaimed. 'Is that little Arlette from the Golden Gate?'

'The very same. She always was a gabby little cow. She talked too much on the job one night to one of our boys. Dead proud she was of how her regular boyfriend was fucking up the Boche, begging your pardon, gents. Funny, but once we got her here, she stopped being so gabby. I thought a good gurgle might clear her throat.'

Boucher looked down at the distorted face and desperate eyes. She was a tart, acquisitive, unrepentant, had been nothing else since she was twelve. But she'd sheltered him when he had no money and nowhere to go.

He said, 'For Christ's sake, does it have to be like this?'

196

'If you've got any better ideas, better tell us, Miche.'

He didn't reply but turned abruptly and left. As he walked along the landing, Pajou came after him, still dripping water from his arms.

'Miche, what the hell's the matter? Too strong for your stomach, is it? You amaze me. I'd have thought you were just the lad for the rough stuff.'

'Rough stuff? Don't lecture me about rough stuff, Pajou,' snarled Boucher.

He clenched his fist and studied it as he tried to articulate his feelings. There was a line of reasoning which started there somehow . . . a fist was a fist . . . and a face was a face . . . and sometimes it was natural they should meet . . . but buckets, and women . . .

Pajou said, 'Look, mate, don't take it so hard. There's no lasting harm done, she'll be back on the job tonight.'

Boucher looked at him in disbelief.

'True,' asserted Pajou. 'She doesn't know all that much. Bait for Boche soldiers, that's her game. But she's picked up from her boyfriend that his gang's planning a raid on some canal barges soon, and I reckon if she can squeeze the details out of him, we can scoop up the lot.'

'You mean she'll betray her man?' said Boucher indignantly.

'No,' laughed Pajou. 'She's done that already. He's the only one whose real name she knows. Now we get her working for us so she can *save* him! Clever, eh? We promise he'll come to no harm and she co-operates.'

'She didn't look like she was co-operating in there.'

'Just a final taste of what she can expect if she double-crosses us,' said Pajou. 'Love and fear, that's how you tame 'em, old Fiebelkorn says. I'd better get back. I'll tell 'em you'd eaten a dicey oyster, turned your stomach. Regards to the lovely Hélène.'

Whistling cheerfully Pajou turned and re-entered the room.

Boucher went down to the car. It wasn't so bad, he reassured himself. Arlette was going to be all right. Christ,

197

she'd probably had worse times with some of the kinky customers she got. All the same, it made you think. If this was the way things were going, it wasn't going to be so easy to kiss and make up after the Boche had gone. And they *would* go, of course. No one stayed for ever.

Suddenly he made up his mind. He would buy the house at Moret. Not in his own name, though. In Hélène's name. He would be her respectable businessman husband, working all week in the city. For once in his life he'd look to the future. For Hélène a nest, for himself a bolt-hole.

He got into the car and accelerated away to tell her.

A few miles to the south beneath the leafy dome of the great Cedar of Lebanon which Jussieu had planted in the Jardin des Plantes two hundred years before, Michel Boucher was the topic of conversation.

Mai had offered the subject as one of neutral common interest, and Janine had gladly accepted it for the same reason.

'He's got a good heart,' she said. 'But he doesn't think. Working for you people could bring him a lot of trouble one day.'

He sucked deeply on his pipe and glanced sideways at her.

She interpreted his glance as the comment it was.

'Yes. I know it's incongruous, me sitting here saying things like that. That's the trouble with life isn't it? It's all mixed up instead of being clear-cut and simple. Miche is kind and generous, but he's also a Géstapiste. Maman is prejudiced and grasping but she's still my loving caring mother. You're the enemy. Yet, though I'm here against my will, I somehow feel quite willing to be here, talking to solid, reliable Monsieur Scheffer from Alsace whose company I almost enjoy.'

The pleasure Mai felt at hearing these words was far from professional, but inside him, the *Abwehr* officer, the enemy, was telling solid Monsieur Scheffer, 'She's vulnerable. Work on her. She wants to talk. Squeeze her!'

Sadly he listened. But where should he push her to? Now that she was out of Valois's flat (definitely at Delaplanche's instigation; he'd established a link between the lawyer and the owner of the new apartment) what was the best way to use her? With the hold he had on her, he could probably force almost anything from her; what did she know of any interest?

He said, 'Yes, I see what you mean. And your husband too . . .'

'More than anyone he's two people,' she agreed sadly. 'Loving husband, loving father. And the other, the cold, distant unremembering man your bullets turned him into.'

'He's no better?'

'Sometimes he's almost his old self again,' she said. 'But I daren't relax because he can change to the other almost in a breath. It's the children I worry about . . . Céci's too young to really notice but Pauli, he notices . . .'

'How does Jean-Paul pass his time?' asked Mai casually. 'Does he see much of his friend, the one whose flat you stayed in?'

'Christian? No, not since we moved on. To tell the truth, I don't know what he does or where he goes . . . sometimes I think . . .'

She shook her head, not in denial but in exasperated self-reminder that this was not some old family friend she was talking to, but a German intelligence officer. It was odd, though; with everyone – her parents, Sophie, Christian – she had to hold something back. Not always the same thing, but something. Yet with this man, where she must always be most on her guard, she somehow felt most relaxed.

It was his job, she reminded herself bitterly. And he was good at it.

And by her side Mai caught her hesitation and guessed its cause.

Jean-Paul went she did not know where, returned late, ignored her questions. Normally the answer would be obvious – another woman. And Janine must have considered this answer and, even though neither the man nor the times were normal, had not been able to discard it.

But the man and the times suggested other possibilities, and Günter Mai's heart sank as his professional mind computed the likelihood that a Boche-hating former soldier like Simonian would be recruited by the Resistance.

And if he had been, it was *his* job to pursue and destroy him.

7

It was a bright, clear night of early July with a slice of moon lighting up the poplar-lined towpath like a stage spot.

'This is no good,' whispered Pierre. 'It's like the Rue de Rivoli at Christmas.'

André looked upwards and sniffed the air.

'It's all right,' he said. 'Wind's in the east, and that bank of cloud over there will black us out long before we need to move.'

'Are you sure?'

'Your trouble is, you're not an angler, Pierre! When you've spent as long as I have on exposed river banks, you get to understand the weather.'

'I spent long enough this afternoon.'

'Yes, and a right idiot you looked. I had to tell people you were a bit simple!'

The canal like the majority of the waterways in and around the city was lined with fishermen most weekends and evenings. What had formerly been a sport was now a method of supplementing meagre and monotonous food rations. That day André's group had used their fishing as a cover for concealing weapons and explosives along the banks to be picked up that night. This meant that if one of their number happened to be stopped on his way to the rendezvous, at least he wouldn't be carrying anything incriminating. Curfew breaking was always serious, but sometimes you could persuade a sympathetic cop that sex or booze had been your downfall and get away with it. Sympathetic Germans were becoming harder to find, however, as acts of sabotage and assault increased.

The heat of the July day had long since vanished. The night breeze quickened along the length of the canal, bringing with it a dank chill which gave more than one of the men waiting a welcome excuse to shiver. There were eight of them in the team; André, Pierre and Jean-Paul Simonian plus four others were the attack force, while Henri was providing back-up in a wood two kilometres to the east. The plan was for the raiders to join him there, pass the night in the open, then filter into the great Sunday rush of hopeful anglers and so get back to the city unnoticed on Sunday night.

Personally Simonian thought it was all too clever and they'd have been much better advised to head straight back to Paris under cover of dark. Nor did he care for the complication of leaving their weapons hidden on the canal bank for collection at night. But he had resolved to take orders till he felt sufficiently accepted to voice opinions.

He glanced impatiently at his watch and then up at the sky. The cold breeze was taking its time in dragging the blanket of cloud across the moon.

'Relax, Jean-Paul. Plenty of time,' said André soothingly.

Fifteen minutes later his fears about the complexity of André's plan had been partially allayed. They'd successfully picked up all the weapons and explosives where they'd been hidden and were now approaching the main waterway where, if André's information was right, the three supply barges would be moored above the lock. Part of the plan was to blow open the lock gates and sink one of the barges right in the middle of the basin.

'There they are!' whispered André. 'One, two, three. What did I tell you?'

He sounded as gleeful as if the job were already done. Simonian viewed the squat hulk of the silhouetted barges with less enthusiasm. He'd always found canals with their unnatural straight lines, and flat-bottomed boats with their lack of either power or grace, simply depressing.

They were attacking two to a barge, with André in support with his Sten gun wherever he might be needed. This part of the operation had been meticulously rehearsed. Timing was of the essence. The German deck guards had to be gunned down simultaneously so that the attack on one barge wouldn't alert the next. Four Germans to a barge, two on watch, two below sleeping. The deck secure, the next move was to get below and take the other two before they were fully awake. Pierre, who was very nervy, was all for dropping a couple of grenades down the hatch first, but André said, 'No. The crew are French lads, doing their job. What's up with you, Pierre? Arlette giving you a bad time?'

'She had bad feelings about this job,' admitted Pierre. 'She didn't want me to come.'

'First time ever!' joked André, relieving the tension. But Simonian, who was paired with Pierre, didn't rate very highly the French crew's chances. Pierre was going to blast anything that moved.

Now they were in position, crouched behind the low wall which separated the towpath from the plantation of plane trees they'd just come through. Pierre was checking his watch, mouthing figures as he counted them down to the agreed deadline. Simonian focused his gaze on the familiar yet fearsome silhouette of the nearest German guard, great-coated, rifle slung over the shoulder with its fixed bayonet rising like a steeple above the smooth cupola of the coal-scuttle helmet. The other German joined his comrade, offered him a cigarette. They lit up. Their faces looked young, almost childlike, in the glow of the match. They'd had it too easy, thought Simonian. Such indiscipline wouldn't be found among trained and experienced men, expecting trouble. These two probably congratulated themselves every time they heard a bulletin from the Eastern Front. A cushy job on a cushy posting. France, the young man's dream, where the German soldier with his endless Marks was king. Well, soon they would realize their error.

'. . . three . . . two . . . one , , , GO!'

Pierre's scream took Simonian by surprise and he was a second behind the other man in going over the wall. He had his pistol ready, however. André was the only one of them with a truly automatic weapon, the Sten, so they had to get close to their targets to make sure of them. It was no use blazing away from fifty feet with a pistol. On the other hand, there was nothing like the rattle of gun fire to spread fear and alarm, so as he ran forward he let off a couple of snap-shots towards the barge.

Or tried to.

He was pressing the trigger but nothing was happening. Jammed, perhaps? It happened easily. But that easy explanation was crowded from his mind by the awareness that neither to left nor right was there any sound but rushing feet and the clicking of useless hammers on unresponsive cartridges.

And then the moon came out. No, not the moon, which before had merely seemed like a theatrical spotlight. These were genuine lights, blossoming from either side along the towpath and now joined by beams from the barges themselves as the grinning soldiers pulled back tarpaulins from search lights and from the machine guns that were mounted alongside them.

'Hands up! Stand still!' called a voice in fluent French. 'Resistance will be useless. Don't make things worse for yourselves.'

They'd slowed down as the shock of the lights hit them. The wise thing was now to obey, to stand quite still, to wait for the triumphant Germans to herd them away to some quiet cell where they could sit and ponder who had betrayed them, and who they would betray in a few hours.

That is probably what they would have done. But from somewhere behind them in the plantation came a pathetic flurry of shots from a hand-gun. One of the search lights shattered. But there was still more than enough light from the machine gunners to mow down the line of attackers as they turned to flee. Simonian was already diving for the ground. A bullet clipped his shoulder as he fell, but he felt no pain. Pierre too was down and hit. Perhaps not badly? There was only a thin trickle of blood down his back. Then he rolled cumbersomely over as if desperate for a last look at the sky, and revealed the shattered ruin of his chest. 'Arlette . . .' he breathed, whether in accusation or simple farewell Simonian had no way of knowing. In any case, he was himself no longer there by the canal. He was in a trench, a shallow defensive scrape on the foothills of the Vosges, and all around him his companions of more than a year lay dead or dying. Their deaths would bring more pain than he could bear, and part of his life and his soul would be cut away beyond all hope of retrieval.

Not again! Not again! He pushed himself to his feet with his right arm, aware for the first time that the left was useless. The German guns had for the moment swung from the fallen men and were devastating the plantation in a blind effort to destroy their unexpected assailant, who had to be André; André who had kept his own revolver with him after all. A leader wasn't bound by his own rules, Simonian would remember that. But not now. He was off and running, not towards the plantation where bullets were pumping into tree trunks with a noise like cleavers on a goose farm at Christmas; no, he went in the only direction possible, towards the water.

He had surprise on his side, but not for long. The soldiers on the barge missed him with their first two shots, but the third caught him in the side and the fourth burnt through his thigh. He fell forward. No ground came up to meet him but a long space, then cold black water. He'd reached his goal but with one leg and one arm out of action his success looked likely to be his death also.

Deep down he went. Instinct sent him reaching up in search of light and air, but each time he tried he crashed against an obstacle as long and solid as a coffin lid. He was under a barge, moving with the slow current down its whole endless length. He kicked out with his good leg and arm but felt no respondent surge of speed. Slowly he tumbled and turned, felt long tongues of weed lick and caress him, pushed upwards once more in fear and revulsion, hit the coffin lid, sank down again. He knew he was finished because his mind was seeking a god to pray to. The current drifted him slowly down the pale line of classical deities, marble whitely gleaming in long neglected arbours; past the palest of them all, the grey Galilean with his blood-stained palms; plunged him suddenly into a whirlpool of colour where the human form was parodied instead of perfected in a welter of limbs and animal heads; sank him briefly into a pool of serenity where a peaceful buddha contemplated his own smooth belly; and then all too soon the current dragged him out of that peace and began rushing him at ever-increasing speed through a tumult of water towards what he had known from the start was the end of this journey, to where the first god he had rejected, the god of his fathers, the god of their persecution, the unrelenting, unforgiving, unforgetting god of blood and birth and a thousand years was waiting.

He opened his mouth to scream denial, to drink oblivion, anything rather than this humiliating return. His mouth and nose and lungs and belly were full of water and still that fire of fear and hatred could not be quenched.

He screamed, 'No!'

It wasn't much of a scream, which was a good thing, he realized. For the waters had parted above his head to reveal not the god of Moses clearing a way through the sea to the promised land, but a plain French moon coquettishly flashing her bosom through a rent in the clouds.

He looked back and was amazed to see how very far

past the barges he had come. They would have been invisible if the air around them had not been stained with light. The gun fire had stopped except for an occasional crackle as someone imagined he saw something move among the trees. He turned over and with an awkward side-stroke made obliquely for the bank. When he reached it, he saw instantly that he might have spared his effort. The bank here was steep and crumbly. Even if his good hand had had the strength to pull his body upwards, the shallow-rooted grasses lacked the strength to support it. He would have to go further downstream. But when he tried to resume his side-stroke, he found that his body which had been promised dry land and safety if it reached the bank had withdrawn its labour.

He clung to the bank one-handed while his mind harangued his flesh. There was no response. You'll be sorry, he threatened. Get yourself moving, or it's all up with you!

He pushed himself off once more, realized at once that his plea had been in vain, sank, drank deep of the foul and chilly water, rose spluttering, grabbed at the bank again and felt it crumble like English cheese under the puny pressure of his nerveless fingers.

Have it your own way, he told his recalcitrant body. See if I care.

And let himself go.

His wrist was seized. An illusion, of course. He tried to pull it under to join the rest of his departing body. But an opposite and superior force was pulling upwards, dragging his whole sodden body up the canal bank.

'For Christ's sake, make an effort!' hissed a voice.

Weakly he dug his good leg into the yielding clay and pushed upwards. It wasn't much but it was enough. Next moment he was out of the water and lying alongside the towpath.

'I thought it must be you making all that noise,' said André. 'I saw you go in the water.'

'The others?' he gasped.

206

'Dead, I think. I hope, for all our sakes,' said André grimly. 'Come on. We can't stay here. The Boche are still searching the plantation, but one of them may decide to wander down this way any moment. Can you walk?'

Simonian consulted his body. The bank disagreement having reached a satisfactory conclusion, channels of negotiation had been reopened.

'I can hop,' he said.

'Let's hop,' said André, pulling him to his feet, or rather to his foot.

Leaning heavily on the older man, Simonian let himself be led away. His wounds and the tangled undergrowth made progress painfully slow. From time to time they were helped by the moon's brief appearance, but when in one of these periods of illumination, Jean-Paul glimpsed André's face, he realized that the weakness was not all his own. André's left cheek was ripped open by a wound which jagged round the jawbone to the throat. A kerchief round the neck acted as a bandage but clearly the blood was pumping out at a debilitating rate.

'This is crazy,' he gasped. 'You can't lug me along in your state. We'll both end up dead.'

André didn't waste strength arguing.

'I'll hide you up here,' he said. 'Then I'll try to get Henri. We've got contacts in the area if you can just hang on.'

'Don't worry about me,' said Simonian. 'I'm good at hanging on.'

They were moving parallel to a small stream which ran towards the canal. Its banks were too heavily wooded to have any attraction for fishermen. With André's help, Simonian slid down almost to the water's edge and pulled a tangle of low-growing bushes across his body.

'I'll be back as soon as I can,' said André.

'I'll be here,' said Simonian.

He heard the other move away, then he was alone, as he'd been alone in the German hospital, concentrating all the resources of his heart and mind on simply staying alive from minute to agonizing minute.

When at last the dawn came, he knew he was going to survive. Birds sang, the air grew warmer, flies buzzed around his leg, attracted by the scent of blood. The narrow stream dimpled with sunlight. He watched its waters flow by barely a foot from his face, and in his imagination he followed them, bubbling into the broad, smooth-flowing canal which in a few miles became the Marne and slid down to Charenton where it joined the Seine, whose long and winding course bore his mind through Paris, his birthplace, and across the sullen face of captive France, till finally it spilled into the grey swell of the open sea whose long waves beat on that so close but so inaccessible shore where men still walked, and talked, and fished, in freedom.

8

It was Bastille Day.

Some used the holiday as an occasion for defiance, flying tricolours, getting quarrelsomely drunk, singing songs patriotic and martial. The Boche largely ignored such acts, with the contempt of hard reality for empty symbolism.

Christian Valois had been invited to lunch at his boss's home in Neuilly. He observed no dancing in the streets on his way there. His boss, Marc du Prat, had returned to Paris a month after the Occupation, but Valois noticed that the Corot sketch hadn't returned to its place on the office wall. Trust in the Occupiers clearly only went so far.

It was a dull lunch. Even the most collaborationist of guests seemed inhibited by the contrast between the occasion and its circumstance. A lot of shop was talked. General approval was voiced for the fiscal policies Laval had introduced in the three months since his return to power. Professionally, Valois agreed. It seemed to him imperative to defend the franc against the ever-present threat of runaway inflation.

On the other hand, he understood why Delaplanche's reaction to the prospect was delight.

'That's the way to radicalize your petit-bourgeois!' he said. 'Devalue his savings and let him know it's the Boche to blame.'

'Yes, but Laval . . .'

'Laval's a collaborating bastard who'll be guillotined from the ankles up when this war's over,' said Delaplanche grimly. 'Don't start seeing both sides of *anything*. You're an actor. Play your part, but don't ever forget the real world.'

'That's all right, but I never get into that real world,' said Valois stubbornly.

'Shooting squareheads, blowing up trains, is that what you mean? Each man must offer what he's best at, Christian. What you are doing – will do – is worth any amount of blood and mayhem.'

Valois was not convinced and even less so after the Bastille Day lunch. He left early, pleading pressure of work.

When he got back to the flat the phone was ringing. It was impossible to say, of course, but he had a sense it had been ringing for a long time, and immediately found himself thinking 'It's mama, she's ill; it's Marie-Rose; she's had an accident; it's . . .'

It was Janine. He recognized the voice at once and with considerable irritation, as though she had got him to the phone by a confidence trick.

'What do you want?' he said angrily.

'It's Jean-Paul . . . oh please, Christian, can you come round here? Please!'

'Is he ill? Can I speak to him?'

'No!' she cried wretchedly. 'No! Please. I don't want to talk . . . I'm in the hallway . . .'

Suddenly he saw her quite clearly, her thin expressive face full of pain, standing in the draughty hallway of her apartment building, aware of God knows what attentive ears behind every doorway. He had hardly seen the Simonians at all since they moved. In this too he had obeyed Delaplanche's injunction, helped by a slight but unmistakable chill which had touched his friendship with Jean-Paul.

Now he was overcome by a longing to see him again, and to see Janine also, to be with someone who, in joy or in pain, was simple, direct, whole-hearted and completely open.

'I'll come at once,' he said.

She met him on the landing. They embraced and she almost dragged him into the flat.

'Where's Jean-Paul?' he asked.

'He's gone,' she said. 'That's why I rang. I'm so worried, I don't know what to do . . .'

'Where are the children?' he intervened sharply, thinking quite rightly that this was a question guaranteed to steady her down. He was right.

'I took them to the bakery this morning to spend the holiday there,' she said. 'I told my parents I was spending it at Bubbah Sophie's with Jean-Paul. That didn't please my mother, as you can guess . . .'

'No. All right. Tell me about Jean-Paul.'

'He's been gone since Saturday. Before he went out, he said he'd probably not be back that night, perhaps not Sunday either. Naturally I asked him where he was going.'

'And he said?'

'He just laughed and said, *Fishing.*'

'Fishing? Does he fish?'

'Not that I know of. He seemed very excited. I was very unhappy. I imagined all kinds of stupid things . . . even another woman . . .'

Christian Valois shook his head. For him this kind of secretive behaviour by his friend meant only one thing. Delaplanche had carried out his implied promise and once Jean-Paul was out of the apartment, he'd made sure he was recruited into an active Resistance cell. He felt a pang of pure envy.

He wanted to comfort Janine with this more likely theory, but hesitated. For a man not to return from a dirty weekend could simply mean he'd enjoyed it so much he'd decided to make it a dirty week. But not to return from a sabotage attack . . .

She saved him from the debate.

'I don't think it is a woman,' she resumed. 'It doesn't feel like a woman. It feels more like . . . something sinister. Oh Christian, I think he may have got mixed up with the Resistance! You'd think he'd done his bit, what he's been through, and he's not well . . . how could they use him? How did they contact him?'

Valois said guiltily, 'Perhaps it's not . . .'

'The house is being watched.'

'What? Are you sure?'

'Oh yes. Last night there was a man. I saw him. Well, Pauli noticed him actually. He doesn't miss much, Pauli. But I kept my eyes skinned after that. He was there for hours.'

'Has he been there today?'

He couldn't keep the note of accusation out of his voice.

'No, of course not. You don't think I'd have asked you to come round if he had been, do you?'

'It didn't occur to you they might have more than one man?' he said sarcastically, going to the window. The street seemed deserted.

'No,' she said, stricken. 'Oh God, Christian, you're quite right about me, I'm stupid. Who do you think it is? The Gestapo?'

Curiously his mind was less concerned with that than with the revelation of her knowledge of his past assessment of her.

'I don't think you're stupid,' he said. 'And I think if the Gestapo had any interest in you and me, we'd be down at the Rue des Saussaies, or somewhere worse.'

He spoke with more confidence than he felt and his next

211

question was in contradiction to that alleged confidence.

'Janine, have you spoken to anyone else, either since Jean-Paul went, or before, about your worries, I mean?'

'No!' she said emphatically. 'Who would I speak to? I wasn't going to worry his mother with it and I'd get precious little sympathy from my mother, I'm afraid.'

'I see that. But what about, well, someone else, someone not so close, but close enough,' he said gently.

For a moment of sheer horror she thought, he knows I've seen Mai! Then he added, 'Like your cousin, say.'

'Miche! You don't think I'd say anything to Miche?' she cried almost gaily. 'Not because he works for the Boche. Oh, I do know all about that, Christian, I'm not completely dense. But because he's feckless, that's why. No, I haven't told a soul. I couldn't. That's why I was desperate. That's why I had to involve you. I'm sorry, I really am.'

Valois was embracing her, murmuring unwanted consolations. He was also holding her a little too close.

She broke away and said, 'It's not a shoulder to cry on I need, Christian. It's practical help. What can I do?'

'Nothing,' he said, immediately businesslike. 'I'll ask around, see if I can find out anything. And I'll call back here tomorrow night, all right? If anything happens in the meantime, ring me at the flat, or at my office tomorrow.'

'Yes,' she said.

She made no effort to detain him. There was in her a strength which had merely needed to touch one other person to be renewed.

He kissed her on the cheek and left.

In the next twenty-four hours he discovered very little and nothing of comfort. His main hope for help and assistance was Delaplanche, but it turned out the lawyer was away on another of his 'business' trips. And a carefully accidental encounter with an old acquaintance working in the Ministry of the Interior elicited the news that there'd been an abortive terrorist attack on some canal barges at the weekend.

212

'Happily they were expected. I gather some gabby tart opened her mouth as well as her legs.'

'They were captured, you mean?'

'Killed, my dear chap. Our squareheaded friends don't mess about, you know,' replied the other, almost admiringly.

What was it Jean-Paul had told Janine he was going to do? *Fishing?* The link between that reply and the canal attack was too strong to be ignored.

He went round to Janine's flat that night uncertain what to tell her. It was a desire to postpone the moment as much as natural circumspection which made him check out the neighbouring streets thoroughly for signs of surveillance.

There was nothing. He went in and rang the bell.

The door opened. Janine stood there, her face pale and enigmatic. There was a mark on her brow, like a circular weal.

'Janine!' he said, stepping forward, his arms outstretched.

He never reached her. His right arm was seized at the wrist, twisted downwards so that he was spun round, screaming in pain. Then he was dragged into the room and hurled forward on to a sofa. When he twisted round and tried to get up, a pistol muzzle stamped its cold circle into his brow. Behind it stood a bullet-headed middle-aged man in stained and smelly overalls who looked ready to kill him.

'It's all right! Please, it's my friend. The one who I told you about. Christian, are you all right?'

Valois nodded uncertainly as the gun was slowly withdrawn. He didn't speak; at the moment he couldn't speak. He knew he'd come very close to soiling his trousers.

'This is Henri, Christian,' bubbled Janine, both frightened and excited. 'He's been with Jean-Paul. He's hurt, but he's alive. Thank God, he's alive!'

Valois pushed himself upright.

'Where . . . where is he?' he stammered.

213

The man called Henri described what had happened swiftly and succinctly.

'Everyone bought it, except André and Jean-Paul. Our whole group wiped out, just like that!'

He shook his head at the horror of the thought.

'There's the three of you left,' urged Valois.

'Two.'

'What . . . ?'

'No. Not your friend. *My* friend,' said Henri dully. 'André. Our boss.'

They'd got a local doctor with the right attitude to look at the wounded men. He'd transferred them to a house in the area whose owners were also sympathetic. But they had to be moved out by Friday.

'Their son-in-law's a gendarme; he'll be visiting this weekend. They're not sure how he'd react. I came back on Monday. I was due in at work, I'm with the Sanitation Department, and I didn't want to be noticeable by my absence. They were checking us very carefully, I noticed that. I didn't know why, but it bothered me. Still, there was no sign of activity round my house, so I thought it might be all right. I checked André's place and that seemed all right too. Then I came on here, just to be sure.'

'We noticed you,' said Janine.

'Did you? Not so bloody good, am I? Not so bloody good at all!' He spoke with a bitter vehemence which seemed out of all proportion.

'It was my son who spotted you. He misses nothing,' said Janine soothingly.

'Then I wish to hell he'd been with me when I checked André's place!' exclaimed Henri. 'I told him it was OK. He wasn't so badly hurt, you see. He wanted to get back as soon as possible to repair the damage and make arrangements to get Jean-Paul back too. So he came back yesterday. I didn't try to see him. Act normal, he said. That meant a day with my in-laws. So I didn't go back to André's till this evening. Oh Christ, you should've seen it!

Everything smashed up, blood everywhere. They'd been waiting for him, the bastards, waiting!'

He put his head in his hands and let out a racking sob.

'What about his family?' demanded Janine aghast.

'A daughter. She was away, thank God. I've sent a message to her telling the poor kid to stay away. After that, all I wanted to do was find out who'd betrayed us.'

'So you came round here!' exclaimed Valois indignantly, understanding the mark on Janine's brow.

'Yes. I'm sorry. I soon realized it couldn't be her. Sorry, love. Then you came, Jean-Paul's best friend, the lady said. People often confide in their best friends.'

'And they often confide in their tarts!' said Valois. 'For God's sake, what kind of ramshackle organization are you?'

He passed on what he'd gleaned from his friend in the Ministry of the Interior.

'Oh shit,' said Henri wearily. 'Arlette.'

'You know her? Then why haven't you been arrested?'

'Because André was the only one whose address she knew. Me she'd know as a dustbin man, nothing more, and there's hundreds of us. As for Jean-Paul, she'd know nothing at all about his background, he was so new to us.'

'But André knows all about you, and Jean-Paul too?' cried Janine in alarm.

'André won't talk,' he said sadly. 'I saw the blood, remember? I doubt if they got him to Gestapo Headquarters alive.'

There was a moment of silence, intense as prayer.

Then Janine said, 'Please. What about Jean-Paul?'

'He'll live, but he has to be moved. We need transport. All I've got is a sanitation truck!'

'I can get a car,' said Valois quietly.

'What? With a proper permit, you mean?'

'Oh yes. A proper permit. Very proper.'

He'd never used the car since his father got him the permit. Despite even his pretended reconciliation, he baulked at openly joining the small privileged bunch of

215

private drivers. Delaplanche had agreed, saying, 'We want you well placed when this is all over, and I don't mean well placed dangling from a lamp-post!'

'You must be important, mister,' said Henri, regarding him distrustingly.

'He is,' said Janine. 'Christian, you can't get mixed up in this. It could ruin you. All right, lend us the car and the permit. If we get caught, we'll say we stole it.'

'It's in my name,' he said flatly. 'I can get away with it. You can't.'

'He's right,' said Henri. 'We've no choice.'

'All right,' said Janine. 'When do we go? Tonight?'

'We?' said Valois.

'I'm coming too,' she said coldly. 'No argument.'

'But you mustn't!' he said. 'The children . . .'

'I'll leave them with Sophie,' she said. 'I'm coming, Christian, and there's an end to it.'

Henri laughed and said, 'Not married, are you, monsieur? Thought not, else you'd know you were wasting your breath.'

The altercation seemed to have persuaded him to trust Valois and he now outlined his plan for picking up Jean-Paul.

'Tomorrow night, Thursday,' he said. 'We'll time it so that we're driving back in the dusk. You can get away without lights still, and it makes cars so much harder to spot.'

Soon after the two men left. At parting when he offered to kiss her on the cheek she surprised him by kissing him full on the lips.

'Thanks, Christian,' she breathed. 'You're a real friend.'

Story of my life, he thought as he turned away. The only time I see the light of joy in that woman's eyes is when she hears her husband is still alive.

He walked to the Monge métro station with Henri, chatting inconsequentially with the man. It soon became clear that Henri was no political animal.

'André, he was a bit political,' he conceded. 'The rest

216

of us, like your mate Jean-Paul, all we wanted to do was kill a few of them bastards.'

He was looking at a group of young German soldiers chasing each other drunkenly round the empty market stalls in the Place Monge before tumbling down the stairs into the métro.

'Master race!' said Henri contemptuously.

They discovered they were going in different directions so shook hands and separated. Valois stood and watched the other walk away, a plump, middle-aged, shabbily dressed working man, one of millions. But he was unclutttered by self-doubt or Party dogma. And he had a gun in his pocket and was an active Resistant.

Suddenly he was glad that Delaplanche with all his cool calculation and his reasoned advice was far, far away.

9

The pick-up went perfectly.

The middle-aged couple who'd taken Jean-Paul in were at the same time relieved and apologetic.

'We would have kept him longer,' explained the woman, 'but our son, Jacques . . .'

'No names,' growled Henri. 'The less we all know the better. How is he?'

'The doctor's been today. He's very weak still but he can be moved,' said the man leading them upstairs.

Janine went into the room first. On the journey out she had convinced herself that Jean-Paul would have regressed to complete amnesia and now she steeled herself for the heart-tearing lack of recognition.

Instead the pale head raised itself from the pillow, broke into a joyous smile, immediately replaced by a look of irritated concern, and he said, 'Janine, you shouldn't be here!'

'She's come to take you home so shut up and be grateful,' said Henri.

'We're using Christian's car, he's got a permit,' said Janine trying to cover her emotion by being very business-like.

'Christian. You too. God, what risks you're taking,' said Simonian.

'No risks,' said Valois. 'First sign of trouble and you're out in the ditch.'

Simonian laughed and gripped Valois with his good arm as he stooped over him.

'It's brave of you to come, Christian,' he said. 'Thanks. I'll not forget this.'

The light was beginning to fade as they got him into the car. The movement caused him some pain. He didn't cry out or even wince, but Janine felt it in the tension of his body. His hosts stood anxiously around, knowing that these moments, with the injured man in full view of anyone passing the house, were for them the most dangerous. At last the car was ready to depart and Janine embraced them with tears in her eyes.

'Thank you, thank you,' she said. 'When this is all over, I'll come to thank you properly.'

And then they were on their way.

With light fading fast, they drove slowly so that they didn't need headlights. Janine sat in the back with her arm round Jean-Paul. Soon after they set off he said in a low voice, 'How are the children?'

'Fine. They're with your mother. They missed you.'

'Does she know about this?'

'No. I don't know what she guesses, but I've told her nothing.'

He smiled his approval, then slipped into a silence which hovered on the edge of unconsciousness.

In the front, Valois drove, while Henri, who seemed to have a cab driver's knowledge of roads, navigated. It was growing quite dark now and as they penetrated further into the unlit suburbs, Valois said, 'I need to use my side-lights, I think. Besides being dangerous, without them we'll look bloody suspicious.'

'Wait,' said Henri. 'Slow down, turn left here.'

'What's up?' said Valois, obeying.

'Didn't you see? Up ahead there was something going on. It looked like a road block to me. Right in about two hundred metres should bring us back on course.'

'Where are we?' asked Janine, trying to hide her fear.

'Well, we've passed the Buttes Chaumont, must be on the edge of the Tenth Arrondissement. Right here, I think. Jesus, there they are again! Left, left! Just turn off, but don't hurry!'

This time they were close enough for them all to see quite clearly the activity ahead. Two police cars. Half a dozen gendarmes. They looked towards the car and watched it as it turned off the main road once more.

'All right. Straight on. Fast as you can, but don't kill us!' commanded Henri, twisting round to look for signs of pursuit.

There was none.

They were heading east and Valois kept going till they hit the Boulevard Davour where they turned south. Several times when he was contemplating turning west towards the city centre again he glimpsed gendarmerie cars parked across roads intersecting the boulevard.

'Shit,' he said. 'Henri, what's going on? We can't be that important!'

'Don't flatter yourself, we're not!' said Henri. 'They're not interested in us. God knows what's going on, though. What the hell's that?'

A convoy of three green and white Paris Transport Company buses went speeding by. Their interiors were dark, but they seemed to be packed.

They crossed the Seine by the Pont National. It was pitch dark by now and Valois was forced to use his side-lights, but once on this side of the river, all signs of a police presence seemed to evaporate and they crawled west to the Quartier Mouffetard without further alarm.

'Jean-Paul, we're home,' whispered Janine.

The words seemed to act like a reviving injection, as if he had deliberately lapsed into suspended animation to preserve his strength for this final effort. Even so, Valois had to half carry him up the flight of stairs, and when they laid him on the bed he was as quiet and still as any piece of funebrial marble.

Henri checked the dressings. There were signs of fresh bleeding but now he was lying down it seemed to have stopped.

'He'll be all right,' he assured Janine. 'Let him rest quiet, that's best. Your kids are away? That's good. Peace and quiet are what he needs. I'll fix for a doctor to call. He's good with bullet wounds and even better at keeping his mouth shut. But I think we'd better be off now, monsieur.'

Valois was stooping over Jean-Paul who opened his eyes for a moment and smiled. Then he turned to Janine and said, 'Look, I'd stay, only I have to get the car back in the garage. Out there, it could attract attention.'

'Yes, of course. Thank you, thank you both from the bottom of my heart for what you've done. I'll never forget it. Never.'

She embraced them both, then accompanied them down the stairs to the front door and checked the street was clear.

'Take care,' she said anxiously. 'Those gendarmes will probably still be about.'

Valois nodded, kissed her cheek and got into the car.

Henri grinned and said, 'Don't worry, lady. Without your husband, we're just a couple of good citizens in a car with a permit. Besides, like I said before, whatever the flics are up to tonight, one thing's for sure; it's nothing to do with us!'

*

220

The knock at the door came just after Pauli had got into bed.

Sophie Simonian twitched more in irritation than alarm. It was probably that idiot concierge complaining once more that Charlot was howling outside her kitchen window. Then a movement on the sofa told her that Charlot was sleeping there in his favourite spot having dragged down the old heavy antimacassar on top of him.

'Who's there?' she called at the door.

'Gendarmerie, madame,' replied a courteous voice. 'Please open the door.'

She obeyed, but left it on the chain till she was sure the uniform matched the claim. Then she let them in.

There were two of them, a sergeant and a younger constable. The constable smiled apologetically but the sergeant wore the stern face stupid people adopt who are happy to accept instructions as a reasonable substitute for independent thought. Outside on the landing, Sophie could see two more men, hardly more than boys really. They were wearing blue shirts, with cross-straps, and they had armbands on, but she could not make out the symbol on them.

The sergeant was consulting a printed sheet.

'You are Madame Sophie Simonian of this address?'

'Yes, monsieur. I have my papers here if you wish to see them.'

She moved towards her old bureau but the sergeant said impatiently, 'No, don't show them to me. But bring them with you. They will need to be checked.'

'*Bring* them, monsieur?' said Sophie. 'When?'

'Now, of course.'

He flourished his sheet of paper at her. She saw it was a list of names and addresses. The sheet was headed *Census of Jews and Foreign Nationals 1941*, and she recalled her visit to the police station to register.

'I have done nothing wrong,' she said.

'No one's saying you've done anything wrong,' he said impatiently. 'It's just the law, madame. Now please get

221

ready. Bring some clothes with you, a bundle, you're not going on a world cruise.'

'Clothes? You mean I shall be away all night?' she said in alarm. She was thinking about the children. She could trust Pauli to look after his sister for an hour or two, but all night . . . ! She was opening her mouth to say something of this when the constable cried, 'Hey sarge! In here!'

He had wandered through into the little bedroom. Céci was still fast asleep, but Pauli was sitting up, wide-eyed, regarding the policemen with that grave disconcerting gaze.

The sergeant consulted his paper.

'There's nothing about them down here,' he said in irritation. 'Are these your children, madame?'

Sophie laughed and said, 'Hardly!' and the constable grinned.

The sergeant wasn't amused.

'Here, lad,' he said to Pauli. 'What's your name?'

'Pauli. Paul.'

'Paul what?'

'Paul Simonian.'

'Oh, I see. So this lady is . . . ?'

'She's my grandmother,' said Pauli. 'Is something wrong? Have you brought bad news?'

'He's a real old-fashioned one!' laughed the constable. 'No, sonny, it's all right. Nothing to worry about.'

'No,' said Sophie ushering them back into the living-room. She saw that the two young men had ventured through the door in the interim and were examining her ornaments and giggling together. She could see now that their armbands bore the initials PPF. Parti Populaire Français. She knew little of politics but she knew that this party and its leader, Jacques Doriot, were virulently anti-Semitic.

'With permission, sergeant,' she said quietly. 'I will ask the concierge to keep an eye on the children while I'm away.'

222

The gendarme was blocking her way to the door. He didn't move.

He said, 'Their parents, where are they?'

'Not here. I'm looking after them for a little while.'

'Oh yes. It's your son who's their father, right? I don't see his name down here. Or is he registered somewhere else?'

'I expect so. I don't know. He is not Jewish, so perhaps he will not have registered.'

'Not Jewish?' the sergeant exclaimed. 'What do you mean?'

'He abandoned the faith many years ago,' she explained. 'He has no religion. He is no longer Jewish.'

'It doesn't work like that, madame, as I think you know,' said the sergeant with grave stupidity. 'We'll check on him, never fear. Now, you get yourself ready quick as you can.'

'Shall I see the concierge about the kids?' offered the constable.

But the sergeant's attention was diverted by a small movement on the sofa.

'Hello,' he said. 'Not another of them?'

He reached down to tweak aside the antimacassar.

Charlot, rudely awakened and detecting a stranger, sank teeth and claws into his hand. Then with a farewell miaou counterpointing the sergeant's scream of pain, he shot away out of the room and down the stairs.

'Jesus Christ!' cried the gendarme. 'I'm bleeding.'

His hand and wrist were badly scratched.

Tut-tutting in sympathy, Sophie said, 'Here, monsieur, let me bathe it in a lysol solution. He's very nervous, Charlot, but very clean too. I don't think you need worry about infection.'

'I'll see to it myself,' barked the sergeant. 'Savier! You get yourself upstairs. That special case we've got noted, the one who isn't registered, see if there's any sign of him. And take this pair of delinquents with you in case he's locked himself in.'

223

'Yes, sarge. And what about the kids?'

The sergeant looked at his bleeding hand.

'They'll have to come,' he said grimly. 'They're family, aren't they? No, it's no use making a fuss, madame. I've got my job to do, and I'm bound by more regulations than you'd believe. I can't just go around letting people go on my own responsibility.'

'But these are *children*!' protested Sophie.

'Yeah, sarge. They're only kids,' echoed Savier.

'*Jewish* kids,' said the sergeant. 'Or have they given it up too, madame? Savier, didn't I give you an order!'

'Yes, sergeant.'

The constable left with the two PPF youths. The sergeant said, 'Now get yourself packed, and those children too, madame. Fifteen minutes, that's the most I can give you.'

Sophie obeyed. She recognized the kind of man the sergeant was. There was no point in arguing with such people. All she could hope was that wherever he was taking her, there would be someone there with greater power and enough sympathy to recognize that the little ones ought to be at home, safely tucked up in bed.

Upstairs there was the sound of loud knocking. She called to the sergeant who was at the sink, bathing his hand, 'Monsieur Melchior is not at home. He has not been home for many months.'

The man ignored her and with a shrug she went through to the children. They were both awake now; Céci had probably been disturbed by the noise above and she was close to tears. Pauli had his arm around her and was talking to her in that low-pitched incomprehensible buzz which, even though Céci was now quite articulate, still remained their private form of communication.

'Children,' said Sophie. 'We're going out now with the gendarmes. Don't worry, it won't be for long, but the night air can be chilly even in summer, so you must dress up warm. Pauli, will you help your sister while I pack a few things together?'

'Yes, Bubbah,' said the boy.

Upstairs the knocking had stopped, but now came a violent crash and the sound of splintering wood. Céci began to cry in earnest. Sophie said, 'There, there, child. It's nothing. They're here to protect us, the gendarmes, you know that, don't you Pauli?'

Their eyes met. Hers moved away.

'Yes, Bubbah,' he said.

Swiftly they made preparations to the accompaniment of footsteps and bangings from above. After a while, she heard the constable return and report to the sergeant that the flat was definitely empty. But the two youths obviously hadn't come down with him, and the sounds now crescendoed to the discord of wanton destruction.

Finally they were ready, their belongings crammed into an old carpet bag which had come with Sophie and Iakov from Russia all those years ago. The PPF bully boys were back in the flat, their faces flushed with the joy of vandalism. At the door, Sophie produced her key and stood and stared at them. There was a long pause. One of them made an obscene gesture with his arm.

The constable said, 'Right, you two, out! Can't you see the lady wants to lock up?'

The youths came out with very ill grace and Sophie locked the door. She had scribbled a note to Janine and left it on the stove where she'd be certain to see it. In her heart she was beginning to have grave misgivings. These grew when she got down into the street and saw several other little groups being shepherded along by uniformed policemen. There were old men with paper parcels, old women on sticks, younger women pushing prams, whole family groups, all of them neat and tidy despite the unexpected summons, the rapid preparation, the late hour, all silent or talking only in low murmurs, inaudible except to those nearest.

By the time they'd crossed the little Place de Thorigny and were walking down the Rue Elzevir, they had becor a procession. 'Where are we going?' someone asked. 'Only to the Rue des Rosiers,' someone said reassuringly. There

225

were spectators now, one or two on the pavement, several at open windows. Someone made a remark, there was a laugh. At another window a woman was sobbing uncontrollably. Most just watched in silence. A drunken voice screeched, 'It's pork every day where you buggers are going!' A gendarme cried, 'Shut up!' This comforted Sophie and she felt even more reassured when Constable Savier, noticing that Céci was so tired she could hardly walk, scooped the little girl up in his arms.

Then a man in the uniform of an inspector of gendarmerie stepped out in front of them. 'What the hell do you think the force pays you for? Not to carry Yid kids around the streets, you'd better believe that!'

Flushing, Savier gently lowered Céci. She tried to hold on to his hand, but with the inspector keeping pace alongside them, his angry eyes taking in every detail of the scene, he had to ignore it. Finally, with a glance of shamefaced appeal at Sophie, he dropped back and she saw him no more.

When they turned into the Rue des Rosiers, she saw a long line of buses. The sight of these everyday green and white vehicles in this most familiar of streets where she had shopped and chatted for over thirty years should have been reassuring. It wasn't. Everything seemed transformed by the hour and the atmosphere into something at the same time unreal and terrifying, like the landscape of an evil dream.

As the queues of people slowly shuffled forward into the gaping doors of the buses, a middle-aged man suddenly stepped out of line and began walking away towards the Rue Pavée. He didn't run or even walk very fast and the very normality of his gait disconcerted the supervising police. Then a couple of gendarmes ran after him. For a few paces they fell into step alongside him and they spoke as they walked. Then one of the officers seized his arm and brought him to a halt. He tried to wrestle free and punched the officer, making him stagger. The other pulled out his truncheon and struck him in the belly. Doubled up and sucking air into his grey lips with a bubbling, rattling sound, he was dragged back and hurled on to a bus.

Finally the Simonians' turn came. The bus was jampacked, but a man rose and gave Sophie his seat. She drew Céci on to her lap and the little girl promptly fell asleep. Pauli leaned against her shoulder with his arm round her neck. Elsewhere on the bus, children were crying and mothers were making crooning comforting noises, but there was no attempt at adult conversation.

The bus sped swiftly through the deserted streets. Sophie was vaguely aware that they crossed the river but otherwise she had little sense of where they were going. Her mind was going years back with Iakov Moseich, when she had lain on the floor of a crowded swaying train with her head pillowed on this very bag now jammed between her legs, and her ears drinking greedily the remorseless clack of the engine wheels bearing them westward to their long-dreamt-of new and better life.

The bus stopped. A gendarme yelled at them to get out. They found themselves standing before a huge building she didn't recognize.

'What is this place?' she asked no one in particular.

'It's the Vél d'Hiv,' said Pauli whose secret wanderings had familiarized him with the far corners of Paris.

'What?'

'The Vélodrome d'Hiver,' he expounded. 'Fifteenth Arrondissement. It's a cycling stadium, Bubbah.'

Another youngster recognizing the place said seriously, 'Are we going to see a race, papa?'

Once more they joined a queue and filed forward in an orderly fashion. But once they were inside the huge open-air stadium all sense of order vanished. There were people everywhere and more pouring in by the minute. Sophie was instantly aware of the first great danger which was separation. From all sides there came the cry of voices calling out the names of those they'd lost and most piteous of all, the voices of children calling simply, 'Maman! Papa!'

'Pauli,' she said sharply. 'Here, you must carry the bag. Can you manage it?'

'Yes, Bubbah,' he said.

'Good. Now put your other hand in my pocket. There. Clench your fist. And don't take it out, you hear me now, boy? Good.'

She stooped and picked up Céci, who was fully awake again, staring round-eyed at this mad, crowded world she suddenly found herself in.

'Now let's try to find ourselves somewhere to sit.'

They made their way across the centre of the arena. It seemed a long walk; they stumbled on unseen obstacles in the dark and people were continually crossing their path and colliding with them, while Pauli had to rest from time to time as the bag felt as if it was dragging his arm out of its socket. When they finally reached the other side, Sophie's hope that they might find the grandstands there less crowded proved delusory. Finally she halted out of sheer exhaustion.

'This will do nicely,' she said as if she had been searching for just such a spot, and they all collapsed to the floor.

It was Céci who spoke first.

'Go home,' she said plaintively.

'Yes, darling. You shall go home. Very soon, shan't she, Pauli.'

'Yes, Bubbah,' said Pauli leaning over his sister and murmuring into her ear. Finally she closed her eyes and fell asleep again, resting against his arm.

'Bubbah,' said Pauli. 'How soon shall we go home, do you think?'

'Oh, tomorrow I expect. What a boy for questions! Tomorrow when it's light they'll come, the authorities, and sort this chaos out, you'll see. Now get some rest, Pauli. You're a growing boy. You need your rest.'

'Yes, Bubbah.'

He closed his eyes but their lids became a screen on which memories of that strange night flickered like images cast from a magic lantern. And when sleep

228

finally came, he bore the images into its shallow depths with him.

And still the buses drew up outside the Vél d'Hiv and still the people poured in.

10

Janine awoke.

She found herself lying in Pauli's bed and for a moment was filled with a paralysing panic. *Where were the children?*

Then she remembered, and sighed with relief. And remembering why she was sleeping in her son's bed, she rose swiftly, and went through the open door into her own room.

Jean-Paul lay as if he hadn't moved all night. Then panic came oozing back. With the beginnings of terror she reached out to touch him.

He opened his eyes. There was no recognition there, only blank bewilderment. He spoke. She couldn't understand the language but recognized it as German. Then he tried to sit upright and the smooth marble of his face crazed with pain as his head fell back on the bolster.

'Jesus Christ!' he said.

'Jean-Paul, are you all right?' cried Janine, hovering helplessly.

'Oh yes. I am now. I thought for a moment I was back in hospital and those German bastards had started chopping pieces off me for fun!'

He stretched out his good arm and she took his hand in both of hers.

'You came for me,' he said. 'Thanks.'

It was a good moment. Then she felt his hand pull away from hers and he clutched his side and grimaced.

'I feel hot,' he said. 'Could I have some water?'

She went to pour a glass. When she returned he was in a high fever.

The next few hours were an agony. The doctor who'd treated him had left him a few tablets. For a while there seemed to be an improvement, then the fever flared up again, bearing Jean-Paul into a confusion of other worlds. In no particular order, he slipped in and out of childhood, student days, marriage, the war, hospital, and his contact with the Resistance. Janine was too concerned with his comfort to pay much heed to his often incoherent babblings, but he kept coming back to one incident with such passion that in the end it forced itself upon her consciousness.

'. . . two of them . . . bastards! Two of them . . . on a French street . . . with French whores . . . they're happy . . . they're laughing . . . let's see how you laugh at that *mein' lustiger Knab'*, let's see how your Aryan blood looks on the pavement, *mein' schöner Held*!'

And his hand came up as if aiming a pistol and jerked back with the recoil twice.

By midday, Janine was in despair. Where was Henri's doctor? If he didn't come soon she would have to take the risk of sending for someone else. An hour later she had made up her mind.

She ran to the door, opened it, and almost screamed. A man was standing there, heavy-jowled, badly shaven, with a cigarette drooping from the side of his mouth. He wore a crumpled black suit and carried a scuffed imitation-leather attaché case.

'Henri sent me,' he said. 'How's the man?'

She took him through without question or demur. He looked down at Jean-Paul for a moment then said, 'Where can I wash my hands?'

When he returned, the cigarette was still in his mouth. He caught her glance, removed it, nicked it economically and put it in a small tin box he took from his pocket. She saw it contained many others. Next he opened the old attaché case. In it were crammed the essentials of his trade.

He remarked, 'Can't lug a doctor's bag out on jobs like this, can I? By the way, I let on to the concierge that I was selling you insurance.'

He began removing the dressings, assuming without question that Janine would act as nurse. The arm and thigh wounds were clean and dry but the wound in his side was red and angry.

'There's your trouble-maker,' he said with satisfaction. 'Let's see what we can do.'

He worked swiftly and efficiently despite the fact that, as Janine had come to realize, he was dog-tired.

'There,' he said. 'With luck that ought to do the trick.'

'Luck, doctor?'

He smiled ruefully and said, 'Madame, I should like there to be a lot less luck and a lot more medicine. A few days in hospital is what he really needs, but with three palpable bullet-holes in him, someone's going to start asking questions.'

He washed his hands again, lit a fresh cigarette.

'I'll call again in two or three days. In an emergency you can contact me through Henri.'

'I don't know how to contact Henri,' she said.

'I shouldn't worry about that,' he smiled. 'He'll keep in touch.'

He left. She went back in to look at Jean-Paul. He was sleeping peacefully. She went out into the living-room and sat down and wept, long and silently, for fear of disturbing the patient.

Then she thought, Oh God. The children!

She took another look at the still sleeping Jean-Paul then ran down the stairs to the telephone in the hallway. Three times she tried to call the concierge's number at Sophie Simonian's building but the line was clearly out of order. This was annoying but not unusual. Sophie would probably try to ring the other way, so would know what had happened.

She returned to her husband's bedside.

231

At six o'clock that evening, Christian Valois appeared. His thin handsome face looked tired and worried.

She greeted him with a smile, saying, 'Henri sent a doctor like he promised. Isn't he marvellous? Jean-Paul had a fever, but he seems much better now. He's still weak, but I persuaded him to have a cup of soup. Come on through. I'm sure seeing you will cheer him up.'

Her uncomplicated and unselfish delight should have been irresistibly contagious, but Valois seemed untouched by it and not in too much of a hurry to see his friend either.

He stood in the living-room doorway and looked around.

'Children not here?' he said.

'No. I told you. They're with Sophie. I haven't had time to go round there and collect them, as you can imagine. Besides, thinking about it, I wonder if it mightn't be a good idea to let them stay with their grandmother a bit longer. I don't want them to see Jean-Paul while he's ill again. And he could probably do without the noise.'

She laughed.

Valois said, 'That's OK, is it? I mean for them to stay. You've talked with Sophie on the phone?'

'No. The line's out of order again.'

She was looking at him closely. Open natures might find evasion difficult to contrive, but they were quick to spot it.

'What's up, Christian? There's nothing wrong, is there?'

'No, no. I'm sure not,' he said unhappily. 'It's just that, well, you remember as we drove back last night, we kept on hitting those road blocks, and we thought at first they were for us, but no one seemed much bothered when we turned off? I found out the reason for that this afternoon. It seems they weren't road blocks to stop traffic getting in, they were to stop people getting out. The police evidently sealed off half a dozen *arrondissements*, north of the river, last night. I got this from a friend at the Ministry of the Interior.'

'But why?' asked Janine. 'Has there been a big robbery or something?'

'No,' said Valois wretchedly. 'They were rounding up Jews.'

'Jews? But . . .' She was merely puzzled till visibly her mind moved from the general to the particular and she cried out, 'Oh God! Which *arrondissements*? The Fourth? Was one of them the Fourth?'

He nodded and said, 'I believe so. I may have got it wrong, but I believe so.'

'But why? You say it was the police? The French police, you mean? *Our* police? No Germans?'

'That's what I was told. Just our own. Over a thousand of them. All French.'

'Then that must be all right, mustn't it? If the Boche weren't involved, I mean,' she said, her eyes fixed unblinkingly on his as though she hoped to mesmerize reassurance out of him.

It was tempting to give in, tempting to take her hands and smile and talk soothingly. But this was not the time.

He said, 'The Boche *were* involved, of course they were involved! Who do you think organized the whole thing? They just think it looks better if they can get us to do our own dirty work. And they don't find that too hard.'

'But the police are fair, aren't they? They wouldn't do anything that was going to hurt anyone not a criminal?'

'Crime is what the rulers say is crime,' said Valois. 'Listen; of course there'll be plenty of cops who find all this as disgusting as we do. But there's plenty more who are too stupid, or frightened, or just don't care. And there were several hundred PPF thugs backing them up.'

As he spoke, Janine was struggling into a light summer coat. Now she ran into the bedroom to peer down at Jean-Paul.

'He's asleep,' she said to Valois, 'but he'll wake up soon. There's some soup to heat up.'

She made for the door.

'Wait!' cried Valois. 'Where are you going?'

'To Sophie's, of course. I've got to see about the children.'

'Wait! I'll come with you.'

'No,' she said as if talking to a simple child. 'You stay here, someone has to stay with Jean-Paul. I'll be back as soon as I can.'

Then she was gone.

As she cycled through the evening streets, Janine forced her mind away from what might lie ahead. She was going too fast, she knew that: too fast for safety, too fast for endurance. Down the steep slope of the Rue Lacépède she sped with the Jardin des Plantes ahead, straight across the Rue Geoffroy Saint-Hilaire without a glance to left or right, into the long straight Rue Cuvier, still downhill, still gathering speed.

Soon the Seine's oily surface gleamed like a stream of metal in a foundry through the rails of the Pont de Sully. She kept up her speed till she was across the river, but as she turned along the Quai des Célestins she was already flagging and up the slight rise of the Rue Saint-Paul her breath began to burn her chest. It was dark in the canyons of the north-south streets, a darkness accentuated by the explosions of sunlight at east-west intersections. Above, the sky was bright but down here the shadows lay so thick that her tyres seemed to sink into them like wet sand. Rue Malher, Rue Payenne . . . and now at last Rue de Thorigny and Sophie's house.

Too tired and too fearful to go through the usual ritual of chaining up her bike and removing the pump, she let it slip into the gutter and went inside.

There was no sign of Madame Nomary, the concierge. She went upstairs, each step requiring a real effort of strength, and of will. The apartment door was ajar.

'Sophie?' she called. 'Pauli? Céci?'

She pushed open the door, fearing the silence.

'Oh Jesus, help me!' she said.

The room was in chaos with furniture overturned, curtains ripped down, and every drawer and cupboard door burst open. There was a smell of urine. She ran through into the bedrooms, the spare one first, then Sophie's. A movement beneath a tangle of coverlets set her heart pounding, but what emerged was the head of a cat, wide-eyed and fearful.

'Charlot!' she said, reaching out her hand.

The animal snarled, struggled out of the bedding and dashed past her through the door. She turned to follow it and stopped dead at the sight of a woman in the doorway.

'Madame Nomary!' she cried. 'What's happened here? Where are my children?'

'It's you, Madame Janine?' said the old woman as if in doubt. 'The police came last night. They took everyone away. Everyone who is Jewish, that is.'

'The police did *this*?' exclaimed Janine, gesturing at the wreckage.

'No. That was the young men, the PPF they call themselves. They did some damage upstairs, but no one was there. Here they did nothing till your mother-in-law and children were taken. Then they came back without the police and asked for my key. I told them I would not give it, I would call the gendarmes, but they broke my phone and said they would break my arm too. I had to give in . . .'

Janine realized that the old woman was trembling.

'Please, Madame Nomary, don't upset yourself,' she said. 'But the children . . . is there nothing you can tell me?'

'Madame Sophie left a note. I found it on the floor.'

Janine recognized Sophie's writing at once though it showed every sign of haste.

Janine, two policemen are taking us away. The sergeant won't let me leave the children. The constable is kinder but not in charge. Don't worry.

Sophie.

235

'Where? Where have they taken them?' cried Janine.
The old woman could only shake her head helplessly.
'Oh God,' moaned Janine. 'Oh God.'
And she did not know if it was a prayer or a curse.

11

'Pauli,' whispered Céci. 'I want to do pi-pi.'

Pauli Simonian sat up. Beside him, his grandmother
stirred but did not waken. They were huddled close
together, partly for warmth, but mainly because of the
sheer lack of space. Everywhere he looked the dim starlight
showed him people, vague outlines of darker grey against
the greyness of the night.

He stood up carefully. He was dressed in his outdoor
clothes plus a thick cardigan of his grandmother's, worn
like an overcoat. She didn't feel the cold, she assured him.
Old people had less sensitivity.

'Careful,' he admonished his sister as she too got up.
He took her hand and gingerly they picked their way
among the recumbent bodies towards the distant lavatories
beneath the stand. The stench hit them long before they
got there. The lavatories had packed up within the first
twenty-four hours under sheer pressure of usage, and now
they were open sewers. The only reason they were still
used was the virtual impossibility of finding anywhere else
that didn't involve the risk of fouling someone's sleeping
space – or sleeping person.

'Pooh,' said Céci wrinkling her nose. 'Like Charlot when
he got shut in. Oh, sorry, madame.'

The woman she had stumbled against didn't protest or
move, not even when Pauli close behind made the same
error and almost fell on her, putting his hand against her
shoulder to steady himself.

236

'Come on, Céci,' he said. 'Over here. Hurry up.'

They reached the lavatory door. It was pointless going on. The room was literally overflowing. Céci squatted down and quickly relieved herself.

On their way back, she said, 'I'm hungry.'

'We'll get some food soon.'

'Why doesn't maman send us some food? Granpa would send us some biscuits if he knew we were here, wouldn't he, Pauli?'

'Of course he would. Lots,' assured Pauli. He'd told his sister that they were camping here for a few days while their mother went with daddy to get some fruit from the countryside. It was a story the little girl was ready to accept as she had absolute faith in her brother. But he couldn't talk her out of feeling hungry.

Sophie Simonian had packed a little food in her old carpet bag, inspired by distant memory of her flight from Russia. She eked it out to them in dribs and drabs once she realized that no one seemed interested in feeding them. But it couldn't last for ever and already they'd been here in the Vél d'Hiv three, or was it four nights? Dysentery was already rife. It couldn't be long before even worse epidemics broke out. There'd actually been a doctor in the place yesterday. She'd got within earshot of him and heard him respond angrily to a woman demanding more of his time and attention, 'There are two of us, madame, two for all these people. The Germans won't let any more of us in at a time. What can I do?'

You can go home at night, thought Sophie. Go home and sit with your family and try to put us out of your mind.

This was the hardest thing to bear, the knowledge that out there within only a few yards there were French families eating, drinking, laughing, playing. This sense of abandonment, of devaluation, was potentially the most dangerous thing of all. Yesterday a young woman had somehow got on to the grandstand roof and with one last

237

scream of despair plunged out of sight. Sophie could never forget that scream. She seemed to hear it now . . .

Violently she erupted out of her fitful feverish half-sleep. The echo of a scream did hang on the air, and about fifty yards away there was a lot of commotion. Swiftly the word passed . . . another jumper . . . woman . . . five children . . . not dead but dying . . .

Then with a coldness which made the night air like a jet of steam, Sophie realized the children were no longer with her.

'Pauli!' she cried. And sobbed with relief as a voice answered instantly, 'Here, Bubbah.'

Next moment they were back.

'Ceci wanted pi-pi,' explained the boy.

'I'm hungry,' said the girl.

Her attention was diverted by the sudden wail of mourning which rose from close by.

'What's that, Bubbah?' asked Céci sleepily.

'Nothing. Just some people making a noise,' said Sophie.

Already, thank God, the child was going back to sleep. She glanced at her grandson, old eyes somehow sharper in the dark than they had been when she was a girl.

Thank heaven he also seemed too preoccupied to pay much attention to the noise.

'What are you doing, Pauli,' she asked.

'Nothing. Just cleaning my hands, Bubbah,' he explained.

'Good boy. That's good. You have to keep clean,' she approved. 'Then go back to sleep.'

'Yes, Bubbah.'

Satisfied, she let her own head sag back and soon the shallow waves of time-breaking sleep lapsed around her again. While in the darkness by her side her grandson, Pauli, tried to cleanse his hand of the blood that had stained it ever since he stumbled on the woman and steadied himself with his fingers against her deep-gashed throat.

*

238

'No!' said Delaplanche. 'Definitely no. I cannot help her. You even less. You must not even try!'

'I must do what I can,' retorted Valois angrily.

'And what's that? Make enough fuss to draw attention to yourself and in the end achieve nothing? Listen Christian, they've rounded up God knows how many Jews, fifteen thousand minimum I'd say. Now just imagine how many of them have got friends, often influential friends, trying to help them. And if one half of one per cent achieve anything, I'll be amazed! And this man, your friend, he's lying in bed wounded by German bullets, you say? God, man! Suppose you draw attention to *him*? Suppose they discover that the head of this family you're so anxious about is what they call a terrorist? What then? You'll be a marked man!'

'It's no good,' said Valois defiantly. 'I have to do what I can. I've already written to my father asking for help.'

He stood, fists clenched, expecting anger.

Instead, to his surprise, Delaplanche began to smile.

'To your father? That's good. If *that's* what you mean by help, write all you will my boy. To your father! Write away, write away!'

And chuckling still, in a much better humour than when they had encountered, Delaplanche left.

Madame Crozier threw her apron up over her head and rocked to and fro crooning, 'Oh the children, oh the poor poor children.'

Claude Crozier held his daughter tight.

'My poor girl,' he said. 'My poor girl. This is too much to bear. You should have come to us earlier. Why didn't you come to us earlier?'

Before Janine could answer, his wife's flour-smudged, tear-streaked face surfaced from the apron.

'Because she doesn't trust us, that's why. Because she's cut herself off from us and doesn't think we've got any rights in the welfare of our own grandchildren. Oh the poor children!'

Janine broke free from her father's grip. Five days of suffering showed on her face; five days of nursing Jean-Paul, who kept on sliding back into fever, five days of listening to meaningless reassurances from Christian that they were being held in the cycling stadium and would be quite safe; five days of using every rare minute she could get away from the flat to beg for news at the police station or to wander with many hundreds of others, disconsolately, desperately, in the streets outside the Vélodrome d'Hiver, hoping somehow for a message, a glimpse. Five days of this, with the fear in her heart all the time that to press too close, to make too much of a fuss, might draw the attention of the authorities to Jean-Paul, unregistered, unstarred, lying between life and death with three German bullet holes in his body.

Even her relief at Jean-Paul's lucid intervals was soured by his enquiries after the children, his puzzlement that his mother didn't bring them to visit him.

All this had pared the already meagre layers of flesh on her face almost to the bone and her eyes shone huge at the promised luxury of burying her grief for a moment under an outpouring of fury at her mother's accusation. Then she recognized the impulse for the indulgence that it was, recognized too that her mother's intemperate words were her attempt to build a shield against the pain she felt. Her anger drained away and with it her strength.

'Oh maman,' she said, collapsing on to a chair. 'I should have told you sooner only there's been so much . . . and I didn't want to cause you pain . . . I thought it might all come all right . . . children, why should they want to lock up children . . .'

'Because of their name,' flashed Louise. Then she caught her husband's gaze over their daughter's head and for once was cowed by it.

'I'm sorry, I shouldn't have said what I said. It's not Jean-Paul's fault that . . . nor old Sophie's . . . it's just that if you hadn't . . .'

240

'If I hadn't married him, you'd have no grandchildren to worry about,' said Janine dully.

'Oh the poor children,' wept Louise. 'Crozier, what are we going to do?'

As Claude Crozier stood there regarding his wife helplessly the door opened and Michel Boucher's sunburst of red hair appeared.

'What's all this then? You've got a bigger crowd of people listening in your shop than if you'd announced an extra baking of baguettes!'

'Oh Miche!' cried Janine and ran and embraced him.

'Hello,' he said. 'Trouble again, is it? I'm away in the country for a few days and this family's up to its neck in trouble. Tell me everything.'

His natural jollity faded then vanished altogether as he heard what had taken place.

'Pauli and Céci!' he exclaimed indignantly. 'The bastards. Do they not know who they are? We'll have to see about this!'

Janine looked at him hopefully.

'You think you can help, Miche?'

He opened his mouth to give her the big reassurances, the all-embracing promises which so naturally arose there. Then he saw her desperate face, and behind her, Claude's sad and warning eyes.

'Maybe,' he said gently. 'Who can tell? But I'll try. I promise you that. No one will try harder. And at least we know where they are, cousin. That's a start, eh? At least we know where they are!'

'Yes,' said Janine dully. 'We know where they are.'

'Up! Up! Up! Hurry! Hurry! Hurry! Come on there! For God's sake, you people have been moaning about this place for days, now we're trying to move you, all you want is to sit around enjoying the view. Up! Up! Up!'

Sophie Simonian rose slowly, leaning heavily on Pauli's shoulder. It was just old bones, she told herself, nothing more. It had rained the previous night, the wind drifting it in under the scanty protection of the stand roof. Old bones soaked up cold and damp, but it was nothing that a bit of exercise wouldn't loosen and lubricate.

She took a step forward, swayed and almost fainted.

'Bubbah, are you all right?' said Pauli anxiously.

'Yes, my dear. Fine. I think I've forgotten how to walk, that's all. Never mind. I'll soon leap again.'

'Can you really forget things like that? How to walk, I mean?' said Pauli.

'Of course you can! You can forget your head if you're not careful. You can forget everything.'

'I don't think I'll ever forget this place, Bubbah,' said Pauli seriously as he helped his little sister up. 'Céci, you'll have to walk. Bubbah can't carry you and I've got to carry the bag. Take Bubbah's hand.'

'Where are we going, Pauli? Are we going home?'

Pauli looked up at his grandmother.

'I don't think so,' she said. 'Later perhaps. But not today. The holiday's not over yet. Come on, children. Come on.'

Slowly they joined the long shuffling queues winding towards the stadium exits. Slowly the huge stadium emptied, but not completely. The detritus of all those days remained blowing around in the summer wind, and amidst it here and there lay crumpled forms of those too decrepit to obey the instruction to rise. Policemen moved among them, prodding with foot and truncheon to diagnose the seriousness of each one's condition. Gradually they were lifted or dragged away and men and women with brooms and buckets started the long task of clearing up.

Two cleaning women went beneath the stadium to the toilets. The stench as they approached made them gag. One pushed open the door.

'Oh Jesus Mary!' she exclaimed. 'Look at that! That's disgusting!'

The other peered in.

'Yeah,' she said. 'Filthy bastards, these Jews. My husband always said it. Plain naturally filthy.'

12

'Günter. Back already? Isn't it strange how other people's leave seems to pass even more quickly than one's own?'

Mai was sitting in the Lutétia's lounge enjoying a coffee, which he'd found almost unobtainable at home. He'd just got back, having travelled overnight. Fortunately he had the gift of being able to sleep anywhere.

'And how was Offenburg? Dull as ever? But perhaps you've got some really interesting addresses in that little black book of yours. I don't suppose you even had time to pop down the river and see my mama.'

Ever since Mai had been foolish enough to remark on his grandfather's buttons with the horn and Zed, the major had mockingly urged him to take a trip along the Rhine to Schloss Zeller for a chat about old times with his mother. One of these leaves he'd take the bastard by surprise and do it.

'Sorry,' he said. 'Next time perhaps. I spent a lot of time in Strasbourg. I always preferred that side of the river. Funny, it feels even more French now it's not.'

'Careful, Günter. You never know who's listening.'

'I think I do, sir,' said Mai, lighting his pipe. 'Has anything interesting happened since I've been away?'

Zeller laughed and said, 'What? Asking me for information, and you must have been back all of thirty minutes? You're slipping.'

Ignoring the sarcasm Mai said, 'Before I went there was a rumour about our friends planning a big anti-Jewish operation.'

'Oh yes. Operation Printanier. It missed its target by fifty per cent I gather, but they still locked up fifteen thousand.'

'Good God. And how did the French authorities react?'

'React? It was the French who did it. Not a single German in sight, wasn't that marvellous? Operation Spring Wind. A thousand French cops using French census lists to gently waft French Jews into French concentration camps guarded by French guards.'

'And once in the camps, what then?'

'A trainload went east earlier in the year. No doubt there'll be more.'

'What a waste of time, manpower, transport!' exclaimed Mai indignantly. 'Forced labour I can just about understand. Sending them out to mend bomb-damage or build the new sea-wall might make sense. But this locking them up and guarding them for evermore, it's just crazy! You don't say anything. Don't you agree?'

'My dear fellow, who wouldn't agree? It's just that what I've heard makes "crazy" an . . . understatement.'

A mess orderly approached and clicked his heels.

'Begging the major's pardon, a telephone call for the lieutenant. A French lady, I think.'

'Good Lord, Günter, hardly off the train and already they're after you!'

'Excuse me,' said Mai, rising.

He moved over to the telephone and picking it up said, 'Hello? Günter Mai.'

'Hello! It's Janine Simonian. Lieutenant, can I see you? *Please.*'

The voice was urgent, pleading. She sounded desperate. Best procedure now was to be doubtful, suggest delay, span her nerves to the point where she'd make any bargain for his help. That was what she wanted, he was in no doubt.

He said, 'I'll come at once. No. Give me ten minutes to change. Where?'

She said, 'I can't go far. The Jardin des Plantes, by the big cedar. In fifteen minutes then.'

The phone went dead.

He made his way to the switchboard and asked, 'I've

just had a call from a woman. I wondered, has she perhaps rung before?'

The operator looked at his log.

'Yes, sir. There's been some woman trying to get hold of you several times in the past couple of days.'

'Thank you.'

He'd guessed from the sound of her voice that she was far past the stage where this would have been her first call. Perhaps it hadn't after all been kindness that made him agree instantly to meet, but a professional awareness that she'd done all the necessary nerve-twisting for herself.

Or is that what I want to think? he wondered.

By the time he had changed out of uniform, he was late arriving at the Jardin, even though he got a car to drop him in the Rue Linne, just a hundred yards from the north-western gate. A sudden fear came upon him that she would not have waited, not the fear of a professional who dislikes having his time wasted, but something much more irrational. He broke into a trot without thinking. As he passed beneath the amused gaze of the pair of rather mangy bronze lions just inside the gate, he said to himself, 'This is ridiculous! I'm trying to look inconspicuous!' But he didn't slow to a walk till he'd turned up the track towards the cedar and saw her slim figure standing impatiently beneath its magnificent spread of summer-heavy branches.

She started speaking rapidly as soon as he arrived, but now he was in control again, the trained *Abwehr* man playing with the potential agent. He waved her words aside without even looking at her and collapsed on the stone bench round the bole of the tree.

'All right, all right, give me a minute,' he said breathing heavily. It came easy, playing the part of a man much older and much less fit. After a moment, he took out his pipe, filled it and putting it in his mouth said as he struck a match, 'Now you can begin.'

He looked up at her as he spoke and his voice faltered a little as he saw close the face which matched the desperate voice. Sunken cheeks, bloodless skin, deep-shadowed eyes, all combined to make her look more like some spirit of the underworld, begging release, than the lively young woman he remembered.

'Madame Simonian, please, won't you sit down. You're ill.'

'No, no, I'm not ill,' she said, sitting by him. 'Please, listen to me, you must help me. There's no one else.'

The story came pouring out – the arrest of Sophie and the children, their imprisonment in the Vél d'Hiv, her vain attempts to see them – and then her discovery that they'd been moved out of the stadium.

'I can't find out where,' she sobbed. 'Some say it's somewhere in the Loiret. Are there camps there? What do you want with them? What *can* you want with little children? People near the stadium said you took them away in cattle-trucks. Why should you do that? Why should you put children and old women into cattle-trucks? It's monstrous, monstrous! Oh please help me, lieutenant! Please, please, you've got to, I beg you – I'll do anything!'

Her tone switched from bitter accusation to desperate pleading and back again without modulation as she spoke. Tears ran down the wasted cheeks. People walking past were looking towards them and Mai put his arm around her shoulders and said helplessly, 'Please, please . . . Janine . . . I beg you . . .'

She leaned against him and sobbed without restraint.

'I've tried everything . . . asked everyone . . . Christian tried to get his father to help but he said he couldn't interfere . . . *interfere!* . . . Miche tried to find out but he was too late . . . they'd gone . . . and the people he works with won't help . . . they hate Jews, he says . . . it was their idea . . . but he suggested you . . . and I rang and they said you were away . . . but I kept on ringing . . . because I don't know what else to do . . . please . . . help . . . me . . .'

Were there men of his race, or of any race, who could have resisted such an appeal? He had to believe there were, and yet he could not believe it and feel that there was anything in humanity worth fighting for.

He said, 'Of course I'll help. Believe me; trust me. I'll do everything in my power. Now give me all the details please. We Germans are above all a bureaucratic nation. Everything will be correct, everything will be recorded. But I must have the details.'

It was the right approach. For a second she threatened to be as devastated by her joy at his promise as she had been by her despair at her loss. But his businesslike manner as he produced the black *Tagebuch* and questioned her and made tiny illegible notes about the children's age, history and description, brought her back to something like normality.

Only when he mentioned her husband did he immediately sense a reticence.

'He must be desperate, the poor man,' he said casually. 'His mother *and* his children. Desperate. How's he taking it?'

The hesitation.

'He doesn't know,' she said.

'What?'

'I haven't told him. He's been ill, very ill. The wound he got in the war, it's been bothering him again.'

Liar, he thought almost tenderly. You shouldn't try to lie, my sweet; better still, you shouldn't have to need to lie.

She was looking at her watch in alarm.

'I have to get back to him,' she said. 'I left him sleeping. Please, when will you know something? When shall we meet?'

Her impatience touched and amused him. It was tempting to fuel her joy at his promise of help by saying tomorrow. But it would be a selfish suggestion. His anticipation would be satisfied by seeing her again so quickly; but hers, so much more exhausting and essential, could only be disappointed, with God knows what new wounds to her spirit.

247

'Seventy-two hours,' he said. 'Three days.'

He held up three fingers to reinforce what he was saying. Her face showed dismay.

'Three days? So long?'

It was too short. He hadn't been lying when he said the machine was efficient but it could also be very slow. Christ! How slow it could be!

He said, 'Three days to our next meeting. And there's no guarantee that I will know anything by then.'

Now she surprised him.

'Oh but you will, Günter, you're so clever, I know you will,' she cried almost coquettishly. 'Thank you, thank you so very much.'

She leaned forward and kissed him on the cheek, then began to hurry away down the hill. After a few yards she turned, still moving backwards so that she almost over-balanced, and cried, 'Same place, same time, by the cedar!' and waved and was gone.

He remained for a little while, lighting his pipe and sending curls of pungent smoke into the ancient branches above. And when he finally moved off, he didn't go straight back to the Lutétia, but strolled around the garden, watching the old men playing cards, the children playing *boule*, and gently nursing the image of Janine running away down the hill and turning to call and wave, like any young woman parting from her lover.

He put such stupidities from his mind when he got back to the hotel. Zeller had been preparing a comprehensive situation report to be sent to Admiral Canaris. He gave Mai a draft for his comments.

'Excellent, sir,' said Mai. 'I look forward to seeing the rest.'

'The rest?'

'Yes. Surely this is only Part One? Our successes. Resistance groups we have infiltrated or smashed. British agents who have parachuted into our hands. Radio sets we have located and are using to mislead the enemy. Excellent. I'm all for blowing our trumpet. But surely we will also be sounding our warning bell? The rise in acts of terrorism and sabotage. Our awareness that *they* have *infiltrated* us, or at least our French co-operators. Our suspicion that most of the information radioed to us out of England is false.'

Zeller threw up his hands in mock alarm.

'Dear boy, do you really want copies of *that* kind of report to drop through the letter-box at Berchtesgarten? Of course, there will be a Part Two which the Admiral will receive for private consumption, and in addition there will be a Part Three about the activities of the *real* enemy, and *that* won't even be written down.'

He gave a gross parody of a knowing wink.

Oh God, thought Mai. He's so pleased with himself, so cocky. He thinks that ultimately he and his class, or rather his caste, must succeed, for breeding is bound to tell.

'I'll have a word with my tame Frenchman,' he said. 'See if he's got any new snippets.'

'That would be most kind of you, Günter,' said Zeller. 'It won't be forgotten, believe me.'

What are you going to do? thought Mai in irritation. Give me a job mucking out the stables after the war's over?

At lunchtime, he went to the bar he knew was one of Michel Boucher's favourites. The red-head came in with a group of friends and gave no sign of recognizing Mai. But an hour later when the others left, he wandered across to the German's table and sat down.

'Some of my lads,' he said. 'Good boys, most of them. Slit their mothers' throats for a sou, or sell me out to Pajou for less.'

'You're right to be careful,' said Mai.

'You don't have to tell me. Hey, have you had a good leave, lieutenant? Plenty of hoop-la? Or are you getting so much here in Paris that you go off home for a rest?'

'It was fine. Now tell me, what have you been up to?'

'Well, there was this exotic dancer at the Scheherezade.

Tits like mangoes . . . All right,' he laughed, 'I know that's not what you mean. On the work front . . .'

He launched into a detailed account of his own activities and what he'd been able to pick up about other SD operations and plans. As Mai listened it came to him that corruption was insidious and irresistible. He had seen it at work in Frenchmen at all levels – politicians, civil servants, policemen, shopkeepers – everyone who started off by saying, 'This far, I can go this far along the path of necessary co-operation and still stop well short of active collaboration.' But slowly, gradually, in all but the strongest-willed the contagion spread far beyond what they wished or believed. In Boucher's case, every time the red-head talked it was clear he had gone another half-step towards full acceptance of the Gestapo outlook.

His views on the Great Raid, as the round-up at the Vél d'Hiv had come to be known, were typical. Token sympathy (*poor sods, it's a bit rough being dragged off out of your nice comfy house to sleep on a bench!*) was allied with reasoned justification (*mind you, it'll do some of those bastards no harm to find out how the other half live; did you ever know a poor Jew?*).

Only when it came to Janine's children did indignation surface.

'Now that's not right. They're lovely kids. They shouldn't be shut up with that lot. Jews! If them kids are Jewish, you can skin my old man and call me Micah!'

He paused and looked at Mai with the complacency of one who knew he'd made his case.

'I saw your cousin,' said Mai.

'Good! I told her you were the man. Can you help?'

'I don't know. It may be difficult.'

'Yeah, I know,' said Boucher sympathetically. 'Them bastards at the Rue des Saussaies can generally speaking run rings round your lot, present company excepted. Do what you can, won't you? If you want any help breaking them out, don't hesitate to ask. Don't look so taken aback! None of your lot would get hurt. It's French cops that seem to be looking after them, and I don't mind smashing a few of their heads in!'

'That's kind of you. I'll bear it in mind,' said Mai.

'Right. And by the way, remember I mentioned my mate, Maurice, to you? Any joy there? He's turning into a liability. I was away for a few days recently, and he takes to wandering off. Nearly got picked up too. You know what he did the day after the Great Raid? He went back to his old flat to see if they'd been there!'

'And had they?'

'Oh yes. Wrecked it by all accounts. And here's a funny coincidence. It turns out he used to live upstairs from the old lady, Janine's ma-in-law, where the kids were that night they got taken. It's a small world, isn't it. So, what do you say, lieutenant? Will you be able to help the little twerp?'

'For God's sake, man, I'm not in a position to help the whole Jewish population of France!' snapped Mai. 'They're *your* people. What are you and others like you doing to help them?'

'Well, nothing,' said Boucher, clearly baffled by the question. 'I mean, it's you buggers that are in charge, isn't it? *We*'re not locking them up.'

'No? I got the distinct impression that's exactly what you were doing.'

Mai finished his drink and got his irritation under control.

'I'll do what I can, Miche,' he said. 'For everyone. But don't expect too much. Keep in touch, won't you?'

He rose, shook hands and left.

I should never have gone on leave, he thought as he strolled towards the river. It's unsettled me. Christ, everyone's getting to me today. Zeller, Boucher, and above all Janine. They've all got under my guard. Perhaps what I need is a change of scene, a posting a long long way from here. I can just imagine what they'd say. *Jawohl, Herr Leutnant.* The Russian Front's a long long way from here. How would that suit you?

251

He smiled. There were still worse places to be than Paris on a pleasant summer day.

And wherever Céci and Pauli Simonian were was certainly one of them.

It was time to put the search under way.

13

While the memory of the Vél d'Hiver was strong, the new camp seemed almost luxurious by comparison. They were in huts; they had beds; there were toilets that worked and taps that gave out water; they were fed.

But remembered pain was not long a standard for judging. The huts leaked, the beds were bare boards, the toilets stank and were infested with flies, the taps produced only a thin trickle of rust-coloured water and the food was only just preferable to fasting.

The guards were French. They glimpsed Germans occasionally in the distance, but their only immediate contact was with Frenchmen, usually police. Some were kinder than others. From one of these, a middle-aged man who took a fancy to little Céci, Sophie learnt where they were.

'Pithiviers in the Loiret,' she echoed. 'No, I don't know it. But it seems very beautiful here.'

She was talking to the man through the barbed strands of a tall fence. Behind him she could see rolling countryside in the full flush of summer greenery.

'It's all right if you like that sort of thing. Me, I'm a city man,' said the guard. 'I like streets, lights, crowds, action.'

'Yes, it must be very boring here for you,' agreed Sophie. 'A pity the Germans chose to build this camp in such a place. And already it is so dilapidated!'

She was building up to a request for help for the children – extra food, milk, blankets, *anything*, but the man gave her no encouragement, only laughing and saying, 'No, you've got it wrong, old woman. The Germans didn't build this place. Our own government did. They used to stick undesirables in here, aliens, refugees. If I were in your shoes, I'd wait till I saw the inside of a real German camp before I started knocking this place.'

With a cheerful wave, he wandered away.

Oh God, thought Sophie, is this the limit of kindness we can expect?

She turned and looked back inside the camp. There was despair here, plainly visible in the shuffling gait and blank eyes of so many of her fellow inmates. But there was also life and indeed liveliness, people moving around helping and organizing; others standing in small groups arguing and debating.

Perhaps the cop was right. This might seem like hell but it was still only a suburb. If they were left here for the duration of the war, there was hope of survival.

'Bubbah,' said Pauli. 'Can we leave this place?'

She looked down at him in surprise. He usually didn't ask such pointless questions.

She started to explain that no, they couldn't leave for the obvious reasons that the gates were locked and the fences were high, but he interrupted, 'I just thought it might be better to escape here than somewhere else where there was maybe moats or big walls with spikes.'

He was right, of course.

She ruffled his dusty and matted hair and said, 'If you think of a way to escape, you tell me, cabbage. But perhaps we'll be OK. Perhaps we'll be here a long time, eh?'

He looked up at her, his eyes huge in his shrunken face.

'I don't think so,' he said with that disconcerting certainty.

That night at roll-call they were ordered to get ready for moving off within the hour.

'Drancy!' Janine did a little sedentary jig of delight. 'Near le Bourget airport? Oh, thank God they're back in Paris!

That's something, isn't it? That's better than being stuck out in the middle of nowhere.'

Mai looked at her gloomily. It had been in little spirit of celebration that he had brought his news, first that he had tracked them down on paper to Pithiviers, and next that when he attempted to confirm their presence in the Loiret, he had been told that they had just been transferred to Drancy.

All that this meant to Janine was that once more they were close to her.

But Mai had contacted a friend on the staff of the Military Governor in France at the Hôtel Majestic.

'Tell me about Drancy,' he said.

'The camp you mean? What's to tell? It was a building project, apartment blocks mainly, down-market stuff, none of your luxury penthouse suites, as you can imagine. It was only half-finished when the war started, but it was perfect for a camp. Easy to fence off, throw up a few watchtowers, plenty of accommodation for the prisoners, but not too comfortable! Good communications, east and west . . .'

'East and west?'

'West to the city centre. And east to wherever you like. There's a railway station just round the corner. They ran a trainload of Jews out of there last March: you know; those terrorists they rounded up before Christmas. And they've started shipping this latest lot east for resettlement too. Basically all Jews are orientals so it makes sense. What's your interest?'

'It's just that an agent of mine inadvertently got picked up and I'm anxious to help. Good agents are hard to come by.'

'Is that it? And I bet you believe those twerps in the SD did it deliberately? I wouldn't put it past them. But no problem, Günter. Just pop round here with the details some time and we'll fix up an *Ausweis*.'

'I'll do that,' said Mai. 'Incidentally, this resettlement, where is it, precisely?'

'If you're thinking about asking for your agent back if he's already gone, forget it!' laughed the other. 'They're shipping them off to some God-forsaken hole in Upper Silesia, would you believe? Auschwitz, I think they call it. Dear God, Günter, imagine being posted there! Let's thank our lucky stars and meet for a drink some time soon, shall we?'

He pulled his mind back to the present and was disconcerted to find Janine looking at him as if he had just given her champagne, her eyes sparkling with hope.

She said, confidently, 'What do we do now, Günter?'

He could detect nothing premeditated or self-seeking in the use of his name. It slipped out as naturally and easily as any friend's name on the tongue of any friend.

He said, 'I can get them out.'

If he expected a dance of joy, arms around his neck, passionate gratitude, he was disappointed. But what he got was more disturbing. She merely nodded with the serene confidence of the acolyte who has entertained no doubts about the power of her deity.

'But there's a price,' he added harshly.

Again she surprised him.

'Of course there's a price,' she said. 'Do you think I imagined you were doing this out of the goodness of your heart?'

If she'd chosen deliberately to strike at him she could not have aimed a better weapon. Pain rose in Mai and must surely have shown in his eyes. A ball came bouncing down the hill past the cedar and two children pursued it, laughing. Janine's gaze followed them out of sight and when she turned to Mai once more he was back in control.

'No, I don't think that,' he said quietly. 'But tell me why you did imagine I was doing it.'

She fixed her clear, candid gaze on him and said, 'Please, don't think I can't see that you *do* have much goodness of heart, and you'll try to keep it in balance with the needs of your job. I wish all your soldiers were like that. But you'll also *do* your job. I don't think you want sex with me, not this time. I'm not sure how much you wanted it last time.'

He felt himself flushing and said, 'More than I realized. But not like that.'

'No? How then? No, don't answer that. What I imagine you want this time is to help me all you can in return for whatever help I can give you professionally. I've no idea what that may be, and I'm not sure if you have. I think perhaps deep inside, you hope it may not be very much. So do I. But I'll give what I can, and I know you will not be able to refuse what I can give. You've got me in a trap, lieutenant, but I half-suspect you're in there with me.'

He shook his head slowly, not in denial but in admiration, and in self-exasperation too.

'What's the matter?' she asked.

'I've been stupid,' he said. 'I made a misjudgement of you. I should have grasped from what I know of your husband that he was not a man to make such misjudgements.'

Again the mention of Simonian brought a veil over her expression.

He said harshly, 'So we understand each other. To get an *Ausweis* for your children and the old lady, I shall need to affirm that you are a valued agent of the *Abwehr*, your name will appear in our files, and this will not simply be for show. As you say, anything you can tell me, I shall not hesitate to use. Anything I think you can do for us, I shall not hesitate to ask.'

He had never contemplated so open an approach. He had always thought of himself as the manipulator, the puppet-master. But now, with this woman, in these circumstances, he could see that nothing else was possible. He had to state exactly what he wanted, except of course that he wanted her. He could never ask her for that again and he could not imagine a situation in which she would offer herself to him freely and with love. The knowledge made him cold and angry.

'Now, when can you do it?' she cried. 'When can I have them home?'

'I should have the *Ausweis* by tomorrow. Then I have to arrange for a release order to be sent to the camp.'

'Tomorrow?' Her face fell. 'Can't we go for them to-night?'

He said brusquely, 'Tomorrow at the earliest. It takes time.'

She said, 'Of course. I'm sorry, I'm just so impatient. Günter, whatever you want, thank you, thank you more than I can say.'

She leaned forward and kissed him lightly on the lips.

'Till tomorrow,' she said, standing up.

Once again she turned and waved as she ran lightly down the hill.

He didn't wave back.

14

'You smiled, Bubbah,' said Pauli. 'What did you smile at?'

So my smile has become such a rare thing that this sharp-eyed grandson of mine instantly spots it, thought Sophie sadly.

Bending over Céci's hair which she was combing for lice, she plucked one out, held it up and said, 'I was just thinking, there's such a one! Must be the grandfather of a whole family! Crack, and there's an end to him.'

Her lie seemed to satisfy the boy. What she had actually been smiling at was a sudden memory of Iakov singeing lice from the seams of his clothes with a candle after their long flight from Russia and accidentally setting his shirt on fire. Such memories were precious sustenance for the soul here in Drancy.

For Drancy was an abomination. The food was vile

beyond description. They slept like animals on straw infested with parasites. Every day, new arrivals poured in, including vast numbers of children, many separated from their parents. When she saw them herded out of the trucks and left to mill around, aimless and hopeless as lambs in an abattoir, Sophie wanted to rush forward and comfort them, pressing to her thin bony body as many as possible.

But she did not dare do it. All her energy was directed to keeping Pauli and Céci with her. She'd seen families ripped apart after dawn roll-calls when those picked out had been marched away to the station.

At first she'd been sure there must be protests. Drancy was a complex of apartment blocks surrounded by other apartment blocks. People at their windows could look into the camp. People out shopping or going to work must see the lines of deportees plodding by.

Then she remembered the walk from her home to the Rue des Rosiers. She must not look for help from anywhere but within. Only the children mattered. Keeping them with her was her only function.

She concentrated all her attention on her granddaughter's hair.

'Bubbah,' said the little girl idly. 'When will it be our turn to go to Pitchipoi?'

'Pitchi-what? Where's that, cabbage?' she asked.

'Pitchipoi!' repeated Céci. 'When are we going?'

'Pauli?' said Sophie, turning as always to the boy whenever she couldn't grasp what Céci meant.

'It's a name,' said Pauli, who was sitting trying to repair his worn and torn trousers. It would be much easier if he had a needle or even a knife. He thought with regret of the super knife that Uncle Miche had given him. He'd left it at home the day his mother had suddenly and inexplicably decided they should stay with Bubbah. He wished he had it now. Even though he'd promised maman he would never open the blade till he had her permission, there were still all those other bits and pieces which would have been so useful.

'I know it's a name,' said Sophie sharply. 'I may be ancient but I'm not antique. A name for what?'

'It's the name some of the children give to the place they're going to send us,' said Pauli casually.

'What place? You mean it's a game?' demanded Sophie in alarm.

'It's an awful place,' announced Céci, happy to be forthcoming now that her brother had shown the way. 'It's a dreadful place where they do dreadful things. They make stew out of the little girls and steak out of the little boys.'

'Céci!' exclaimed Sophie almost choking on her alarm. 'That's just silly.'

'No it's not,' said the girl indignantly. 'Everyone knows. It's an awful awful place and it's miles and miles from home and you never never ever come back, 'cause if you try to run away there's big dogs like wolves to eat you. Isn't that right, Pauli?'

Her brother looked up at his grandmother then looked away. Céci took the silence as assent and cried triumphantly to Sophie, 'See, Pauli knows it's true!' and in the very moment of her triumph, the implication of having her worst fears confirmed by her infallible brother hit her.

Bursting into tears, she squeezed tight against Sophie as if trying to get inside the old woman's body and sobbed, 'I don't want to go, Bubbah. I don't want to go to Pitchipoi.'

'There, there, cabbage, there's no such place, it's just a silly game,' crooned Sophie rocking the child to and fro. 'We're not going anywhere.'

The next morning in the corpse-light of a grey, drizzling dawn, their names were called out in the list for departure.

She tried to protest, but all she did was draw attention to herself and the gendarmes were only too pleased to satisfy their masters' bureaucratic demands by ticking off three names.

'Quickly, over there. Do as I say, old woman!'

They had collected their pathetic scraps of belongings. The old carpet bag was long gone. Now what they had was contained in a ragged square of cloth tied together at the corners. Now this was opened and searched but not even the magpie instincts of the searchers could find anything left worth stealing.

'Over there! Get on the bus!'

The old green and white buses were being used today. There was a larger than usual number of unaccompanied children being deported and it was felt there was a slight risk that the sight of them being herded along the rain-soaked pavements might provoke some kind of protest.

One or two gendarmes were visibly affected. Most hid their feelings under a shield of anger. They shouted and swore and brandished their sticks as though there was a constant threat of resistance. Sophie realized why they were doing this but felt no sympathy. This was not work fit for decent men.

On the bus she sat near the door and pulled the children close to her. They didn't speak but sat by the rain-spattered window, fearfully watching the confusion outside.

Whatever system there was had clearly broken down. Harassed French officials with lists were trying to check names. The guards were herding people towards the buses with growing brutality. A German officer appeared, a comparatively rare sight within the camp. He began to shout angry instructions, adding to the confusion. A girl of about ten ran from the doorway of one of the blocks and spoke to him. She kept on gesturing towards the buses. Her dirty face was streaked with tears. The officer spoke to a French official who studied his list and shook his head. The officer pointed back to the block, the girl persisted, and finally the official dragged her, screaming in grief and protest, back into the building. It was like watching a vision of madness, then realizing you were no spectator but a part of it. And over everything rose the cries of weeping children.

Céci's face at last crumpled and she said, 'Bubbah, are we going to Pitchipoi now?'

'No, of course not,' said Sophie, but her voice carried no conviction even to herself. She had to do something.

She closed her eyes in prayer for a moment, opened them again and saw through the window the young girl who was desperate to get on a bus being driven back by the angry official once more.

'Pauli,' she said. 'Don't ask questions. Take Céci back to the block. If anyone stops you, tell them you want to go on the bus because there's a nice lady who's been kind to you on the bus. But don't tell them your name. Can you do that, Pauli?'

He looked straight into her eyes with that unblinking gaze he had inherited from her son. Then he nodded.

'Yes, Bubbah,' he said, and flung his arms round her neck and kissed her. Then he took Céci by the hand. Their bus was full and their guard was round the front, smoking a cigarette and talking with the driver. The door was slightly ajar. Pauli pushed it so it slid just wide enough for them to squeeze out.

Sophie watched them walk away. Pauli had his arm around his sister, holding her tight against his side. They looked so small, so defenceless. The old woman half rose from her seat to call them back. This was stupidity. At least they had been together. All that was likely to happen now was for the children to be transported separately, out of reach of any small protection she could afford them.

But she slumped down again without calling. In her mind she was seeing that sad, already defeated queue shuffling over the hall of the police station to register what no civilized state could have any reason for wanting them to register. Even then she had known but not been able to admit where that queue led to.

Now it was her unavoidable fate to travel east at the end of her life just as she and Iakov had travelled west at its true beginning. But for the children any delay must increase their slender chance of rescue from this nightmare.

They had almost reached the nearest block. Perhaps they would simply walk in unchallenged. But just as it seemed they had made it, a gendarme planted himself in front of them and began shouting at them and pointing back to the buses.

Sophie felt her old frail body ready to collapse in on itself and die at this last disappointment. She sank back in her seat and put her hands over her face.

Pauli looked up at the man who was yelling at them to get back to the buses. He let him go on a bit, then began to yell, 'We want to go! We want to go! But he won't let us! He won't let us!'

At last the gendarme realized what was being said.

'What do you mean? Who won't let you?'

'The man on the bus! We want to go with the lady, but he said we can't! The lady was kind to us. We want to go with the lady!'

He now screwed his face up, and made himself cry, and through the tears continued his refrain, 'We want to go with the lady!'

Céci had no idea what was going on, but tears are infectious, and anything Pauli did was good enough for her, so she soon joined in, 'We want to go with the lady!'

'Shut your row, boy!' ordered the gendarme, but his tone was now less angry than his words. 'What's your name?'

The man had a list.

Pauli thought desperately. All names except his own vanished from his mind. Then he saw the door of his grandfather's shop, and smelt the glorious smell of fresh baked bread, and his eyes filled with genuine tears.

'Crozier,' he said. 'I'm Claude Crozier and this is my sister, Louise.'

The gendarme studied the list. Suppose there was some-one called Crozier on it? Pauli clasped his sister's hand so tight, she squealed in pain.

'Poor kid. You really are upset, aren't you?' said the gendarme paying attention to Céci for the first time. Men were always delighted with the little girl's wide-eyed, appealing face framed in blonde curls, and even in her present state, the charm still worked. Suddenly Pauli foresaw a new danger. Success.

He flung himself forward against the gendarme, butting his head against the man's crutch.

'Let us go with the lady! You've got to let us go with the lady!' he cried, beating his fists against the policeman's thighs.

'Yes, you've got to, you've got to!' yelled Céci, adding her tiny fists to the tattoo.

'Jesus Christ, you little bastard!' gasped the gendarme, doubled up with pain. 'Get out of here before I break your fucking neck! Go on, you nasty little Yid! Get out of here!'

In the bus, Sophie took her hands from her eyes. She saw the gendarme straightening up with difficulty, saw the backs of Pauli and his sister as they disappeared back into the detention block.

'Thank God!' said Sophie, certain beyond reason that this was no temporary escape for the children, that some-how they would be freed completely from Drancy. 'Thank you, dear God. Now I can die.'

She meant it. It seemed an easy thing, now that she no longer had the children to care for, to release her hold on life and slip quietly away, perhaps even before the cattle-wagon into which they were herded at the railway station trundled its way eastwards out of France.

But when she lay back against the rough wooden slats and closed her eyes, she felt fingers tugging at her arms and her legs and her shoulders and her hair. Opening her eyes, she saw she was the only adult in this wagon full of children. Slowly their touch and their cries drew her reluctantly, painfully, back to life.

She reached out and put her arms around as many as possible.

'Be silent, my cabbages,' she said. 'Dry your tears. It's a train we'll be travelling on, not a boat, so who needs a river, eh?'

Some of the nearest children tried to stop their tears. A

263

small boy asked fearfully, 'Will the train take us to Pitchipoi, madame?'

'Who knows where a train goes these days? Only the driver. Do I look like a driver, eh? But don't be afraid, cabbage. Be sure, wherever it takes us, I'm going with you all of the way.'

The wagon lurched forward. The journey had begun. Paris was soon falling behind them, Paris where people were stretching, and yawning, and eating breakfast, and grumbling about the coffee, and going to work; Paris where Günter Mai was already in his staff car, heading to the Majestic, eager to collect the *Ausweis* and the release order for the Simonian children and their grandmother from the horror of Drancy.

15

Three months after Sophie Simonian's train had crawled into the east, the rescued children stood on a cold, wind-swept platform of the Gare de Lyon and prepared to journey south. Once more their destination was the home of their Aunt Mireille in the Ain, and this time the journey made even less sense to Pauli than it had in 1940. Then at least their mother had been going with them.

Towering over the children on the platform, one huge hand resting on each small head, was Michel Boucher. With his beard and locks tousled by the wind, he looked like a red-headed Moses giving them his benison. To protect Janine, not to mention his own interest, Günter Mai had suggested that Boucher be given the credit for obtaining the Drancy release order, and it had made sense to maintain the deception when it came to the children's permit to travel into the Free Zone.

While Boucher had been delighted to play the role of

264

benevolent provider, he hadn't omitted to use the occasion to his own advantage. The children needed an escort, at least as far as Lyon where his sister would meet them. He knew just the man. And there was no need for Mai to worry. He, Boucher, would supply all the necessary identification papers if the German could arrange the *Ausweis*. Although feeling he was being sucked from bending the rules into active illegality, Mai finally agreed, and the result was Monsieur Roger Corder, commercial traveller who stood there, wan-faced, anxious-eyed, in a grey fedora and an astrakhan coat.

Boucher had said, 'For God's sake, Maurice, dump that coat! It's a dead giveaway. You look like a mad poet heading south to die of consumption!'

'Do you know how much this coat cost me?' replied Melchior passionately. 'Nothing! Do you expect me to give up so easily something which was a gift from God?'

Janine had been more than relieved to learn that Melchior was travelling too. Worried at the thought of the children having to make such a long trip by themselves, she had been tempted in many ways to obey Jean-Paul's harsh instruction and Mai's gentler urgings to go with them. But her greater fear was that if she made the trip, she would not have the strength to come back.

She looked at her husband now, so much slighter, so much less flamboyant than Michel Boucher. But to those close enough to feel it, the intensity of passion and menace emanating from that still body made him the group's dominant figure.

He had taken the news of his mother's deportation with the same terrifying immobility of feature. She'd kept it from him as long as possible, waiting till he got some of his strength back. That night, he rose from his sick bed and went out, returning hours later with no explanation. But she noticed that the toes of his heavy boots were stained brown and the backs of his hands were scored with scratches such as a woman's long nails might make trying to loosen a strangler's grip.

Next day there were red and black notices everywhere announcing heavy reprisals for the brutal murder of a German sergeant. Not mentioned, because not thought significant, was the fact that he had been killed at the apartment of a blonde Pigalle prostitute, and that the woman had been throttled so violently that every bone in her throat was shattered.

Since then Jean-Paul seemed to have settled into a creature of stealth, as though acknowledging that to take unnecessary risks might cut short his chosen career of destroying the enemy. Janine and the children he either ignored or looked at with baffled despair like a man watching birds through a barred window.

There was danger here, she could feel it. For herself, she did not mind. But the thought of having the children brought into peril again became too much and finally she had embraced the lesser pain and opted to send them away.

Jean-Paul had not reacted to the decision, but when she added the lie that Boucher was arranging the *Ausweis*, then he reacted.

'That Nazi-loving bastard? No! He's having nothing more to do with us. I don't want his dirty hands getting near anything of mine, do you understand?'

'What do you suggest then? If *we* apply, we just draw attention to ourselves. I want the children safe, not arrested again!'

'I've got friends now. We can get them out,' he said.

'Without risk? Do you guarantee that?'

When he didn't answer she called, 'Pauli.'

The boy came from his bedroom, rubbing his eyes. It looked very convincing, except that the speed of his response suggested he'd been listening rather than sleeping.

'Pauli,' she said. 'We were just talking about what it was like in the Vél d'Hiv and those camps. Your father hasn't heard. Would you like to tell him?'

'Yes, maman,' said the boy.

She hated herself for doing this, but she was determined

266

that the danger to her children was going to be minimized, and that meant travelling on the train with Mai's *Ausweis* rather than wandering round the countryside with any of Jean-Paul's new wild friends.

Pauli described his experiences and his words were all the more powerful because of their matter-of-fact tone.

When he had finished, his father did not speak but turned away, his face working with grief and rage. Then he took the boy in his arms and pressed him close to his chest saying, 'They'll pay, Pauli, that I promise.'

But he no longer objected to Michel Boucher's involvement.

Now at last the time had come for the train to leave. Melchior had gone ahead to claim seats, causing a considerable disturbance by assuring the passengers opposite that if he were not allowed to travel with his back to the engine, he would assuredly vomit on them all the way to Lyon.

Now the children joined him. Whistles blew, flags waved, steam jetted sideways, smoke billowed up. Slowly the locomotive began to move.

Distantly two pairs of eyes observed the scene but did not observe each other. They saw Janine run helplessly a little way after the train, saw the small pale faces of the children, their arms stretched out and waving; saw above them a large adult arm languidly flapping a pale-pink kerchief; saw Jean-Paul turn away like a soldier on parade and begin marching towards the barrier, saw Janine squeeze Boucher's arm then set off after her husband.

The watchers turned away also, Alphonse Pajou because he did not wish to be seen, Günter Mai also because he did not wish to see the pain that must be scored on the woman's face.

He didn't go far, however, and when Michel Boucher came off the platform, whistling a bravura version of *Lili Marlene* full of trills and grace notes, Mai fell into step beside him, though it involved two of his steps to one of the red-head's.

'Lieutenant! So you did come. Hey, listen, come and have some champagne. I'm a father! How about that. The loveliest little girl you ever saw. We're calling her Antoinette. Classy, eh?'

'Very,' said Mai. 'Congratulations. How was everything? On the platform, I mean.'

'Oh, it was fine. That Pauli's cool as a butcher's slab and as long as he's OK, the little girl will go anywhere. They'll make fine cousins for my Antoinette.'

'And Janine?'

'Well, what do you think? Upset naturally, but she'll be OK. She's got strength, that one. No, the only fly in the ointment was that husband of hers. Could hardly talk to me, and after all I've done for the family! I reckon that Boche bullet's left a permanent hole in his head, poor devil. Now, what about that drink?'

'Later,' said Mai. He hesitated then added, 'Perhaps a lot later. Look, Miche, I've got to leave Paris. I've been posted . . .'

'Jesus Mary! Not to the Russian Front?' said Boucher with an alarm which made Mai smile.

'No. I'll still be in France. And I hope to get back here eventually. I just wondered if you'd mention it to your uncle and aunt. I'd hate them to think I was taking my business elsewhere! And to your cousin too, of course. Tell her the file is cleared. She'll understand.'

It was self-interest not sentiment that had made him erase Janine's name from his records, he assured himself. If his successor got interested in what precisely this female agent was doing for the Reich, explanation would not be easy, whereas anyone could explain a small gap in the files.

'Good luck,' said Boucher. 'I'm really going to miss you.'

They shook hands and he walked quickly away.

There, it was done. Perhaps after all it would be better if he never came back to Paris, but he knew that Zeller had been furious when the official notice of his posting came through. It had been rather flattering to hear his superior swear he wouldn't rest till he had his lieutenant back in his section once more. Mai sometimes suspected that Zeller sat on his promotion to keep him close. Well, this time he'd got it. Captain Mai. And with it the highly responsible job of helping to set up a new *Abwehr* centre in Toulouse.

Toulouse. That was why he didn't wish to give the news of his posting to Janine himself. She was bound to ask why it was that he was being posted into the so-called Free Zone to which with his aid she'd just despatched her children for safety.

He could have lied of course. In fact, as an officer of the *Wehrmacht* he was duty bound to lie to an enemy alien. But he'd have had to tell her; and he hadn't the courage to be the man to give her the news which he himself had only learnt the previous day.

Four days hence on November 11th, the twenty-fourth anniversary of that painful armistice, a second Army of Occupation would sweep south to secure the Africa-threatened Mediterranean shore.

The Free Zone and its comparative security would cease to exist.

PART FIVE
March–December 1943

La jeune fille poussa un petit cri: 'Oh! il
m'a piquée sur le menton! Sale petite
bête, vilain petit moustique!' Puis je lui vis
faire un geste vif de la main. 'J'en ai
attrapé un, Werner! Oh! regardez, je vais
le punir: je lui – arrache – les pattes – l'une
– après – l'autre . . .' et elle le faisait . . .

Vercors, *Le silence de la mer*

1

Day broke, grey and cold.

Janine watched it as she had watched many days break that winter. This was her time of despair, but by an effort of will she had not thought possible, she had contrived to make it also a time of renewal. The despair was unavoidable, waking her despite all soporifics between the Gestapo hours of four and five. Recognizing that it was going to destroy her, she had ceased to flee it and had started instead to face and embrace it, squeezing every scrap of inner blackness into a single ball and hurling it away with the sun.

It was far from easy, especially on days like this when there was little promise of sunlight. She lit a cigarette. Previously she had smoked only occasionally. Now she smoked twenty or thirty a day. It was a bad time to acquire the habit but Miche got round this as he got round most shortages. She needed something to massage her taut nerves and did not care to put her control at risk with alcohol.

She was rarely disturbed in her early morning vigils. These days Jean-Paul slept soundly, like a man satisfied with his day's work, or else he was not at home to sleep. Outwardly their relationship was now fairly stable but it was a stability she got little satisfaction from. In the months since the children's departure she had realized just what a softening effect they had had upon their father, just how much of a buffer they had been between herself and Jean-Paul. Sophie's deportation and the children's departure had confirmed him in a role which left only a subordinate place for her. She had accepted it unquestioningly at first. Let nature take its course sounded the best advice. There was even the renewal of their sexual relationship to give further hope. He had come home late one night, flushed from exertion and smelling of cordite, and had taken her before she was hardly awake. This had set the pattern for all subsequent couplings, short, savage, purely physical, a far cry from the slow tender love-making of their early years. From the start she had sensed that there was no path here back to the way things once were, but what other choice did she have? And even now the gleam of his old smile, a brief relapse into his old manner, could set her heart pounding with renewed hope and give her the strength to hold on till dawn when next her terrors roused her early.

Such a moment came unexpectedly this morning.

'Got one of those to spare?' said his voice behind her.

She turned. He had come silently into the kitchen where she was sitting. She had no idea how long he had been watching her.

'Of course,' she said passing over the packet.

He took a cigarette, lit and drew in the smoke with a sigh of pleasure.

'Classy weed this,' he said. 'None of your barber's floor sweepings.'

Often such a comment would have been the prelude to a sarcastic attack on her collaborationist cousin and his blackmarket empire. This morning it was accompanied by a smile of shared enjoyment.

'You're up early,' she said. 'I've put some coffee on. Like some?'

'Please,' he said. 'I've got to go out shortly, that's why I'm up. I was watching you sitting here.'

'Oh, were you?' she said busying herself at the stove.

'You looked, I don't know, as if you were . . . well, you certainly didn't look happy.'

'Didn't I?' she said lightly. She felt at the same time full of happiness and full of tension.

'What were you thinking about? The children?'

'Yes,' she said to keep things simple. 'I miss them so much.'

'I miss them too,' he said with just the faintest hint of surprise. 'And I worry about them.'

'You don't think they're not safe?' she said, fearful that he had heard some news she'd missed about the situation in the Ain. There'd been a period of combined rage and fear when the Boche had occupied the Free Zone so soon after the children's departure. Günter Mai would have suffered if she could have got near him at that moment, and when Miche told her of his posting, it had seemed to her like flight. At first she had wanted to fetch the children home but had been dissuaded. Whatever happened in the old Free Zone, the dangers in Paris hadn't changed, and next time things went wrong there was no Günter Mai to offer his ambivalent help.

Letters from Mireille had reassured her that the German presence in the countryside was minimal and the children were getting on OK with her three boys and at school. It was safer and healthier down there. Why didn't she come to join them?

Paradoxically travel was rather easier now there weren't two zones, but she delayed making even a short visit in case it unsettled the children. Also, to be honest, in case it unsettled herself too much. She didn't trust her strength to make the return. And if she weakened and stayed, what would there be left of their relationship to return to?

'Oh yes, I'm sure they're safe,' he said. 'It's just that they must miss you too, Jan. Why don't you join them?'

Here it was again, the pressure. She felt her moment of happiness slipping away.

'And would you come too?' she asked quietly, pouring the coffee with a steady hand.

'I can't,' he said. 'I have work to do here.'

'Your precious Fishermen, you mean?'

And now the moment was gone completely.

'What do you know about the Fishermen?' he demanded.

'Nothing specific. But I've heard you and Henri talking.

275

Am I supposed to be deaf or something? Or stupid? Or not to be trusted?'

The thought flashed unwanted across her mind that it was easy for her to wax indignant about trust with Günter Mai safely out of the way. She stared defiantly at her husband, expecting anger. Instead he reached to her and took her hands.

'One thing I've learned since coming back is who I can trust,' he said. 'You, Christian, Henri; after that I take care. But I don't want you involved in this any more than I want Christian involved. He leads his own life, serves in his own way. That's what I want for you.'

Only the awareness that this was as close as he'd yet come to expressing real concern for her soothed her irritation at being lumped once again with Valois in his affections.

'I'm your wife, whatever you may or may have not forgotten,' she said. 'While I live with you, of course I'm involved.'

'Yes,' he said nodding, as if she were agreeing with his argument. 'You see what I mean then. Jan, when all this is over then there'll be a time to sit at leisure and mend things. Just now there's no time for ourselves, no time for *personal* relationships. We can't afford to divert energies.'

Before she could respond he looked at his watch and said, 'See what I mean? Now I've got to go. You'll think about what we've said?'

He was gone with a swiftness which was typical, leaving Janine holding the percolator from which she had not yet filled her own cup.

Well, at least it had been a real conversation, even if the net outcome was that he wanted her to leave. Perhaps she was wrong and everyone else was right. Perhaps he would be better off, safer even, in Paris by himself while she took care of the children at Mireille's.

These thoughts stayed with her as she got ready and set off for the boulangerie. She had tried to get a job after the children went but there was little call for her skill of pastry

276

cooking in these days of shortages. So she helped in the shop and the bakehouse first thing in the morning. There was very little to do there either and she knew it was simply a device by which her parents could subsidize her. Jean-Paul seemed to have other sources of subsidy. Les Pêcheurs. The Fishermen. Such a childish name. She could only guess the kind of work they did. Sabotage, theft, disruption. Perhaps it needed to be done but it seemed to have precious little effect on the stranglehold the Boche had on Paris.

She was on foot. Jean-Paul had taken the bicycle they shared. Despite the fact that spring was officially here, the morning was gloomy and a thin cold rain had begun to fall. Normally she would have walked to the shop but today the weather drove her into the métro. The nearest station to the bakery was in the Boulevard Raspail, not far from the Lutétia. She thought again of Mai. There was no reason why they should ever meet again so she could look objectively at the relationship. On balance she had profited largely from it, there was no doubt of that. On one side, her husband and her children safe; on the other, one act of sex and the threat, since removed, of having her name on an *Abwehr* agent list.

'Janine!'

Alarmed by the sudden summons she halted uncertainly. She was just off the boulevard in a side-street. A man was standing in a doorway at the corner. He leaned forward slightly out of the shadows and was instantly recognizable as Miche Boucher.

'Miche. What are you up to?'

'Saving your life mebbe,' he said. 'Do you always wander round in a dream?'

'I'm on my way to the bakery,' she said, piqued. 'What are you hiding from, Miche? The flics?'

The gibe stung.

'Listen, lady, can't you get it into your head that I'm on the side of the law now?' he said indignantly.

'Hiding in doorways?'

277

'On watch,' he corrected. 'We've had a tip that some bunch of terrorists are planning to hit a staff-car. We're here to clear up the mess.'

He opened his expensive jacket dramatically and showed her a Luger in a shoulder holster.

'You mean after they've attacked the car? Why don't you just warn the men in it?'

It was a good question and one which Boucher had put to Pajou.

'Because one of the guys in the car is that jumped-up *Abwehr* poof, Zeller,' Pajou had said with relish. 'Basically old Fiebelkorn don't mind how many *Abwehr* shits get hurt so long as we sort out these terrorists afterwards. Why do you think it's us lot on this job? Whatever happens, Fiebelkorn gets all the credit and none of the blame.'

Boucher didn't try to explain any of this to Janine.

'Never you mind, just move on quick. This won't be a safe place to be very shortly. Oh, shit.'

In a window overlooking the boulevard a man struck a match to light a cigarette. This was the signal. The staff-car was in sight. Grabbing hold of Janine, Boucher drew her roughly into the doorway.

'Stay there,' he ordered. 'Keep back.'

As the car approached their intersection, a cyclist wobbled out of a narrow entry on the other side of the road. He looked like a workman on his way to work. His dirty old raincoat was sodden wet and over his shoulders was a canvas tool bag.

He seemed to be having trouble with his brakes and slid sideways on the greasy road right into the path of the German car. It skidded to a halt alongside the fallen cyclist. The driver leaned out of the window and began shouting. The two officers in the back looked unconcerned. The cyclist rose with difficulty and started yelling back at the driver.

And then another cyclist appeared, a gendarme. Attracted by the commotion, he halted on the other side of the car, saluted the officer and started asking questions.

278

'What the hell's that idiot doing?' groaned Boucher. 'Never around when you want the buggers but the moment you don't . . .'

The gendarme addressed the workman, who grumblingly stooped and picked up the bicycle. Another salute to the officers and the two cyclists moved slowly away alongside each other. The car started up and set off in the opposite direction.

'Trust the flics to cock everything up,' groaned Boucher stepping out of the doorway and looking desperately for some signal to indicate the next move.

And then in the same instant two things struck him.

The workman no longer had his tool bag. And there had been something dragging along beneath the car.

He opened his mouth to yell, but his words were drowned by a huge explosion followed by the scream of tearing metal and a second flash as the petrol tank went up.

The two cyclists stood on the pedals and raced away up the boulevard. But now the trap was sprung as Pajou's men came out of a building ahead of them and began blazing away with machine-pistols. The gendarme was hit instantly and went flying over his handlebars. The workman wrenched his bike round, the front wheel rearing as though he were riding a horse. He held himself low and bumped up the pavement to give himself the protection of the lamp-posts. Windows shattered alongside him as the stream of bullets whiplashed in pursuit.

Boucher's Luger was out. The fugitive was being driven straight towards him. Janine had come out of the doorway and was standing close behind, watching with horror.

'Right, you bastard,' said Boucher raising his gun.

And Janine cried, 'Miche! No!' and flung her arms around his body, as the cyclist went hurtling past them down the side-street and out of view.

Shaking himself free, Boucher turned to Janine and said disbelievingly, 'That was him. That was your husband, wasn't it?'

She nodded, hardly able to speak from the shock.

'Did you know, Jan?' demanded Boucher. 'Quick. Tell me!'

She shook her head and gasped, 'No, Miche, I swear it.'

Men came running up, among them Pajou.

'What the fuck are you playing at, Miche? You must have been within spitting distance of him.'

'Spit was all I could do,' said Boucher. 'Bloody gun jammed.'

'Yeah? Did you get a look at his face?'

'Not much. He was all muffled up.'

'Great.' His eyes turned suspiciously towards Janine. 'Who's this?'

'My cousin, Janine. She works close by. I saw her and told her to keep her head down.'

Another man joined them.

'The one we got's dead,' he reported. 'Also the car driver and one of the officers. The other one's still alive, the major. But he's all smashed up. Burnt too. He'll be lucky to make it. Or maybe not so lucky.'

'That should please the boss anyway,' said Pajou. 'Better get back and report. Coming, Miche?'

'I'll catch you up.'

He waited till his companions were out of earshot then said disbelievingly, 'Look, Jan, are you sure you had no idea what Jean-Paul was up to?'

'Of course I had some idea,' she retorted. 'But I didn't realize . . .'

'That it involved blowing people to pieces?' Boucher completed the sentence for her. 'One thing's sure; he'll get caught or killed sooner or later. Get out while you can. The Gestapo won't believe you're not in it too. Join the kids at Mireille's place and sit the war out there, that's the wise move.'

Of course it was the wise move. She'd heard it from both sides now so it must be so. But now more than ever she knew she had to stay. Her cousin had finished her sentence wrongly. It wasn't the slaughter, shocking though it was, that had appalled her. It had been the sight of

Jean-Paul's face as he raced past. Fear she would have expected to see there, and perhaps even excitement. But all that she had seen was wild exultation, a glow of sheer joy, giving him the face of a prophet who had just been vouchsafed a vision of paradise and was now more careless than ever of the grey shadows of mortal existence.

There was no way that she could think of leaving him now.

2

'Hey, Paris-piglet!'

Pauli Simonian ignored the cry. He was sitting on a stone by a pond watching a flotilla of ducks and wondering what it must be like to spend most of your life with your legs and belly in cold dirty water.

'Are you deaf as well as stupid, *youpin*?'

It was Christophe calling, the youngest of 'Aunt' Mireille's three sons. The two older boys had accepted the arrival of the newcomers with indifference, but Christophe, a burly nine-year-old, had been antagonistic from the start. Somehow he'd picked up that their father was a Jew and he'd taken to calling Pauli *yid* and *youpin*. A clout round the ears from Mireille had shut him up at home, but his persecution continued at school, and set the pattern for the other children's attitude to Pauli. He bore the abuse stoically, happy to see that Céci's open, guileless nature had worked its usual charm and made her everybody's friend.

'See if your dirty ears can hear that then!'

A stone struck the water in front of him, splashing droplets in his face. Another larger one followed. Céci, playing a few yards away, looked up in delight at this new game and laughed merrily. But the next stone hurled by Christophe went astray and instead of splashing Pauli, sent a spray of cold water over his sister. Laughs turned to sobs. She began to move away from the water's edge, slipped, fell to the muddy ground, and cried even harder. Pauli rose, fists clenched. Christophe, seeing that he had at last found a way of stinging his unwanted 'cousin', now began to aim at Céci. Pauli ran towards the other boy, who regarded his approach with pleasurable anticipation. A year older, two inches taller and a stone heavier, Christophe didn't doubt he could put the Paris-piglet in his place. He planted his feet firmly in the earth, leaned slightly forward and raised his already brawny arms to ward off the expected frontal onslaught.

Instead, Pauli came to a halt a couple of feet in front of him, then with great force and accuracy kicked his cousin just beneath the left kneecap.

Christophe screeched in pain and hopped on his right leg which Pauli's right foot immediately scythed from under him. He fell on his back. Pauli dropped both knees into his belly and proceeded to beat him savagely about the chest. Finally, still not having uttered a word, he rose and, leaving his blubbering cousin prostrate on the dank grass, he went to collect Céci and took her back to the farmhouse to get dry.

Next morning at school, Pauli approached Christophe and addressed him in a friendly fashion. Normally Christophe would have replied with scornful abuse. Today he hesitated. A playground fight no longer seemed the attractive proposition it once had. To everyone's surprise, when he replied his tone was almost as friendly as Pauli's though his mind stored up its resentment.

After that, things got much better. Pauli still didn't make any close friends but as long as Céci was happy, most of the time he preferred to be alone. Soon he was almost as familiar with the surrounding countryside as he'd been with the streets of Paris.

Mireille was at first unhappy about his long absences.

'Janine said he was a bit of a wanderer, but that was in the town where he knew his way around.'

'Less chance of coming to harm in the country,' said her

husband with the sympathy of one independent mind for another.

'Less chance than in the town? What do you know about it, you don't spend more time in the village than you have to!' mocked his wife.

'I went to Paris once and look what happened to me there,' said Lucien Laurentin. It had been during a holiday visit to Paris that he'd met, wooed and married Mireille in the course of a week. That had been twelve years ago. She had borne him a son in each of the first three years of marriage and local opinion was cautiously moving towards the possibility that Laurentin might have done all right for himself.

'Well, keep an eye out for him in your wanderings. There's too many wild men with shotguns up in the hills for my liking.'

It was a double-edged remark. Since the Occupation there'd been a steady trickle of men taking to the hills and woods. Their reasons varied but their cause was common: hatred of the Boche. These were the Maquis. At first the largest threat many of them offered was to tobacconist shops, which they raided whenever the cigarette ration came in. But as organization improved, they began to prick the Germans with acts of sabotage and there'd already been reprisals against the families of men known to be involved.

'I promised you, I'm not going to join,' said Laurentin wearily. 'I'll not put my family at risk for a gesture. But these lads have got families too. I've known their mams and dads since I was a boy. I'll not turn my back on them. Dropping the odd sack of vegetables is the least I can do.'

'As long as it stops at that,' said Mireille who had observed how deep these country loyalties could go and was determined to put her family first.

'I'm going up today,' said Laurentin bluntly. 'Old Rom will be working in the barn if you want anything.'

Rom was the farm labourer, a taciturn man of unguessable years.

Despite the burden of a sack over his shoulder, the farmer made his way rapidly up into the hills which rose gently at first on all sides of the farm. After half an hour he stopped for a breather, resting against the vegetable sack.

Twenty yards behind, Pauli halted too. His heart was pounding from exertion and excitement. He guessed where his uncle was going and was longing to glimpse these wild outlaws the boys at school talked or, if they were lucky, boasted about. He lay on the cold earth and watched the outline of the knobbly sack against which his uncle was reclining in the long grass. Above, grey clouds played with a pale sun, alternating patches of dark and bright across the rolling landscape. He lay in sunlight but now a shadow swept over him, more intense somehow than a cloud's shadow, and he screamed like a young rabbit in terror as the nape of his neck was seized by a strong hand and he was dragged roughly to his feet.

'Watch the beast not the burden,' said Laurentin's voice in his ear. 'Next man you follow may reckon it's safer to blast away with his shotgun than come crawling back here to trap you live.'

He released the boy whose legs felt so weak he almost collapsed back to the ground. But he forced himself to stay upright and stood looking silently at his uncle, waiting for his verdict.

'Straight back to the farm,' ordered Laurentin. 'Don't mention this to anyone, least of all your aunt. Understood?'

'Yes sir,' said Pauli.

'Then go. I want to see you run.'

Twenty minutes later a breathless Pauli came running down the long meadow which sloped towards the farmhouse just as an old truck spluttered into sight round the bend of the farm track.

Non-military vehicles were rare enough to bring Mireille to the door and old Rom out of the barn. The truck halted noisily. There were two men in it, one round and gross and untidy, the other small, slim and dapper. This one got out first, leaping nimbly to the ground.

'Madame, how pleasant to meet you again,' he said

walking up to Mireille. 'How are you? Do you hear from that reprobate brother of yours?'

As recognition struggled into Mireille's face, Pauli arrived, driving his flagging legs into a sprint.

'Monsieur Melchior! Monsieur Melchior!' he cried.

'Monsieur Corder, you mean,' said Melchior reprovingly, but he smiled as he swept the delighted boy up into his arms.

Two minutes later, he was seated in the kitchen drinking coffee with his companion whom he'd introduced as his business partner, Octave Timbal.

'But monsieur, when you left the children with me at the station last year, I thought you said you were travelling on to Marseille?'

'Such was my plan,' said Melchior. 'But first I needed rest. My nerves were quite ragged. I took a room in the Hôtel Terminus just across from the station. A short respite of perfect peace, then on I would go to join the dear matelots of Marseille. Can you imagine how I felt a few days later when I heard this dreadful din of grinding engines and marching feet and looked out of my window to see the Cours de Verdun filling up with the fearful Hun? How it took me back to 1940. Naturally I tried to leave but they had taken over the station and all travel was restricted. Worse, when I returned to the Terminus, they had taken that over too and my luggage was in the lobby. Naturally I refused to pay my bill. I found other lodgings and resolved to leave as soon as things settled. But it soon became apparent that it wasn't just Lyon which had been infested but the whole of France. Why flee when there is nowhere to flee to?'

'So what did you do, monsieur?' asked Mireille, delighted after so many years of slow country conversation to be hearing this rapid, lively Parisian flow again.

'Happily I make friends easily. Also I had a few sous set aside for emergencies. So eventually I decided to set up in business with my dear friend Octave here.'

Mireille had been eyeing Timbal with some misgiving.

He had risen from the table and started wandering round the room, peering into cupboards and drawers. Now he went out into the yard and seemed to be examining the barn and the byre.

'And what is your business?' asked Mireille, beginning to guess.

'Retailing,' said Melchior. 'We bring surpluses and shortages together, particularly in the field of fresh comestibles.'

'You mean you're in the black market,' said Mireille.

Melchior spread his hands and smiled.

'We are suppliers,' he said. 'Octave was fortunate enough to get a small supply of petrol from a grateful client. We decided to invest it in a buying trip into the countryside and I recalled that you lived somewhere in this vicinity and I thought how nice it would be to see my young friends again.'

He ruffled Céci's hair and winked at Pauli.

'And you thought we might have something to sell, eh?' said Mireille.

'Good Lord. It never crossed my mind. But of course if there should happen to be anything . . . a ham perhaps, some fresh vegetables . . . we would offer the very best price, or even better to a friend.'

Mireille began to laugh. Melchior joined in. Soon the children, not knowing what they were laughing at, but with spirits lifted by this visitor from their previous life, were laughing too.

Now Mireille lowered her voice and said, 'All right. But I'll want a favour. Janine's coming to see the children soon. She says she'd rather see them in Lyon than come out to the farm. Something about getting more time with them that way, but I reckon . . . well, that's family business. But if you could find somewhere for them to stay a few days in town, somewhere half-decent . . .'

'My pleasure,' said Melchior.

'Thanks,' said Mireille rising. 'Now let's see what we can find.'

They went out into the yard. Most of the clouds had cleared now and the sunshine was beginning to have some warmth in it.

Céci had taken Melchior's hand and as he stood and enjoyed the sun on his face, he felt his free hand grasped too.

He looked down and smiled.

'You see, Pauli, everything works out for the best. Bearing gifts of gold, that's me, my boy. Never forget it. I think I've fallen on my feet at last!'

3

Early in the summer Günter Mai returned to Paris.

The *Abwehr* chief at the Lutétia said, 'I'm sorry if you feel mucked around, Mai, but Bruno Zeller was always adamant that you knew as much about the work in his section as he did.'

Mai smiled secretly at the under-estimate.

'How is the major?' he asked.

'Lucky to be alive. Or perhaps not,' said the chief, an anxious, melancholy man with the look of an overworked academic. 'He's lost his right arm and the best part of his left foot and he was badly burnt about the face and the upper torso. They've shipped him back home for treatment.'

Mai felt a cowardly relief. He had not relished the thought of visiting that once handsome young man whose elegance and poise he had always resented.

'Anything special I ought to know, sir?' he asked.

'It'll all be in the files,' came the reply. Mai doubted it.

'And our friends in the Rue des Saussaies and Avenue Foch, how are they?'

'Cock-a-hoop that they caught Moulin,' said the chief gloomily.

Jean Moulin had been de Gaulle's emmissary, given the

task which he'd almost accomplished of co-ordinating the various conflicting arms of the Resistance. He'd been caught in Lyon and had died under interrogation.

'Caught and killed,' said Mai. 'Before he told anything, I gather.'

'It still comes out as a triumph. We'll have to be alert, Mai, or they'll steal all our thunder.'

Was the man a fool, or just ultra-cautious? wondered Mai as he returned to his room. The battle with the SD was long lost. All they could do now was fight the rearguard action with enough spirit to gain an honourable settlement, preferably somewhere not on the Eastern Front.

His conclusions about the way things were going were confirmed as he slipped back into his old work. Perhaps his short absence had wrought large change or perhaps simply sharpened his perception. But Paris was now definitely the capital of a conquered country and the techniques of persuasion had been abandoned almost entirely in favour of the threat of terror. The pretence of partnership had gone; the hope of neutralization was dead; they had lost France just as certainly as they were losing Italy. News of these external defeats had had its inevitable effect upon the great passive majority of the people. Content to make the best of the Occupation, or even a profit out of it, when it seemed a permanency, now the good burghers of Paris were cautiously shifting some of their eggs into the Resistance basket.

Others felt the shift in the wind too. It wasn't that hope was greater. If anything the German grip was tighter than ever before. But none but the out-and-out fascists could still pretend that the stranglehold was a loving embrace, and when hope lay in only one direction, that's where you had to look.

This gentle shift made Christian Valois even more unhappy with his role. In obedience to Delaplanche's command, he had almost broken off contact with the Simonians, but he knew that Jean-Paul had cobbled together his own group out of what was left of André's after the canal fiasco, and every reference to Les Pêcheurs filled him with envy. The memory of his one piece of action, the shooting in the métro, now seemed like an adolescent's day-dream. He sought out Theo Laffay who'd been his group leader then, pretending the encounter was accidental. The man looked weary and ill but his mind was still sharp enough to see through Valois's pretence.

'If you don't vanish from my sight in thirty seconds, I'll have to ring Delaplanche,' he said not unkindly. 'Grow up, eh, kid?'

Valois had felt angry and ashamed. The following week he had visited his parents for a few days. Vichy was now a dead and dispirited place. Since the occupation of the Free Zone its function was manifestly an empty pretence. He found his father silent and depressed, his mother drinking too much, and even Marie-Rose seemed off-hand and self-absorbed. He pressed her to tell him what was the matter but all that she replied was, 'I've just got to get away from here.'

'Come and see me in Paris,' he said. 'At least that should be OK now there's no Free Zone.'

To his surprise she shook her head.

'I can't,' she said. 'Not yet. Soon perhaps.'

'Why? Is there something the matter?' he asked.

She shook her head and laughed but as he sat on the train home the sense that Marie-Rose was no longer completely open with him was a further cause for depression.

Coming out from the platform in Paris, a man collided with him and forced him into an involuntary embrace.

As he tried to pull loose, Jean-Paul's voice hissed in his ear, 'It's me, idiot. Head for the old bistro by the Cluny.'

Then he was gone.

There was no doubting where he meant. The bistro near the Cluny Museum had been a haunt of their student days. But what he meant was something else. By the time he reached the bistro, his mind had invented a hundred reasons, all bad.

Jean-Paul was there already with two drinks in front of him.

'What's happened?' asked Valois, sitting down and trying to conceal his anxiety. 'All this cloak and dagger, it
must be important.'

'It is. They've taken Laffay.'

'Oh shit! What happened?'

'There was a meeting. It was blown. One guy didn't
appear. Presumably they got him and kicked his balls till
he talked. They shot another. With a bit of luck, he's dead.
But Theo got taken, alive and well.'

'Theo won't talk,' said Valois certainly. 'He'd die first.'

'Don't talk shit,' said Simonian contemptuously. 'Everyone talks. Twenty-four hours is what we usually expect to
be given. Hold out for twenty-four hours, then spill your
guts out. Trouble is, the Gestapo know this as well, so
they do everything possible to start the talking earlier. In
this case I reckon they've got Theo's family. I rang to warn
them. There was no reply. He's a very uxorious man, this
Laffay. His wife screaming in the next room may loosen
his tongue ahead of schedule.'

'Good God. I'd better warn Delaplanche!'

Valois began to rise. Simonian grabbed his arm and
pulled him down.

'Sod Delaplanche,' he said wearily. 'He can look after
himself. He's a big man, too big to go under easily. Some
day, they'll send the Géstapistes in to blow him up, maybe.
Meanwhile, he'll get by. No, it's you I'm here to warn.
Theo knows about you, right?'

'He's met me,' said Valois, suddenly cautious.

'Don't go coy! He knows about your Boche, doesn't he?
He was there! Don't look surprised. I'll tell you something
about me, Christian. Nine months ago I was taking risks
that make me shudder when I think about them now. But
I've learned a lot. And one of the things I learned is to
reconnoitre your allies as thoroughly as your enemies. So
I know about Theo. And he knows about you!'

'But we only met briefly. In his eyes, I'm not important
at all,' protested Valois.

'Perhaps not. But he'll be grabbing for scraps to feed

those bastards by the time they finish with him. And once he mentions that you killed one of them . . . !'

Valois picked up his empty glass and attempted to suck the last few drops out of it.

'What shall I do?' he asked desperately.

'Lie low. Ring your office, tell them you've had to stay in Vichy – sick relative, anything. Come and stay at my place for a couple of days. We'll watch and wait. Perhaps it will blow over. Cheer up, old friend, there's always a silver lining.'

'You say so? Well, show it to me.'

Simonian grinned. He looked young, carefree, like the student who had so often sat in this very bistro those few, short, life-long years ago. Valois felt a small surge of hope. Perhaps his friend had some genuine consolation to offer.

'I told you I know all about my allies,' said Simonian. 'Well, Theo has a heart condition. With a bit of luck, you're so unimportant that his ticker will give out before he dredges you up!'

4

It was strange to be living under the same roof as Janine again. Last time it had been his roof, and she had always been on the defensive. Also the children had been there, and her mind had been preoccupied with doubts and fears about her newly returned husband.

The doubts and fears had not diminished but Valois could tell they had changed. Jean-Paul was a different man, full of life and energy, constantly on the move. He had found a role and was living it to the full. But he was not the same man Valois had known in the old days; there was a new hardness and to make room, something gentle and loving and sensitive had had to give way.

He spent a whole week closeted in the Simonians' apartment, much of it alone with Janine.

'Should I be here?' he asked anxiously. 'Wouldn't it be better to put me in a safe-house somewhere? I don't want to bring you danger.'

Simonian had laughed.

'If they come looking for you here, we're all in danger anyway,' he said. 'And this way, I don't waste a good safe-house. You know where I live already!'

'He's enjoying all this,' he said to Janine as they sat together one night.

'Yes.'

She'd gone very quiet, very introspective, as if her husband's vitality had been derived, vampirishly, from her own veins.

'But you're not?'

'I live in fear,' she said very simply. 'Night and day, waking and sleeping. I have nightmares full of terror and when I wake up, the terror wakes with me. I didn't think you could grow used to terror, but I have.'

He wanted to reach across and take her in his arms but he knew that this would be useless. All her passion was reserved for Jean-Paul.

He suddenly came close to hating his friend.

'What are you afraid of?' he asked. 'That he'll be caught?'

'Yes, but not just that,' she said. 'I'm not so saintly that I don't fear for my own sake. In fact, I sometimes think that Jean-Paul would quite like to be caught so that he could tell the Boche just how many of them he has killed. But what I really fear is what they may do to me to make me tell what I know.'

'What *do* you know?' Valois asked gently.

'About Jean-Paul? Next to nothing!' she answered. 'I've stopped myself from knowing, stopped myself from hearing, though I can't stop from guessing.'

'But if you don't know anything, why be so afraid?'

'Because the only way to stop the pain is to tell them

what you do know,' she said patiently as if to an idiot. 'If you've nothing to tell, the pain goes on for ever. So I fear I would tell them something. Anything. *Everything!*'

'What?' he asked, smiling despite himself at her earnestness.

'I don't know. About you perhaps. Or about my parents. But what I fear most of all is that I'd tell them about the children.'

'What's to tell about the children?' he said in surprise.

'Their father is a Jew and a Resistant. Their grandmother has been deported. They left Paris on an illegal *Ausweis*. Their mother is . . .'

'What?'

'What's it matter what their mother is?' she asked sharply. 'She'll be the one who'll be doing the telling.'

He reached over and took her hands in his.

'Janine, don't upset yourself like this,' he urged. 'They're not interested in the kids, honestly. Why should they be? They've other things to worry about.'

'They arrested them and put them in Drancy, didn't they?' she demanded.

It was unanswerable. He said, 'Janine, you went to see the kids last month. OK, I know you don't like to talk about it, but tell me one thing. How could you bear to come back?'

She stared at him resentfully. It was true. She could hardly bear to think let alone talk about her short visit. The way Céci's face had crumpled as she got on the train . . . and Pauli's eyes . . .

'Why don't you go back now and stay on there?' Valois pressed.

'Because! Because I might take danger with me where there is none now. Because I don't know what might happen here if I left!'

She jerked her hands up to cover her face. He didn't release them instantly but let his own hands be drawn up with them, so that when he did loosen his grip it seemed natural to run his fingers through her hair.

'It'll be all right,' he said. 'I know it will. This can't go on for ever. You and the children will be together again soon, I'm sure of it. How are they anyway? You've got to talk about them. Honestly it does no good bottling things up.'

With a great effort she said, 'Yes, you're right. You usually are. It's me. I'm so weak. You know I didn't go out to the farm? I stayed in Lyon and Mireille brought the children in to be with me. I said it was to give us more time together. Liar! It was because I didn't trust myself to . . . but next time, Christmas, perhaps things will be better . . . Mireille gave me a photo. Would you like to see it?'

She rose, breaking the contact. He looked at his hands as though he'd just let a precious fragile vase slip out of his grip.

'See. Those are Mireille's three boys, they're older than my two, of course. And there's Pauli and Céci. Look at her smiling, she's always smiling and laughing. Not Pauli though. He's like his father . . .'

Valois looked at the frowning intensity of the boy's expression. He seemed to be looking beyond the camera as if disdaining to acknowledge its existence.

So he would probably look at a firing squad.

The thought was so macabre he felt for a moment he'd said it out loud. It must be these crazy times that brought such thoughts into his head. But surely the very craziness of the times meant that ordinary patterns of behaviour no longer applied? In a world where boys might face firing squads, grown men were foolish not to speak their hearts while they still had the chance.

He reached forward to take her hand once more and looked deep into her eyes.

'Janine,' he said.

A door opened and banged shut.

Valois let her go and sat back in his chair. She remained where he left her, pulled slightly forward, regarding him with bewilderment.

The room door opened.

'Here you are then. Very comfortable you look!' proclaimed Jean-Paul. 'Very cosy. Pity you can't stay longer, Christian.'

'Can't . . . ?'

'No need to. It's been confirmed. Poor old Theo's heart gave out three days ago. There's been no sign of the Geste round at your place. So it looks as if everything's clear. You can go home and resume the even tenor of your ways!'

'*Now*, you mean? *Tonight?*'

He must have sounded querulous, like an old man frightened of being pushed out on to some long and perilous journey rather than a young man being invited to take a short métro trip home. The Simonians glanced at each other and shared their amusement, an event rare enough to surprise them both and to fill Valois with resentful jealousy.

All the way back to his apartment the picture remained with him. Jean-Paul with his arm draped loosely over Janine's shoulders, she smiling with pleasure at the contact, he with that expression of mocking bewilderment he used to wear when he was puncturing his friend's student pomposity.

If the Gestapo had been waiting for him he'd have walked straight into their hands. He found himself putting the key into the lock with no recollection of how he'd got there.

Well, it was too late to worry now. If the Boche got him, maybe that would wipe the smile off their faces!

He went inside. The place felt cold, unused. He closed the blinds and put the lights on. It was just as he'd left it. A half-full coffee cup stood on the telephone table reminding him that as usual he'd left in a rush, fearful of missing his train.

He poured himself a drink and walked around. It was good to be back, he decided. Good to get out of that poky little flat in the Quartier Mouffetard. A man got silly ideas cooped up like that. Obsessions rubbed off and by Christ, the Simonians were certainly an obsessive pair! There was Jean-Paul, reduced by rage and mental damage to playing at gangsters. And Janine, the little shop-girl, who only lived through her connection with this madman . . .

He paused in front of a mirror and regarded his reflection

for almost a minute. He looked pale and unkempt but it was deeper than this that his gaze was trying to penetrate.

'You mealy-mouthed shit,' he said finally. 'Tell the truth to yourself at least. You are sick with envy of his courage, his role, and you're even sicker with desire to bed his wife. But you won't do anything about it. You won't do anything about *anything*!'

He felt an impulse to hurl the glass at the mirror, but it would have been artifice, a contrived gesture, not in his nature.

The telephone rang, startling him out of his little self-dramatization.

He picked it up but did not speak. His mouth was dry.

A voice said, 'You all right?'

It was Jean-Paul. 'Yes, I'm fine. Look I really didn't say how grateful I was . . .'

'That's OK. Go to bed.' The phone went dead.

Bed. It was good advice. Suddenly he realized he was exhausted.

He awoke to darkness and the sound of rain lashing the window-panes and a wind rattling a badly closed door. He glanced at the luminous dial of his watch. It was five a.m. Gestapo time.

He pushed the unpleasant thought from his mind and rolled over.

In a corner of the room a torch flashed on.

He sat up, holding his hand against the jet of light.

'Mr Valois, so you've come home,' said a soft, friendly voice. 'I said you would. Don't go crashing into his flat, I said, smashing up his nice things, tearing up the floor-boards. What would a nice young man, son of a deputy, be hiding there, anyway?'

'Who are you? What do you want?' demanded Christian fearfully.

'Come now. You can answer both those questions yourself. Just as I was able to say, watch and wait, watch and wait. When all seems safe, he'll come wandering home. And here you are, as I forecast.'

Valois struggled out of bed. The torch was his enemy. He plunged towards the disc of light. A forearm caught him round the throat. A knee drove into his crutch. His mouth gaped wide, gasping to take in air, to let screams out. A gloved hand fastened on it and squeezed so tight he thought his cheeks would tear. His nostrils sucked in air, but not enough. He saw the torch disc dwindle to a pin-point as a new darkness invaded his sight.

'Now let us go quietly,' said the soft voice. 'No need to disturb the neighbours, is there?'

5

Mai sat under the great cedar in the Jardin des Plantes and filled his pipe for the third time. A bitter damp wind was rasping through the bare branches making it hard to light the pipe which in any case tasted sour from oversmoking. The few people who had passed him in the last hour had glanced at him with amusement, clearly thinking he was a lover who'd been stood up. Good cover, except that that was just what he felt like.

Since his return to Paris he had only seen Janine distantly but he had been kept up-to-date on her by her cousin, Miche, with whom he'd resumed the old relationship.

Then Miche had passed on a problem.

'That stuck-up mate of hers, Valois, he's gone missing it seems. She seems to think he might have got himself arrested, God knows why. I've checked as best I can. No trace, but there's a lot of people doing a lot of arresting these days.'

'And she asked you to ask me?'

'No. That was my idea. Would you mind asking around?'

'You've got a cheek!' said Mai. Inside, he was suddenly hit by a powerful desire to see Janine again.

He said, 'All right. I'll see what I can do. But she'll have to come herself. Tell her tomorrow afternoon, three o'clock, the usual place.'

'The usual place?' Boucher raised his eyebrows and grinned. 'We'll make a Frenchman out of you yet!'

A fool was all that had been made out of him, thought Mai gloomily looking at his watch. It was four.

He got up stiffly and set off down the steep path. As he turned the corner at the bottom of the slope, there she was, standing by the railings.

'You're late,' he said shortly.

'This wasn't my idea. I didn't have to come.'

'Why did you?'

She thought seriously of the answers she wasn't going to give. She was worried sick about Christian, but Jean-Paul seemed to regard her concern as a kind of self-indulgence, reserving all real feeling to himself. Her attempts to win a role in the hunt for information had been dismissed and she found herself expected to be available in the kitchen at all hours to provide Les Pêcheurs with coffee and food. They'd moved out of the Quartier Mouffetard as soon as they realized Christian had vanished and were now living in a dilapidated flat in Clichy. It had seemed clever to try to steal a march on the men by asking Miche for help, but her reaction when he told her about Mai had been anger. She didn't want to get involved there again.

But today, furious at being left alone after an urgent message had taken Jean-Paul from the flat without explanation and scarcely a farewell, she had gone out herself. In direct contravention of her husband's instructions, she had headed back to the old apartment. By the time she got there, discretion had returned and she had resisted the temptation to go in and pick up some more of her things. Then, though she'd resolved not to keep the appointment with Mai, finding herself so near the Jardin, she'd come here anyway.

She said, 'Curiosity. And Miche said you offered to find out about Christian.'

'Offered?'

298

'Look, I'm not buying, not this time,' she said.

'And I'm not selling. Your friend was arrested by the Gestapo. He is presently in Fresnes Prison, unharmed as far as I can ascertain.'

Taken aback by the ease with which she'd got the information, she stammered a thank you.

'What for? It's not good news. And please don't tell me he's innocent. Even more, don't tell me he's guilty. I know that already and I don't want any details.'

'If you're so sure, why are you helping me?'

'Why do you think?'

'I don't know. Because you still hope you can turn me into a collabo like Miche?'

He laughed to hide his absurd hurt.

'That would require surgery,' he said. 'So, you're convinced Germans aren't capable of altruism?'

'I'm not sure what Germans are capable of,' she said in a low voice.

'Just Germans? It was *your* gendarmes who rounded up your kids and put them in Drancy.'

'There are always idiots who will follow orders,' she said dismissively. 'But you've got to be sick or evil to give those orders.'

'And which am I?' he asked. 'Sick or evil?'

'Not evil,' she replied at once. 'But to be part of it, even just to be on the very edge of it, you must be just a little bit sick, I think.'

'You do, do you?' said Mai feeling himself driven into a corner by the simple intensity of her reasoning. 'And what does Nurse Simonian prescribe as the cure for this sickness?'

He saw a smile touch her lips at his effort to escape into ponderous sarcasm.

'Simple,' she said. 'I would prescribe a long, long rest. At home.'

He opened his mouth to destroy her with some fine German metaphysic but instead he let out a huge roar of laughter. And after a moment, seeing that it was her joke he was laughing at and not her, she joined in.

'Thank you for coming to give me this consultation,' he said, still chuckling. 'I'll pass your recommendations on to my superiors.'

She took his amusement as the cue for release.

'Now I must go,' she said. 'Goodbye.'

She turned away but he was alongside her in a couple of paces.

'Not so quick,' he said, taking her elbow. 'Where're you rushing off to?'

'Home,' she said.

'You kept me waiting for an hour,' he said. 'I'm very cold and rather damp. What I need is hot coffee laced with brandy and in addition I claim at least ten minutes of the hour of your company you've cheated me out of.'

She said, 'Really, I can't.'

'Think about it as we walk through the Jardin,' he said. 'How are the children? Miche tells me you went to see them.'

'Yes. It wasn't easy arranging it but Miche helped. Mireille brought them to Lyon and we stayed a few days in a boarding house. They were fine, really fine.'

He could tell it was painful for her to talk about them.

'Why not go to the farm?' he asked.

'It seemed better. This way I could have them to myself . . .'

And also he guessed she'd wanted to avoid the additional pressure likely to be on her at the farm to make her stay permanent.

Could this fellow Simonian have any idea of the demands he was making on her love and loyalty? Obviously not. From what Boucher reported, he seemed as keen as anyone for his wife to join the children.

'I'll stay at the farm next time,' she went on. 'I'd like to go at Christmas.'

'Let me know,' he said. 'I'll fix the travel papers. And before you ask, no conditions. Except perhaps that coffee.'

As they passed through the exit from the Jardin, she said, 'All right. Ten minutes. No more.'

'No more,' said Mai, delighted.

A car was parked at the kerb. Two men got out. His attention was focused on Janine and he scarcely registered them until one of them stepped in front of the woman and said, 'Madame Simonian!'

'Yes.'

'Come with me.'

The man seized Janine's other arm. She turned on Mai an expression uncertain whether to be an appeal for help or a Medusa-stare of accusation.

'Hold on!' cried Mai.

But before he could take more than half a step forward, his left arm was seized from behind, twisted round and forced up between his shoulder-blades till he doubled forward, screaming with pain.

The man holding him didn't relax his grip, but relaxed his attention to look towards the car for instruction.

'Bring him too,' came the order.

But the relaxation was enough for Mai, who drove his heel hard beneath his captor's right knee, then stamped viciously on his left toe as he hopped in pain. The man crashed to the ground needing both hands to break his fall. Mai straightened up. Janine, inspired by his example, had flung herself at the man holding her and her nails had drawn blood from his face. Mai's impulse was to go to her aid, but a third man was emerging from the car and in his hand was a pistol.

'You idiots!' screamed Mai in his best parade ground voice. 'You blockheads! You stupid, half-witted botchers! I'll have you on the Russian Front for this. I'll see that you're still up to your arseholes in snow when your mates back here are ankle-deep in daffodils!'

The man with the gun looked at him in bewilderment modulating to concern. Janine's captor released her. Even the man on the floor showed signs through his pain of a suspicion that all was not as it should be.

Janine, bewildered by events and all this incomprehensible yelling, was leaning against the parked car, drawing

301

in deep shock-absorbing breaths. Her first cogent thought had been that Mai had led her into a trap. His behaviour now seemed to disprove that. Or perhaps it was just that the trap had been sprung too soon, the men hadn't waited for his command?

The man with the gun spoke. His voice was respectful but he still held the weapon loosely ready and it snapped up into the aim position as Mai reached inside his overcoat.

What he came out with was a leather wallet. He opened it, took something out, probably his card of identity, and handed it over. The gun man examined it, returned it, put the gun away and, stiffening momentarily to attention, spoke in a conciliatory voice. Mai replied in kind. The gun man gestured towards Janine and spoke again. Mai's reply this time was emphatic and urgent. The gun man looked dubious. For a couple of phrases, Mai returned to his earlier, frighteningly authoritarian manner. This seemed to do the trick. A few more words and some rudimentary salutes were exchanged. The man Janine had scratched helped the man Mai had kicked into the car and it accelerated away.

Mai watched them go. As he stood there he felt Janine's hand take hold of his arm.

'Günter,' she said. 'Who were they? What's going on?'

It occurred to him that never before had she addressed him so familiarly, so naturally. Nothing like a bit of fear for breaking down barriers, he thought cynically. Well, she was right to be afraid.

'Gestapo,' he said. 'Who else? They were going to arrest you.'

He paused then went on, 'No, not arrest you in the legal sense. If they'd had a formal warrant with the signature of a high-ranking officer on it, nothing I said would have stopped them. They were just going to take you in for a little unofficial questioning. People have been known to survive.'

'But why? What have I done?'

He turned to her, looked into her eyes and said sadly,

302

'Janine, stop playing the innocent. There's no protection in it, not from us, not from your own people.'

'My own people? Why should I need protection from them?'

'You're standing here talking to a German officer, for a start. Don't you imagine there'll be Frenchmen willing to believe what I hope those Gestapo hoodlums believe?'

'And what's that?'

'How do you think I got rid of them? I told them who I was and said that you were one of my best agents. Janine, I'm afraid you're back on my books again.'

She showed neither gratitude nor surprise. Her mind was still occupied with working out what had happened. Why her? Why here?

They must have been on watch near the flat in the Quartier Mouffetard.

She felt faint at the thought of what would have happened if she'd abandoned the rendezvous with Mai entirely and headed straight back to Jean-Paul. The Geste agents must have decided that while one was worth following, two were worth picking up. Thank God the other had been Mai.

Impulsively she leaned forward and kissed him on the cheek.

'Thank you,' she said. 'Now I've got to go.'

Rushing off to warn her precious husband, thought Mai. And why should he need warning?

Alarm bells were sounding in his own mind. He'd been right in his suspicions about Christian Valois. And from the sound of him, Simonian was an even more likely member of the Resistance, and not in any passive, sleeping capacity either.

How deep was he willing to plunge in his increasingly ambiguous relationship with Janine? Mai asked himself. When did he reach the point where protecting her meant also protecting men whose main aim was to kill German soldiers?

Meanwhile, talking of protection he'd better set about protecting himself. The Gestapo men were probably reporting in already.

Janine was turning to go.

He said, 'Hold on. If you want to see me, ring the Lutétia and just leave a time. I'll meet you an hour earlier at the Balzac the same day.'

'An hour earlier?' she said puzzled.

'Just so you won't keep me waiting,' he joked. Then, because it was no joking matter, he spelt it out. 'For security. You're one of my best agents, remember?'

He watched her run away along the damp pavement towards the Jussieu métro. Slim-hipped, she ran with an athlete's grace, like a winning runner.

'One of my best agents,' he repeated without irony.

Then he set off up the steep incline of the Rue Lacépède with the short aggressive steps of a man who may not go fast but knows that he can keep going for ever.

6

'Where the hell did you hear that?' demanded Jean-Paul Simonian.

She'd been full of her news. It might not be good but she'd got it herself despite their attempts to freeze her out. Now all her elation drained away.

'Miche found out,' she said. It was a believable lie. She hadn't been able to think of one to cover her close escape from the Gestapo.

'That treacherous bastard! I've told you to keep away from him.'

'At least he can find things out which none of your patriotic friends can manage,' she retorted.

'You think not,' he said. He looked pleased with himself.

'Well, at least we can confirm that for once your Géstapiste cousin is telling the truth.'

'Jean-Paul! You've found out something too?'

He sat beside her, his outburst of temper forgotten as he spoke of his friend.

'Yes, he's in Fresnes. There's a warder there who wants to keep on the right side of the Resistance against the day he's called to account. He says Christian's in the German section of the prison. He looks a bit bruised about the face but otherwise all right. The word is that Vichy father of his got on to it quick enough to pull strings before the Gestapo really got to work.'

'So he's safe? Will his father be able to get him out?'

'Don't be stupid. Once Theo talked, and he must have said something, Christian was a dead man. Old Valois can hold things up for a bit, but the Geste will be given a free hand eventually and once that happens there's no way that Christian won't tell everything he knows.'

'Is that all you're worried about?' she cried. 'That Christian may break and tell them something about your precious group?'

He rushed forward and grabbed her arm, pulling her towards him. His grip was so tight she cried out in pain. His face only a few inches from hers was no longer emotionless.

'Who the hell do you think you are?' he said in a voice low with the effort of restraint. 'What do you know about what I feel for Christian? He's been my friend, my dearest friend, for years. I know the risks he took to get me back home after the canal raid. I know that if I were in Fresnes, he wouldn't rest till he got me out. Don't tell *me* what my reasons are for wanting to rescue him.'

'Oh I'm sorry, I'm sorry,' she said, trying to turn their closeness into an embrace. 'Rescue him, you say? But how? From Fresnes? Surely it's impossible!'

He let her go and turned away to light a cigarette.

'That's a word the Boche like to use,' he said. 'They haven't realized yet it doesn't mean the same here as in Berlin.'

'And what does it mean here, Jean-Paul?' asked Janine.

305

He let out a joyful laugh.

'It means Christian will be back safe with us tomorrow!'

The Department of Sanitation truck coughed its way under the arch of the main entrance to Fresnes Prison. It slowed almost to a halt so that the guard could scan the driver's familiar face. They exchanged greetings, the man next to the driver joining in, then the truck accelerated laboriously across the courtyard, following the familiar route to the kitchen block where the greatest concentration of refuse was stacked.

The passenger got out, stretched, beat his mittened hands against his chest against the winter chill, then wandered round to the back of the truck. After glancing casually around, he rapped on the tailboard. A moment later, a man slipped down from the truck. He was dressed in the uniform of a warder. He made no effort to move away but stood chatting casually to the garbage man, as if he'd just come out to supervise the loading.

'How do I look?' said Jean-Paul Simonian.

'Not bad,' said Henri, eyeing him critically. 'Except maybe for that cabbage leaf on your hat.'

'What?' Simonian raised his hand, found nothing, realized his lieutenant was joking. A great respect had grown between these two since the débâcle at the canal. 'He's a mad bugger and he may get us all killed yet,' Henri would declare to others of Les Pêcheurs. 'But not without getting himself killed first, trying to save us.'

Now the two men smiled at each other.

'I'll be on my way.'

'Don't forget your parcel.'

'I've got it.'

He reached into the truck and extracted a neatly wrapped box with the name of a well-known *pâtisserie* on it.

'Back in twenty minutes,' said Simonian.

'Make it fifteen,' said Henri. 'This is one place we don't hang around on the job. Good luck.'

He watched the Fisherman stride boldly away.

'Good luck,' he repeated to himself. They were going to need it. In fact, they were going to need a whole year's supply of it for this crazy scheme to succeed.

Simonian had no such doubts. It was at moments like this that he felt most truly in control, most passionately alive. He could do anything, be anything. For the moment he felt that he actually was a prison warder who'd just taken delivery of a cake addressed to the guard commander of the German prison block at Fresnes and who was rather irritated at having to waste his time carrying the thing around.

He burst through the door with a suddenness which had the corporal at the desk leaping to attention before he spotted the inconsequential uniform.

'A cake,' he announced, banging the box on to the desk.

'A cake?' said the corporal. 'Oh yes. It's his birthday.'

'Is it?' said Simonian, who'd obtained this and much more information about lay-out, procedure and timing, not to mention his uniform, from the warder who'd first revealed that Christian Valois was here.

'He must have rich friends,' he continued. 'Ask me when I last had a decent slice of cake. Shortages, they say. This doesn't look very short to me.'

He shook the box.

'Careful,' said the corporal, alarmed. 'He'll play hell if you muck it up.'

'No. It's all right, I'm sure. Let's take a look.'

He undid the elegant bow, lifted a corner of the box, smiled his approval, then, to the corporal's round-eyed shock, he inserted his hand into the box as though to scrape at the icing.

'Here, none of that!' said the corporal. 'None of . . .'

He stopped speaking as a second and more powerful wave of shock stifled his voice. Simonian's hand had come out of the box with a revolver in it.

'Open up,' ordered Jean-Paul. 'Take me to the prisoner Valois. Shout, resist, even delay, and I'll put a bullet right

307

at the base of your spine. It won't kill you. It will just paralyse you from the neck down for the rest of your life. Move.'

He spoke quietly but with the same utter conviction as he'd brought to his previous role.

The corporal was pale and trembling slightly. For a second Simonian feared he might have got himself a true Teutonic hero. Then the man rose, took his keys and, with the swiftness of one who wants to get an unpleasant duty over, he began unlocking the inner door.

Using the cake box to conceal the gun, Simonian followed close behind. They passed a couple of German guards coming the other way but the men paid no heed to the common sight of a French warder's uniform. Fresnes was a big enough prison for the Occupation Force to have its own section, but overall administrative control still lay with the local authorities.

The corporal stopped and opened a cell.

He stood aside as if to usher Simonian courteously before him.

'Get in,' snarled Simonian.

The man entered. Simonian followed close behind. As the corporal's leading foot touched the floor of the cell, the gun barrel came down on the nape of his neck. He slumped to the floor and Christian Valois, squatting on the end of his trestle bed, had to leap upright out of his way.

'Jesus Christ!' he exclaimed in alarm. 'What the hell . . . Jean-Paul!'

'That's right. You OK?'

'Yes. Fine. Just a few punches . . . Jean-Paul!'

The two men embraced. When they drew apart, there were tears in Valois's eyes.

'Jean-Paul,' he began, but Simonian shook his head testily.

'No time. Put this on.'

He opened the box fully and took out of it another warder's tunic.

Stooping he lifted the corporal, dropped him face down on the bed, gagged him with a length of cloth, then pulled his dangling arms together under the bed and joined them with a pair of handcuffs taken from his pocket.

'That should keep him quiet,' he said, throwing a blanket over the body. 'Now let's go. Just look as if you owned the place!'

In fact Christian Valois's powers of acting were very little tested. They left the block without encountering a soul, and though they saw one or two other guards and officials on their way towards the kitchens, no one spared them a second glance.

Henri was just emptying the last bin.

'In you get,' he said.

With a glance around to make sure they were unobserved, Valois slipped over the tailboard.

'Now you,' said Henri.

Before Simonian could obey, the kitchen door opened. The driver emerged, took in Simonian's presence with relief, and called out to someone inside, 'Thanks for the coffee!'

As he made for his cab, the kitchen door opened once more and a man in a cook's apron appeared, yawning in the cold sunlight. Simonian was just clambering over the tailboard. He paused and stared at the cook, who grinned back.

'Think they're escaping in the rubbish, do we?' he called mockingly.

Simonian dropped to the ground.

'Maybe,' he said.

Henri coughed. He was standing by the cab and could see round the side of the building. Simonian stepped forward and followed his gaze. On the far side of the courtyard, a prison officer and a German soldier had come out of a building and were talking together. He willed the cook to go back inside. Perhaps he was OK. He looked at the driver, who was looking very unhappy. If he didn't trust the fellow, then certainly Simonian wasn't going to.

The officer and the soldier split up. The soldier was heading to the German detention area. The officer was walking towards the kitchen block. There was little time left.

He went up to the still smiling cook, pulled out a long-bladed knife from its sheath in his belt and drove it into the man's rib-cage.

The driver hissed involuntarily, 'Oh Christ! He was my mate!'

'You should've trusted him then,' gasped Simonian. 'Henri, help me. *You*, start up!'

They tipped the dead man into the rubbish. Simonian plunged in after him and covered up the body, then himself. Valois stirred. Simonian whispered, 'Lie still.'

The truck set off towards the main gates, which opened as they approached, and they were waved through without an inspection.

As they drove under the arch, Henri glanced back. The German soldier had turned towards the barrack block well short of the detention area. The prison officer too had turned back well before the kitchen.

As they left the prison behind, he should have felt elated. But somehow elation didn't come very easy these days.

7

As soon as he'd got back to the Lutétia from the Jardin Mai had composed a formal complaint to the office of the *Höherer SS und Polizeiführer* in the Avenue Foch. It was not a conventional channel of communication between the *Abwehr* and the SD but he worked out that if a fuss was going to be made, he'd better do the lion's share as the alleged injured party.

When news of the daring rescue of Christian Valois reached him the next day, he was stricken with guilt and fear.

The guilt was soon disposed of. His reason told him that merely telling Janine where Valois was imprisoned couldn't have anything to do with his escape a mere twenty-four hours later.

But the fear remained. If the Gestapo decided to make an issue of his interference in Janine's arrest – as, enraged by the humiliation of losing Valois, they might – then anything could happen, to him and to the woman.

There was nothing to do but wait.

A few days later as he sat in his office, the door opened and he rose swiftly to his feet as Major Nebe, the Head of Records, appeared, ushering in Colonel Fiebelkorn who wore a smile like a hangman's, with more in it of relish than reassurance.

'Heil Hitler!' said Mai smartly.

'Heil,' replied the colonel. 'How are you, Captain Mai? And poor Major Zeller, how is he?'

'I'm well. The major is improving, thank you, sir. He has been taken back to Berlin for specialized treatment.'

'Excellent. We can ill afford to lose such a man, though from what I hear, his work has passed into the very best of hands.'

Gold teeth glinted in another smile. You could almost hear the mouth muscles creak in protest at this unusual activity. But not even gold could glitter bright enough to touch the dark dead eyes.

Suddenly he became businesslike.

'I was here on a small matter of shared interest, exchanging information. We should do more of this, don't you think?'

'Yes, colonel.'

'Yes. Then perhaps if we did, embarrassments like trying to arrest each other's agents would be avoided!'

'Yes. I'm sorry, colonel . . .'

'No, no,' said Fiebelkorn holding up a pale pudgy hand in remonstrance. 'There is nothing for you to be sorry about. I can understand your anger. I have been glancing at the woman Simonian's record, with Major Nebe's per-

311

mission of course, and I can see how much you must value her. Informants are plentiful enough. You can't spit out of your window without hitting half a dozen! But reliable ones, trustworthy ones – only the best intelligence officers can recruit those.'

'Thank you, colonel,' said Mai bewildered. He'd worked all night after the incident outside the Jardin to give Janine real substance as an agent, expecting the row to explode almost immediately. Instead of which, he could have taken his time; and in any case, far from a row, he was getting what amounted to an apology!

'So let's say no more about it,' said Fiebelkorn. 'The idiots who caused you this embarrassment are now relearning their basic skills in the Ukraine. And let us try to be more sharing and co-operative in the future. We need to unite our strength against all the enemies of the Fatherland. Agreed?'

'Agreed, colonel,' said Mai.

'Good. Anything you learn from your good agents, like this Simonian woman, that would be very interesting to us. And should you ever wish to restructure your career, Captain Mai, give me a ring. There's always room in the SD for any man with the skills to persuade a woman to stay with her terrorist husband so she can keep on betraying him!'

He laughed as he spoke and the two *Abwehr* men laughed too, like a trio of untuned cellos.

Mai, alone, sat down heavily and soon had the room foggy with tobacco smoke, but for once the outer fumes brought no compensating clarity to his thoughts. He realized now he'd made a mistake in not insisting that he had some means of contacting Janine. He wanted to see her, to make sure she was safe. No. He just wanted to see her.

He tried to will the phone to ring. It didn't. He went back to work.

Two days later, the phone rang when he was out. A woman, the message simply *two o'clock*.

He got there at ten to one. At two he was still sitting in

the Café Balzac with the patron making sympathetic grunts every time he brought another drink.

At two forty-five, he gave up. This was absurd. He tried to feel annoyance, but all he could feel was terror.

He stood up, looked down the café for the patron. And there she was. Standing in the doorway. Like a slim, pale flame in the gloomy atmosphere of the shabby café.

She came to him and sat down.

'Where've you been?' he demanded.

She looked at him in surprise.

'What do you mean?'

'Mean? You're so late!'

'No I'm not!' she replied indignantly. 'Don't you remember, you said I should give a time an hour before the real time? I'm early.'

He began to laugh, but the laughter didn't sound right, like the cracked notes he'd produced from Fiebelkorn's joke. So he stopped laughing and clasped his hands together in an effort to control their sudden trembling.

'Are you ill?' she asked with real concern.

'No, not at all. Just relieved,' he said. 'I was so worried.'

'About me?' She looked at him closely.

She sounded surprised. But concerned too. And perhaps even, though this might have been his imagination, pleased.

'Let's walk, shall we?' he said.

'If you like.'

The patron opened the door for him, his congratulatory leer concealing his melancholy musings on the weakness of man. Monsieur Scheffer was obviously putty in the hands of this woman. She wasn't even a beauty! A skinny, undernourished thing, like a frightened rabbit! But she must have something . . . He watched them stroll away in the wintry gloom and tried to warm himself up by imagining what it was.

As they walked along he asked, 'What happened when you got back that day?'

313

'I told him that I'd learned from Miche where Christian was.'

'*Was* is the operative word.'

'That had nothing to do with our conversation, believe me.'

'I worked that out for myself.'

Relieved, she moved away from that delicate topic.

'What about you? What happened about those Gestapo thugs?'

'Is that why you rang? To find out?'

'Yes. I got more and more worried.'

For the sake of that precious husband, no doubt, thought Mai. She felt guilty at hiding things from him and wanted at the very least to make sure that her silence wasn't endangering him. He told her briefly of his visit from Fiebelkorn. Ahead lay the Tuileries Garden. Mist seemed to hang in the leafless trees like the ghost of some old decoration. There were few people about, stick-figures with little plumes of breath trailing behind them. Our breath too, thought Mai, suddenly melancholy. Our life. A little vapour. How many exhalations to go?

A bunch of soldiers passed them as they entered the gardens. They looked so young. It wasn't just his own sense of ageing that was doing this. They really were young, seventeen, eighteen, nineteen. We're spreading ourselves so thin, he thought. Italy, the Ukraine, the whole of France. The pot's not bottomless.

One of the soldiers glanced at Janine as they passed, made a phallic gesture with his forearm, and the sound of his companions' laughter drifted eerily back as the mist swallowed them up.

'Don't be annoyed,' said Mai. 'Boys, a long way from home, trying to pretend they're so experienced, so sophisticated.'

'I'm not annoyed,' said Janine. 'I'm not some provincial schoolmarm you know. But don't ask me to feel sorry for them either. I know what your "boys" are capable of when the occasion demands.'

'And yours?' said Mai gently.

'You mean the Resistance? That's different. That's . . .'

'. . . morally justified? Like the Crusades? We won't argue that. But I met some of your other *boys* when I was down in Toulouse. The Milice. You've heard of them? They're not in Paris yet, but don't worry, they will be, next year at the latest. To start with, the SD trained them but the ones I saw were already outrunning their teachers!'

The grey tendrils of mist curled around them, weaving a curtain which shut them off not merely from sight and sound of the great city but from time and circumstance too. He took her hand as they walked, held it loosely and was not surprised when she did not pull it away. Why should she? They were in suspense. What was said and done now didn't count.

Or rather it might count more than anything they had ever said or done before.

She said gently, like a grown-up reasoning with a child, 'What can you tell me that justifies you, I mean the Germans, being here? That justifies the things you've done?'

Treated like a child, he found himself swinging her hand like a child as he wrestled with the problem.

He said, 'Humiliation, perhaps. You humiliated us at Versailles back in 1919. That's what made 1940 possible.'

'That's a cause not a justification,' she corrected. 'And I hope you're wrong. Because you're going to be humiliated again.'

She spoke with such certainty that he halted and peered into her face as if hoping to see there the source of such firm prophecy.

'Why do you say that?'

'Because you boast so proudly and behave so meanly,' she declared. 'Everybody knows what empty boasts they are! You were going to destroy England, weren't you? Well, it's still there. Half of Paris listens to its broadcasts every night and every night we hear British and American planes droning away overhead. It's the sound of our victory, your defeat. And it won't be a noble defeat either. That's when the full story of your barbarity will come out. God knows how vile the whole truth will be! The little bit I know is enough to humiliate you all for a thousand years.'

He tried to meet the steady gaze of those wide eyes but he couldn't. He'd never felt homesick before but suddenly he realized that like those boys who'd just passed them, he too was a long way from home.

He spoke, trying to keep his voice as even and controlled as hers had been.

'I won't argue with you. Perhaps I can't. But one thing you should know is whatever we've done here in France, we've had our job made easy. We've had people queueing up for jobs, everything from political administrators to paid informers. And then there's tens of thousands who didn't want any pay. The letter writers, the telephoners, the anonymous tipsters. We've been snowed under. I sometimes think it must be a Resistance plot to break down the system! Perhaps that's what they'll claim later. They'll have to claim something because when the world finds out that the Germans have got more than their fair share of madmen, they'll also learn that France had more than its fair share of collaborators!'

He fell silent. It was a cheap point he had made even though he believed it to be true. But he wasn't using it as an argument here, merely a diversion. He felt ashamed to see in her face that she was taking it so seriously.

She said, 'Do you count me as a collaborator?'

'No,' he said, recognizing the truth as he said it. 'Of course not.'

'Then,' she said never taking her eyes off him, 'if I'm not, you must be.'

He was surprised only for a moment. He turned his head away and strove to force his sight through the mist back to the real world, back to the Rue de Rivoli where the crimson swastikas still flapped lazily in a triumph as empty as the shops beneath them. But it was no use. That part of his mind which, despite everything, could still pretend that he was leading her on simply would not function here.

He said slowly and with effort, 'I'm not a collaborator. I'm in love with you.'

Immediately he felt a vast sense of relief.

He was still holding her hand. He raised it, played with her fingers, kissed them gently.

She said sadly, 'Yes. That's what I was afraid of.'

'Afraid?' He wanted to laugh out loud in his strange exultation. 'You mean you'd rather I was the enemy manipulating you to betray your country?'

'No. Of course not. Günter, what I meant was I'm afraid for you.'

Her voice was soft with sympathy as if he'd just revealed he'd got a fatal illness. But how clearly she saw things, he realized. For him that's what it probably was. There was no place in her life for him other than as a source of help in the enemy camp. By his declaration of love, he had removed all threat from that help and transferred it to himself. She had been right after all. Being in love did make him a collaborator.

He drew her towards him. She did not resist but bowed her head away from his lips and he buried his face in her mist-damp hair.

'I love you,' he said taking pleasure from speaking the words again.

'Poor Günter,' she murmured almost to herself. 'Poor Günter.'

8

In the days that followed his rescue, Christian Valois was moved around so much that he began to lose track of place and time.

'For Christ's sake,' he protested, as they moved yet again. 'Is this really necessary? I mean if *I* don't know where I am, the Boche are going to be hard put to trace me, aren't they?'

'Someone's put the bastards on to me,' said Simonian grimly. 'And with relatives like my wife's I'm taking no chances.'

'You really think it was Janine's cousin?'

'Why not?'

'Well, he helped get the children away safely, didn't he? That shows he's still got some scruples.'

'Sentimentality is not a moral quality,' said Jean-Paul.

'But he got papers for that little Jew, Melchior, too,' protested Valois.

'Perhaps he's perverted as well as being a traitor,' said Simonian shortly. 'You're very defensive of this piece of shit, Christian. Do you owe him money or something?'

'It's just that, without proof . . . I know he's a collaborator, but that doesn't mean he'd betray everything. And he *is* Janine's cousin.'

'You're a bit sentimental yourself,' observed Simonian. 'We'll have to knock that out of you. You've spent too long in that ivory tower at the Louvre.'

'Well, I'm out of it now for good,' said Valois almost sadly.

But when they reached the new safe-house, there was a reminder of the past waiting for him.

'Christian, it's good to see you!' said Maître Delaplanche rising from a chair.

'And you!' said Valois, surprised and pleased. 'I didn't think I'd see you . . . I'm sorry . . . all your plans for me kaput!'

'It wasn't your fault,' said the lawyer. 'Theo pointed the finger. Don't blame him. I heard what the bastards did to him. It was enough to make a man betray his own mother.'

'So he gave them Christian but he didn't give them you. Odd, that,' said Simonian staring at Delaplanche speculatively.

'He gave them everyone he knew, including me,' said the man calmly. 'We got the others safely hidden as soon as we heard the news. When I heard Christian had gone to ground, I guessed he'd been warned too.'

'So why didn't the Boche pick you up?'

'They did. They interrogated me. They let me go.'

'Just like that?' said Simonian incredulously.

'Not quite. There were phone calls, in and out. Angry scenes. Threats on both sides. Then they let me go.'

'Why?'

'Because so far, I've managed to confuse the issue. I can't work underground like you, Monsieur Simonian. I'm a public figure. I must move publicly. That in a way is my security. My name appears on no party list. I have voted for all the centrist parties at some point. When this war started and I saw what my role must be, I planned for it. If I could not rise above suspicion, I would smother myself in it! From the very beginning I've had accusers. Not an act of terrorism occurs without a stream of anonymous delations against me pouring into the Majestic and the Rue des Saussaies. Men like Theo have instructions if they are caught and questioned about me to babble out agreement with whatever suggestions the Boche make. Thus by being manifestly innocent of ninety per cent of what I'm accused of, I've so far managed to keep my head above water.

'I've also got friends. And there are people in power on both sides that I know enough about for them to value my silence. But there are more ways than one of ensuring silence. Perhaps the Gestapo's patience will finally snap and they'll simply send a bunch of their French friends round to blow my head off in a fit of patriotic fury.'

He concluded and watched for Simonian's reaction with a faint smile.

'You're a brave man, monsieur.'

'Am I? If so, it's a finite quality and I think I've almost drained the barrel.'

'I think not. You've been frank with me. Now I'll be frank with you. What plans have you got for Christian?'

319

'Plans? All my plans for Christian are ruined, you must see that!'

'So you have no plans? Good. Then you'll have no objection if he transfers his allegiance to my group?'

Suddenly Valois erupted.

'It's me you're talking about!' he yelled. 'Me! I'm here, in the same room! I've got ears. I'm a man, not a beast in a cattle market.'

Delaplanche turned to him and said gently, 'Don't be so offended, my friend. I'm sorry if we seem high-handed, but Monsieur Simonian is right. Your future is too import-ant to be left solely to you. Look at yourself! You look dreadful. It's a real strain this kind of thing. Later, you must make your own decisions about the detail. But the broad movement and direction is down to your friend and me. After all, if neither of us wants you, then that would leave you very awkwardly placed, wouldn't it?'

He turned back to Simonian without waiting for an answer.

'Agreed. He's yours. I think it's best. Now I must go. I've been here too long already. Christian, goodbye. I hope we'll meet in happier times very soon. Any message for your parents?'

'You'll be seeing them?' said Valois eagerly.

'Yes. I saw them a couple of times when I was in Vichy recently. I was able to advise them how best to react to the news of your disappearance, where to put pressure on, how to inhibit an immediate and energetic interrogation from the start. It seems to have worked.'

'Are they well?'

'Concerned, naturally. A double concern as it happens. Your sister . . .'

'What about my sister?' interrupted Valois fearfully.

'It's all right! Nothing's wrong. She just ran away from home, that's all. She's bored by Vichy, it seems. Well, who can blame her? And there was an attachment, to an "unsuitable" young man, which I presume in Vichy means someone who supports the Resistance! Your parents broke it up. She disap-

320

peared. They've had a postcard from Besançon saying she's there. She knows someone in Besançon, I gather?'

'An old school friend,' said Valois.

'Well, let's hope she stays there and doesn't try to get into Switzerland. But she sounds a determined young lady. Goodbye, Christian. Take care.'

He shook hands and left. Simonian followed him out of the room and spoke in a low voice to one of his men in the hallway. When he returned he found Valois slumped forward with his head between his hands.

'Christian! Cheer up! You're alive and free. Your sister too. And your parents. So why so sad?'

Valois said, 'My parents. What do you think will happen when the war ends, Jean-Paul? To people like my father, I mean. Men who've gone along with the Marshal and collaborated.'

Simonian said neutrally, 'It depends how far they've gone, I'd say. But they must pay something, you can see that can't you, Christian? And as for rubbish like my wife's cousin, I wouldn't even waste the expense of a trial on him!'

Valois laughed humourlessly.

'So, token trial or summary execution for everyone tainted with collaboration, eh? I hope no one's in a hurry to rebuild France after the war, Jean-Paul. From the sound of it, for the first year or so you won't be able to move for bodies in the streets.'

'Perhaps,' said Jean-Paul. 'Let's hope that for the last year of the war you won't be able to move for German bodies. Talking of which, are you really interested in joining us? Or would you rather let your tally stop at one?'

For a second Valois looked at him without comprehension. Then he said, 'I'm sorry. I'm not quite . . . yes, of course, Jean-Paul, that's what I want more than anything.'

'Good,' said Simonian. 'Then it's back to school for you. Excuse me.'

He went out and returned a moment later with a gun in his hands.

'This is what they call a Sten gun,' he said. 'It doesn't look much, but this particular weapon has done more for France than General Big-nose sitting in London. It's killed at least a dozen Boche. Let me show you how to strip it down.'

Two hours later they were still sitting in the room surrounded by a confusion of weapons.

Simonian watched critically as his friend assembled a machine pistol, loaded the magazine and rammed it into place.

'I think I've been underestimating you, Christian,' he said. 'You know it wouldn't surprise me if by the end of the year you weren't even better known to the Germans than your father!'

Valois looked at him then began to laugh.

Soon both men were laughing together. But it was not a harmonious sound.

9

'Another year,' said Marc du Prat. 'Not perhaps the best.'

'Fiscally speaking, you mean?' said Léon Valois.

'Of course. What else?'

The two men were well matched, of an age, both going grey with distinction, both wearing anonymous grey suits of immaculate English cut. But du Prat's lean intelligent face showed little sign of stress except for a certain watchfulness about the eyes.

Léon Valois by contrast looked worn and haggard. It was understandable, thought du Prat with a pang of sympathy. He must be worried sick about that crazy son of his. Who'd have thought it? Christian a terrorist, high on the Gestapo's wanted list. It must have ruined Léon's standing in Vichy. Though looked at another way, a year

322

from now a Vichy politician might be very glad indeed to have a Resistant son to shelter behind!

'None of our friends here tonight?' said Valois looking round the crowded room.

The occasion was a semi-formal Christmas reception given by a few senior civil servants. Rumour had it that its real function was to provide those wishing to escape German invitations with an alibi. There was to be no repeat of the glittering parties of 1940, but celebrations there were in plenty, and men of prudence were beginning to be careful who they were seen with.

'No,' said du Prat. 'We're a simple homespun crowd.'

He felt there was something contemptuous in the way Valois was looking at him and let himself grow indignant. For God's sake, if the man was so proud of his German friends, what was *he* doing here tonight?

The indignation faded as he acknowledged its artificiality. He'd promised himself not to mention Christian but now he said impulsively, 'Any word of your son?'

'No,' said Valois shortly.

Meaning, he's not going to tell *me* even if there is!

'If you hear from him, give him my best wishes,' he said. 'My wife and I are very fond of him, you know.'

True, as far as it could be. And there was never any harm in casting a bit of bread upon muddy waters!

But it was time for a change of subject.

'Good lord,' he said. 'See who's just come in? Delaplanche!'

'Who? Where?'

Valois turned to look. The stocky figure of the lawyer stood in the doorway, his leathery features set in the veiled amusement of the peasant at the sight of these upper-class antics. But he hadn't strayed in by accident. One of the hosts went across to greet him with a fond embrace and led him to a group of equally senior men.

'I don't know how he does it!' said du Prat admiringly. 'Three and a half years, and he's still wandering loose. They've pulled him in half a dozen times, of course, but

323

he's always either talked his way out, or pulled strings to get himself hauled out. Very strange!'

'You're not suggesting he's really working with the Germans, are you?' said Valois uneasily.

'Who knows?' said du Prat cynically. 'Most people are. But I can't really believe Delaplanche is in their pockets, not unless he's picking them! He's just bloody clever, that's all. The trouble is, the Germans have several simple cures for cleverness. Or so they tell me. Another drink, Monsieur le Deputé?'

'No thanks,' said Léon Valois. 'I'd better circulate.'

Strange fellow, thought du Prat as he watched him move away. I really can't understand what he's doing here.

An hour later, Léon Valois had achieved the real purpose of his visit. He went out to the toilet and found Maître Delaplanche waiting there, smoking a strong sweet-smelling cigarette.

'Turkish,' he said. 'All I could get.'

'Can we talk?' asked Valois.

'Until someone comes. But most of that lot are so retentive, they even hang on to their piss as long as they can! No, this is the safest place for you and me, Léon. Neither of us wants to risk a private meeting. Too compromising, eh?'

He laughed. Valois didn't join in.

'You said you had news of my son?'

'He hasn't been in touch direct? No, he wouldn't want to risk getting you involved, would he? Well, first, understand I haven't seen him for some time, but I've heard from reliable sources that he's in good health.'

'And safe? Is he safe?'

Delaplanche laughed. 'Don't be silly, Léon. Your boy has left safety far behind. He is a highly active, highly effective, highly respected and highly wanted Resistant, or terrorist as they call them in Vichy. I must say I'm surprised. I didn't really think he had it in him, to be a successful man of action, I mean. Depending on who wins

324

the war, you've fathered a very great criminal or a very great hero, Léon. How does that make you feel?'

'All his mother and I want is that he should stay alive,' said Valois, gripping a washbasin so tight that his knuckles were almost as white as the marble.

'Yes, I know,' said Delaplanche, touched by the intensity of the other's feelings. 'Léon, a word of advice. In my mind there's no doubt how this is all going to end. Do yourself a bit of good, eh? I think personally you've been absolutely, indefensibly wrong in the path you chose. But at least I think you've been honest and honourable in your choice. But that won't turn aside many bullets when the clean-out starts. So get yourself a few credentials, eh? Don't be so Simon-pure. Do a few favours, and get them on record! You've never been afraid to speak up, but make sure you speak up in the right causes *now*. A few months from now, I reckon the Gadarene rush to join the Resistance will be such a stampede, you'll have to shoot Hitler to get yourself noticed!'

Valois looked at him scornfully and shook his head.

'You want me to be like that pathetic creature, du Prat? God forbid!'

Delaplanche returned his gaze unblinkingly.

'No,' he said calmly. 'Politically what I want is people like you dead, Léon. The du Prats I can easily deal with. I don't know what came over me. A fit of bourgeois sentimentality! But back to our onions. In case I get the chance to pass a message to Christian, what can I tell him about the family? You don't look too well, Léon.'

'Don't tell him that!' urged Valois. 'I'm in good health, really. His mother too. Excellent health.'

'And his sister, Marie-Rose.'

Valois passed his hand wearily over his face.

'Almost as much a worry as Christian,' he admitted. 'But for God's sake, don't tell him that either.'

'No, but I have to say something. Is she still with her friends in Besançon?'

'So her cards say. But I know it's not true. A friend

visiting Besançon went to the house and found it shut up and empty. Evidently the family left almost a year ago. I think she may have done something crazy like joined a Maquis. Oh Christ, what have I done to my children to make them like this!'

He looked close to tears. Delaplanche pulled a flask from his pocket.

'Drink some of this,' he said. 'Tell me all about it, eh? I've got a lot of contacts. Perhaps I can find something out. After all, what are old friends for?'

A week later it was New Year's Eve. Delaplanche sat in his apartment on the top floor of a block in the Rue de Monceau overlooking the park. He was alone, but an open bottle of Saint Émilion and two glasses showed he was expecting company. While he waited he studied some papers with the care of a lawyer who knows on how fine a point matters of profit and loss, of life and death, can depend.

A single knock at the door came. He didn't move. There came a double knock, another pause, then a quadruple knock, all evenly paced.

Now he rose and went to the door and said, *'Chile?'*

'China,' came the whispered reply.

Satisfied, he unlocked the door.

'Come in,' he said to the muffled figure outside. 'I've got something very interesting for you.'

'Me too,' said Alphonse Pajou pressing the trigger of his Mauser automatic pistol. 'Happy New Year.'

When Jean-Paul Simonian arrived twenty minutes later, he found the lawyer's bullet-riddled body lying by the door in a lake of blood. He glanced briefly round the flat. No one else was there. The glasses still stood on the table, but the wine bottle and the papers had gone.

He stepped carefully back over the corpse, closed the door behind him and ran lightly down the stairs.

PART SIX
January–July 1944

Que voulez-vous la porte était gardée
Que voulez-vous nous étions enfermés
Que voulez-vous la rue était barrée
Que voulez-vous la ville était matée
Que voulez-vous nous étions desarmés
Que voulez-vous la nuit était tombée
Que voulez-vous nous nous sommes aimés

Paul Éluard, Couvre-feu

1

'For God's sake, woman,' said Mireille Laurentin. 'Why don't you give that one his marching orders!'

It was New Year's Day. The two women were sitting alone at the kitchen table. A glass of wine had set all the vapours of the previous night's celebration stirring and Janine, urged by her cousin to extend her stay permanently, had spoken more freely of her situation than she intended.

'He's my husband,' she said. 'I love him. He needs me.'

'Funny way he has of showing it,' said Mireille.

'Because he's a Resistant, you mean?'

'Not exactly. A man's got to do what he thinks is right. But he's got to take everything into consideration, hasn't he? I mean, your fellow doesn't seem to consider anything but himself from what you say. Look, we all hate the Boche, right? We all want to see 'em chucked out and they know it. So the bastards put notices up in Lyon and round the villages saying what they'll do to the families of anyone caught with the Resistance. Men get shot, women get hard labour, kids get sent to a reform school, that's the gist of it. Makes you think, doesn't it?'

'So Lucien decided not to join the Resistance?' said Janine, relieved to be assured once more that her children weren't staying in an endangered home.

'With a bit of help from me, he decided,' grinned Mireille. 'Oh I don't say he doesn't drop the odd sack of vegetables to those maquisards up in the hills. But as for going around shooting people and blowing things up, Lucien's got more sense than to get mixed up with that. No, no one's going to bother us for the odd sack of potatoes, are they? But from what you say, your Jean-

Paul's gone a lot further than that! If he gets caught, that's you and the kids dropped right in it.'

'Perhaps he won't get caught,' said Janine unhappily.

Now the children came in, wet with snow. They'd been sledging. Céci was red with exertion and excitement, full of tales of thrills and spills, and Mireille's boys were obviously delighted to be presented as such heroic figures.

Mireille said, 'She twists lads round her little finger already, that one. Just wait till she's sixteen or so. That's when the trouble starts!'

Pauli was wet too, but showed no other sign of exertion. After he took his coat off, he sat quietly in a corner from which his dark eyes in their pale setting were able to watch everything else in the room.

He looked so like his father, self-contained, watchful, assessing.

She said, 'Pauli, come here and give me a kiss for 1944.'

He rose instantly, with no boyish embarrassment, and came to her and embraced her. She tickled him and he threw back his head and laughed, and that happy laughing face was so like his father's too, but not a version of his father that she saw often these days, that her heart contracted and she felt hot tears burning her eyes.

She knew then that she had to go back. She was no longer sure if the old Jean-Paul was retrievable, but while there was the faintest chance, she could not abandon him.

Not all the resolve in the world could render the final leave-taking any less painful. Céci looked set to cry her heart out until Pauli took her aside and assured her that all was well and maman would soon be back and there were honey-cakes for tea. But there was no one to do the same comforting service for him, and more than anything else it was the sense of tight control in his slim body as she kissed him goodbye that almost persuaded Janine to change her mind even at this stage.

But at last she was on the train.

Mireille said, 'We'll see you in the summer then.'

330

'Yes. July.'

'Come earlier if you like. Stay longer.'

It would have taken little to make her get off the train there and then. But now it started. She waved from the window, smiling, till her cousin and the two little heads on either side dwindled to nothing.

Now she cried, quietly but passionately. A man offered her a handkerchief. She took it unthinkingly. Only later as she returned it did she see it belonged to a German soldier, a warrant officer. A French family, two middle-aged women and an old man, glared at her as if accepting the hanky had been the ultimate patriotic betrayal.

It was a slow journey, full of stops and starts. So much for the famous German efficiency. She caught the soldier's eye and he smiled ruefully as though reading her thought. She looked away.

She was several hours late getting into Paris.

As she descended from the train, she felt herself seized in a tight embrace and for a second thought it was Jean-Paul who'd come to meet her. Then Christian Valois said, 'Janine, welcome back!'

'Christian? Where's Jean-Paul? Has something happened?'

'No, of course not,' he said releasing her. 'Jean-Paul's busy. I said I'd come. Then the train was so late and there was talk of air attacks and I started to get worried.'

'You're so sweet, Christian,' she said.

A hand touched her shoulder. When she turned she saw the German warrant officer. He smiled at her and said in heavily accented French, 'Good night, madame.'

'Good night. And thank you,' she replied.

He went on his way and she turned back to Valois to find he'd turned aside and buried his face in a handkerchief.

'What's the matter?' she said almost gaily. 'Did you think I was going to turn you in?'

'Don't even joke about it!' he said.

'He was kind to me in the train, that's all,' she said.

'Don't worry, Christian. Your own mother wouldn't recognize you now!'

It was true. The elegant young civil servant had disappeared. Now, dressed in a baggy old suit, with a heavy moustache and a fringe of beard, he looked like an illustration from *Les Misérables*.

His manner had changed too. There was a new alertness about him, a sense of command. He had rapidly become Les Pêcheurs' mouthpiece, their linkman with other members of the Resistance Council. But from the start he had insisted on being operational too. Soon he had matured into a brilliantly effective field commander with a consistently low casualty rate.

This was highly valued by his men. The Resistance trumpeted its successes but those involved knew the cost. Loose security, bad planning and Gestapo infiltration were wreaking havoc. Raiding parties walked into traps. Whole networks got swept up. Agents and suppliers parachuted into enemy arms.

Simonian reacted by taking ever greater risks. His loyal lieutenant, Henri, might disapprove, but would never oppose. Janine knew that the only person with any hope of holding her husband in check was Christian Valois.

He took her back now to the flat in Clichy. This was her home now, though it seemed to her that Jean-Paul used it more like an animal uses a bolt-hole. He hadn't returned from his 'business' and Christian said apologetically that this was one of those nights when he probably wouldn't be back at all.

Janine collapsed into an armchair. The well of energy which had kept her going since leaving Lyon was completely dry.

'Jan, you look dreadful. Are you ill? Shall I get a doctor?'

Valois's concern was so genuine, it made her smile. It was good to have someone caring about you. She held out her hand to him.

'I'm all right, Christian. Just so tired.'

He took her hand and knelt before her and it seemed

332

perfectly natural to take his head and draw it down on to her bosom, then to close her eyes and slip into sleep.

She awoke as often she'd awoken in the first years of her marriage out of a dream into its reality. She'd dreamt she was lying passive beneath Jean-Paul and he was beginning that old, long, unhurried journey which would end in her arousal. Warm lips were at her breast, gently nudging her nipple to firmness, a soft hand stroking the curve of her thigh. She stretched, arching her body sensuously to thrust the nipple deep into his mouth, to let the hand slip easily beneath her buttock. She half-opened her eyes to look down at the dear narrow head with its crown of jet-black hair.

And instead found herself looking into a tangle of nut-brown curls.

'Christian!' she screamed, trying to sit upright and push him away. 'What the hell do you think you're doing?'

He raised his head and looked at her, his eyes blank with desire.

She opened her mouth to shout again, but his lips caught hers half-open and pressed bruisingly down on them. She caught hold of his hair and dragged his face from hers.

'Christian!' she screamed again. 'No!'

And suddenly he heard her and saw her clear. He pushed himself to his feet in a single spasmodic movement, his face full of shock.

'Janine, forgive me, I'm sorry, I thought . . .'

'Thought? What did you think?'

'I don't know. I thought . . . Janine, I love you, I'm sorry, I can't help it.'

Another one! What is it about me? My husband's enemy first, and now his best friend! thought Janine in horror. And somewhere in there was the edge of a disturbing awareness that as a woman she responded much more positively to the German than to the good-looking young Frenchman.

She pushed all such notions from her mind and said, 'Christian, please go now.'

'Yes, I will. Of course. I'm sorry. Jan, can't we talk . . . ?'

She said, 'We'll talk later. Not here, not now. Please, Christian, just go!'

He went. She locked the door after him. Usually she would have sat up late just in case Jean-Paul did come home. But tonight she hurried to get into bed, pressed by an impulse she didn't understand till she found herself curled foetally with the covers pulled tight above her head and recalled that this was how she'd sought escape as a child when all the pressures and disappointments of her young life seemed too much for her.

She sought now as she'd sought then for consolations and compensations. Then, they'd usually been found in a promised treat, or an approaching birthday, or a good mark at school. Now, they were much harder to find. The Occupation seemed endless. In her mind, like most people she knew, she was accepting it and all its dangers and horrors as a permanent state of existence. So must a criminal serving a life-sentence come to terms with the limits set on his movement and his actions.

But there was a consolation. At least the children were safe.

Clutching this to her mind as in younger days she'd clutched a rag-doll to her breast, she fell asleep.

2

Paris in the springtime. Of all the clichés about the city, this was the one Günter enjoyed most.

1941 had been best; triumph still tasted sweet on the lips and there'd seemed to be some correspondence between the blossom on the trees and the shape of things to come. 1942 hadn't been too bad, the daffodils and lilac speaking of a second chance to remedy lost time and opportunities missed. In 1943 he'd hardly noticed the spring. Down there in the south he'd been too concerned with other matters; on the one hand, the Maquis, in his eyes the greatest danger yet to the Occupation Forces; on the other hand, the Milice, who seemed bent on outstripping the Gestapo and SS in their repressive measures.

Now the Milice were in Paris at the instigation of SD Headquarters in the Avenue Foch. What an admission of failure, thought Mai bitterly. It was no consolation to know from Michel Boucher that there was one person who resented their presence more bitterly still – Alphonse Pajou, who saw in these new Géstapistes a threat to his own power and profits!

From Boucher he also got news of Janine, though he never asked directly for it. He'd seen her distantly from time to time, arriving at or leaving the boulangerie where he still sometimes enjoyed a croissant and coffee. He knew she used the house as a poste restante for mail from the Ain, the regular postcards which confirmed the children were well. They had never exchanged more than a formal greeting since that day he had declared his love. Now with the end of May in sight, he decided that memory had been a cheat. The blossom lacked colour and scent, nor were the skies as blue, the air as wine-like as he had recalled. He felt a sense of mockery everywhere, of scornful farewell. And he felt no sense of romance whatsoever, which confirmed what he wanted to believe – that this absurd, potentially destructive passion for the Simonian woman was dead.

So he did his work, ate, drank and had the occasional security-vetted whore.

And from time to time he updated Janine's 'agent' file to be on the safe side in case the Gestapo had their plant in the Lutétia just as he had his in the Rue des Saussaies. It wasn't for her sake he was doing this, he assured himself. It was for his own safety. Also the children's. If he'd done nothing else worthwhile in this war, at least he'd helped two innocent kids to a place of safety where the sounds of spring could still fall without distortion upon responsive ears.

All afternoon there had been the crackle of distant gunfire in the hills.

Hunters, Mireille told herself. But she had lived too long in the country not to know the difference between hunting rifles and automatic fire.

As soon as the firing had started she had gone to look for Lucien, hoping to see his sturdy silhouette as he toiled in the nearby fields or hear his axe at work in the copice. But there was no sign.

She asked old Rom, the farmhand, if he knew where his master was, but he merely shook his head. The villagers had a joke which said that Rom had found he'd got some life left over at the end of his words.

She now went into the living-room and looked at the old clock. It was time to eat. In fact, as she well knew, it was rather late. The table was set, the food was ready. Céci had been sitting there impatiently for some time. She went to the door and called, 'Boys!'

They came at their own pace as boys do, the elder pair first, then Christophe, all red-faced and hot from their exertions.

'Where's Pauli?' she asked.

'Don't know,' said one of the older boys.

'And don't care,' added Christophe with the surliness he still showed at the mention of Pauli's name.

His campaign of persecution might have ended, but his old resentment was never far beneath the surface, even after more than a year.

'He's here now,' said one of the others.

His sharp young ears had caught what Mireille now heard a moment later, Pauli's voice calling, 'Aunt Mireille! Aunt Mireille!'

She went to the window. The boy was running across a field towards the farm. She realized she'd rarely seen him run before. He wasn't slow of movement, in fact his reactions could be amazingly quick, but the general impression he gave was of a calm passivity. Now his speed, his exertion and his voice caught her heart in a spasm of fear.

Now he was in the farmyard, running past old Rom whose weatherbeaten face was provoked to something like surprise, and tumbling through the kitchen door.

'The Boche are coming, the Boche are coming!' he gasped through deep ragged breaths.

Even as he gave his news, the noise of vehicles could be heard and when Mireille looked through the doorway she could see a covered truck and a German staff car bumping down the track towards the farm.

'Stay inside, children,' she commanded.

She went out, shutting the door behind her.

'What's happened?' demanded the eldest boy. 'Pauli, what's going on?'

'They attacked the Maquis,' said Pauli, beginning to regain control of his breathing. 'They killed some of them, captured the rest. I saw them. And they captured Uncle Lucien.'

'Papa? Why did they capture papa?' The boy's voice was shrill.

'He was up there. He'd taken some vegetables I think. He often did it.'

He sat down by Céci and, putting his arm around her said, 'Eat your meal, little one. Eat it all up.'

And seizing a hunk of bread himself, he began to chew vigorously.

'Why are you eating? Pig, pig!' cried Christophe. 'How can you eat now?'

But Pauli just looked at him and continued chewing.

Outside, the vehicles had come to a halt. Two soldiers sprang from the back of the open car, one of them knelt with his gun aimed at Rom, the other ran past the old man, kicked open the kitchen door and went inside. A little while later he emerged.

337

'Just some kids, captain,' he said to the officer in the car who now got out. Mireille's heart contracted even further as she recognized the SS insignia on his tunic.

He saluted her and said, 'Madame Laurentin?'

'Yes.'

'Wife of the terrorist, Lucien Laurentin?'

'What do you mean? My husband's no terrorist!'

'You must come with us, madame,' said the captain who looked no more than twenty.

His youthfulness deceived her into making a plea.

Going close to him she said urgently, 'Please, monsieur, it's all a mistake. My husband's not a maquisard. A few vegetables he gave them from time to time, that's all. What's the harm in that? They're local boys, we've known their families for years . . .'

'And will have the chance to renew the acquaintance. In the truck!'

He turned away, she caught at his arm, he pulled it free, then swung the back of his hand into her face with a force that broke her nose.

She screamed and almost fell. The kitchen door opened and her sons tried to come out, but old Rom blocked their way.

'No, no,' she cried to them. 'I'm all right. I'm all right. Stay inside. I'll be back soon.'

She held her hand over her face in an effort to conceal the blood gushing over her lips. One of the soldiers took her arm and said, 'Come on, missus. Let's get you inside.'

There were more soldiers in the truck. Grumbling, they dragged her over the tailboard and now she saw they were not alone. There were half a dozen men lying on the floor, most of whom she recognized. At least two were unconscious and the others close. All had blood soaking into their clothes either from visible or invisible wounds.

The engine started. She went to the tailgate; the soldiers grabbed her arms but she thrust her head out and cried, 'Rom, take care of the children! Children, take care of each other!'

A glimpse, then the soldiers threw her to the floor alongside the wounded men and the truck was grinding round the bend and out of sight of the house.

Back in the farmyard, one of the soldiers said, 'What about him, captain?' pointing his weapon at Rom.

'Him? Of course not,' said the officer with distaste. 'We're not in the business of collecting scarecrows.'

The soldier laughed dutifully and went on, 'And the kids?'

'They'll be sorted out later. Corrective schools most likely, so they don't grow up like their terrorist parents. You didn't notice such a thing as a bottle of wine in there, did you, trooper? It's been a thirsty kind of day.'

'I'm sure we can find you something, sir,' said the soldier, jerking his head at his mate, who winked in reply. They'd been fearful that the captain would be in such a hurry to get back to his comfortable quarters in Lyon that their chance of a bit of booty would go begging.

They went into the kitchen, the three boys and the old man retreating before them. The captain followed. Pauli and Céci were seated at the table. Pauli was still eating.

'Hello, more of them. They farrow well these country sows,' observed the captain to his driver, who was close behind. 'But hold on. Five? Surely our information was three, all boys?'

He took out some papers and examined them.

'Yes. So, we have two over? Is that you two, the hungry ones?'

His French was excellent. Pauli nodded.

'And who may you be?'

'We're visitors, monsieur. From Paris. Madame Laurentin is my mother's cousin.'

'I see,' said the captain, assured by the boy's rather pedantic way of speaking. 'Then what stories you'll have to tell when you get back home, eh?'

He smiled as he spoke. His friendliness to Pauli, his casual reference to their return home combined with all the other sources of resentment in Christophe.

339

Bursting from the restraint of Rom's long arm, his face red with shock and terror and fury, he burst out, 'It's all their fault! It's all their fault! It wouldn't have happened if they hadn't come! They're Jews, they're filthy Jews, that's why this has happened.'

One of the soldiers appeared with a bottle of wine and a glass which he filled.

The captain took it and drank it.

'Not too bad,' he said. 'Jews, you say, boy? But they're your relatives. Does that mean you too are Jews?'

Christophe's fury was spent. Only the shock and terror remained. And increased. He shook his head but couldn't speak.

'Well, boy, what's your name?'

The question was to Pauli, who was thrusting pieces of bread into his pockets.

'Paul Simonian, monsieur.'

'Simonian? Now, that has a flavour, certainly. And are you Jewish, Paul?'

The boy's eyes met his unblinkingly.

'We're Roman Catholics, sir, like maman.'

'Ah yes. But your father, this Simonian, what about him?'

Before Pauli could reply, Céci piped up, reassured by the captain's relaxed manner, 'Bubbah Sophie is Jewish, she told me so. The bad men took her away to Pitchipoi.'

'Bubbah Sophie? Your grandmother?'

Pauli nodded.

'And your grandfather? He was a Jew also?'

Pauli put some more bread into his pocket but didn't reply.

The captain finished his wine.

'Time to go,' he said. 'Fetch them.'

'All of them, sir?' asked the soldier.

The officer hesitated, looked at the brothers.

Pauli said, 'Madame Laurentin is my *mother's* cousin, monsieur, not my father's.'

The captain laughed.

'No wonder we need to deal with you people!' he said. 'Even the children are cleverer than half of our own adults! No. Just the young professor here and his sister. Quickly!'

Pauli and Céci were seized and dragged from the table and out of the kitchen.

'Should we get them some clothes?' asked one of the soldiers as they dumped the children in the back seat of the car.

'Don't be stupid,' said the captain languidly. 'Hello. What's this?'

An ancient truck had come creaking into sight down the farm track. It shuddered to a halt as its driver saw the staff car. Then, realizing that retreat was impossible, he set the vehicle bumping slowly forward again. It stopped by the barn. One of the soldiers approached and raised his rifle.

The passenger door opened and out climbed Maurice Melchior. He nodded at the soldier and strolled across to the car, his sharp eyes taking in the frightened children at the door and the young Simonians in the car. He tried to send a warning to Pauli and probably it got through. But Céci was too young for warnings. Delighted to see a familiar adult face, she cried, 'Hello, Monsieur Melchior.'

Melchior ignored her.

'Good day, lieutenant,' he said. 'A fine day for . . . almost anything.'

'Who are you?' said the officer, lighting a cigarette.

'Corder. Roger Corder. My partner and I do a little business with these good people. We're privileged to help keep many of your brave fellow officers in Lyon supplied with the fresh produce they deserve.'

'You mean you're a blackmarketeer. Why did this child call you Melchior?'

'A childish nickname. She thinks I come bearing gifts of gold.'

'Is that so?' The officer smiled. 'Go back to your truck, monsieur.'

'But of course. So pleased to have met you. If I can ever be of service.'

'Trooper,' called the officer. 'Get in that truck with these gentlemen and accompany them back to camp. If they lose their way or if the truck breaks down, shoot them both instantly. Driver, move on.'

The car pulled away, leaving Melchior pale-faced but still smiling. As they climbed the track, Pauli got a last glimpse of Christophe. But it was too distant to see if the boy, so early acquainted with grief and terror, had yet had time to savour the still more bitter and longer lasting taste of guilt.

3

Janine woke up. The bedroom was full of sunlight. She glanced at her watch and realized that it was only five forty-five. These nights of early June were short. Too short. She rolled over, realized that Jean-Paul was not by her side, and suddenly knew what had awoken her. A noise at the door, voices in the next room. Five o'clock in the morning. This was Gestapo time.

She jumped out of bed and rushed to the bedroom door and flung it open.

Jean-Paul still in his nightshirt, Henri and another man looked at her in surprise.

'I'm sorry,' she said. 'I thought . . .'

'. . . it was a raid!' To her surprise Jean-Paul laughed. Interruptions of meetings of Les Pêcheurs on any pretext usually filled him with irritation. Something must have put him in a good humour.

'Well, I suppose it is a raid in a manner of speaking,' continued Jean-Paul gleefully. 'But if you are expecting the Geste, I think you ought to wear something a little more formal, eh?'

She glanced down, realized she was naked and retreated

342

full of embarrassment. Beyond the door, the men laughed. She didn't mind. It was good to hear laughter in the house especially if Jean-Paul was part of it.

She went back to bed for an hour, but the meeting didn't end. Indeed there seemed to be more voices. Finally she rose and got dressed. The living-room was now full of smoke. She saw at once that the full council of Les Pêcheurs was here, including Christian Valois. She smiled at him and he nodded. He'd been very wary of her since she'd rebuffed him. He'd lost a lot of weight, looked older.

'Shall I make some coffee?' she asked.

'*Real* coffee?' asked Henri.

She smiled and shook her head and he groaned in mock disappointment.

'You'll get plenty of real coffee soon,' said Jean-Paul. 'Yes, Jansy, if you would.'

His rare use of his private name for her delighted her. Henri came into the tiny kitchen to drink some water to ease his talk- and smoke-roughened throat.

'Henri, what's happened?' she asked.

'Hasn't he told you? The message was broadcast from London last night. *The dice are cast.*'

'Meaning?'

He scratched his bullet head in bewilderment and said, 'He doesn't tell you much, does he? It means the invasion's close! We've got to do our bit to tie up the Boche from behind. There'll be high-level conferences later on, but you know Jean-Paul. He'll want to be sure Les Pêcheurs get their fair share!'

He went back through. The invasion! thought Janine. She was filled with hope, with fear, and also with some resentment. Jean-Paul's use of her in connection with Les Pêcheurs was almost solely on the domestic level. Like now. She occasionally carried low-key messages, made phone calls, left signs chalked on doors or walls. She didn't object. The less she knew, the less she could betray.

But he might have come to her himself with this tremendous news!

343

She shook the thought from her head and went through with the coffee. After she'd made sure everyone was served, she went back into the bedroom and left them to their planning. At eight-thirty she re-emerged and said to Jean-Paul, 'I'm going to my parents'! There should be a card from Mireille soon.'

'OK,' he said with a wave.

As she stood in the crowded métro carriage, she wondered how many of those around her had heard and understood the BBC message. There was no way to know. That was one thing this war had changed for ever. No one who had lived through it in France would ever be able to look at another human face and be sure he knew what was going on behind the eyes.

The thought frightened her. She prized openness so highly. This barrier of secrets which lay between her and Jean-Paul – not Resistance secrets, but reservations of thought, restraint of emotions, concealment of purpose in their everyday relationship – it was this which was the most painful change from what had existed before.

There was a smell of baking coming from the boulangerie but nothing like the rich perfume which used to make mouths water two streets away. Her still expert nose told her that her father was using potato flour. Even her mother's influence with the authorities must be waning in face of the ever-growing shortages.

Louise Crozier was in the shop. They embraced and Janine said eagerly, 'Any card?'

Her cousin Mireille had written to her care of the boulangerie ever since they'd been forced to abandon the flat in the Quartier Mouffetard. Only open cards were permitted and she'd written three since last she got one from Mireille, but such vagaries of the post were too commonplace to be a cause for concern.

'No,' said Louise. 'But there's a letter for you.'

'A letter.'

'Yes. It was posted through the door the night before last.'

344

Her mother's voice was displeased.

'I hope you're not getting mixed up with the wrong sort, Janine.'

'Oh, maman!' said Janine in exasperation. 'Where is it?'

They went into the living-room. Louise, of course, was right to some extent. A letter delivered anonymously in the night must have come through a subversive channel.

It was addressed simply to Madame Simonian. Janine examined the seal.

Her mother said, 'It's all right. It hasn't been opened. Don't think I didn't want to but *he* wouldn't let me.'

'I wasn't thinking of you, maman,' said Janine. 'I was checking if anyone official had been at it.'

Now she ripped the envelope open and began to read the single sheet of paper it held.

Madame Simonian,

Monsieur Laurentin's farmhand, Rom, who cannot read, has brought me your cards from the farmhouse. It is my sad duty to tell you that Monsieur Laurentin and his wife have been arrested on charges of terrorism. Their sons are being looked after by neighbours, but your children I regret to say were also taken into custody, I believe on the suspicion that they are Jewish. Since their arrest, I have been unable to discover anything further of their fate.

Madame, if your family is not Jewish, I advise you to apply to the authorities, with all haste and with every written proof you can furnish, for the return of your children. If, however, you are Jewish, then all I can recommend is that you pray to your God, as I will surely do to mine, that He delivers them safely from this ordeal.

It was signed by the curé of the local village.

Janine read it once. Read it twice.

Then she turned her stricken face to her mother and said, 'Oh maman . . .'

'Child, what is it? Oh God. Crozier!'

345

She caught her daughter as she fell. Crozier came in from the bakehouse, wiping his hands on his apron, and froze in shock in the doorway.

'What's happened?' he cried.

'Shut up and help me. Quickly, quickly!'

Together they eased Janine on to the sofa. Louise loosened her clothing and raised her feet on to a stool.

'Fetch the smelling salts. And the brandy. And a blanket. Hurry.'

Crozier rushed away, and, with her arm supporting Janine's head, Louise read the letter.

'Holy Mary, Mother of God,' she said, letting the single sheet flutter to the floor.

Her husband returned with the blanket and salts. She held the bottle under her own nose for a second before administering it to Janine, while Crozier draped the blanket over her. Then he stooped and picked up the letter.

Through tear-filled eyes, Louise saw his pasty face go even whiter.

'Where's that brandy?' she said sharply. 'Can't you do anything I ask?'

He went out again. Janine coughed and rolled her head away from the salts. With consciousness came memory and she started to sob wildly.

'There, there, child,' said Louise, pulling her head on to her bosom. 'It'll be all right, you'll see. It's just a mistake, a dreadful mistake.'

Crozier returned with the brandy bottle.

'I've closed the shop,' he said.

'What's to sell?' said his wife. 'Pour that brandy, will you? We all need it.'

He poured three generous glasses. Louise downed hers in a single draught, but Janine shook her head and pushed the offered glass away. Freeing herself from her mother's embrace, she sat upright, her gaze fixed on her father as if trying to force some reassurance from him. His face was full of love and pain as he said, 'We'll find them, never fear. We'll take advice, get a lawyer, everything that can be done, we'll do, don't worry, we'll find them . . .'

And Louise, trying to fill out the hollowness of these words, chimed in, 'I'll go down to the Majestic myself and ask them what they think they're doing, persecuting the families of honest citizens . . .'

But Janine knew that they had moved beyond a world in which love, and shared pain, and protest, and promises, could deter monsters.

Jumping up she cried, 'I have to tell Jean-Paul. He'll know what's best.'

'Wait!' cried Louise.

But it was no use. The young woman was already out of the room and next moment they heard the front door slam.

Crozier turned to his wife. For a moment she looked ready once more to heap on his head blame for all that had happened, was happening and might happen in these terrible times. But when he put his arms around her, she did not speak or resist.

How Janine got back to the flat in Clichy, she did not know. The meeting was still going on, but her entry was so sudden and violent that all talk stopped instantly. Jean-Paul, who'd been in mid-flow, regarded her with all his cold irritation at being interrupted. Henri tried to lighten the moment by saying, 'God, you nearly gave me a heart attack, coming in like that.'

She opened her mouth to speak. She believed almost superstitiously that if she could only present the facts rationally then a rational solution must be possible. But all that came out was a torrent of sobs in which all rational explanation was drowned.

Jean-Paul, his face twisted with alarm, took her in his arms but this only made things worse. It took Henri's unconscious imitation of her mother – 'Brandy! Fetch some brandy!' – to give her a focus for her chaotic emotions. Her parents loved their grandchildren enough to die for them, but they lacked the knowledge, the experience, the expertise, to help them live. These men, Henri, Christian, and above all Jean-Paul, were intimately acquainted with the world that was trying to destroy Pauli and Céci. They devoted their lives to fighting it. Here if anywhere she would find help.

Pushing herself away from her husband's embrace and this time accepting the brandy glass Henri offered her, she told them what had happened as baldly as she could.

Jean-Paul seized the letter and read it with a scowling intensity.

Henri swore softly.

'The bastards, I heard they'd blitzed the Maquis down there last month. Didn't you know that your cousin was . . . I'm sorry, I didn't mean to suggest . . .'

'It's all right, Henri. No, I didn't know. Mireille said that Lucien dropped them the odd sack of potatoes. If I'd thought there was any real risk, do you think I'd have . . .'

She was close to sobbing again. She took a deep breath. Valois took her hand.

'It'll be all right,' he assured her. 'They're running out of time. The invasion force will go through France like a knife through butter, you'll see.'

'But if they've been sent to Germany . . .'

'They won't have fuel and transport to spare to send kids to Germany,' he said.

She looked to Jean-Paul for confirmation of this theory.

He said bleakly, 'They had fuel and transport for my mother.'

'For God's sake,' protested Christian angrily.

Henri took his arm and gestured with his head towards the door. Simonian caught the gesture and said, 'No. Don't go. We'll go through here. But wait.'

He took Janine's hand and led her through into the bedroom.

They sat on the bed and for a minute or more simply held each other in silence. She was the first to break it.

'What are we going to do?' she asked. 'Should we go straight to Lyon?'

'To Lyon?' He sounded as if the suggestion surprised him.

'Yes. That's where they're likely to be, isn't it?'

'Perhaps. But they could be anywhere. We don't even know how long it's been. There are plenty of camps. They could even be back in Drancy by now.'

'Drancy?' Her eyes lit up with sudden hope. Drancy was vile but it was close. And she'd already got them out of there once.

'Don't worry. I'll check,' he said, with the quick confidence she'd been looking for. 'And I'll get word out to the network in Lyon to see if they can find anything.'

'You don't think we should go there then?'

'Jan, the invasion's just about to start, there's going to be chaos . . .'

She drew away from him now and said incredulously, 'You're not saying that you're going to be too busy to look for your children?'

'Don't be stupid!' he said angrily. 'What I'm saying is, the Boche will be expecting an upturn in Resistance activity and by Christ they're going to get it. But it'll mean a clampdown on travel, a tightening of security checks. Anyone vaguely suspicious is bound to be taken in. That's probably all that's happened to Pauli and Céci. Or some kind of protective custody. Who's to look after them now that the Laurentins have been arrested? It could just be some bureaucratic thing.'

'The letter said that Mireille's own kids weren't taken, just ours,' said Janine. 'Why should the authorities be so concerned about Pauli and Céci?'

She was trying to stop herself from growing angry. She was trying to tell herself that these apparent irrelevances were all part of that rational process which she had convinced herself was so desirable. But they still sounded like empty consolations.

'The letter! Some senile country priest taking dictation from some half-witted peasant. No, let's find out what's really happened first.' Jean-Paul was sounding angry too.

What was his anger concealing? Her mind reached for a solution, found one, didn't like it, tried to draw back from it.

'Jean-Paul,' she said quietly. 'What are you going to do?'

No longer *we. You.*

He turned to her, took her head in his hands and looked straight into her eyes.

'Jan, I'm going to do everything possible, believe me,' he said with a fierce intensity. 'And one thing you can be certain of, if any harm comes to the children, the bastards who did it, or allowed it to be done, will pay a thousand times over.'

She stood up and looked down at him.

'And you take some consolation from that thought, do you?' she said thoughtfully.

'Yes, I do,' he answered, not flinching from her gaze. 'It's not much, but it works. It's worked with my friends. It's worked with my mother. But, Jan, I'm not saying I believe anything's happened to the kids, far from it. I'm sick to my stomach about them but I'm ninety per cent certain we'll find they're OK . . .'

'No,' she interrupted. 'No, you're not. I understand you now, Jean-Paul. I thought at first you were being either incredibly stupid or incredibly callous. The truth's both better and worse, isn't it? What you're ninety per cent, even ninety-nine per cent sure is that the *worst* has happened, that there's nothing we can do. Or perhaps you simply have to believe that because that's your way of dealing with life now.'

'For Christ's sake,' he said angrily. 'This is no time for cut-price psychology.'

'Why not?' she said. 'Because it's wasting time we could spend trying to save our children? Or because it's wasting time you'd rather spend saving western civilization? Jean-Paul, they've got our children again. Hasn't it penetrated? Last time I had to face it alone. This time help me, please, I beg you.'

'I will,' he cried in an anguish almost matching her own. 'But I can only do what seems best . . .'

'Like carrying on with your precious meeting, you mean?'

'*Yes!* That's one of the ways, yes. Everything we can do to help the invasion brings everybody's freedom closer . . .'

'I don't give a damn about *everybody*, or *anybody* except Pauli and Céci,' she said harshly. 'Those German bullets did a lot to you, but the worst thing they did was make you forget how to love your children. You must have forgotten or else you'd know that there was nothing and nobody more important in the world. Well, I'll leave civilization in your safe hands. I've got other things to do!'

She turned and marched through the living-room where Les Pêcheurs were sitting with the embarrassed expressions of men who'd heard every word. Valois half-rose and said, 'Janine,' but she didn't even pause in her stride.

Simonian came into the room a moment later and sat down heavily.

'For God's sake, go after her, man,' urged Henri.

'Why? You heard what she said. She was right. I'll do all I can, but inside I fear the worst. Later, I'll talk with her later. Now isn't the moment, can't you see that?'

'Yes,' said Henri uncertainly. 'Look, shall we go now, leave this till later?'

'No,' said Simonian harshly. 'There's work to be done.'

Valois shook his head and said softly, 'Janine was right. Those bullets really changed you, didn't they?'

'They taught me to face up to the truth,' said Simonian. 'They taught me there are no short cuts to winning.'

'I see. It's the *Cause* that's all important! And you, Jean-Paul, you wouldn't betray that Cause, not even to save your own flesh and blood, would you?'

'No,' came the reply.

'I don't know whether to admire or despise you,' mused Valois.

But Henri said softly, 'From the bottom of my heart, I pity you.'

4

Günter Mai also received a letter that morning. The envelope bore Zeller's hunting horn emblem and, as required by military law, had the sender's address on the back. Nevertheless it had been opened and resealed. Censorship of officers' mail was unusual, especially from such an influential source. *Was it because of me or because of him?* wondered Mai uneasily.

It was a relief to find the contents were not even comically subversive. Zeller, now promoted colonel and, he modestly noted, awarded the Iron Cross, said the doctors had finally finished with him. He'd returned from Berlin to the family estate where he was convalescing. One of the pleasures of convalescence was entertaining old friends. He hoped Mai would spend a few days of his next home leave visiting him.

Had it not been for the censorship, Mai might have jokingly replied that he'd possibly look in as the whole army retreated across the Rhine. He too had been told of the BBC's message the previous night. More than 50 per cent of these coded messages were known to the *Abwehr*. *'The dice are cast'* merely confirmed what had been anticipated for weeks. The only question was, where would the landings be? Mai guessed Normandy but he hadn't been asked. His job was going to be coping with the support the Resistance would be giving the enemy.

'Excuse me, captain,' said a corporal sticking his head round the door. 'There's a woman says she wants to see you.'

'A woman?'

'Yes. She just walked in, bold as brass and asked to see you. They're holding her downstairs.'

'I'd better take a look.'

The corporal held the door open for him and didn't quite manage to conceal his grin as Mai passed.

He reckons I've put someone in the club, thought Mai.

He ran down the stairs into the sumptuously decorated vestibule of the Lutétia.

Standing quietly by the desk with an armed guard in close attendance was Janine Simonian.

He said, 'It's all right,' to the guard and to Janine he said, 'Come.'

He led her into the lift. As they sped upwards he said, 'What is it? The children or Jean-Paul?'

He knew that it must be some grave family crisis which had caused her to walk so openly into *Abwehr* HQ. When she said, 'The children,' he was relieved. To tangle with the Gestapo over Simonian, a terrorist Jew, was more than he could undertake. Yet he feared if she'd asked him, he might have tried, even though he knew she saw him only as a last resort, a lesser evil, when desperate needs made desperate demands.

They went into his office.

'Sit down,' he ordered, going round his desk. When he turned, she was still standing.

'You look different in your uniform,' she said.

She'd grown used to seeing him in civilian clothes, perhaps had even half grown to think of him as Édouard Scheffer, the dubious Alsatian businessman. Here, in uniform, he was indubitably the enemy and she was beginning to believe she must be crazy to have come.

'Janine, sit,' he said gently. He undid his tunic, removed it, rolled up his shirt sleeves, lit his pipe.

'Thank you,' she said and sat.

'Now,' he said.

Silently she handed him the curé's letter.

He read it without comment and handed it back.

'What do you want from me, Janine?'

'Find them,' she said. 'Get them released. You helped me last time.'

'Last time,' he echoed. He marshalled his thoughts. He should be telling her that last time they were in Paris and there was still some semblance of military control of internal security; he should be telling her that last time he had a favour to call in and could arrange for an *Ausweis* with little difficulty; he should be telling her that last time the children had been picked up because they were staying with their Jewish grandmother, not arrested because they were illicit members of a terrorist household.

And perhaps he should be telling her too that his country was about to face the most important, most deadly, and most desperate battle in its history, and every fibre of every nerve of every German officer ought to be straining to win that battle.

Above all he should be telling her that in the months that had elapsed since their last meeting, he had gained control of his emotions, that the love he had declared for her then had died of exposure, that he owed her nothing.

He looked at her and considered in his mind what he should be telling her and wondered how so much deception could have got mixed up with so much truth.

'I'll see what I can do,' he said.

'Thank you,' she said rising. 'I'll be at the boulangerie.'

'You're living with your parents again?'

'I shall be from today,' she said heading for the door. 'Thank you again.'

She's so certain I'll help her, so certain I'll succeed! he thought. Partly he resented this certainty, wanted to puncture it. But how much more he treasured it as the most direct and personal link between them!

He said, 'Wait. I'd better get someone to see you out.'

He summoned the corporal who looked in surprise at his shirt sleeve order.

'Please escort madame to the street,' he ordered.

She regarded him seriously for a moment, then she was gone.

He reached for the phone and asked to be connected with Lyon. The exchange operator told him there was very heavy traffic that morning and also that several lines were out of commission, meaning, he guessed, cut. It had started already, the terrorist back-up. The operator wanted to know his priority so that she could fit him into the order of precedence.

He hesitated, then gave the highest *Abwehr* priority he was authorized to use.

When his call got through about midday he kept it short. Two children, Paul and Cécile Simonian, had been taken by the occupying authority from the house of an Ain farmer called Lucien Laurentin some time in May. What had happened to them? Where were they now?

The captain in Lyon who took the call seemed disposed to wonder if, in the present state of the war, the whereabouts of a pair of French kids was worth very much *Abwehr* time.

'Do it!' barked Mai. 'Top priority.'

'All right,' said the captain reluctantly. 'But if it's a Gestapo matter, it may take a little time. Their right hands are never sure what their left hands have got hold of. Montluc's packed jam-tight.'

'Montluc?'

'It's a prison. A fortress really. The Frogs had closed it on health grounds, but the Gestapo had a grand reopening. From what I hear, compared with what it is now, it must have been like a Swiss sanatorium when they closed it.'

'Do what you can,' said Mai. 'It's urgent.'

He replaced the phone. It didn't sound good. He'd heard many reports of the barbarity of the SD regime down in Lyon. It sounded repressive even by Gestapo standards.

He hadn't heard anything by midnight. He'd felt a strong urge to walk round to the bakery earlier but the picture he had of hope lighting up that pale, thin face, then fading as she realized he brought no news, kept him from such foolishness. Besides he was very busy. Everybody was. There was an electricity in the air. Everyone, French and

355

German alike, knew it was coming, knew it was close. Rumours mushroomed; exploded, they sprouted up somewhere else.

But Mai knew it was no rumour that made his corporal shake him awake in the early hours of the following morning, June 6th.

'Sir, it's started,' he said. 'We've just had a signal.'

Mai rubbed his eyes, stretched.

'Where?' he asked.

'Normandy.'

'Thanks,' he said and went back to sleep.

Next morning the atmosphere had changed from electric to explosive. *They're getting news quicker than us*, someone complained. *And it's all good!* He meant the people of Paris. This good news was probably just about as accurate as the version of things the Propaganda Staffel in the Champs-Élysées was trying to feed them with, which told of enemy landing parties being driven back into the sea and showed the first pictures of Saint-Lô, destroyed by 'barbarian' bombers the night before.

Mai sat in the Café Balzac at midday and absorbed the atmosphere. It was the day of his regular meeting with Michel Boucher. He wondered if the big red-head would turn up. News of an allied invasion must have sent tremors of fear through the more blatantly collaborationist community.

But Boucher turned up, dead on time and sat down simultaneously with the arrival of his drink. Mai eyed the patron thoughtfully. There was a good weather-vane. When *he* decided that Miche should be struck from his list of most favoured customers, then it was time to worry.

'How are you, Édouard?' asked Boucher.

'I'm fine. A lot of patriots here today, I see.'

'Patriots? Yes, that's what we all are really, when it comes down to it,' said Boucher with apparent sincerity.

Mai smiled and wondered if Janine had gone to Boucher with her problems too. Seeking a way to prompt, without

356

arousing suspicion, he said, 'Ever hear from your friend, Melchior?'

'Little Maurice?' grinned Boucher. 'A postcard last year. He must have stayed on in Lyon after he got rid of the kids.'

'I thought he was going on to Marseille,' said Mai with a frown.

'What? Oh, you're worried he might split on the kids if he got picked up in Lyon, are you? Or on you, even. You never did fancy him going along with the kids, did you? Was that because he was a queer or because he was a Jew? Don't worry yourself, Maurice is all right. I wouldn't have had him working for me else, would I?'

Mai was more annoyed than he cared to show at having to sit under Boucher's mocking reproach. It was true, he didn't trust Melchior, never had; but it was because the man was clearly an amoral opportunist. Wasn't it?

Anyway it was clear Janine hadn't yet talked to Boucher.

'How's your family?' he asked to change the subject.

'Great!' said Boucher, his face lighting up. 'Hélène loves it down in the country. And she's having another! We just found out. Next January. It'll be a boy this time.'

'It must be great to be so certain of the future. Many congratulations.'

'Thanks. The future's what you make it, Günter. That's the one thing I've learned these last few years,' said Boucher with apparent confidence.

Mai smiled ruefully, almost enviously; lit his pipe and signalled to the patron who replenished their glasses. This was the signal that social chit-chat was over.

'How're *they* taking things?' enquired Mai.

'Running around like blue-arse fleas,' said Boucher. 'Blaming your lot for not knowing where the landings were coming.'

'They may be right. Any action?'

'They're going after terrorists heavy-handed,' said Boucher. 'They reckon this invasion will trigger off all the loonies, so they're going to pull in everyone they know.'

'Anything specific?'

'There's some meeting tomorrow morning, a Resistance council or some such thing. They're going to take it. They've got the address, timing, everything. I got details.'

He passed over a piece of paper. Mai studied it.

'Good intelligence,' he said with professional admiration. 'Are you on the raid?'

'No. Germans only. They're not even letting Pajou and his mob in on this. They must want some of these buggers alive!'

'What's Pajou up to these days?'

'He's in with that Milice lot, didn't I tell you? He took against them at first, but in the end he realized he couldn't beat 'em at their games, so he dealt himself in. He wanted me to stick with him, but I didn't fancy it somehow. Nasty sods. You've got to draw a line somewhere.'

I hope your countrymen make such fine distinctions, thought Mai.

He slipped Boucher his money a little later. The redhead didn't put the envelope out of sight with his usual speed.

'What's up?' said Mai rather sharply. 'Not enough?'

'What? No!' laughed Boucher. 'I'm not going to try to push you up. Though you're right, it's not enough to be worth bothering about! No, the thing is, Günter, the way I'm placed, I've got more than enough cash. I don't need this.'

'You mean, you want to break our connection?' said Mai.

To his surprise, Boucher said, 'No! I mean, it's not much of a connection really, professionally speaking. I never have much to tell you. And in any case, it's no contest any more between your lot and the Avenue Foch boys. They're in charge, aren't they? Christ, you're ten times brighter than me, so you must know it! Me, I enjoy meeting you, having a chat whether I've anything to report or not. I hoped mebbe you felt the same.'

Mai was at first amazed. Then as he examined what the

other had said, he was forced to acknowledge the truth. Partly it was Boucher's relationship to Janine that kept him coming to these meetings; but also it was because he enjoyed slipping into the clothes and character of Édouard Scheffer and relaxing for a friendly chat with this amiable, uncomplicated collaborator!

'Yes, I do, Miche,' he said.'Where does that leave us?'

'Same place, same time next week,' said Boucher cheerily. 'But keep your money to spend on booze.'

He tossed the envelope back.

Mai said, 'I'll buy the baby something with it.'

'That'll be nice. Hey look, I've been thinking. You must get local leave some time. Why not come and stay with us for a couple of days? Hélène doesn't see much company. We keep very quiet down there. To tell the truth, no one knows anything about me. I've kept what I do, who I am, pretty quiet. Some people react funny, don't they?'

Intrigued at this glimpse of a new domestic and discreet Boucher, Mai thought, Why not? He'd been working at full stretch for too long. With the Battle of Normandy still to be fought, there was no hope of home leave, but being in charge of the Section now meant it was easy enough to slip away for a couple of days.

He said, 'I'll see what I can manage. If we keep the invasion pinned down in Normandy, perhaps they'll be able to spare me briefly next month some time.'

'And if you can't keep the invasion pinned down, then you'll take a real holiday,' laughed Boucher. 'Fine, that's fixed. I look forward to it.'

'Yes,' said Mai, rather surprised. 'So do I.'

The next morning the phone rang at last.

'Mai? Bruch.' It was his opposite number in Lyon. 'They're here. At least they've got two Jewish terrorists called Simonian listed, so I presume that's Gestapo longhand for the kids. The Gestapo here seem to have taken the invasion personally. They're rounding up everyone. Montluc's bursting at the seams, but the only way they know of releasing anyone is down a gun barrel into a grave.

I thought the bastards were going to take *me* in! So next time I hear from you, it'd better be with a written order with a big *big* signature. Otherwise, my hands are tied, if you'll excuse the phrase.'

The phone went dead.

Mai sat unmoving for several minutes.

Then he picked up the receiver once more.

Ten minutes later he was in the office of his *Abwehr* chief.

'This had better be important, Captain Mai.'

'I think it is, sir,' he said producing the paper Boucher had passed him. 'One of my agents, a woman, she's always been most reliable in the past, well she's just come through with information about a high-level Resistance council meeting this afternoon. I've got everything – timing, location, security, escape routes, the lot. This could be a real coup for us, sir. And for free! All my agent wants in payment is . . .'

Half an hour after this he was at the Hôtel Majestic. Always go to the top.

He got two copies of the release order. One he delivered personally to Gestapo HQ with a request that they expedite the release. The other he despatched to his *Abwehr* counterpart in Lyon. His final act was to attempt to get a direct connection with the Administrator at Montluc, but this proved impossible and he had to be content with talking to Bruch once more.

'Well done. I'll get round there as soon as it arrives,' the captain promised.

Mai put down the phone and slumped back in his chair. He felt exhausted. It wasn't surprising. This had all started at nine-thirty that morning. It was now about three. He hadn't stopped to eat or drink or even smoke a pipe in that time.

But he hadn't finished yet.

As he stood up, the phone rang. It was the chief.

'Mai, that intelligence you got.'

'Sir. Nothing wrong, I hope.'

'No, it's all fine. The trouble is, the SD have it already. They got a hint somehow we were setting up an operation and rang to request us to hold off.'

Request. Mai could tell from the bitterness in the other's voice what kind of request it had been.

'I'm so sorry, sir,' he said. 'I didn't know . . .'

'Of course not. How could you? Not your fault. I sometimes wonder . . .'

What he sometimes wondered he decided to keep to himself. With a brusque goodbye, he signed off.

Mai sighed with relief. If for one moment the man had suspected how he'd been manipulated . . .

But there were still tracks to be smoothed over before he could feel safe.

And best of all there was the good news to pass on!

When he reached the bakery, however, his heart sank with disappointment. The shutters were up and there was a *Closed* sign on the door.

Disconsolately he rapped on the glass. After a couple of minutes he was just turning away when the blind twitched. Next thing it had flown up like a startled bird and he saw Janine pulling at bolts and twisting at keys in her desperate haste to open the door.

'What's happened?' she was demanding even before he'd got across the doorstep. 'Is there news? Please, please.'

'It's all right, it's all right,' he said. 'They're alive and well.'

'Oh thank God,' she said, swaying forward into his arms. 'Thank God.'

He held her for a moment then she broke away and taking his hand pulled him from the open doorway into the living quarters behind the shop.

'Please, please, tell me everything,' she begged.

'Are you alone?' he asked.

'Yes,' she said impatiently. 'There's no flour, nothing, so maman and papa have gone to visit some friends. Please, tell me!'

361

He told her what he knew, what he'd done.

'And they'll let them go, you're sure?' she demanded.

'Absolutely,' he said, with more confidence than he felt. With the Gestapo, who could be sure? But he knew he could do no more.

'Oh thank you. Thank you,' she said. She was aglow with relief, with joy. He could have sat and simply watched her for the rest of the day. But there were still things to do and, in any case, any moment now she would be wanting to rush off to share her joy with Simonian.

He said rather brusquely, 'One more thing. To get this release, I've had to make out you're one of my top agents. Well, you know that already. Only this time, I had to claim you'd given me details of an important terrorist meeting. It would be useful to have this supported by written evidence in your file. I've jotted down the details.'

He handed her his jottings and a blank sheet of paper.

She said, 'You want me to copy this and sign it.'

'Yes.'

'And that will help the children?'

'The children's release is already on the way. This will help me in the not unlikely event that the Gestapo decide to check my files again.'

'So it's just to help you?'

He thought he was being accused of selfishness and said sharply, 'Yes, but if you don't want to copy it, I'll understand.'

'No, no,' she said shaking her head, taking up the pen he'd given her and beginning to scribble. 'But tell me, why didn't you bring this to me first? Wouldn't that have been the clever thing, to make sure you had your cover-up fixed in advance?'

'The release form was the important thing,' he said. 'Time might be of the essence.'

She scrawled her name at the bottom of the sheet and blew on it to dry the ink. When she passed it over to him, he folded it without looking at it, thrust it into his tunic and stood up.

'Are you going?' she asked.

'Yes. You'll want to tell your husband. What will you tell him by the way?'

'I don't know,' she said. 'The truth perhaps. Anyone can stay pure by hiding from dilemmas, can't they?'

'I'd avoid the truth,' he said uneasily. 'Can't you give Miche the credit for finding out the children are alive?'

'OK, I'll tell him that. When I can find him. And if it happens he's not too busy.'

Her bitterness was unmistakable.

Mai said, 'I'm sorry.'

'Why?' She rose now and stood before him, studying him curiously. 'You said in the Tuileries Garden that you loved me.'

'Yes.'

'I didn't know what to believe. Now you've put yourself at risk again for me, and only thought later of how you'd cover yourself.'

He tried to turn away, thinking he couldn't stand much more of this, but she caught at his arm and pulled him back to face her. Now she stepped so close to him that he could feel her warmth though they were not actually touching.

'I don't want a *reward*!' he cried.

'Don't you?' she said. 'That's your affair. What I want is to be held by a man who loves me and puts that before everything.'

Her face was raised to his. And now they were touching.

'Janine,' he said.

'No words,' she said. 'No nationalities. No deals, no rewards. Just love.'

5

Christian Valois struck the table so hard that a glass fell off it and only Jean-Paul's instant reflexes prevented it from hitting the ground.

'Calm down,' he said, replacing the glass. 'You'll get us arrested for creating a disturbance and then neither of us will get to the meeting.'

They were sitting outside a café on the Avenue d'Italie. Christian's fury was caused because during what he'd thought was a last-minute briefing before an important meeting at which he was Les Pêcheurs' accredited representative, Jean-Paul had casually announced he was coming along as well.

'What's the matter?' he demanded. 'Don't you think I can argue our point of view?'

'Better than me, probably,' said Simonian. 'Only, I've got things to say which I have to say myself.'

'They're only expecting one. They won't want two,' argued Valois. 'It's not democratic, it's not good security.'

'All right. Then I'll go by myself,' said Simonian equably. 'You stay here and drink a bottle of this terrible stuff they call wine.'

Christian thought, then shook his head.

'No,' he said. 'I'm the delegate.'

'So you are. The delegate of Les Pêcheurs. But I'm Le Pêcheur himself, Christian, never forget that. When you joined, I told you what I tell everyone. What I say goes!'

The friends locked gazes.

'Janine's right. You have changed,' said Valois looking away.

'You too, Christian. And everyone else. Right, shall we go?'

'It's not for an hour. We'll be early.'

'Then perhaps we'll arrive at the same time as the Gestapo if they happen to be coming!'

'For Christ's sake, this is no joking matter,' snapped Valois. 'There's always danger, especially if people start changing the arrangements.'

Simonian looked at his friend curiously.

'Don't let it get to you, Christian,' he said. 'I've noticed you showing the strain a bit lately. Look. I'm sorry I've upset you, but I really do think I should attend this one. And we'll take extra care, I promise.'

And in fact so cautious was the approach mapped out by Simonian that they needed almost the full hour even though the house where the meeting was being held was only ten minutes' walk from the café.

As they entered the shadowy hallway, a man confronted them with his hand in his coat pocket. Hastily Christian gave the password.

'There's only supposed to be one of you,' said the man.

'Now there's two,' said Simonian.

'He's our group leader,' said Christian.

'The Fisherman? Well, I suppose that'll be all right.'

'Kind of you,' said Simonian.

They climbed to the second floor. It was the waiting-room of a dentist's surgery. This was the cover in case of accidental interruption. The dentist and a 'patient', both Resistants, would be in the surgery next door.

The last representative arrived on the stroke of three and the meeting got under way. Below in the hallway, the guard smoked a home-made cigarette and tried to identify the wide variety of tobaccos from which it had been constructed. It only lasted as long as a slow fuse. Outside in the breeze it would have been more like a fast fuse, he consoled himself, peering through the peephole he'd poked through the curtain. He was wondering whether to light another awful fag when he saw a couple walking along the pavement, the woman with a piece of towel held against

365

her mouth, the man with his arm around her shoulders, talking sympathetically, encouragingly.

'Shit,' said the guard as they paused uncertainly. Deciding that positive action was best, he opened the door and made as if to step out. Then, glancing at the woman, he said, 'Not looking for the dentist, I hope? He's away. All shut up. Won't be back for a week.'

'Bloody hell!' said the man. 'It's just about killing her. Is there another dentist round here?'

'Well,' said the guard, 'I've seen a sign, but whether there's anyone still working there. If you go down the street, take the first left . . .'

He turned to point and gesticulate. Something hard rammed into his spine.

'Keep quiet,' hissed the man.

He said in as loud a voice as he dared, 'Now what's all . . .'

The woman hit him with amazing strength in the belly so that he doubled up, belching his words out as he was forced back through the doorway. He was dimly aware now she'd dropped the towel that the woman needed a shave. He was also aware that at least two more men had slipped into the hall.

'Let's go,' said one in German.

They went quiet as snakes up the stairs.

Some instinct for danger made Simonian begin to rise a single second before the door burst open and the armed men rushed in crying, 'Gestapo! No one move!' He stared at them like a cornered animal, his body tensed to leap. But Christian cried, 'Jean-Paul, no!' and, grabbing his arm, pulled him back down. The Resistant nearest the surgery door suddenly made a dive for it. No one offered to fire at him, but he stopped as though hit on the threshold. The dentist and the 'patient' were crouched on the floor with their hands on their heads and three more armed men stood behind them.

'Let's get them downstairs,' said the group's leader. He seized Christian by the collar and hurled him towards the door where one of the others spun him on to the landing and pushed him down the stairs. He almost fell, only just managing to keep his balance, but his uncontrolled impetus carried him into the hallway with such force that the Gestapo man at the bottom had to jump aside, tripping over the guard's recumbent figure as he did so.

Valois didn't stop but flung himself out of the street door. A car was coming to a halt just outside. He turned and ran in the direction it had come from. The passenger door opened and the man seated there got out without haste, drawing a pistol from his pocket. But before he could aim, he screamed with pain as another figure rocketed out of the house and crashed the car door against his legs.

It was Jean-Paul.

Christian had reached a corner. He glanced back to check on pursuit as he rounded it. For the first time he became aware that Jean-Paul was behind him.

And behind Jean-Paul two – no, *three* – of the German raiders were bringing up their guns.

Christian screamed, 'Jean-Paul! *No!*'

The guns fired. A rackety volley like an old motorbike trying to start. Ten yards from the corner, Jean-Paul threw up his arms. But he kept coming, his heart pumping blood to desperate straining muscles, three yards, two, and he flung himself into Christian's arms like a runner breasting the tape.

The heart still pumped madly and Valois felt the blood spurting out against his hands which he clasped around his friend's back.

Jean-Paul turned his face up to him like a lover seeking a kiss.

'Tell Janine . . .' he said but could manage no more, and the hot orgasmic spurts against Christian's fingers died to nothing as the body became dead weight in his arms.

He looked back towards the house. The gun men were still standing there, guns outstretched, as though frozen in a movie frame. Then the reel jerked into life again and they came running towards him, shouting.

Gently he laid Jean-Paul Simonian on the pavement. The face looked young again and the scar of his head wound from that hopeless battle back in 1940 was almost invisible.

The Gestapo men were closing fast. Christian reached inside his jacket and pulled out an automatic pistol. The Germans seemed nonplussed to find him armed and standing his ground, and he had killed the first two before the third managed to get a retaliatory shot in. It ripped along Christian's left shoulder, but his right arm remained steady as he shot the man through the head.

Now there were more men in the street, running, firing. He dropped his gun into the gutter, clutched at his wounded shoulder, turned and ran.

He had no conscious idea of where he was going but he knew where he had to go, so it was no surprise when he started taking notice of his surroundings again to find himself approaching the Crozier Boulangerie. It was a surprise, however, when his eye caught his watch to see that it was not yet four o'clock. Less than an hour had passed since he and Jean-Paul had entered the dentist's house an eternity ago.

The shop door was open. He walked in and through to the back. There was no one there, but he thought he heard a noise above, so he went to the foot of the stairs and called, 'Janine.'

There was silence but it was the silence of listening.

'Janine!' he called again. 'For God's sake!'

A door opened and she appeared at the head of the stairs. She had pulled a cotton wrap about her body and was tying it at the waist. Her hair was loose and trailed like sun-bleached silk over her shoulders.

'Christian. What is it? I was asleep.'

He pushed himself away from the wall as his swimming mind sought the words to convey his terrible news.

Janine let out a cry of horror and he realized that his palm had left a bloody imprint on the wall.

'You're hurt,' she said starting down the stairs towards him.

But her cry had reached other ears. Through pain-filled eyes Christian saw another figure appear behind her on the landing. His first thought as he recognized the uniform was that he had been followed here. Then his eyes and his mind cleared and he recognized the man buttoning up his grey tunic as the stocky *Abwehr* officer who was always hanging round the bakery.

Janine reached him. He swung his good arm with all his strength and struck her backhanded across the mouth.

'Bitch!' he cried, as she fell back on the stairs, her lips bloody.

Mai started to descend, shouting angrily, his hand plucking his gun from its holster, but Janine half-rose to block his way.

'For Christ's sake, what's happened?' she asked thickly.

'Jean-Paul's dead,' said Valois with vicious clarity. 'Our meeting was raided. They shot him down in the street. Your lovers slaughtered him in the street!'

Then with one last despairing, contemptuous look at the stricken woman, he turned and staggered out of the house.

Mai put his hands on Janine's shoulders and turned her towards him, flinching away from her accusing gaze.

'I didn't know. I swear I didn't know,' he said urgently.

She shook her head in disbelief and mouthed but could not articulate the words, 'Go! Just go.'

He had no resources for dealing with this, he, Günter Mai, Captain of Military Intelligence, master of agents, manipulator of men. He could find nothing to do but fasten his buttons and put on his cap and sneak away like any squalid philanderer caught in an act of betrayal.

Betrayal of whom? he asked himself that night as he drank alone in his room. There had been betrayal, that was true, but not that which Janine accused him of. There had been a wanted man, a terrorist who had been involved in the murder of many Germans, standing wounded and

369

unarmed within easy reach of him, and he had done nothing. That was betrayal, surely?

He was drinking brandy by the tumblerful, but drunkenness was a long time coming and at eleven o'clock he had a telephone call which put it completely beyond reach.

'Mai? Walter Fiebelkorn here. Look, I've just been dining at the Raphael and your chief had been invited too. We had a chat. We were amused that we'd both wanted to ambush the same terrorist meeting today. He told me you'd got the details for the *Abwehr*. Good work. If we'd known you were on the trail too, we could have worked together. But I thought you might like to know that it went fairly well. A few casualties on our side, I'm afraid. One dead, one escaped on the other side, but we got a good haul. The interrogation's been going on while I've been having dinner and I'm sure they'll begin to break soon.'

'Congratulations, colonel. Thank you for calling.'

'Wait. A moment more. The dead man was called Simonian, also known, I believe, as the Fisherman. Your Colonel Zeller will be pleased to hear that. His gang were responsible for the attempt on his life, I believe. But I was interested to learn that it was this man's own wife who gave you the information! Excellent work, Mai. Didn't you once rescue her from us before? I seem to recall it. It just shows how right you were! And also, I gather, as a reward and an incentive, you were trying to get this woman's children released from arrest. Quite right. A couple of Jewish children for an agent like this, it would be a bargain.'

Now Mai was as sober as he ever had been in his life.

'That's right,' he said. 'I hope perhaps you can help, colonel. There's a release order on the way. I left a copy at Gestapo HQ.'

'Yes, yes. I have it before me now. That's really why I was ringing. Knowing how energetic our officers in Lyon are and what a rapid turnover of prisoners there is down there, I took the liberty of ringing Montluc myself to ensure your order was expected.

'Captain Mai. I'm sorry to tell you this, but I was too late. Alas, these miserable children have already been put on a transport.'

'When? Where to?' shouted Mai.

'Who knows? It was a bad line. And with such large numbers as are dealt with daily, there is always some vagueness. But their ultimate destination is certain enough. Perhaps we should redirect the release order there. To Auschwitz, Captain Mai. To Auschwitz Camp in Poland. Would you like the address?'

6

'Pauli,' whispered Céci. 'Is it Christmas yet?'

'No. Not yet.'

'It's just that we've been here such a long time, I thought maybe it was nearly Christmas.'

'No, but don't worry. I'll tell you when it comes. I won't let you miss it.'

Pauli knew exactly how long they'd been in Montluc. He kept a count of the days scratched in his sandal leather with his thumb nail. He could have scratched more efficiently if he'd wanted, for deep in the lining of his trousers he had the knife which Uncle Miche had given him for Christmas two, or was it three years earlier. He kept it hidden, however, doubtful if his fellow prisoners could resist the temptation to steal it, certain that the guards wouldn't even try to resist. They had only been perfunctorily searched on arrival, nothing like the thorough and repeated body searches given at Drancy where every last item of value was stripped from the inmates before they were packed into the cattle-train for the east.

There were three imprisonment buildings in the fortress

371

of Montluc; the main cell block, three storeys high; a single-storey block referred to though not used as the refectory; and a building made of yellow painted wood where the Jewish prisoners were 'housed'. It was into this that the Simonian children had been pushed. A mutter of protest went up at the sight of the youngsters, but it was stilled by a man called Stern who seemed to have some authority.

'Let 'em be,' he growled. 'Draw attention to them and God knows what may happen. Each day any of us sits quietly here is a day nearer the end of the war, remember that.'

Somehow, contact was kept with the outside world, and the fever of anticipation of the expected invasion had touched even these men who guessed how little they personally were likely to benefit from it.

The Gestapo guards sensed this traffic of news in and out and did everything they could by way of punishment and infiltration to halt it. The inmates always required any new prisoner to give a full account of himself to convince them he was not a German stoolie. Not even the bright evidence of recent beating visible on the face of the thin little man hurled into their midst a couple of days later was enough. Anyone could stand a beating.

'What's your name, friend?' enquired someone.

'Now that's a matter of some small dispute,' said the newcomer, massaging his badly bruised jaw. 'Magus I am, but I fear my gifts of gold have been knocked from my teeth!'

'Anyone know this joker? No?' The questioner grew angry. 'So what's your sodding name?'

The newcomer's hand had moved from his jaw to a cut on his cheekbone.

'Do you have a mirror?' he said in alarm. 'Has anyone got a mirror? Oh dear. What do you think, sir? Will it leave a scar? Oh God. Wrinkles I can resist, but not another scar!'

His interrogator seized him by the throat.

'It'll scar all the way down to your toes if you don't start answering!'

To the surprise of those with the strength left to be surprised, the little man laughed.

'My dear fellow, after what I've been through, after what I've been threatened with, do you imagine a scarecrow like you can frighten me? Now, remove your hand or at least put it somewhere more friendly.'

The man looked at Stern, who nodded.

'Thank you,' said the man. 'And now, to those who have a sympathetic soul, let me bring pain with my most melancholy story.'

But before he could start his narration, he felt a small hand slip into his. Looking down, he encountered a gaze whose steadiness was more disconcerting here than ever before.

'Good morning, Monsieur Melchior,' said Pauli.

'What? Pauli? Is it you? And Céci. Oh God, have they thrown you too in this awful place, my dears?'

His attempted insouciance ripped to shreds, Maurice Melchior knelt down and embraced the children with tears streaming down his face.

'You know this man, kids?' said Stern.

'Yes, sir. He brought us from Paris to Lyon. He lived upstairs from Bubbah Sophie, my grandmother in Paris.'

That established Melchior's credentials for most. Only Stern showed any interest in his story now.

He told it without embellishment, conscious of Pauli drinking in every word.

'Even then, I may have persuaded them I really *was* Corder if Octave, my business associate, had not decided he could save his own skin by offering them mine,' he concluded. 'Since this war began, I have not been fortunate in my choice of friends. But at least it has brought me in touch with these unfortunate children again. I owe Pauli at least two debts. We must get them out, and ourselves too!'

Stern shook his head.

'Forget it. Only one man has escaped from Montluc, André Devigny last year. There are only two ways any of us are leaving this place. *Avec bagages* or *sans bagages*.'

'I'm sorry?' said Melchior, puzzled.

'If your name is called *avec bagages* it means you're on your way to a concentration camp in Germany,' said Stern.

'And *sans bagages*?'

'Shorter journey. Quicker end,' said Stern laconically.

'Oh God.' Maurice Melchior closed his eyes. Despite his show of bravado, he was utterly terrified. Always before in his life, even during the worst periods, his capacity to relax in a sea of troubles and grasp at whatever straws of pleasure floated by had always kept him going. Now at last he found himself completely waterlogged with his prospects reduced to a choice between a quick and a slow drowning.

Céci moved against his chest and whimpered. He opened his eyes and adjusted her head so that she was once more comfortable.

Now he glanced at Pauli and tried to smile. His purpose was to reassure, to offer hope and encouragement, but the smile would not come. After a moment he closed his eyes once more. It was strange, but if there had been any reassurance in that brief eye-contact, it had passed not from him to the boy, but from that steady, thoughtful gaze into his hectic mind.

Days passed, became weeks. It was good when they were allowed to pass in utter passivity. A world of stinking air, overflowing toilet buckets, vile food and the complete and uncontrollable infestation of person, clothing, bedding and woodwork with every kind of crawling, burrowing, flying vermin imaginable made itself bearable only when the mind was anaesthetized into accepting this as the best, and the worst, there was. But there were disturbances, prisoners dragged out for interrogation, or for deportation, or worst of all the four a.m. *appels sans bagages* which were followed a short time later by the rattle of rifle-fire.

And even disturbances of a different kind, like the ripple of joyous excitement that ran through the prison when news penetrated of the Allied landings in Normandy, only brought more pain, as the image of an outer world touched with a hope they could not share trembled like a heat-mirage before the prisoners' minds.

Then late one night the guard opened the door and cried, 'Simonian. Paul. Cécile. Out!'

Maurice Melchior was roused from what passed for sleep by the call. He struggled to his feet in time to see the children going through the door.

Heedless of the men he trampled on, he rushed after them saying, 'Wait!'

The guard watched his approach indifferently then swung the butt of his rifle into his skinny rib-cage and sent him crashing backwards on top of the sleepers he'd just roused with his feet.

The guard looked down at his list again and rattled off some more names. Last among them was Melchior. When he saw Maurice approaching again, he laughed.

'If you'd waited, you wouldn't have got hit, would you? Oh, by the way, *avec bagages*, if you've got any.'

Encouraged by the guard's albeit brutal attempt at humour, Melchior asked, 'Where are we going? Is it to Drancy?'

The guard looked at him closely, clearly wondering which would cause more pain, another blow or an honest reply.

He opted for the reply.

'No,' he said. 'Usually you lot go to Drancy first, that's true. But this time you're privileged. Straight to Germany, or should I say, straight through Germany? Lucky sods. Wish it was me! Now get out before I smash your head in.'

Behind him he heard Stern's voice calling, 'Good luck! Remember, there's no way out from within!'

If that was a hint, it ought to have come with a printed diagram, thought Melchior bitterly as they were herded by soldiers armed with sub-machine-guns across the short distance which separated the prison from a complex of railway sidings. Here a line of cattle-wagons awaited. They were driven into them. Melchior saw the children ahead and managed to close up behind them so that they got into the same wagon.

The wagons were crowded, but not jam-packed and it was possible for everyone to squat, though not to stretch out. The children were accorded a corner and Melchior by asserting his status *in loco parentis* joined them.

'Let's get comfortable,' he said trying for cheerfulness. 'I daresay it will be a longish journey.'

'Let no one wish it shorter,' said someone with gloomy foreboding.

'Don't worry. We'll probably be stuck here till tomorrow at least.'

It seemed he might be right. The night passed by and the sun was beginning to make the temperature in the wagon uncomfortable and they still hadn't moved.

Melchior tried to sleep, but his mind seemed to have been jerked into frenetic and useless activity by the move, like an old clock whirring into life for a little while when shaken. Also there were too many noises, new and therefore distracting noises, to keep him awake. Among them was a gentle scratching, perhaps the least of all the sounds that disturbed him, but the most regular and certainly he decided, the closest.

He finally tracked it down to Pauli, who lay almost doubled up, apparently sleeping.

He touched the boy gently and he opened his eyes.

'Monsieur?'

'Pauli, that noise . . .'

The boy shifted his leg slightly and looked down. Melchior followed his gaze. His eyes rounded as he saw in the boy's hand a knife.

'I promised maman I wouldn't use the blade until she said I could,' said Pauli guiltily.

'I think if she knew, she wouldn't mind at all,' said Maurice Melchior.

The boy was scratching away at the floorboards. To Melchior it looked like a hopeless task. The boards were thick, close-laid, solidly nailed and constructed from hardwood beaten even harder by the stamp of shifting hooves over the years.

'Let me know when you're tired,' he said.

And now the long wait was on their side. Inevitably, it seemed like no time at all before they felt the jolt of a shunting locomotive being attached and then the movement of the wagons beginning to roll.

They only went a few miles, however, before they came to a halt again. Melchior guessed they were being linked with another train, possibly a supply train. They wouldn't want to waste a precious locomotive on a few Jew-filled wagons.

But even with these hours of delay, the impression made on the floorboards still seemed little more than a scratch when after another series of bangs and jerks, they at last started up once more. Matters weren't helped by the need to keep their efforts secret. Melchior would have liked to think otherwise, but he knew there was no guarantee that they wouldn't find a majority of their fellow prisoners more terrified of probable reprisals than interested in possible escape.

The train stopped again. They heard a guard on the roof of their wagon call, 'What's happening?' and the distant reply came, 'It's the line. Fucking terrorists have blown it up!'

Some time later, the train went into reverse for several miles then stopped, either waiting to be re-routed, or because it had sought the shelter of a tunnel from possible air attack. The work went on, always more carefully and therefore more slowly when there wasn't the sound of the train to cover the scratching. But the extra time was invaluable and shortly after the train started again, Pauli gave a little cry and when Melchior looked, he saw that the knife was moving quite freely at one end of the by now deep groove.

Blowing the wood-shavings aside, he pressed his eye to the slit and saw beneath the wagon the railway sleepers rushing by.

But all this had drawn attention. A bald middle-aged man who'd been sitting close by with his eyes half-closed reciting prayers for most of the journey suddenly said in a frightened whisper, 'What are you doing?'

'Sh,' said Melchior, putting his finger to his lips.

'Are you crazy?' said the man who'd now glimpsed the knife and the damage to the floorboard. 'You'll get us all killed, you know that! They won't ask who's in, who's out! They'll blame us all!'

'All the more reason to keep your mouth shut!' said Melchior.

Another thirty minutes had the break extended across the whole width of the floorboard. Now they picked a point about twenty inches along the same board, just before it reached the next cross-joint, and set to work again. Where they were, how far they'd gone, Maurice had no idea. But Stern's parting words, you don't get outside from inside, were echoing in his mind and he worked like a man obsessed with the idea that here was their last chance. Surprisingly, though his strength was greater than Pauli's, he lacked the boy's stamina and they soon evolved a system of thirty minutes' steady scratching from Pauli followed by a quarter-hour's hard assault by himself. At one point he offered the neighbour the knife, but the man turned away as though it was a fresh dog-turd.

The train began to slow again and finally came to a halt. Could they have arrived already? It was dark again outside, they'd been on the train for at least twenty-four hours with nothing to sustain them but a couple of buckets of dirty water. These were long since empty and one was being used as a toilet bucket, its vile stench almost visible in the heavy air. Suddenly the wagon door slid open. Bright lights shone in. Melchior shifted his position to give Pauli who was working at the floorboard maximum cover. The man who had objected moved as if to stand up and even began to speak. Then he seemed to change his mind and sat down, silent, once more.

Melchior waited in fear for the order to get out.

Instead, a couple of new water buckets were dumped on the wagon floor and a cardboard box containing several hard German loaves.

Just before the door slid shut again, Melchior glanced towards the bald man to show his gratitude. In the glare of the electric light he saw that Pauli was sitting, blank-faced, with the point of the knife pressed against the man's kidneys. Then the door closed and darkness returned.

It took some time for their eyes to get accustomed to the gloom once more. In that time, someone managed to knock over one of the buckets and the bread box too was overturned and the loaves scattered. There was a lot of angry shouting and recrimination.

Fools, thought Melchior. On the other hand, you couldn't fight the Boche without sustenance.

He crawled towards the bread and water and by calling out, 'The children! The children!' he managed to get a reasonable share.

Refreshed, they worked even harder and as the grey light of dawn began to seep through the gaps in the side of the wagon, the blade of the knife slipped completely through at one end of the second groove. Another ten minutes and all that held it in place was a thin splinter. Carefully Melchior sawed through this and withdrew the knife. The section of floorboard remained in place. Impatient suddenly, he stood up and drove his heel down hard. The cut-away square vanished and there a couple of feet beneath them was the stone-filled track rushing by like a pebbly torrent.

By now almost everyone in the wagon was aware what was going on. Men crowded round the aperture and peered down. It took some time for someone to voice the general thought.

'Who's going through *that*? A rubber dwarf?'

It was true, now it was finished, the aperture looked remarkably small. Eighteen inches by twelve perhaps. And it was also true that, even if it were possible to squeeze through, to drop on to that rushing track looked like certain death.

'You'll need to cut a section out of the next board too,' advised someone.

'Suddenly everyone's an expert!' said Melchior. 'Where were you when we were sawing already?'

For answer the man snatched the knife from Pauli's hand and began hacking at the next board. Another knelt down and tried to wrench the broken board upwards by main force, but it would probably have defeated a fit man, let alone this emaciated scarecrow.

Céci who, happily for her, possessed a cat's power of being able to sleep at will and apparently for ever, was woken up by the activity and, because Pauli was not clearly in view, began to weep. Her brother went to her immediately and tried to comfort her.

'We're slowing down again,' someone said.

'Bugger! What is it? A station?'

One of those peering through the slats in the side of the wagon said, 'No. It's a bridge. I can't see much. It's dark. But there's a river. Yes, definitely a river. A big river. It just goes on and on. Oh God. It must be the Rhine! We're over now. We must be in Germany.'

The news chilled their hearts disproportionately. France which had done so few favours for most of them still felt like the land of home and freedom. Here they were in the beast's own terrain.

Some time later, the train came to a halt. Again not a station, the man at the spy-hole reported. Nothing but trees were visible. At first the halt seemed a stroke of luck, giving them more time to work, but suddenly a couple of guards stretching their legs came to a halt outside the wagon, and their conversation was so clear that the man working with the knife was shushed to silence. It became clear this was a mere signal delay. The guards talked happily of having a real German breakfast half an hour up the line. But the worst news came when one of them said, 'Jesus! What a stink from these wagons!'

'Not to worry,' said the other. 'We'll get 'em out and have a bit of fun with the hoses when we reach the station!'

Laughing, they moved away. Maurice whose German was now excellent, translated what had been said.

'That does it,' said the man with the knife. 'It's now or never.'

He sat down and thrust his legs into the hole. It was at once clear that he wasn't going to be able to get his thighs through, let alone his hips.

'Get out, idiot,' someone said. 'Let someone try who's got a chance.'

They all looked at Melchior. He dropped his skinny legs through the hole and slid downwards. When he reached his hips, he got stuck. The others pressed his shoulders but it was in vain.

Finally he said, 'This is wasting time. Get me out.'

They pulled him upwards not without difficulty. He turned to the children.

'All right, Pauli. Down you go.'

The skinny boy got through without difficulty. Next he passed down the little girl, her eyes wide at this latest extraordinary game she and Pauli were having to play.

'Right, Pauli. Lie down between the tracks. Don't move till the train has gone right away. Understand?'

'Yes, monsieur. Please, Monsieur Melchior, can't you come too?'

Whether the appeal was based on concern for the adult or the child, Melchior didn't know. Either way it moved him greatly.

'I'm sorry, I can't,' he said. 'All this rich living has made me fat. Now, if I had some nice goose grease, I might slip through!'

He saw the direction of the boy's eyes. With a child's clarity, he had identified the only possible source of lubrication in that wagon. Melchior rose and looked down into the slop bucket. His stomach turned over.

'What the hell are you thinking of?' asked one of others, revolted.

Melchior looked around at their faces, barely visible in the grey light, good faces, weak faces, bewildered faces, fearful faces, incredulous faces, defeated faces. What precisely lay at their journey's end, none of them knew, but it came to Melchior then that there could be a time when he would recall his squeamishness standing over this slop bucket, and weep.

He began to slip off his clothes and toss them through the hole to Pauli.

Naked he bent with a handful of straw; retching, he plunged it into the bucket and then began to anoint his hips and skinny rump with the noisome slimy mixture.

There were cries of horror and disgust, but they didn't bother him. His own feeling of nausea ceased. He knew he was right.

'Stand aside Pauli,' he said.

He stepped into the hole. The vile lubrication worked and he got much deeper than before. But still he could not pass completely through, still there was a quarter-inch too much.

Suddenly there was shouting outside and the guards could be heard clambering back on board as a steam-whistle blew.

'Help me!' he cried at the watching men.

The bald man moved forward and flung himself on to Melchior's shoulder. There was a moment of pain, then he was through. After him the bald man tossed a lump of bread.

'Take this!' he cried.

Melchior had no time for thanks. He felt the train beginning to lurch forward. He flung himself down. Pauli was already lying between the tracks, almost covering his sister. A foot from his head a huge wheel strained round. He watched it without flinching. If this child can bear this,

382

what cannot I bear? Melchior asked himself as he buried his face in the gravel between the sleepers. On either side, the wheels found traction; the train began to move, gathering speed; the sound of metal kissing metal rang in his ears, the ground trembled beneath his belly.

Then it was past and away and fading.

The trio lay still a little longer. Then Melchior and Pauli rolled over on their backs and looked up at the dawn-grey sky. After a while Melchior rose and, stepping off the track, began to pull handfuls of dew-damp grass to clean the evil-smelling lubrication from his body.

'What do we do now, Monsieur Melchior?' asked Pauli.

'We walk,' said Melchior, pulling on his clothes. 'Back that way towards the Rhine. Then we cross it and get back into France and go home. How does that sound, little prince?'

The boy didn't speak but nodded enigmatically and turned to help his sister.

You're right, thought Melchior. That's how it sounds to me too. Hopeless! But now he came to think about it, he'd given up any hope many years ago and had always managed very well without it!

'Arc you ready, children?' he asked brightly. 'Then west we go. Homeward bound.'

7

It was more than a month since Mai had been to the Balzac.

Michel Boucher greeted him with undisguised pleasure.

'Hey, I was beginning to think you were avoiding me.'

'No,' said Mai sharply. 'Pressure of work.'

'Yeah? The Resistance has certainly been busy since the invasion. Auntie Louise was saying you never go down to the bakery now. I think she'd have liked to ask your advice about the kids. Ask! I think she'd have got down on her knees and begged. I never thought I'd feel sorry for the old battle-axe, but she's really taken it bad. Janine said there was nothing you could expect a German to do. Only she wasn't as polite as that.'

The big man's keen eyes were regarding him shrewdly.

'She asked if I could help. I couldn't,' said Mai.

'That's what I reckoned. But I know you'd do your best, Günter.'

'And how is Janine?' asked Mai in a voice only just under control.

'What do you think? The kids. Then Jean-Paul. I wanted to get her out. You know how it is with the Geste. Once they get their hands on a Resistant or his body they usually go looking for the rest of the family. But she wouldn't. And they didn't. Funny that.'

'Yes, funny,' said Mai.

'People said some nasty things. I had to slap a couple of mouths.'

It occurred to Mai that Boucher was not the most convincing champion a woman accused of collaboration might select.

He said, 'Is she ill?'

'Ill? She ought to be dead by the look of her,' said Boucher bluntly. 'But she'll keep going till she finds out something. She's been wandering around everywhere. The Majestic, the Kommandantur, Avenue Foch. She even goes to Drancy, stands and waits for convoys to leave. Günter, are you sure there's nothing you can do for her?'

Only destroy her completely, thought Mai. He had used and abused every bit of authority he had. The SD had blocked his every move. Fiebelkorn may or may not have been lying when he said the children had already been transported, but one thing was clear. Mai wasn't going to find out anything different, and each passing day made it more likely that Fiebelkorn's claim had become true.

So all he could say now to Janine was, *The children are lost. Believe it.*

She would make him say it one day. No matter how much she despised him, in the end desperation would drive her to seek him out. For the past few weeks he had simply been avoiding the inevitable.

'I've done all I can,' he said. 'There's nothing more I can do.'

He must have sounded desperate for Boucher patted him sympathetically on the arm and said, 'Don't take it to heart. It's not your fault. It's those other bastards. You look a bit run down to me, Günter. I'd say a few days in the country is just what you need.'

Boucher had renewed his invitation to come and stay at his house at Moret. Mai would have loved nothing better. The invasion forces were still being held, though at great cost. There was a false sense of calm in the city at the moment. Perhaps he could sneak a day or two . . .

'You'll love it,' said Boucher sensing his weakening. 'Peace, booze, and lots of lovely grub. Hélène's a marvellous cook. She's really taken to the life. So what do you say?'

Mai was saved from answering immediately by the approach of the patron who whispered, 'Monsieur Scheffer, your friend is here . . . I've seen her outside a couple of times recently . . . Do you want me to . . . ?'

He made a gesture of dismissal.

Mai looked up. Standing in the doorway of the café was Janine. Framed by the light, she appeared only as a slim silhouette, but unmistakable.

The patron obviously thought there'd been a rift, followed by a refusal on her part to accept her marching orders.

He said, 'No,' stood up, went down the length of the café with the step of a man walking from the condemned cell to the execution chamber.

'Janine,' he said.

'Where are the children?'

385

Her voice sounded calm. He wasn't deceived. Now was the time to kill the hope.

He said, 'Janine, I'm doing all I can . . .'

'This too,' she said. 'Even in this, you deceived me.'

'Janine . . .' He couldn't do it.

She turned and walked away. Hysterics, assault, abuse, anything would have been better than this cold certainty that he was beneath contempt. He wanted to run after her, but something in his will failed, and his muscles would not move.

'Hey, was that Janine? What did she want? Are you all right?'

Boucher was standing by him looking anxious.

'Yes, it was Janine,' he said. 'And yes, I'm all right.'

'Shit. I know how much you'd like to help,' said Boucher. 'Me too. I'd do anything.'

The man's sincerity shone out of him. They stood together united in helplessness. Suddenly Mai made up his mind. He had to get away or he'd go mad, or perform madness.

'I'll come to Moret,' he said. 'Next week, if that's OK?'

'That's great,' enthused Boucher. 'I'll pick you up and run you down in the Hispanola. You'll have a great time, just you wait!'

For once the red-head's assurances proved totally reliable and Mai enjoyed the stay even more than he expected. The sun shone and he spent most of the time walking or sitting in the extensive garden, reading books, playing with Boucher's tiny daughter and eating huge meals.

It was only thoughts of Janine which darkened these sunlit days. He found himself imagining her in Hélène's place and himself in Boucher's, with Pauli and Céci playing on the grass, and he would drift so deep into these reveries that it often took a vigorous shake of his shoulder to bring him back to the painful reality.

Boucher was no great intellect, but it didn't take him long to fathom the cause of his guest's distraction. Over a

386

bottle of Armagnac on the last night of his stay Mai found himself confiding in the man. Boucher's response was both comforting and devastating in its directness and lack of complication.

'I've always seen you were sweet on her,' he said. 'And she fancied you too, even if she didn't want to.'

'Did she?' said Mai, amazed.

'Oh yes. I reckon I saw it before she knew it herself. Not that you had any real chance while that Jew-boy of hers was alive. She was obsessed with him.'

Mai reached for the bottle.

'It's empty,' said Boucher. 'I'll fetch another.'

The next day, Mai didn't wake up till noon.

'Oh shit,' he said.

'What's up?' asked Boucher from the doorway.

'I should've been back this morning.'

'Are you sure? What do your papers say?'

'Leave of absence till the twentieth.'

'There you are then. It's the twentieth all day! And they won't expect you to check in at midnight will they? Come and have some breakfast and then some lunch! I'll see you're back in your office by eight sharp tomorrow morning.'

What strength and what weakness lay in such a simplistic approach to life and its problems, thought Mai.

'All right,' he agreed.

Another idyllic day went by, free from pressures, free almost from the painful memory of Janine as he sat in the sunshine and allowed its heat to drug his already hangover-anaesthetized mind.

That night he was very temperate in his sampling of Boucher's excellent cellar. The big red-head laughed at him and drank with his customary enthusiasm. Mai forecast to himself that in order to get back to Paris for eight in the morning, he would have to take upon himself his host's reveille duties.

But when he was woken by a loud knocking, he thought sleepily that he'd done the man an injustice. It took a little time to realize that the knocking was downstairs at the main door. He glanced at his watch. It was still very early. The light coming through his curtains was the pearly luminescence of a summer dawn. He heard Boucher's door open further along the landing and his voice booming, presumably to Hélène, 'It's all right, go back to sleep, it'll just be some idiot gendarme checking on the black-out now the sun's coming up!'

Mai went to the window. There was a long black car parked across the driveway. Two men leaned against it. One was smoking a cigarette. Both were armed.

His first thought was – Resistance raid!

He ran out on to the landing to warn Boucher but looking down the stairs into the hallway he saw it was unnecessary. His grumpy reassurances had been for Hélène's benefit. He was moving swiftly and quietly towards the door with a machine-pistol in his hand.

There was a spy-hole fitted on the door. The big man applied his eye to it, and let out an exclamation.

Then he stepped back, undid the bolts and the lock, and flung the door open.

'Pajou!' he said. 'What the hell do you want?'

The weedy little Géstapiste stepped inside uninvited. He didn't seem to be armed. He wore an ingratiating smile but his eyes behind the wire-rimmed glasses were darting glances everywhere.

'Miche,' he said. 'Morning. Sorry to disturb you. Hey, it's a lovely place you've got here!'

'How the hell did you know about it?' demanded Boucher angrily.

'It wasn't a secret, was it?' said Pajou with mock surprise. 'Well, you know me, Miche. Sharp eyes, sharp ears. But if it was supposed to be secret, then I'm glad I came myself.'

'What do you mean?'

'It's just that there's a bit of a flap on among our Boche mates, and they seemed to want Lieutenant – sorry, *Captain* Mai in a hurry, and I happened to know he was down here enjoying a spot of leave, so I offered to fetch him.'

He never looked directly up the stairs but Mai knew he'd been seen and the contemptuous reference to 'our Boche mates' had been dropped in for his benefit.

But for God's sake, what could have happencd to make this little rat so impudent in the presence of a *Wehrmacht* officer?

It was time to speak.

'Pajou, what the hell's going on?' he demanded.

'There you are, captain,' said Pajou, advancing to the foot of the stairs and shielding his eyes as though from a great light. 'You haven't heard then? Well, how could you, down here, enjoying your leave? That's a mark in your favour. You see, there's bad news and good news. The bad news is someone tried to blow up the Führer.'

'What?' exclaimed Mai, knowing as he saw Pajou's cynical smile that he didn't sound surprised enough. Why should he? Anyone with half a mind had known that it was only success that had made the old militaiy families like Bruno Zeller's put up with vulgar little Adolf so long. With the invasion forces established and advancing, some kind of revolt was inevitable. If Zeller had still been in Paris, he'd almost certainly have tried to involve his lieutenant. He'd dropped enough hints of disaffection in the past. So; a lucky escape or a missed opportunity, depending on how things had gone. Not that Pajou's presence left much doubt of that.

'*Tried*, you say?' said Mai.

'Oh yes. That's the good news. The Führer was uninjured. A little annoyed, so they say, but completely safe! Heil Hitler!'

The revolting creature threw his hand in the air in a parody of a salute. Mai's heart sank. Nothing was more ominous than Pajou's confident impudence. But he couldn't believe that even the SD would depute a French collaborationist to arrest a *Wehrmacht* officer.

He said, 'Who sent you, Pajou?'

'Well, Colonel Fiebelkorn, sort of. I'll explain in private, shall I?'

Uninvited he came running up the stairs. Mai led him into his bedroom and quickly got dressed, the annoyance of being watched by those lizard eyes being preferable to the disadvantage of holding a conversation in his night-shirt.

'Civilian clothes, eh? Very good. And no doubt you've got Monsieur Édouard Scheffer's identification somewhere about you? That could be useful.'

Did this little bastard know everything? Mai recalled he'd once dismissed him as being not very bright. Something else he'd been wrong about.

'All right, Pajou. Spit it out,' he said brusquely.

The man had no intention of saying anything directly, but by hints and obliquities, he soon made his purpose clear. There'd been several hours during which it was believed Hitler was dead. The *Militärbefehlshaber* had ordered the arrest of senior SS and SD officers to prepare the way for the expected assumption by the Army of all powers, political and military. But news of the Führer's survival, confirmed later that night by his voice, hysterical with fury, on the radio, had changed everything. Released, the SD were bent on revenge. The principal high-ranking officers involved would be returned to Berlin to be dealt with there. But smaller fry would be disposed of locally.

'I just happened to be around while all this was going on,' said Pajou. 'I was at the Avenue Foch when some *Wehrmacht* chaps were invited in for a chat. That's when I realized Colonel Fiebelkorn was keen to see you too, captain, and as I happened to know where you were . . .'

But he was here under his own steam, that was clear. And his reasons were soon clear too.

For a 'consideration', he would give Mai a running start to disappear into the countryside. For a larger consideration, he would even help him across the border into Switzerland.

When Mai packed his bag and announced his intention of returning to Paris, Pajou only laughed, assuming this was part of the haggling process.

'Come on, captain,' he said. 'You must be loaded! I mean, you've been here from the start.'

The man really believed it! He could not envisage that a man with Mai's opportunities wouldn't have laden himself with plunder during the past four years.

But when it became clear that Mai meant what he said, his ingratiating manner ceased.

'You're a fucking idiot,' he said. 'But you can't help that. All right, in the car! Sooner we get you back the better.'

'Pajou,' said Mai softly. 'You forget yourself. To talk to a *Wehrmacht* officer in that insubordinate tone is a criminal offence. Men have been shot for less.'

This was the real test. For a moment Pajou looked uneasy and Mai felt triumphant. But when he turned to Boucher and said, 'Right, Miche. Let's go,' Pajou said, 'Oh no, captain. With me, not him.'

'I prefer to choose my own transport.'

'There may be less choice than you think. Eh, Miche?'

Boucher was sitting on a sofa with Hélène, whose face was heavy with apprehension. She had hold of his right arm and now her grip visibly tightened. The red-head's gaze met Mai's then slipped away.

'I'm sorry, captain,' he said miserably. 'But mebbe it's best . . .'

'Never mind, Miche,' said Mai, smiling. 'I understand.'

He did. Pajou's keen sharp nose must have sniffed out Boucher's special arrangement with the *Abwehr* as well as his country hideaway, so poor Miche was in no position to make empty gestures on behalf of a German officer in trouble.

As they approached Paris, Pajou renewed his offer. Mai didn't respond. There hadn't even been a moment when he felt tempted. He couldn't envisage a worse fate for a man than to become a fugitive from his own country. In

391

any case, why should he? Whatever he had guessed, he had *known* nothing.

Of course there would be a witch-hunt, there would be unpleasant moments ahead; but ultimately even the fury of the SD must wane and acknowledge that some of those under suspicion were telling the truth. At worst he might find himself under officer's arrest in the Lutétia for a couple of days. He could use them to weed out his files before the withdrawal from Paris – a withdrawal he now accepted as certain. An intelligence officer had loyalties to his agents. Some, like Boucher, were too prominent in their activities to be protected. But others, more clandestine in their work, did not deserve betrayal by their employers.

And there was one more, whose name must be expunged completely. He'd kept Janine's file on record so that her alleged *Abwehr* status could protect her from the SD. Now suddenly he wished he'd anticipated matters and destroyed it before his trip to Moret.

He wished it even more a little later. The streets of Paris were full of soldiers in full battledress. The car was stopped several times, but Pajou's papers obviously carried a weighty authority. Mai, deep in gloomy thought, paid little attention till he realized they were crossing the river.

'Hold on! Where are we going? I want to go to the Lutétia!'

But Pajou only smiled at him, and fingered his gun. A few minutes later, the car came to a halt before SD HQ in the Avenue Foch.

'Wishing you'd made a deal now, eh, captain?' said Pajou, opening the door. 'Sorry, but it's too late.'

They went in. Pajou talked urgently to an SS major who went away, and returned a few minutes later. Mai tried to address him, but the man ignored him. For the first time, Mai wished he'd been wearing his uniform.

Now he felt his arm seized by Pajou in a grip which was close to the point where friendly directive pressure became arresting force. They went out into the avenue again and entered another building a little further along. Here they were expected. An NCO led them down a flight of stairs and opened a door into a brightly lit though sparsely furnished room in which Colonel Fiebelkorn was talking to a Gestapo man.

'Captain Mai! So here you are,' said Fiebelkorn, little black eyes glistening behind his glasses. 'Sorry that your leave has been interrupted. Thank you, Monsieur Pajou, for your assistance. Though if you'd told us you knew where to find the captain, we could have saved you the trouble.'

There was a threat vibrating unmistakably behind the words and Pajou retreated before it, smiling ingratiatingly.

'I'm glad to see you do not authorize foreigners to summon *Wehrmacht* officers, colonel,' said Mai boldly.

'Of course not. You can rest assured that I value the honour of the *Wehrmacht* too highly for that,' said Fiebelkorn. 'More highly, it seems, than some of your own superiors.'

'Sir?'

'You must know what has happened?'

'Yes, sir. I learnt of the assassination attempt for the first time from Pajou. It was a terrible shock.'

'It must have been,' said the colonel.

'I was of course delighted to hear the attempt had failed. What I don't understand is why I have been brought here.'

'There are certain necessary investigations. I hope we can rely on your aid.'

'Of course, sir.'

'Good. Now for a start, you can perhaps point out the code phrases in this and tell us what they mean.'

He tossed a sheet of paper on to the desk.

Mai examined it briefly and said in surprise, 'But that's a letter I got recently from Colonel Zeller.'

'Yes, yes, we know it is. What we want to know is its significance.'

'It's just a letter. He was badly hurt, he's been convalescing . . . but you know all that.'

'It's a very friendly letter for someone of Zeller's background to be writing to a subordinate like yourself, wouldn't you say?'

'Perhaps. But as I didn't write it, I don't see why I should need –'

Fiebelkorn cut across him brutally. 'Are you saying it was just coincidence that you decided to bury yourself out of sight in the countryside on the day of this monstrous assassination attempt?'

'Of course. What other reason – '

'A prudent man might think it best to keep his head down till he saw which way things were going.'

'A prudent man who knew what was going to happen, yes! But I didn't. Colonel, I demand to see someone from the *Wehrmacht*'s legal department. If I'm going to be cross-questioned, I want it to be at a properly constituted Board of Enquiry.'

'Someone from the *Wehrmacht* . . .' mused Fiebelkorn. 'Have a look through there, see if there's anyone you fancy.'

He pointed to a door behind him. Günter Mai approached it, then hesitated. Something in him resisted going through that door. The Gestapo man reached past him with a muttered 'excuse me' and turned the handle.

The room beyond was not so brightly lit but bright enough. Two shirt-sleeved men sat on wooden chairs, smoking cigarettes whose vapour coiled around the bare light bulb which hung from the centre of the ceiling. A couple of feet behind it something else hung. Three meat hooks had been screwed into a beam. From them stretched wires so fine that the men hanging from them seemed to be supporting themselves like performers in some grotesque ballet on the very tips of their toes.

Mai looked at the naked bodies in shocked disbelief. Their torsos were livid with bruises and their sexual organs were a scarcely recognizable mass of crushed and bleeding flesh. The thin filaments of wire were digging so deep into their necks that they couldn't be seen, but the pulled and swollen flesh, the gaping lips and protruding tongues, showed that they were there.

'You bastards!' he yelled, turning, his hand going to where his pistol would have been had he been in uniform.

The Gestapo man punched him in the stomach. One of the seated men hooked his legs from under him, and as he hit the floor the other lashed his booted foot against the side of his head. He rolled over and over and came to a halt semi-conscious, with his head resting against a pair of the balletically poised feet.

What could it mean? he wondered dully. When men could do this to other men, *any* men, let alone their fellow soldiers, what could *anything* mean?

Another pair of feet came into view, boots highly polished, toes slightly splayed.

'And now, Captain Mai,' said Fiebelkorn's distant, echoing voice, 'let the Board of Enquiry begin.'

8

Four or it may have been five days after their escape from the train Maurice Melchior and the two children woke high on a forested slope and found themselves looking down on a broad river gleaming in the midday sun.

'Is it the Rhine?' asked Pauli incredulously.

'Of course, my child. What else?' replied Melchior casually.

He thought he concealed his own delight and amazement very well. They had travelled only at night. Mercifully the weather had held fine. They had drunk spring water and eaten whatever of the midsummer vegetation Pauli's recently acquired country lore pronounced safe. They'd made one large diversion to avoid an encampment of soldiers but that apart, they had seen no one. Each morning as the moon faded and the east grew grey, they had chosen a hiding place and snuggled up together to get what sleep they could.

In Melchior's mind they had been completely and irretrievably lost. Thus to wake up this morning and find that by some miracle he had performed what he promised and brought them to this mighty river gave him a greater joy than he could recall and seemed a guarantee of their future safety.

'What do we do now, Monsieur Maurice?' asked Pauli. 'Swim across the river?'

'We'll see,' said Melchior. It was not the time to admit he could not swim a stroke. God would surely provide!

'Don't move!' came a harsh command from behind him. 'Hands up!'

He couldn't believe it, not here, not now, with the Rhine in sight. A man moved slowly by him keeping a safe distance away. He was dressed in a grey-green tunic which for a moment Melchior thought despairingly was *Wehrmacht* uniform. Then he realized that soldiers didn't wear old feathered hats, neither did they carry shotguns, nor were many of them, except perhaps generals, in their seventies.

But for all the man's age, the gun was aimed without a tremor.

'Good day,' Melchior said in his best German. 'The children and I were having a little picnic. I do hope we're not . . .'

The word for 'trespassing' failed him.

'Foreigner?' said the man accusingly.

'Yes, but a friend,' said Melchior disarmingly. 'Italian. An ally.'

It occurred to him as he spoke that most Italians were no longer the Germans' allies. The man was certainly not disarmed.

'Move,' he commanded. And when Melchior stood still, he raised his shotgun menacingly.

Apart from the man's age and his weapon, there was

something else about him which tugged at Melchior's attention and kept his mind off their destination as they marched uphill through the forest. The children walked ahead. Pauli held his sister's hand and she chatted quite happily as she trotted along.

Melchior guessed they would end up in a village where they would be gawked at by rough peasants till the army – or worse, the Gestapo – had been summoned to deal with them. Instead after about twenty minutes they stepped out of the trees on to a rising stretch of mown grass and there ahead of them was a castle.

It wasn't a big castle as Rhine castles go, but it had all the usual absurdly romantic turrets and towers. On another occasion, Melchior might have viewed its exuberance with some pleasure.

There was another old man, who seemed to be pruning some bushes. Their captor shouted at him. He came and peered in amazement at the prisoners then turned and lumbered off towards the house. He too was wearing a sort of uniform tunic. It was this that Melchior now identified as being at the centre of his mental irritation. He tried to divert his mind back to the terrible peril he and the children now stood in, and, as the eye in moving away will often glimpse the object it's been looking for, so now he remembered.

He stopped and turned. The gun came up, the hammer was cocked.

'No, no,' said Melchior soothingly. 'I just want to look at your buttons.'

He looked. They bore a device he had last seen on a ring worn on a hand which was gently caressing his naked thigh. Or had it been clenched in rage?

'And what have we here?'

The voice sounded familiar, but when he turned he saw he had been wrong. The ancient gardener had merely brought another old man to view the scene. This one perhaps had some authority, standing as he did on the steps leading up to the open main door. He looked as if something rather terrible had happened to him. He was leaning heavily on a stick, his right sleeve was empty and pinned to his breast, and as for his face . . . it was heavily muffled, but what Melchior could see had the burnished purpureal look left by severe burning . . .

And then he saw the eyes and recognized their recognition of him. He took a step forward.

'Bruno? Is it you? Oh God. Bruno, my dear . . .'

He felt tears damp on his cheeks.

'Well, well. All things come to those who wait,' came the familiar voice from that dreadful strangeness.

And Melchior looked into those hard blue eyes again and began to think that perhaps he should have saved his tears for himself.

PART SEVEN
August 1944

Il y avait loin de ces mœurs efféminées aux
émotions profondes que donna l'arrivée
imprévue de l'armée française. Bientôt
surgirent des mœurs nouvelles et passionées.
Un peuple tout entier s'aperçut . . . que
tout ce qu'il avait respecté jusque-là était
souverainement ridicule et quelquefois
odieux. Le départ du dernier régiment de
l'Autriche marqua la chute des idées
anciennes: exposer sa vie devint à la
mode; on vit que pour être heureux . . . il
fallait aimer la patrie d'un amour réel et
chercher les actions héroiques.

Stendhal, *La chartreuse de Parme*

1

Janine Simonian looked in her bedroom mirror and wondered why she hadn't gone mad.

It was the same gilt-framed, silver-flaked glass which had faithfully recorded her image since she'd first had to climb on the bed to look into it. Now it showed what could easily have been the picture of a madwoman. Thin by nature, emaciated by malnutrition, her face was now positively cadaverous through grief, and her neglected hair hung in knots and tangles over her sparrow-boned shoulders.

But she knew she was sane. As long as the children were alive she would shun the tempting path down into madness. And the children *were* alive. She knew it with the same certainty she had felt about Jean-Paul during those long months of silence.

But even the firmest faith requires a sign.

During the past weeks she had gone everywhere, confronted everyone, in search of this sign. Curiously the Germans had received her more courteously than the French. Christian Valois must have told Les Pêcheurs of disturbing her in bed with Mai, and it was evident that her other meetings with the man, or at least *a* man, hadn't gone unobserved, and had only gone unreported because Jean-Paul wasn't the kind of man you called a cuckold to his face.

So any sympathy felt at the loss of her children was compounded by the feeling that she'd brought it on herself.

Even Henri, good-natured, solid Henri, couldn't keep the coldness out of his voice as he regretted that none of his Resistance contacts had been able to find any trace of the kids and suggested that for her own good, in the present temper of the city, she'd do well to take a long vacation.

She had in fact travelled to Lyon, not for a holiday or a refuge, but in search of that faith-bolstering sign. All she learned there was that Lucien Laurentin had been shot and Mireille was still imprisoned. Yes, there had been a pair of Yid kids at Montluc some weeks back, but they'd been transported long since. Where? Where the hell did she think!

She returned to Paris and resumed her rounds, meeting everywhere with the same unhelpful courtesy. The fact that the Germans did not seem interested in arresting or even harassing her, the widow of a notorious Jewish Resistant, was not going unnoticed, except by herself. She had no time for any diversion of thought from her search for information, for hope. She went everywhere, the Majestic, the Avenue Foch, even the Lutétia where she demanded to see Günter Mai once more. They held her at the entrance for more than an hour, then told her that Captain Mai had been transferred.

Michel Boucher, when she told him this incidentally in a long account of her efforts, looked grim.

'Transferred, is that what they're calling it now? Poor Günter. It'll be a long bloody transfer, I fear.'

No one, not even Pajou, knew precisely what had become of Mai but there were plenty of stories of the horrific treatment of other suspects in the July conspiracy. What Miche told her of his conversations with Mai at Moret persuaded her that she had probably misjudged him.

'Poor Günter,' she echoed.

But she could not get it out of her mind that being in bed with him had had some kind of causal link with Jean-Paul's death.

So August came and sunny days succeeded each other, and Paris listened to the news from the west, and some watched to see what the Occupiers would do, and others made their own preparations.

'They're leaving! They're going! Oh God, Crozier, is it ending at last? Is our ordeal over?'

402

Madame Crozier burst into the shop where Claude was leaning on the counter talking to a few hopefuls who'd come in vain to buy and stayed instead to gossip.

'We may survive after all. It's been long and hard, but it looks as if we've done it. Not much thanks to you! Thank God I kept my head and did my duty as a French citizen!'

Louise Crozier's conversion to a flamboyant patriotism had gathered pace rapidly since the Normandy landings.

'So, it's happening, eh?' said Crozier.

'Didn't I say so? You can hardly move in the streets. They've got soldiers directing traffic. It's really inconsiderate of the police to pick this time to go on strike when they could be doing so much to speed the Boche on their way!'

The exodus had started the previous day and now it had swollen to flood proportions. But there was not yet any cause for rejoicing. Informed opinion pointed out that this wasn't retreat but a clearing of decks for the battle to come.

It was the administrators who were leaving, the bureaucrats, the office staff, the petty officials who for most Parisians had been the public face of the Occupation.

'I heard the Gestapo and all that lot are pulling out too,' said a customer.

'What do you expect? No stomach for a real fight, those bastards!' growled someone else.

'Don't worry, friend. It's the *Wehrmacht* that's staying and whatever else you say about the Boche, you can't say they don't make good soldiers. You'll get your real fight!'

'Fighting? I hope there's going to be no fighting round here,' said Madame Crozier in alarm. 'Crozier, get the shutters up. I haven't endured so long to have my windows shattered now! Janine, dear, where are you going?'

Silence fell in the shop as Janine entered from the house.

'Out,' she said. 'I'm going out.'

'It might be better to stay at home, my love,' said her father. 'The streets are very busy.'

'That's why I've got to go. If the Germans are leaving, there may be some news.'

Claude Crozier had at first tried to argue in face of his daughter's logic, had tried to steer her gently and with love to an acceptance that perhaps the children were lost for ever. But soon he had given up, recognizing that such an acceptance could only bring about his daughter's complete destruction.

Behind him, Louise burst into tears and rushed into the house. Janine embraced her father and went out into the street.

She was recognized by several people in the immediate neighbourhood. Familiarity with her haggard looks had dulled what sympathy they had initially aroused, and now her passage was marked by threatening and contemptuous glares and sometimes outcries. She gave no sign that she saw or heard anything.

But when she reached the main streets, then she became animated, eyes darting glances everywhere, ears strained to hear everything. Her mother had not exaggerated. In every direction the streets were jammed with German traffic; staff cars, armoured vehicles, supply trucks, ambulances, buses, lorries, even horse-drawn carts, all of them packed with personnel, equipment and luggage.

'The bastards are still taking everything!' said someone angrily.

It looked to be true. No one from the highest officer to the lowliest private seemed willing to leave the loot of four years behind. Quite openly displayed in some vehicles were hastily loaded pictures, ornaments, racks of clothing, cases of wine, and even pieces of furniture.

Suddenly Janine's mind was back on that other refugee-crowded road back in 1940. She saw the long traffic jam between the poplars, felt the children by her side.

She burst into tears and a man by her side, mistaking her grief, put his arm round her shoulders and said, 'Take it easy, lady. We'll make the bastards pay, be sure of that.'

She shook him off and began to push through the spectators peering closely into every vehicle. It seemed possible, indeed likely, that somewhere in this confusion she would glimpse those longed-for heads, hear those yearned-for voices.

Such a glimpse she believed would be enough, even if they then vanished eastward in this great exodus. It would refresh her parching faith, give it strength to carry on for however long God decided she must wait.

Her movement and desperation were in sharp contrast to the general demeanour of the spectators. Their mood was sullen and angry rather than joyous. Occasionally someone called out in mocking farewell, but the Germans either ignored it or waved cheerily and cried, 'Don't worry, mate. We'll be back in a couple of days!' reinforcing the feeling that this was no retreat but rather a military preparation for the battle to come.

And there were other feelings to keep many of the watching Parisians subdued. Like Janine, they too remembered how they had fled in panic and terror four years earlier, leaving their city undefended to drop like a perfect fruit into the hands of the invader. There was a need for action felt by many; in some it was a military need, a belief that what they did now could contribute to the success of the approaching Allies; in others it was a political need, a sense that the last battles of the war were already the first battles of the peace. But for most it had more to do with self-esteem than with tactics or politics; it was the need for expiation, and the hunger for revenge.

A truck had broken down near the Madeleine. The driver had got out and, urged on by his passenger, a middle-aged Gestapo officer, he was peering uncertainly beneath the bonnet. It was an open truck and there were several men in civilian clothes sprawling among the luggage in the back. Their passage had been marked with a perceptible heightening of hatred among the spectators. Many members of the Milice and other French fascist collaborationist groups had decided that soon Paris was going to be no safe place for them and were moving out with their protectors.

405

A young man detached himself from the crowd and strolled forward.

'I'm a mechanic,' he said smiling. 'Here, let me take a look.'

He gently edged the driver aside and stooped to probe deep into the engine. After a moment he stood up, wiped his hands on a handkerchief and with a shrug said, 'Kaput!' then walked slowly away.

The driver looked back into the engine, spoke to the Gestapo man and pointed. The officer looked, turned round, pointed after the Frenchman, opened his mouth to call.

The front of the truck blew up. The driver and officer were hurled to the ground by the blast. One lay there twitching, the other crumpled and still. Flames rolled back from the cab and, screaming and swearing, the Milice fugitives began to scramble over the tailboard, beating at their smouldering clothes or rolling on the ground to put out the flames.

The alleged mechanic had halted and turned. From his jacket he produced an automatic pistol and taking steady aim he began to pump bullets into the burning men. German soldiers, attracted by the noise, began to leap off other trucks and the crowd scattered in panic from the pavement as the bullets began to fly.

Christian Valois paid no heed. When his clip was empty, he turned and walked away at the same steady pace till someone grabbed his arm and forced him into a run. It was Henri, who'd transferred his allegiance whole-heartedly after Jean-Paul's death, but soon found that his new leader was even more dangerous than the old.

Once out of range of the Germans he pushed the younger man into a café and made him sit down while a quick-witted waiter rapidly provided them with two half-filled cups of coffee and a pile of saucers to give the impression they'd been there for hours. Sensitivity to the needs of the Resistants had never been higher.

'Right,' said Henri. 'What the hell do you think you're

playing at? I thought Jean-Paul was bad. He didn't give a damn if he got killed or not. *You* look as if you want it!'

Valois smiled coldly and drank his coffee.

Henri said earnestly, 'Don't cock it up for the rest of us. Another week, we'll all be free or we'll be dead. I know which I prefer. The future stretches a long way beyond getting rid of the Boche.'

'What future?' said Valois.

'Christian, I know it hit you hard, Jean-Paul's death. And then the news about your sister.'

He saw the other's grip tighten on the cup till it seemed the handle must break. The news that Marie-Rose Valois had been executed for terrorist activities had been released six weeks earlier, but no one had dared talk to Valois about it since. He seemed to have decided that single-handed he was going to kill every German in Paris. It was a miracle he had survived so long. And now the end was near, but the killing and the danger were rising to a climax. Henri desperately wanted to preserve the young man's life.

'She's gone, Christian,' he urged. 'Accept it. Never forget it, but accept it.'

He realized Valois was no longer listening. He was staring out at a figure walking slowly by along the pavement, more ghost-like than human.

'Isn't that Janine?' said Henri.

Valois didn't answer but watched his friend's widow out of sight with an unreadable expression on his face. Then he turned to Henri.

'What future?' he repeated.

2

And now at last Paris began to rouse herself. This was the best of times, the worst of times. The police occupied the

Préfecture, the FFI fortified the Hôtel de Ville. It was tanks versus ancient handguns; the outcome for the Resistance was inevitable, but the outcome for the Germans was irrelevant, and they happily accepted a truce within the city the better to confront the danger without. But there were many like Christian Valois who wouldn't accept any truce. They raged through the streets, throwing up puny barricades, firing at any enemy movement whether of men or armour, till it ceased to be clear if they were seeking, or simply offering themselves as, targets.

Other citizens took to the streets too. Fired by a pure vision of justice, or a cloudy lust for revenge, they hunted down, judged and sentenced their errant fellows. Some were beaten, stripped, humiliated; some were executed; some were thrown into gaol to await a formal judgement.

Meanwhile other gaols were being opened, other prisoners set free.

At Fresnes Prison on the southern approaches to the city, a pitched battle took place. It cost the Free French 2nd Armoured Division five tanks to overrun this strongpoint on their way to the Porte d'Orléans. Like the Bastille a century and a half earlier, it gave up very little. Most of the prisoners left behind after the last transports departed had been released when the Germans set about fortifying the strategically placed building.

But there were still a few inmates remaining, too ill to move or set free, or perhaps simply forgotten.

An American medical team took charge of these, transferring them to a nearby civilian hospital. The Americans looked aghast at the evidence of torture they observed on the bodies of some of their new patients, the French with no less revulsion but less shock. In some cases there seemed little hope. In others proper medication and nourishment plus above all the news of the imminent liberation of Paris brought rapid improvement.

And in one case, all these plus a night's rest seemed to produce a really remarkable recovery.

'Hey, doc,' said one of the orderlies early the following

morning. 'We've lost a patient. One of those guys from the gaol.'

'Well, they were pretty badly hurt, poor devils.'

'No, I don't mean he died. He's just up and gone. The bed's empty. He took some clothes too. Took? I mean stole!'

'Perhaps the guy didn't want to miss the celebrations! Which one was it?'

The orderly consulted his list.

'Scheffer,' he said. 'Édouard Scheffer.'

Günter Mai made his way back into Paris in the wake of the 2nd Armoured Division. It was remarkably easy even for a man in his condition. As the liberators drove through the suburbs, the empty streets of early morning suddenly exploded with life far more overwhelming than any German ambush could have been. From every doorway, every window it seemed, poured shouting, singing, laughing, weeping people. Mai had never seen, never heard such joy. Under the cloudless summer sky, this turmoil of flags and banners and cheering and thrown blossoms and spurting wine looked like some great artist's living realization of the spirit of joy. He recalled the stillness, the emptiness, the sense of cold eyes dully watching from shuttered houses, that had been the invading Germans' greeting four years before. How delightful then it had been to savour even that pretence of welcome offered by people like Louise Crozier. But beneath it all had been fear, or greed, or hate – nothing of this pure, untainted upwelling of joy which was exploding all around him.

He was slightly delirious, he realized. Somehow he'd scrambled up on the back of a half-track where he clung, unremarkable in a convoy festooned with men, women and children, kissing the soldiers, waving their flags, singing the 'Marseillaise'. He had to get back to reality, he told himself, to the here and now.

'What's the date?' he asked a young woman who clung by his side, almost hysterical with joy.

'It's Christmas Day! All Saints' Day! Easter Day! It's everyone's birthday!' she cried.

'But the date!'

'August the twenty-fifth, of course! You'll never forget it, none of us will!'

She was probably right. What it meant to him was he'd been in Fresnes for about three weeks. Fiebelkorn's men had worked at him in a leisurely way, pushing him often to the edge of confession to complicity in the plot. That way surely peace and rest lay. But some stubbornness at his core refused to let these bastards make him lie.

'I knew nothing. Nothing!' he repeated through bloodily gaping lips.

And finally Fiebelkorn had believed him. Or got sick of him. Or simply forgotten him. He was transferred to Fresnes. 'We'll be back for you tomorrow,' promised his SS escort. But they never came. And he lay on his prison bed, a cipher to his new guards, who were indifferent to his crime or nationality and indeed to everything except who'd placed him there. The conditions, the treatment, the food here, were not pleasant but they were Hôtel Meurice standards compared with what he'd suffered in the Avenue Foch. Slowly he'd started to explore his ferociously abused body. Cuts, bruises, missing teeth, a broken nose, even cigarette burns he catalogued as minor inconveniences. Cracked ribs and mangled fingertips were more lasting sources of pain, but these too would pass. What had worried him most because they felt most permanent were his left eye, which even when he forced the bruised and swollen flesh around it apart admitted no light, and his testicles, which were so puffed up and painful that walking was almost impossible.

Three weeks' rest had worked no miracles, but at least the swelling round his crotch had gone down enough for mobility, though what the American doctor had hidden beneath the dressing on his eye he did not yet know. Perhaps he should have waited to find out. In fact why hadn't he? What was he doing in his condition clinging

410

precariously to this enemy vehicle? Was he trying to escape?

The thought made him smile. It felt unfamiliar, painful even. It was the oddest escape route imaginable! No, it was some basic instinct that was taking him back into Paris, the sense that the changes exploding through Europe now were so great, so cataclysmic, they might blow him anywhere; the fear that this was the closest to Janine he might ever be again. If there was a last chance to see her, he had to grasp it. And if there was a last chance to protect her, he had to take it. He prayed that all his files at the Lutétia had been burnt or removed or that he could get to them in time to destroy all references to Janine.

And then? Surrender? Escape to continue the fight? The fight for what? He looked down at his mangled finger ends and felt the throb and jag of all his other hurts. These had been inflicted on him in the name and by the authority of the State he served.

'Here, don't fall off,' said the girl next to him, grabbing his arm.

He hadn't realized he'd been slipping.

'Thanks,' he said.

She looked closely at him and said, 'My God, you've been through the mangle, haven't you? Did the Boche do this?'

'Yes,' he nodded. 'Yes. The Boche.'

'Oh, the bastards. But this is the day they get their come-uppance! Think of that! Death to the Boche! Death to the Boche!'

Others took up the chant. And after a while, for the sake of verisimilitude he told himself wryly, he joined in.

And so, on the back of a liberator's half-track, with tricolours flying around him and flower-petals in his hair, Günter Mai returned to Paris.

411

3

They'd come for Janine Simonian the previous night. There were about twenty of them, the men slightly drunk, some of them inclined to merriment. But the women weren't drunk, and they certainly weren't merry.

She put up no resistance. Her father wasn't in the house and her mother had screamed and run and locked herself in the bakehouse when she saw the mob, thinking they were after her.

But once she realized it was Janine they wanted, she reappeared and flung herself into her daughter's defence, both verbally and physically, till two of the men had to restrain her.

'Let's do the old cow too,' suggested one of the intruders. 'She's been arselicking the Boche for years and playing favourites with her miserable lumpy bread.'

'My Crozier's bread's never lumpy!' screamed Louise. 'What would you know about lumpy bread, anyway, you with no teeth!'

The woman thus addressed flew at Madame Crozier and had to be restrained in her turn. Several of the other women urged that Louise should be brought to 'justice' with Janine but their leader said, 'No, leave the old bird. She's not for us.'

'Why not?'

'Never you mind. But her, she's ours whatever anyone says.'

And they dragged Janine out into the street. By the time they reached their destination, a café a couple of streets away, their number had doubled. The café was already packed. In better times, they would have a singer or a musician here and there was a small stage at the back.

412

Tonight it was the focus of attention as if Chevalier himself had been appearing. Huddled together on it were half a dozen women. Their heads had been shaved and their bare feet trod on their own tresses. Their clothes had been ripped from shoulder to waist and on their naked breasts swastikas had been daubed in red and black paint. At least two of them clutched small babies in their arms, presumably the result of their so-called horizontal collaboration. At the front of the stage a fat man in a blue apron stood over a woman seated on a wooden stool. He was cutting her hair with a large pair of scissors, flourishing each tress triumphantly before throwing it over his shoulder, and occasionally taking a long draught from a wine bottle. The audience clapped and cheered, but fell silent when he put the scissors aside and took a cut-throat razor to perform the final shaving.

'Hold still, *liebchen*,' he said. 'I've not cut anyone yet, but if I do, I might go all the way and take off your ears!'

He shaved her swiftly and efficiently and twisted her bald head to display the evidence of his expertise to the wildly applauding audience before stepping aside to let a trio of women get to work with their paint pots.

Janine closed her eyes wearily. This too she could bear.

Now she was up on the stage. She heard her name called to the audience: '. . . Janine Simonian who fornicated with a Boche officer while her husband was being murdered – ' the crowd howled their hate – '. . . and who stayed in Paris to indulge her lusts while her children were sent out into the country to be picked up and deported by the Boche . . .'

'No!' she screamed.

The change from corpse-like indifference to a vital, struggling indignation was so electrifying that for a second it reduced the mob to silence. Then they began to urge the barber on, but his was no easy task. She had to be held down while he used the scissors. Twice she overturned the chair, twice was forced back upright with increasing violence. And when the blue-aproned man came to take

413

the razor, he looked with great unease at the wildly jerking head.

'For Christ's sake, be still!' he hissed. 'It's only hair, woman!'

She spat in his face.

'Cut! Cut! Cut!' screamed the audience.

'Right, you bitch,' he said, pulling at his wine bottle.

He put the razor to her skull. She flung her head from side to side. Next moment there was blood streaming from a long cut on her brow. Now the barber seemed bent on proving that far from being an accident, this drawing of blood had been deliberate. Ferociously he hacked at the stubble and when the razor pierced the skin he did not draw back but removed skin and hair simultaneously. Soon her head was crowned with a bright red helmet of blood.

Then it was the women's turn. Janine kicked one of them in the stomach, bit another's hand to the bone. They retaliated with equal ferocity, tearing her clothes not just to the waist but to the knees and wielding their brushes as if they were chisels. Still Janine resisted and one of her assailants grabbed the barber's scissors and screamed, 'Let's make yours permanent!' Before she could be stopped, she had thrust the point and scored a huge, jagged-edged swastika beneath Janine's breasts across her belly. The barber, already a little ashamed of the havoc he'd created with her head, jumped forward, swearing, to grab at the scissors. But the damage was done.

'For fuck's sake, get her out of here!' he said, looking down at Janine's bloody figure which had suddenly gone quite slack again. 'The sight of her will spoil all the fun.'

They dragged her back through the streets and put her in the boulangerie doorway and left her there after banging at the door.

No one came. Louise Crozier was too terrified, not knowing what madmen might be roaming the streets to avenge imagined wrongs, and Claude Crozier was not yet home. She might have stayed there all night, if Michel Boucher hadn't turned up an hour later.

414

He too was not in the best of conditions. There was blood on his face and his clothing was torn and dusty. But his bruised and swollen knuckles showed that he'd inflicted as well as taken damage.

'Janine, what are you doing out here? Oh Jesus Christ!' He had become aware of her injuries. 'You too! The bastards got you too. Let's get you inside. Come on, open up! Auntie Louise! Uncle Claude! It's Miche!'

He thumped so hard on the door that the glass which had survived all the threats of the Occupation cracked right across. A light appeared somewhere within the house.

'Hurry it up! Oh, Janine, Janine, you poor kid. They've gone mad. What have we done, eh? Me, I've tried to earn an honest living, nothing more. For that they tried to hang me! Would you believe it? They were throwing a rope over a lamp-post! There's a couple of them will feel like hanging themselves when they wake up, I tell you. And that Pajou! He'll wish someone had hanged him when I get hold of him. I should've been long gone, but when I went for my car, it wasn't there. Pajou! The car, and everything else he could lay his hands on! The little shit, I'll tear his head off. Come on, Auntie Lou! Can't you see it's me! Open this sodding door!'

And at last, Louise Crozier, trembling and terrified, unlocked the door and let them in.

Günter Mai found Paris, always a city of contrasts, now displaying to him the greatest contrast of all. Struggling through the joyous celebrating crowds where the most martial sound was the popping of champagne corks, he finally found space and peace. But before he could relax and enjoy it, he suddenly found himself back on the edge of the war.

He'd come in through the Porte d'Orléans. Taking his bearings now for the first time, he realized that the Observatory was behind him and ahead were the Luxembourg Gardens, source of the noise of combat.

That made sense, if anything in this madness could be

called sense. He didn't know who was in charge of defending Paris now; Fiebelkorn had told him that the old military commander and his close aides had gone back to Berlin to be dealt with for their part in the July plot; but whoever it was would probably concentrate his forces in strong-points like the Luxembourg.

He certainly didn't want to be there. He struck off left. He was tempted to make straight for the boulangerie but once seen there and recognized, he would almost certainly find his scope for action limited, possibly permanently. So first it was essential to get to the Lutétia and check what had happened there.

He didn't need to get within more than a hundred yards to see he was too late. That his colleagues would have gone was obvious. Probably the non-fighting element in the Occupation Force had been withdrawn a good week before. But the hotel wasn't deserted. There seemed to be a constant stream of men going in and out. Some of them had rifles. The Resistance had got there before him.

So; the boulangerie. For what purpose? To see Janine once more before he met whatever fate was awaiting him? What he was hoping for from the encounter he couldn't say. Something to dilute the bitterness of their last meeting, that was the most his mind could imagine, and that took an effort.

At the bakery, the noise of the fighting round the Luxembourg was very loud. He stood for a moment and looked at the shop. Soon perhaps it would be back to normal; soon the old promise of 'Pains Français et Viennois, Pains de Seigle, Chaussons aux Pommes et Gâteaux Secs' would be fulfilled. Unless the Croziers were made to suffer for the welcome they had accorded him. That was very possible. This was a family he seemed destined to bring trouble to.

The glass on the door was cracked. Perhaps the trouble had started already. He pushed the door open and went in, passing through the bare and empty shop with the familiarity of use. Last time he had been here, it was to

416

see Janine alone. Last time he was here, she had taken his hand and led him up these stairs . . .

He paused and looked up them. At the top of the stairs stood Madame Crozier.

'You!' she said. 'You dare come here? You!'

'Madame,' he said. 'Where's Janine?'

'You've come to see what they've done to her? Perhaps you should! It's your fault!'

He ran up the stairs, all pain and weakness forgotten. Pushed open the door, looked at the bed where he and Janine had lain.

Now she lay there alone.

'Oh God,' said Mai. 'What have they done to you?'

He advanced towards the bed but a voice behind him said, 'She's sleeping. Leave her.'

He turned. It was Claude Crozier speaking, his voice firmer, more commanding than Mai recalled. And in his hands with the hammer cocked was a large revolver.

'Downstairs, please, lieutenant.'

He urged Mai ahead of him. Behind, Louise Crozier went back into the bedroom and shut the door.

'What have they done to her?' demanded Mai.

'Punished her for associating with you, what do you think?' said Crozier. 'She resisted. They went further than they intended.'

'You sound as if you almost sympathized with them!'

'They're Frenchmen. It's a sense of their weakness not of their virtue that makes them act this way,' said Crozier wearily. 'You look as if you've had your own troubles, lieutenant. Sorry, it's captain now, isn't it?'

'I'm not sure, not after my troubles,' said Mai. 'Tell me, Claude, how have you and your wife managed to escape? Why did these brave supporters of French justice pick only on Janine?'

'Because of you. Because they couldn't stomach her sleeping with you while Jean-Paul was being shot. If I'd been here, perhaps I could have intervened, kept them off her. Perhaps.'

417

'Like you kept them off your wife? God, she's fifty times more a collaborator than ever Janine was!'

'Yes,' agreed Crozier. 'You're right. But croissants aren't embraces. And she is my wife.'

He glanced at his watch.

'I have some friends arriving shortly. We'll be going out on a matter of business. It's probably best that they don't see you. Come this way.'

He motioned Mai towards the bakehouse.

As they went through the door, Crozier said, 'I don't know why I should bother about you. Except that I came to think of you as honest.'

'Because I praised your baking?'

'That too perhaps,' said Crozier. He gestured towards the left-hand oven, the bigger one, the one which shortage of flour and fuel had kept unused for more than three years.

'Get in there,' he said.

'In the oven? What the hell for?' demanded Mai.

'Don't worry. I'm not going to bake you. And you should be reasonably comfortable, at least by Resistance standards. I've had plenty of time to pad it out, haven't I?'

'Pad it out . . . ?' Mai's professional mind was suddenly back at work. He knew what Crozier must be telling him but he couldn't believe it. How many times had he been in this bakehouse? Leaned against this very oven door? Chatted to Crozier and his wife and thought of himself as the great manipulator! 'Oh shit,' he said.

'That's right,' said Crozier allowing himself a brief smile of triumph. 'I've had a lot of interesting people in there. Allied airmen, Resistants, escaped prisoners – and not a single search in all these years, for which I've got you to thank, I believe, Captain Mai.'

'Madame Crozier too?' said Mai disbelievingly. 'Was she . . . ?'

Crozier shook his head. 'No, I'm afraid not. She provided such good cover, I could hardly take her into my confidence. But I made my friends promise she wouldn't be touched afterwards. But Janine . . .'

He fell silent, then sighed and said, 'All right. In you get. I'll be going out when my friends arrive. We have business to attend to.'

'Killing Germans, you mean?'

'If necessary,' said Crozier mildly. 'But not you. Not for an hour, anyway. My wife will release you an hour after I've gone. What you do then, where you go, is your business. Both of you.'

'Both?' said Mai, puzzled.

'Oh yes. You've got company.'

He swivelled the iron bar which held the oven door shut and swung it open.

'Hello, Günter,' said Michel Boucher. 'That little shit, Pajou. You were right not to trust him. He stole my bloody car!'

4

There was fighting yet to do; there was blood still to shed. While to the south of the river they were dancing in the streets and celebrating the victory, on the Rue de Rivoli and in the Tuileries Garden they were still fighting for it.

There were Parisians here too, many of them simply spectators, eager to see the final act of this epic drama. But there were others who weren't content to watch, but who, unasked and sometimes unwanted, rushed forward to join the Allied soldiers in the last battle.

An American infantry section, pinned down by fire from a pill-box close to the Orangerie, settled to wait for the arrival of a tank to remove the obstacle.

A young man with an automatic pistol joined them.

They'd observed him earlier blazing away at the Germans with apparent unconcern for his own safety.

Now he put down his empty pistol and reached out to the grenades which the section leader had dangling from his belt.

'You permit?' he said.

'It's your party, friend,' said the American.

Taking two grenades, the Frenchman stood up and walked towards the pill-box. Perhaps his casual mien baffled the German gunners, or perhaps they thought he came bearing a message of truce.

When he got close enough to throw the grenades, they opened fire. But it was too late, for them and the Frenchman alike. The pill-box rocked, cracked, fell silent. And the Frenchman slid to the ground.

When the Americans reached him, they thought at first he was dead. So did he.

It was with a profound sense of disappointment that Christian Valois opened his eyes to see the anxious faces peering down at him.

'He looks bad, sarge.'

'Yeah. Call up the medics,' said the sergeant. 'This one ought to be kept alive for the shrinks to play with!'

General Choltitz, the German commander, surrendered in the Meurice early in the afternoon. General de Gaulle entered the city at four-thirty. On his way in, he may have passed Michel Boucher and Günter Mai on their way out. When Louise Crozier released them from the oven, Mai had asked to see Janine again. Her mother refused and threatened to call for help. Boucher seized Mai's arm and said, 'Come on, Günter. If they get hold of you today, they'll lynch you! Look what the bastards tried to do to me!'

'Where are we going?' demanded the German as he was dragged, weak and bewildered into the street.

'We'll get a few things together, pick up some transport. You leave it to me. Then we'll head off to my house at

Moret. Hélène will be worried about me. We'll hole up there till things quieten down. Just do what I tell you, OK?'

So they left, the *Abwehr* officer and the collaborator, while Janine lay, her eyes open, staring sightlessly at the cracked, uneven ceiling.

They came for her again in the first month of the Liberation, not a mob of them this time but two gendarmes in neat clean uniforms. They brought an official warrant.

'What the hell is this?' demanded Crozier. 'Can't you leave her alone? Look at her! You can see what they've done already.'

'Sorry,' said the policemen. 'But she's got to come. She'll be safer with us anyway when the news of the charge gets out.'

'What charge? That she was friendly with a German officer? Who wasn't? You lot did more arse-licking than anyone, everyone knows that. Just because you decided to do a bit of fighting in the last few days doesn't mean we've forgotten the years before!'

He spoke bitterly and the gendarme had difficulty in keeping his temper.

'There's no need for that, monsieur,' he said sharply. 'They've been going through files the Boche left behind. It's not just having a bit on the side that your girl's accused of. They're saying she was a paid agent of the *Abwehr*. They're saying it was her who gave away the meeting when her husband got shot!'

Janine hardly seemed to notice her arrest. In a state close to catatonia, only once did she show any sign of emotion. When the enclosed police van into which she was put came to a halt and she was urged out, she stood blinking in the sunshine for a moment. Then it registered where they had brought her and something like a smile floated across her thin, bruised face, but not a smile of hope or of humour. It was more an acknowledgement of what she had known instinctively for a long time. This

421

world her husband had fought and died for, this world she had lost her children and her liberty for, was not too different from the world it replaced. Oppression and blood, revenge and hate; the basic materials were much the same. Even the locations clearly weren't to be very different.

She fell to her knees and prayed to God, any god, to keep her children safe. Once before she had prayed the same prayer in much the same vicinity. Only that time she'd been outside and they'd been in. Now it was the other way round.

They'd thrown her, with the other thousands arrested since the Liberation, into the prison camp at Drancy.

PART EIGHT
March 1945

. . . en effet, la résistance, qui a fini par
triompher, montre que le rôle de
l'homme est de savoir dire non aux faits
même lorsqu'il semble qu'on doive s'y
soumettre.

Jean-Paul Sartre,
Qu'est-ce qu'un collaborateur?

1

On the face of it, the Simonian trial had everything, even in these days when the courts of justice had been resounding to tales of death, deceit and betrayal for several months. But somehow after the first day, it never took off.

The trouble was the prisoner herself. She stood there like a pillar of salt, absorbing all emotion like moisture from the atmosphere. She never raised her voice, never contradicted. She denied nothing, admitted everything. Yes, she had been on the *Abwehr* officer's list of agents; yes, she had accepted favours from him; yes, she had slept with him; yes, she had signed the letter found in his files in which she betrayed her husband's last meeting.

The only time the proccedings came to life was when the prisoner pleaded for news of her children. The judge had felt enough pity for her distress to have their fate checked, but nothing was known except that they had been put on a train carrying several hundred Jewish prisoners from Lyon to Germany.

The judge was finding the woman's dead presence increasingly uncomfortable. The number of spectators had diminished by half, and the newspapers had given the whole thing up as a bad job. Not that the purge did not still have a vast amount of momentum, but the main focus of the public lust for expiation was directed to the promised trials of the Vichy leaders before the new High Court of Justice. Meanwhile the papers tried to direct the country's interest outwards to the re-establishment of France among the great powers and invited readers to rejoice in the news that the Allied Forces, including the Free French, were crossing the Rhine.

The judge shortened matters by refusing to let the prosecutor strut centre stage with his star witness, Christian Valois, the Resistance hero.

'Proof,' he said, 'where there is no denial, merely consumes the court's precious time.'

The verdict was, of course, inevitable. All that was still debatable was the sentence. The prosecutor would certainly demand death. It would be impossible to deprive him of *that* dramatic moment. Death, of course, was pointless even if the prisoner deserved it, which the judge doubted. So far de Gaulle had commuted every death sentence passed on a woman. So it was gaol. But for how long?

For the woman's defence, there was only her father, also it seemed a Resistance hero. Was there anyone who wasn't? wondered the judge. He had little that was material to say, but the judge let him maunder on, disposing of the prosecutor's objections by saying, 'Character testimonial is still acceptable in law, I'm sure you haven't forgotten *that*!'

From the biographical stuff the father gave, it didn't seem likely, even allowing for parental bias, that the woman would deliberately set out to get her husband killed. And the larger part of her association with this German seemed to spring from her concern for her family. Perhaps twelve years would be enough?

He encouraged the father to go on. The woman had been given a defence lawyer, of course, but he seemed totally inadequate. Where were they digging these people up from for God's sake?

So the trial drew to its close. This final morning should see it over well before lunch. The defence lawyer was talking with or rather listening to the father. Now, with evident reluctance, he approached the bench.

Another defence witness! To character? No, to fact!

The judge was doubtful. The prosecutor was scornfully, almost imperiously dismissive.

'By all means, let us hear him,' said the judge.

The man was brought in. He looked rather down-at-

426

heel, with clothes that were manifestly too large for him. But he had an honest, open kind of face.

The judge himself took over the questioning. If there was anything useful to be got out of this fellow, it was silly to leave it to that idiot defender.

'Your name, monsieur,' he said.

'Scheffer. I'm known as Édouard Scheffer.'

For the first time, at the sound of this strong Alsatian accent, the woman's head rose and she turned her eyes to the witness stand.

'You say you're *known* as Édouard Scheffer?' said the judge. 'That implies a sobriquet.'

'Yes sir,' said the witness. 'My real name is Mai. Günter Mai. *Hauptmann* Günter Mai, late of the *Abwehr* counter-intelligence unit stationed at the Hôtel Lutétia in the Boulevard Raspail.'

Now the pall of dullness cast by the prisoner lifted from the courtroom like a morning mist, and the judge sat upright, eyes bright, and he thought, At last! A trial I can tell my dinner guests about without my wife shutting me up for being boring!

Günter Mai had spent the past months at Boucher's house near Moret. That it should prove such a safe place of refuge so close to Paris had seemed unlikely, but the care which Boucher, so careless in most other respects, had taken in establishing this retreat for his family was soon revealed. To the few locals he had any contact with, he was merely a businessman whose work kept him in Paris a good deal. He had complete sets of papers for himself and his wife under her maiden name of Campaux. He shaved off his beard, trimmed his hair and set about giving the appearance of a man taking a rest till the turmoil had settled enough for him to resume his work.

'I thought you didn't think anyone could wish you harm,' said Mai ironically.

'There's always some mad bugger,' said Boucher. 'For myself, I reckon I can take care of anything. But there's

427

Hélène and the kiddies to think of. That's why I set up here in the first place.'

'And very well you've done it.'

'Yes. Foolproof, I'd say.'

'But not Pajou-proof,' reminded Mai.

Boucher's expression darkened.

'That little bastard. I'd love to get my hands on him!'

Summer browned into autumn, blackened to winter. So certain was Mai that each day must be the one on which they came looking for Boucher, or his own thin pretence was pierced, that he felt no sense of time passing or of time stretching ahead. When Hélène started talking of Christmas, he was truly amazed.

'I should try to get away,' he said to Boucher one night.

'Where to?'

A good question. Most of France was now liberated. German resistance was strong and would be strongest of all along the border; but the end, inevitable in Mai's eyes since 1942, was complete defeat, without condition, without honour. He felt no impulse to try to get to Germany and die in arms. What did that make him? A traitor? A collaborator?

'Switzerland,' he said without conviction. 'Or Spain.'

'Yes,' said Boucher eagerly. 'Switzerland, that's what I thought. But it's too dangerous on your own, Günter. Wait till Hélène's time comes and she gets her strength back. Then we'll all go.'

Hélène was heavily pregnant, her baby due at the year's end. Boucher was more worried now than he'd ever been. His naïve self-confidence had suffered a blow in the autumn when, growing tired of these self-imposed restrictions, he'd announced he was going to take a trip to Paris. Despite his wife's protests, he'd gone, but he'd soon come back.

'They've arrested thousands!' he said in amazement. 'They say the Vél d'Hiv and Drancy are packed. Places your lot used, now we're using them! They're going to put 'em on trial, Günter!'

From now on, Boucher kept close to the house. Mai

suggested that if they did come to arrest him it wouldn't help his case if he was found to be harbouring a German.

'Don't be daft,' said Boucher with an unusual flash of lucidity on this point. 'If they arrest me, one German more or less isn't going to help or harm my case, is it? Besides, I need you here, Günter. I'd go mad being stuck here alone; no other man, I mean. I'd start sneaking off for a chat and a drink and God knows what that would lead to!'

So he stayed, needing no persuading. Germany; Switzerland; Spain; the only place he really wanted to be was Paris to find out what had happened to Janine. There was no way of getting news. Claude Crozier had made it clear that hiding in his oven was his last act of kindness; to contact him would be to run a deadly risk.

'She'll be all right,' assured Boucher. 'Like me, tough as old rope.'

'But the children. If she hasn't heard anything about the children . . .'

Boucher gathered his little daughter to him and pressed her close, but did not reply.

The new baby came early in January, a boy. Boucher wanted one of his names to be Günter but Mai advised against it.

'Édouard, then,' said Boucher. 'He shall have your French name at least.'

So the child became Michel Édouard Boucher.

At the end of January there was a second arrival.

Late one wet and windswept night as the two men followed their usual custom of drinking a nightcap of brandy and hot water, they heard a noise outside. They exchanged looks but no words. Rising, Boucher signalled Mai to go out of the back while he took the front. Arming himself with a broad kitchen knife, Mai slipped out into the squally rain and made his way down the side of the house. As he turned the corner to the front, the main door opened, spilling light over the threshold, then Boucher stepped out.

'Who's there?' he called.

'Miche, is that you? Thank God, old friend.'

A figure emerged from a patch of shrubbery and began to move forward. In a second Mai was behind him, his arm locked about the intruder's neck and his knife pressed across the bridge of his nose.

'Don't move or I'll cut your eyes out,' he said. 'Miche!'

Boucher came running, a torch in his hand. He flashed it into the newcomer's face.

'Fuck me,' he said. 'It's a Christmas present come late. Step inside, Pajou, while I unwrap you!'

The little Géstapiste was in a pretty run-down condition. Unkempt, unshaven, he was soaked to the skin though the rainwater hadn't helped clean him.

'God, you smell vile,' said Boucher in disgust when they'd got him into the house.

'You'd smell too if you'd been through what I've been through,' snarled Pajou. The left lens of his spectacles was cracked and there was a suppurating scar down his cheek. Boucher postponed his threatened vengeance while they got the little man cleaned up, but he made it clear it was merely a postponement.

'Now,' he said finally. 'Talk. Why've you come here, you little shit? To apologize? Where's my bloody car?'

'Miche, I'm sorry. Sorry for everything, sorry to disturb you now. But God, you've no idea how relieved I was to find you still here. My last hope! If anyone will help an old mate, it's Miche. I mean, look at the way you're helping the captain here. This is a real surprise, captain, but I'm so glad to see you looking so well . . .'

Boucher took the knife from Mai's hands.

'Talk,' he said.

Pajou talked. Making allowances for embellishments and omissions, it seemed he'd decided that Spain was the best place for him and had headed south in the stolen car with as much loot as he could carry. After narrowly evading the American and Free French forces who'd landed on the Mediterranean coast and were rapidly driving their way

430

north, he'd reached the Spanish border, paid a large sum to a guide to take him over the Pyrenees, spent an exhausting and bewildering couple of nights on the mountain paths, woke on the second morning to find himself abandoned and all his baggage missing, and descended to the valley below to find himself not in the Basque country that he'd been promised but back in Gascogny where he'd started. He'd returned to Paris by fits and starts and with many narrow squeaks because here he'd left hidden the bulkier items of his war loot. But when he went to the warehouse he'd hidden it in, he found he was too late, it had gone. Worse, his presence was reported and for the last week he'd been on the run, in and around Paris, living rough and with his description in the hands of all gendarmerie units.

'They're saying dreadful things about us, Miche,' he concluded indignantly. 'But we're innocent, aren't we? We never did anything to be ashamed of!'

He stressed the *we*, making his meaning unambiguous. He wasn't asking for help and sanctuary. He was stating quite bluntly that if he didn't get it, Miche might as well give himself up too.

If Boucher had decided to slit Pajou's throat there and then, Mai would not have intervened. But despite his threats of violence, the big red-head had no stomach for murder, and so the house at Moret got another guest, but one who had to remain completely hidden for there was no explanation to cover his presence.

He was not good company. He drank everything he could lay his hands on and in his cups he gave up his pretence at innocence and boasted of the disgusting things he'd done with nostalgic glee.

'They'll have your head, you bastard,' said Boucher. 'They'll stretch you out and kill you slow and you deserve it.'

'Don't come the innocent with me, Miche! You may have been a bit more delicate-stomached when it came to the dirty work, but you were always around when it came to the pickings! They all were! Oh yes, the day they try to put me on trial, they'll hear some things about their precious heroes they'd rather not hear! No, they'll send me to Switzerland with a pension rather than risk putting me up in open court!'

'They won't bother with the expense of a trial,' said Boucher. 'They'll kill you in the streets.'

'For what? For doing a job?' said Pajou, suddenly fearful. 'There's no justice. No, there isn't. All right, you think there is? What are you doing hiding here, then? I tell you, Miche, they're trying everyone in Paris. Everyone! They've even got that skinny cousin of yours under arrest, the one you used to meet in the Balzac, captain, and in the Jardin des Plantes.'

He leered and winked at Mai, delighted to show off his intimate knowledge of everything that had gone on.

Mai couldn't speak. Boucher said, 'Janine? She's arrested? What for?'

'She's been under arrest for months,' said Pajou dismissively. 'I went sniffing around that shop her parents run, looking for news of you, Miche. I'd heard nothing, you see, and I was beginning to wonder if mebbe you'd got yourself holed away, safe and sound, down here. I talked with the mother, gabby woman, a bit thick. I buttered her up! All I wanted was to know if she'd heard from you, but I got the whole fucking family history!'

'What did she tell you?' demanded Mai, his eyes blazing.

'All right. Keep your head on! They've accused her of getting her husband killed, of betraying all his Resistance plans to the Boche, mainly you, captain. Funny files those you kept, it seemed!'

'They have the files?'

'Oh yeah. You should've burnt them, captain. Better still, you shouldn't have written them in the first place. What made you go in for fiction anyway? Strange payment for getting your end away!'

Suddenly Pajou found himself on his back with Mai's fingers round his throat.

'What do you mean, fiction?' he said, squeezing. 'How do you know it's fiction?'

'I think maybe he'll speak more clearly if he's not quite dead,' said Boucher mildly.

Mai relaxed his grip.

'All right, all right,' gasped Pajou. 'I'll tell you. No need for this. We're all friends here, aren't we? For God's sake, it's one down, all down, isn't it? So just let me up and I'll tell you a bedtime story that wouldn't put some buggers in Paris to sleep, believe me!'

Later, alone with Boucher, Mai sat in deep silence drinking more than his usual share of brandy.

'Give us a week,' said Boucher suddenly.

'A week?'

'A week's start before you go back to Paris.'

Mai made no effort to deny or even debate his intention.

'I'd not say anything about you, Miche, you know that.'

'Of course. But Pajou will, and you'll be taking him with you, I think. So. A week. And we'd better sort him out now. Once he gets wind that we're moving on, he'll be like a rat in a trap.'

They went for Pajou at Gestapo hour the next morning. He sat up in bed, blinking shortsightedly at the sudden light.

'What's up?' he asked fearfully. 'Are we being raided?'

'You are, Paj,' said Boucher. 'On your feet. No need to bother getting dressed. You're not going anywhere.'

The little Géstapiste obviously thought they were going to kill him. His face turned grey and his legs could hardly support him. Mai felt little sympathy. Pajou must have roused hundreds of his own countrymen at this hour. And Mai hadn't forgotten that it was Pajou who had delivered him into Fiebelkorn's hands.

When he realized they were only going to tie him up, his first reaction was relief. But once he grasped Mai's purpose he went wild.

'You mad bastard,' he screamed. 'They'll lynch me.

They'll lynch us both. We'll never see a court. And if we did, do you think I'm going to say anything?'

They bound and gagged him.

Downstairs Boucher said, 'He may be right. And even if you do get him to stand up in court, you can't make him talk.'

'He'll talk,' said Mai. 'Not for any good reason, but out of sheer malice he won't be able to keep his mouth shut.'

'Let's hope you're right,' said Boucher. 'But you're going to have your work cut out getting him back to Paris by yourself.'

'I'll manage,' said Mai. 'Even if I have to beat the little toad unconscious and carry him over my shoulder.'

A few hours later the house was in a turmoil as the Bouchers prepared to leave. 'We may have to dump a lot of stuff later, but nothing looks more suspicious than travelling light,' said Miche.

At last they were almost ready.

'Has anyone seen Antoinette?' asked Hélène.

'She's probably upstairs,' said her husband. 'Antoinette!'

He ran lightly upstairs towards the nursery bedroom, but as he passed the door to Pajou's room he saw that it was slightly ajar. Carefully he pushed it fully open.

'Oh Christ,' he said.

Pajou had managed to get one arm free and he had it locked tight around little Antoinette's neck.

'A knife,' he snarled. 'Give me a knife, else she stops breathing.'

'Sure, Paj,' said Boucher easily. 'Don't get excited. Here you are.'

From his pocket he took a claspknife like the one he'd given Pauli for Christmas. He pulled out the blade, then he proffered it, handle first. For a second the grip on the child's neck relaxed as Pajou's free hand reached out. The knife spun round in Miche's fingers.

'Bastard,' he said.

A moment later he came out of the room nursing the

434

little girl in his arms. Mai came up the stairs, took in what had happened in a glance.

'Is she all right?' he asked anxiously.

'Oh yes, fine, aren't you, my love? But he's not. Günter, I'm sorry. What will you do now? Will you still go back?'

Günter Mai stood and looked at Pajou's body. Apart from the knife sticking out of his throat, he looked more peaceful than ever before.

'Oh yes,' said Mai. 'I must.'

They tried to stop the trial. The prosecution wanted Mai arrested. The crowds wanted him lynched. The judge summoned the gendarmerie to restore order, and then came to his decision. The trial would go on, and he himself would continue with the questioning.

'Where have you come from, Captain Mai?' he began courteously.

'I cannot say,' said Mai.

'Let us leave that for the moment. Much has been said of your relationship with the prisoner. Can you explain what it was?'

'At first I intended to use her as an agent. Later I changed my mind.'

'Why?'

'I didn't think she would make a very good agent. She was – is – too open, too direct, too honest.'

There was harsh laughter and incredulous whistling.

'I notice you don't say, too patriotic?'

'She attacked me and abused me in our early meetings,' said Mai. 'Yes, I'd say she was patriotic. But I brought pressure to bear. I offered to help get her husband released from imprisonment.'

'So you could get the poor sod murdered!' cried someone.

The judge said, 'If anyone feels unable to control his emotions, please let him leave now. Hereafter he will leave under arrest. In other words, captain, you hoped to blackmail her into working for you.'

'Yes.'

'But you changed your mind because you didn't think she could be of use?'

'Yes.'

'Yet you continued to see her?'

'Yes. Accidentally. Incidentally. And I grew . . . fond of her.'

'Fond? Did she become your mistress?'

'No! Not in any real sense,' said Mai.

'In what sense then? You slept together?'

'Only twice,' he said in a low voice. 'I forced her.'

'You raped her, you mean?'

'No. Not physically. By threats, promises. Blackmail, you called it.'

'Once,' said Janine.

She'd been almost forgotten since Mai took the stand. Now every eye turned to her.

'Once it was against my will,' she said in a listless voice. 'The other time, not.'

'I see,' said the judge. 'Apart from helping to get her husband released, what else did you do for the accused, Captain Mai?'

'I helped get her children out of Drancy,' said Mai.

'Günter, where are the children? Do you know anything about the children?' demanded Janine, suddenly agitated.

'I don't know anything,' said Mai sadly. 'I'm sorry.'

'Carry on, please, Captain Mai,' said the judge.

'I helped get the children into the Free Zone as it was then. And I protected Madame Simonian from arrest by the Gestapo.'

'You did all this for two *encounters*, one forced, one willing, in four years?' said the judge incredulously. 'You do not look like a romantic to me, Captain Mai. Surely there must have been some other consideration. Information? Betrayal?'

'No! Never!' said Mai emphatically.

'But your files . . . these *are* your files, are they? Would you like to examine them?'

He pointed at the files before the State prosecutor.

'No,' said Mai. 'I'm sure they're mine.'

'They state categorically that the prisoner was your agent. What is more, in the matter of the betrayal of the meeting when her husband was shot down, there is a letter giving every detail of the arrangements – place, time, security – and it is signed by the prisoner, who *admits* she signed it. Is this true?'

'Yes, she signed it. She had no idea that the meeting had anything to do with her husband. Neither had I.'

He looked at Janine and repeated with emphasis, 'Neither had I.'

'So why . . . ?'

'Her children were imprisoned once more, this time by the Gestapo in Lyon. I wanted to get a release order. To do this, I needed incontrovertible proof that she was a valuable agent of the *Abwehr*. The Gestapo would not be easily convinced.'

The judge consulted his notes.

'It is my understanding that this meeting was in fact raided by the Gestapo. If you were on such bad terms with them, why did you co-operate with them in this operation?'

'I didn't. They got the information independently.'

'And you, Captain Mai. If, as you say, the prisoner did not give you the information, where *did* you get it?'

Mai sighed and rubbed his face. He would have loved to light his pipe, but it had vanished somewhere between the Avenue Foch and Fresnes. He'd smoked the occasional cigar during his long stay with Boucher but it wasn't the same.

'I got it from the Gestapo,' he said wearily. 'Unofficially.'

There was a single burst of contemptuous laughter.

The judge shook his head and said, 'How unfortunate. I thought at least you were going to offer us an alternative traitor, someone you couldn't name, perhaps, or someone who was dead.'

'No,' said Mai. 'I'll stick to the truth.'

The State prosecutor rose and said, 'Haven't we heard

enough of this rubbish? All this Boche has proved is that he's besotted with the prisoner, thus confirming their intimate relationship which is part of the State's case anyway. Some people might find his willingness to appear here with this farrago of lies touching; I find it merely pathetic. Let's be done with him.'

'Thank you,' said the presiding judge. 'I find I must agree with the prosecutor . . .'

'I'm not finished,' said Mai. 'Yes, I got the information indirectly from the Gestapo. When I got it, I had no idea how *they* had obtained it in the first place. I only found out the truth about that a short while ago. From a man called Pajou.'

There was a stir in the courtroom as the name was repeated by many lips.

'Pajou? Alphonse Pajou, the Géstapiste?' said the judge. 'This man is high on the State's wanted list. If you have information as to his whereabouts . . .'

'He's dead,' said Mai. 'I can tell you where to find the body.'

'Dead? So this man who you claim told you the truth of how the Gestapo got their information is not available for questioning?'

'I said he was dead.'

The judge frowned. He'd bent over backwards to be fair, but now was the time to point out a few legal realities.

'You must see, Captain Mai, whatever you claim Pajou said, it can really put us very little further forward. The court has been patient . . .'

'It was him,' said Mai.

His finger pointed without emphasis or histrionics towards the witness benches.

He said, 'Valois. It was Christian Valois.'

There was a second of silence, then a howl of outrage went up which made the disturbance on his first appearance sound like a lullaby. Valois didn't move but turned deathly pale. Mai looked towards Janine and saw what his accusation had done to her. She was leaning forward towards

438

Valois, her head shaking, her features twisted in disbelief. Mai in his turn instinctively reached his arms out to her but she did not see him. Perhaps to the spectators the gesture looked like one of defiance for now their noise rose in a new crescendo and suddenly half a dozen men came rushing forward. Before the court officers could protect him he was hurled to the ground. As kicks drove into his ribs and crotch and belly, he heard the judge crying distantly, 'Clear the court!'

Then a steel-capped boot, swung with all the strength of four years of hate, crashed against his head, and judge, Janine, court and all went spinning away to a single point of light, faint as a star. Then it was black night.

2

It was spring.

The Allied Armies were pouring across the Rhine. Liberated land had given way to conquered land. Behind them there had to be established a trail of camps, first for the huge number of German prisoners taken, then for the growing numbers of refugees, of workers released from slave-labour, of prisoners released from German camps. And already the advancing troops had begun to find some camps which were beyond comprehension and credibility.

But for most in that spring, Germany was still an enemy capable of fighting to an honourable defeat.

A detachment of Americans mopping up small pockets of resistance on the east bank of the Rhine came under fire as they emerged from the shelter of a pine forest. They hit the ground and looked for their target. Ahead was a castle like an illustration from a children's book. An old man stood before it with a smoking shotgun. Before the soldiers could make up their minds whether to kill him or not, a woman's voice called imperiously in German, and the old man with evident reluctance threw his weapon down.

The woman was not as old as the man but her face was weathered by suffering. One of the soldiers who spoke German talked to her, translating for his sergeant.

'She says she owns the joint. She says Wyatt Earp here is her gamekeeper. She says all her other servants are long gone. I think she's a little nutty, sarge, but harmless.'

'*You* think? *I'll* think, boy. You two, check this place out. And take care even if genius here does say she's harmless. What's she say now, boy?'

'She's asking if we can use our radios to seek news of her son. She says the Gestapo took him away last summer saying he'd tried to kill Hitler or something.'

The sergeant shook his head and began to laugh.

'Know what I think? It's going to be even harder to find a Nazi in Germany than it was to find a collaborator in France. Killing Hitler! The bastards'll be wanting Congressional Medals of Honour next.'

'Sarge. Over here!' cried one of the searching soldiers urgently. He was standing by the open door of what looked like a stable block.

'What's up? Trouble?' called the sergeant, hefting his sub-machine-gun.

'Not for us, sarge. You'd best come and see.'

Christian Valois sat in his room, cleaning a Luger machine-pistol. He had a considerable arsenal of weapons. People seemed to think that they were a suitable gift to acknowledge his heroism. They were right. He had been heroic, there was no denying that. He'd finally overcome that degrading physical fear and become a real hero. Now there was nothing he could not do.

For a while after the Boche's intervention at the trial, he had found his old trembling had come back again, but now . . . he held up the gleaming barrel. Steady as a rock.

It had been good to see the way in which the Boche's

440

accusations had merely driven the majority of people into a fury of indignation. Even those appointed to question him had been deferential and apologetic. And the judge had ordained that it should be done privately to spare him the indignity of a public examination.

He'd told them the truth, that he loved Jean-Paul like a brother. As for the rest, his scars and his medals surely attested to the absurdity of calling him a collabo! They had seemed satisfied.

And he himself, was he satisfied? He should be. A long and illustrious career opened ahead of him. If Marie-Rose's death had not been expiation enough, then a lifetime of service to France must surely be. What did he have to reproach himself for? He'd been forced to work for the Germans by their promise to kill Marie-Rose if he didn't. When he stopped working for them, they kept their promise. He had done all he could to stop Jean-Paul from going to that meeting, just as up till then he had made sure that, no matter who else he betrayed, Jean-Paul's operations went unreported. It had been his friend's own arrogance which put him in the firing line. And Delaplanche, if only he had stuck to his revolutionary plots and not diverted to check precisely what *had* happened to Marie-Rose, why, he too might now be a living legend instead of a dying memory.

Which left Janine. There was no doubt she was the one who had really betrayed Jean-Paul. Lying in bed with that pig's hot hands upon her while her husband . . . Perhaps she had in fact passed on details of the meeting as the Boche's files showed, perhaps she really *had* betrayed him in every sense, and even if he, Valois, hadn't told the Gestapo about the meeting, the *Abwehr* would have been there to arrest and kill . . .

No, there was very little to reproach himself for, he thought as he reassembled the gun with practised ease. He had tried to die and his sacrifice had been refused. All that remained now was to return to the court when the prorogued trial recommenced, and give his evidence, and then he could begin his life's work once more. And Janine?

That was for the court to decide, not him.

The machine-pistol was assembled now.

His finger caressed the trigger almost absently.

Günter Mai lay in hospital, trapped by coarse grey sheets which gripped like a strait-jacket. Two armed gendarmes sat by the door. They needn't have bothered. His own debility was guard enough. He couldn't move his head without his mind dissolving into white mist.

The blow to his skull had reactivated an old concussion from his interrogation by Fiebelkorn. Memory swam in and out of the mists like flotsam in a dark sea. Men came and questioned him. He answered everything they asked. After years of the secret life, he no longer had anything to hide. When he tried to ask them questions, they were not so forthcoming.

Finally, to his increasingly insistent demands about the progress of the trial, one said, 'The trial was suspended. But word is that it will be renewed shortly for judgement.'

'Judgement? But what of my evidence?'

'Evidence? The unsupported ramblings of a love-sick Nazi? You will not be required, Captain Mai. Think yourself lucky. If you showed your face again, you might not get away with a bang on the head this time.'

'But Valois, is he being questioned?'

'Questions were put to Monsieur Valois. He gave answers judged to be sufficient. The nation is desolated to lose such a hero.'

'Lose . . .'

'You don't know? There was an accident with a gun . . . a great tragedy.'

Mai began to laugh. It was a bitter sound.

'You French . . . you sanctimonious cynics!'

'Perhaps, monsieur. But we keep our vices within the bounds of what is human,' retorted the other savagely. 'Your pet monsters have torn us apart. God knows if we can ever be whole again. Every collaborator condemned is a new wound, every hero honoured a new healing. We've got to keep the balance right.'

'And justice?'

'Justice will be done, never fear. Whatever you allege of Monsieur Valois, you will not after all pretend that Janine Crozier is guiltless too?'

Mai did not reply but turned his head to the wall and took no pleasure in realizing that for the first time such a movement brought no obscuring mists.

There was blue sky and the promise of a glorious day on the morning that they brought Janine back to the court for judgement. But inside the dark-painted room with its high shuttered windows it was still winter.

Janine was indifferent to the climate, inside or out. Mai's intervention, far from comforting her, had cast her down into the absolute depths of depression. How could she take comfort from what was impossible to believe anyway – that Christian had been a traitor and betrayed the meeting where Jean-Paul was killed? Even when her father assured her that already there had been talk in Resistance circles that anyone whose sister ended up in Gestapo hands had to be regarded as a risk, she was unconvinced.

But all speculation had ended with the terrible news of Christian's death; and when Claude Crozier tried to suggest that it was no accident but the deliberate act of a guilt-ridden man, she had stopped her ears and screamed at him to shut up.

'At least be grateful you have a man who loves you so much that he is willing to sacrifice his own liberty and risk his life for you,' said Claude, desperate to pull his daughter back from the edge of the pit she was staring into.

'Günter, you mean? If he had stayed away, Christian would be alive and all this would be over. And what have I got to do with love any more?'

Sharing his fears with his wife, Claude got the reply, 'It's the children, can't you see that, you ninny? She's stopped talking about them. She's finally given up hope.'

443

And she put her arms around her husband and they wept.

Now Janine stood in the gloomy courtroom and looked with vast indifference towards the judge. It was a very different atmosphere from her last time here. Determined not to risk a repetition of those disturbances, the judge had denied admission to all the public except Claude and Louise Crozier.

He didn't waste any time.

'Janine Simonian, on the principal charge of supplying information to the *Abwehr* which resulted in the capture or death of many members of the FFI, it is the judgement of this court that you are not guilty.'

There was a shriek of relief and delight from Louise, choked off as the judge glared at her angrily. But sounds of a more distant disturbance outside the door continued. The judge checked his exasperation and continued with his judgement.

'With regard to the subsidiary charge that you gave aid and comfort to the illegal occupying forces of the German Army, it is the judgement of this court that you are guilty.'

He had to raise his voice to make himself heard above the growing level of noise outside. Inside, Louise cried, 'No!' and gripped her husband's arm. Janine's gaze remained unwavering on the judge and her expression did not change.

'It is the sentence of this court that you will undergo five years' national degradation. In case you are ignorant, let me explain what that entails, if I can make myself heard above this din. Officer, would you step outside and arrest whoever it is causing this unseemly disturbance?'

The gendarme on duty before the big double door turned and began to unlock it.

The judge went on, 'During this period you will be deprived of all civic rights, the right to vote, the right . . .' but for the first time Janine's attention had moved from him. Slowly she turned her head towards the back of the court.

The gendarme had got the doors partly open, admitting a shaft of brilliant sunlight and a voice which demanded admission. There was the sound of a scuffle, voices raised in anger, a cry of pain, and suddenly the gendarme was thrust aside as a man burst into the court.

Once inside he skidded to a stop almost immediately and peered uncertainly towards the judge, obviously finding the gloom as blinding as those within found the dazzle of the sun.

'And who the devil are you, monsieur? What is your business here?' demanded the judge furiously.

The man did not answer straightaway. He was a strange-looking figure, not very tall, with a long black rabbinical beard and dressed in American Army fatigues which were several sizes too large for him. His bright eyes screwed up as they focused on Janine, as if in an effort to recognize her.

She moved her head, suddenly feeling faint with an emotion she did not dare name. The movement seemed to act as confirmation, for now the strange newcomer laughed and, turning to the judge, bowed and said, 'Your honour. Melchior's my name. Magus that I am, bearing gifts of gold, from the East I come!'

And with a wave of his hand which was indeed Oriental, he directed their eyes to the doorway.

Janine looked and could see nothing but the glow of diffused sunlight in which floated motes of dust and tendrils of cigarette smoke. She blinked, and merely seemed to add to the dazzle her own internal colours and forms. She closed her eyes, shook her head and tried again. Her heart was beating so fast and so loud that it must have drowned out all other noise, for now she could hear nothing else. Then even the sound of her heart stopped, and the sound of her breathing stopped, and all her strength, all her being, were concentrated into her sight.

And now for the first time she saw a movement in that golden glow, a shape, two shapes, two small shapes advancing uncertainly, hand in hand. She felt as if she

445

were drawing them forward with her eyes, that one flicker, one blink, could send them drifting back through that brightness into the dark once more, beyond all hope of recall.

But now at last they stepped shyly into the solid world of the courtroom, and sound came back to her ears, breath to her lungs, and life to her heart again.

3

They brought Günter Mai out of the hospital as dawn was breaking. His head was still heavily bandaged and beneath his shirt his cracked ribs were swathed so tight that breathing was not so much painful as almost impossible. His legs too felt weak, but despite all this debility, the gendarmes still insisted on manacling his hands.

In the vestibule, two military policemen were waiting to escort him to a POW camp. There was a great deal of form-filling before he was satisfactorily transferred from civil to military custody. Then he was briefly in the open air before being helped into the back of a truck.

Just as it was about to start, one of the gendarmes came hurrying after them.

'What's up?' asked the sergeant in charge of the escort.

'The manacles,' said the breathless gendarme. 'I forgot.'

To the accompaniment of jeers from the soldiers, the man unlocked and removed the manacles, then hurried away.

'Well, Fritz, you're not going to try to escape, are you?' said the sergeant.

'Where to?' asked Mai.

'That's sensible.' He banged on the cab and the truck moved towards the gate.

'Are we going far?'

'Far enough. But it'll be nice for you to be back with your mates, won't it? Sort of a homecoming.'

He seemed to mean his comment to be friendly. Mai tried a smile, but he felt more depressed than at almost any time in the past year. What kind of homecoming was now possible for him when all he wanted, but could never have, lay in this city he was now leaving?

As the truck passed through the gates and swung across the road to turn left, the sergeant pulled open the canvas flap over the tailboard.

'Some people were keen to see the back of you,' he said enigmatically.

Mai glanced out of the truck. It was true. There was a small group of spectators on the pavement outside the gate. Four people, a man, a woman, two children. His mind fought against what it was sure was the madness of recognition. He blinked his eyes as though he had stared into the sun. They were still there, the delusion strong as ever.

He tried to speak but couldn't. The truck was already beginning to move away. He let his gaze run swiftly over Claude Crozier's amiable features, stern now in the dawn light; down to little Céci's round face, her mouth open wide in a yawn; across to Pauli's sallow oval, his eyes unblinking and wary; and finally up to Janine. Her face was thin, so very thin. Even the scarf bound tightly round her head couldn't disguise the ravages of assault and imprisonment.

But there was life in her features now, life triumphing over the deathly despair he had seen in court. He recalled her running down the path in the Jardin des Plantes and turning to wave and smile like a young girl leaving her lover.

She smiled now and as the truck gathered speed, she raised her hand briefly from Pauli's shoulder and waved.

He waved back. It didn't feel like waving goodbye.

Now they were tiny anonymous figures in a long empty street. And now they were gone altogether. But still he peered out of the truck, like a tourist anxious not to miss any of the sights. It seemed their route took them across the city and at this hour it was easy to drive through its empty heart. They crossed the Seine, heavy and fast with the floods of spring. They passed beneath the gilded Victory on the Colonne du Palmier. They drove up the Rue de Rivoli, whose long arcade still bore the shell marks which turned it too into a monument to victory. They passed the Louvre where Christian Valois had made his first act of resistance. And then they drove past the Tuileries Garden where he, Günter Mai, had made his first declaration of love to Janine Simonian.

His eyes stopped seeing outwardly here. He hardly noticed as they climbed the Champs-Élysées, passing Le Colisée where he had sat and talked with Michel Boucher, till they reached the Arc de Triomphe and the Eternal Flame.

Here he took one last look out over the city. It was coming to life now after the long dark night. God knows what these Frenchmen would make of the future. He'd never been able to understand them. But this was nothing to the problems of understanding he feared his own countrymen might be setting the Allied Armies as they drove deeper into Germany's dark heart.

He shuddered and let the flap drop as they descended to Porte Maillot.

'Seen enough?' said the sergeant.

'For now,' said Mai.

'For *now*? You mean you're planning to come back? I'll say this for you Fritzes. You don't know when you're beaten!'

'Oh yes, we do. It's knowing when you've won that's difficult,' said Günter Mai.